Anne Redmon was born
1943 and educated at the University of Pennsylvania. She has since then lived for long periods in London. At present she divides her time between England and America, where she teaches creative writing at the University of Michigan. She is a Fellow of the Royal Society of Literature.

Whilst being a highly intelligent and serious novelist, Anne Redmon also knows how to entertain. Her novels, SECOND SIGHT, MUSIC AND SILENCE, and EMILY STONE, which won for her the Yorkshire Post Prize for the Best First Work, have all received widespread critical acclaim.

Anne Redmon

# SECOND SIGHT

ARENA

An Arena Book
Published by Arrow Books Limited
62–65 Chandos Place, London WC2N 4NW

An imprint of Century Hutchinson Limited

London  Melbourne  Sydney  Auckland
Johannesburg and agencies throughout
the world

First published in England by Secker & Warburg 1987
Arena edition 1989

Printed and bound in Great Britain by
The Guernsey Press Co Ltd
Guernsey, C.I.

ISBN 0 09 9611201

For Benedict, Magdalen
and B.K.S.

Be as a child: be deaf, be blind, for thine own self must cease to be. Leave place, leave time and images, and wander down the pathless ways until you find the wilderness.

O my soul, go out from God till you sink your 'I' into the nothingness of God, till you sink into the measureless flood.

If I flee from Thee, Thou comest to me. If I leave myself, then I find Thee, O goodness supreme.

*God of a Hundred Names*

Thirteenth-century German. Anonymous.
Translated by Barbara Green.
Published by Victor Gollancz.

# Chapter One

I have come back to Baltimore, and to the house on Ashby Street where I was raised, in order to write a full account of the events which led up to the mysterious death of my sister Mathilde, whose body was found in the Gobi Desert last summer. Until now, nearly everybody has made an inquiry except me: the Americans, the Russians, the Mongolians, even the British have had a hand in it. As everyone suspects everyone else of lying, the investigations have bogged down. It seems up to me, the sole survivor of this family, to offer the only evidence I can, no matter how bizarre it may appear. Not only did I accompany Mathilde on the tour through Central Asia from which she disappeared, I also grew up with her here in this house. I have had to ask myself a lot of questions. Was it Mathilde's nature that led her inexorably to an early death? Was it her relationship to Durrand, her dead twin brother that, in effect, murdered her? What I saw and what I heard on that journey could lead to yet another conclusion, but, for reasons which will become apparent, I cannot wholly trust the evidence of my senses. Not even the intensity of my experience can ever fully argue that the nature of my perception is valid. It is for this reason I have come home: to retrieve what I can of my impaired memory and to find out what it really was I saw.

I haven't been back to this house since Mother died and Mathilde decided to let it. She said she couldn't bear to part with it, and that surprised me at the time, as she was very unhappy here. She said she would take responsibility for the place even though she made her home abroad. She had used an agent, who gave me the keys. 'She really let it run down,' he said. 'I think you're in for a shock.' When the taxi set me down on the corner of Key and Ashby, my heart turned for the shabby row house with its early nineteenth-century facade. There it stands − living memory − and my mind began to hum with an immediate concern for every brick. The old bay window of what Mother used to call 'the drawing room' still sags as it juts out over the sidewalk. The wrought-iron sleeping porch, which overlooks the backyard from the second storey, is still twined with honeysuckle.

Several different families have occupied the house since our departure, but nothing much has changed. The marble steps are in a bad state of disrepair and need seeing to. I let myself into the vestibule where a plethora of junk mail littered the floor; but, when I opened the door to the house proper, I discovered to my somewhat hysterical amusement, that there was no furniture. The agent had neglected to tell me we had let the house unfurnished and I had forgotten. I walked cautiously, fearfully, into the empty house; it was cool after the hot sunshine, but stuffy. I recalled things acutely, not so much by vision as by the touch of my spirit, which ran over every floorboard and wall, the intricate tiles in the hall. In the yellowed kitchen, where Lettie used to iron and fry chicken and scold us, nothing remained but the old sink. Large cockroaches scuttled between broken tiles and over dusty linoleum. I looked out into the backyard. It was overgrown with weeds. 'Maybe I shouldn't be alone here,' I said aloud. 'I don't know that I should be alone here at all.'

I miss John acutely, but what I do here is in some sense a preparation for him. Of all people, he is the one to understand why I must finish my business with Mathilde − and Durrand; for John was a part of that journey and knows my dilemma of vision more surely than anyone else I have ever met. He himself is reorganizing his life in London and may make one other trip abroad before we come together. 'You will be careful? You must be careful,' he kept on saying at the airport when we parted. Yet, I must be alone and in this place if my experience is ever to be coherent to us both.

'What shall I do?' I asked myself on my first day back here. My voice rose up into the empty space above the stairs. I opened Mother's old bedroom with trepidation, then mine, then Mathilde's, then Durrand's. The rooms emitted a kind of musk. One of the tenants had painted Mathilde's room green and she never liked green. I started to cry – little, fearful sobs because she is dead and because she hated green. Opening Durrand's room was the worst. I do think I was brave to open Durrand's room, considering everything. Even in the past it was forbidden territory for me. Durrand got it into his head that because I was an epileptic I was unclean; therefore he would never let me cross his threshold. It is only recently that I have realized that Durrand was afraid of me. He looked at me with a loathing that people reserve for insects. He hid everything well away from my contaminating disease: his racks of lead soldiers, his books on the Confederacy. Most of all, he feared my incursion upon his religious life which he adapted to suit his own peculiar needs from the Roman Catholicism into which we were all born. Who knows what went on in that hostile place, his room, now that Mathilde is dead? You could hear him muttering imprecations behind closed doors, sense him feeling the silent air for some palpable vindication of himself. Religion. I cannot quite express what religion was for Durrand and Mathilde – a strange occult hybrid, having to do with zeal and pain, exclusive to the two of them. Their surreptitious rites absorbed them both, and left me on my own to find a different and more orthodox belief. The memory of their half-glimpsed, private ceremonials still makes me shudder.

It is hot. After a short stay in a small hotel, and a few shopping trips, I have settled in Ashby Street. Or, rather, I have perched here. After I have accomplished what I came

9

for, I will let the house go. The minimal furniture I have assembled looks better, somehow, than the old grand pieces which were auctioned off. I never thought I would enjoy cleaning a house so much as I am enjoying cleaning this one.

My other purpose in Baltimore is to make a gift to the Walter's Art Gallery. Mathilde ended up in a profession which illuminates a strange contrast in her life. She was a dealer and restorer of fine icons. If Durrand were still alive; if he had been the sort of man who could have conceived any thought on a matter close to him, he might have been able to say why it was Mathilde chose to give her life to something so at odds with her inclinations. At any rate, I walked into the gallery yesterday and asked them if they wanted Matty's collection and a permanent room for them endowed by me. I stood there, the damp hairs at the back of my neck, cooked by the Maryland sun, congealing in their air-conditioning. At first, I think they did not believe me. I suppose I don't look all that rich. I think I should have written to them first.

'My name is Irene Ward,' I said. 'Miss. My sister Mathilde died and I have inherited twelve icons from her, mostly Russian, some of them Greek. Two are fourteenth-century Novgorod. There is a sixteenth-century Eleussa from the Stroganov School, and a Mother of God of the Sign from Pskov. There is a Birth of the Virgin from Salonica, which my sister believed to have come from Mount Athos, and a number of less important ones. You can have them if you like.'

Before I see them again, I think I will have to buy a linen suit. Mother used to wear a suit to the Ladies Hamilton Street Club where she had lunch with her friends. Mathilde, when she had become a woman of importance, when she lived in London, lectured, restored, bought and sold, travelled to Leningrad or Athens, always dealt with summer matters dressed in a linen suit. In winter, she wore fine, woollen clothing with weighted hems which swung against her ankles, making her seem elegant and poised.

On the other hand, perhaps the gift itself will make me credible. I really do not know.

The gallery people brought me iced tea. They seemed even more surprised when I told them I was Emery Ward's daughter. He is still legendary for his collection of Italian paintings, and even more legendary in Baltimore for the way he acquired it. I met him only once. It was Mathilde who got to know him well, and if she had not made the first move, I do not think he would have left us all that money. When I think of how much his bequest had to do with Matty's death — and Durrand's — I wish he had squandered it, or left it all to cats.

This house. No. I am not sure I can stay. Yet I must stay, even though the rooms seep and bulge with memory, and, what is worse, the loss of it. If I breathe steadily and hold on through the panic of guilt I may arrive at what really happened. The good priest I spoke to on my return from Mongolia spent hours trying to convince me I was not at fault. As Dostoyevsky says, a certain morbid guilt is one of the worst afflictions of epilepsy, but then he was talking about Smirdyakov at the time — Smirdyakov who did the deed. I think this sense of guilt comes from not knowing what one is doing a large part of the time. Certainly, when I was ill in childhood, it was Durrand's particular pleasure to accuse me of things he had done himself; and Mathilde's to project upon me thoughts and feelings that she herself had. I did not kill Durrand. I did not kill Mathilde. As God is my witness.

Today, I took a voyage around the cellar and found the old lamp that used to belong to me. Mathilde gave it to me and I have only recently remembered why. It has a red shade. I have set it on this new table so that I can always have it before my eyes. It is safer to remain always mindful of such an artery to the past. Although I do fear, I am not afraid as I used to be, and I am not sure why. While I was in the cellar, I thought about Smirdyakov. I stood there for a long time. Smirdyakov terrifies me. So, oddly enough, does Prince Myshkin.

The lamp is the presence of Mathilde. The mantelpiece is the memory of a black kitten we had called Figaro, who once got up there and knocked down a Dresden figurine.

The story of my association with Mathilde begins, of course, in Baltimore, but the beginning of the end of it has its origins in Maine where I lived and worked as a schoolteacher until I set off with my sister on the trip which was to end in such a terrible way. If I say I am an epileptic now, it is not what I would have said two years ago. From the age of twenty to the age of thirty-five I had a complete remission from the disease. I think I chose Maine as my home because it was as far north as I could go — away from the lip of the south and the neurological volcano I had lived on there. I liked the neat and ordered ways of the small town where I lived. I enjoyed teaching. It was wonderful to me that I could drive a car.

The night Durrand died eighteen months ago in France, I had, allowing for the time difference between the United States and France, a major seizure at the moment of his death. Or so I think. Or so Mathilde told me. I went into *status epilepticus*. The convulsions nearly killed me.

A very odd feature of this episode is that I can recall the beginning of it. Because of its severity, my memory should have been wiped out completely. This is what I can piece together: I had returned home from school with some papers to mark and had put on the kettle to make some tea. I saw no auras, smelt nothing peculiar. I opened the back door to let the dog out. I had a little terrier then. She saved my life. For the snatch of a moment, it seemed that something wonderful had happened, something liberating and joyful, and then it came: the thunderbolt, the scream I screamed but heard someone else screaming. Everything was torn up like the roots of trees; there was the acrid smell, the evil lights. It was as if the house itself had been taken up and shaken by a wrathful poltergeist; everything reeled and knocked, tearing me away from consciousness and hurling me into the abyss.

I later learned that my neighbour Sam Putnam heard the dog howling while he worked in his field. He came running and found me writhing in froth and spittle.

When I came to in the hospital, I heard about Durrand. Not all at once. I did not hear at once. The first visitor I had, in any case, was the principal of my school. I was so unwell, I found it hard to focus on him. He eyed me, swollen-gummed, no doubt, from drugs, then looked away. I sat with narrowed shoulders in a hospital chair while he brandished gladioli, stiff, white and funereal. I attempted to avoid the multiple-eyed look I know so well, but – could not. There he was, with his duty to behave as if he did not feel horror. I had never concealed my background of epilepsy, but when it came to the actual thing, I could see that a bond was broken between us. It was as if I had betrayed him. 'It's not contagious and I'm not insane,' I said through the blur and he reassured me that he knew this. Was it his hooded look or the jut of his jaw that reminded me of Durrand? Durrand whom I then believed was alive. Durrand, who once 'in nomine' had tried to cast my 'devil' out.

Through the veil of after-images generated by my mind's electricity, I saw people fade forward and retreat. A chaplain came to see me. A numinous aureole attached itself around him, and I closed my eyes against unwanted vision. Snakes, oranges, ghosts burgeoned in and out. The priest sat very still.

Later he returned, when I was better.

'Do you live alone, Miss Ward?'

'Yes.'

'Could you stay with friends after you leave the hospital?'

'No. Yes. I don't know. Is it necessary?' I was worried by his look and I watched him closely. I knew I was about to hear something awful.

'I have bad news.'

Was I caught up in thinking Durrand's name? Or do I remember it all backwards from the event? Did I think about Durrand before he told me? Or did my brain reverse the order?

'I'm afraid your brother has been killed in an accident. Your sister has been trying to reach you. She finally got your neighbours and they called me. I spoke to her on the telephone some time ago, but you were not well enough to hear the news.'

I wondered why he was going into all that. 'Killed? Durrand?'

'I'm afraid so.'

'Killed? How was he killed?'

'He was crushed by a train. I'm sorry, it's very unpleasant.'

'Where? What happened?'

'It happened just outside Paris, in France. He fell under a train. Maybe it will make you feel better to hear that he died saving a child who was on the verge of falling onto the tracks. There was a blizzard and he slipped – saving a child.'

'Durrand always wanted to be a hero,' I said, but something in me rebelled violently against the idea that he had died doing anything noble. At once, I felt guilty at not believing it.

'Mathilde was his twin,' I said. 'How is she taking it?'

'I'm more concerned about you. The doctors said you would be all right, but . . .'

'I wish I could say . . .'

'You don't have to be insincere. Pray for him and leave it all to God's mercy.'

'It was hard for Durrand,' I said. 'He took life hard. I wish I had loved him, but I didn't. I was afraid of him.'

He cleared his throat. 'Don't push yourself,' he said. 'You ought to stay with friends.'

I raised myself up. 'What about the funeral? I must go to the funeral.'

'There has already been a funeral. Your brother died on April the 9th. Ten days ago.'

'That was the day I had my seizure.' I fell back into the chair, a tingling sensation passed through my limbs.

'Your sister seemed very much preoccupied with that coincidence,' the priest said. 'Be careful you don't put the two things together in your mind, particularly if you had mixed feelings about him.'

'Please, how is Mathilde?'

'I think you should take one thing at a time,' he said, and paused. 'She is going to write to you. Don't let her upset you.' From the awkward way he spoke, I gathered that he had found Mathilde a handful.

And she would have given him a hard time on the telephone. Mathilde. Mathilde and Durrand, connected by that invisible trunk of thought always.

Beyond the lamp and through the window I can see Key Street. We used to play up and down it.

*Nyah, nyah, nyah, nyah! I-reen-ie's nutsy cuckoo! I-reen-ie wets her pants!*

It is nothing worse than a memory now.

*Durrand! Don't* broad*cast it to the* neigh*bourhood!* That was Mother.

Mathilde stood like a sphinx. *Watch what you say or I'll tell.* Brother and sister, attack and defence. The boundary between them was sometimes unclear.

Down the track full throttle came the French train with a grinding noise, and he, my childhood persecutor, aghast only for a moment in the late, Lenten snow, cartwheeled down the slope. Crunch, went his neck. I could not see a child in the picture. I closed my eyes to try to stop thinking about it – poor Durrand's flesh finally mortified. I ordered wool and started to knit a complicated pattern. The sweater grew on circular needles until I was well enough to go home, where I waited in bruised shock for a letter from Mathilde.

And, like a letter written in all propriety but left out in the rain, so does my memory throw up fits and jags backwards and forwards across time and space. The images of what I have witnessed and where I have been, ascend and descend in my mind against the patterned order of time and space as others might perceive it. At intervals, I can almost hear the sifting of time against eternity. Sometimes, I feel I am caught in a very loose net of light. Like a narrow bird in a rose tree, I am pierced by a thorn of light which illuminates long, bold patches of darkness. It is hot, so hot. Yesterday, in the seared backyard, I saw a hummingbird in the morning glory; its flashing wings against the dark purple transfixed me. Opening and shutting its visible and invisible wings, the bird drank from the flower.


# Chapter Two


I am glad it is morning. All last night, I lay with my ears alert to the slightest noise or movement. I think I shall get the handyman to move my bed to a less troubling spot than my old room. At four a.m. I nearly called John in England simply to persuade myself that at the other end of this time there is a future for me.

I mouthed a supper in the kitchen. The faucet dripped. There they were, Durrand and Matty in my mind's eye – they must have been twelve or so – screaming and screaming at each other. It suddenly erupted at the table one warm evening in June after Lettie had finished giving us our meal. I, as a rule, sat below the salt nearest the stove and nearest the protection of Lettie, which I needed if Mother was out. I remember no words that passed between them, but words must have passed between them. Suddenly, a violent freak of electricity seemed to separate them, and the china and the glass and the cutlery heaved as if by some innate kinetic force. Milk ran all over the table and before anyone knew it, they were at each other's throats, stabbing with forks so that blood ran, and Lettie was on them. She lifted Durrand up by the scruff of his neck, and locked him away in the pantry: she manacled Mathilde in her strong hand. I remember most of all the uncreaturely howl – a sort of keening they both set up at having been separated, and how the fury was vented on Lettie.

The house when dark pressed still worse shadows on me, worse because they seemed to contain the unseen element of a dread waiting to be animated by some appalling shudder of earth which might exhume them all and give them leave to walk here – Durrand and Mathilde. The doors I had closed I wished open. The doors I had not closed, I was too afraid to shut.

In my old room, a mouse gnawed at the wainscot for part of the night. It gnawed and gnawed at me – that noise of Matty scratching on Durrand's door, Durrand scratching on Mathilde's door in the otherwise profound silence of the night. This stopped when they were adolescents, but for the greater part of their childhood as I recall it, they seemed to have to commune at night, as though they recharged themselves with each other. Unlike husband and wife, it was not the matching of love with love, comfort with comfort, or even like with dislike, anger with forgiveness, anger with anger. As a child, I took it for granted that the bond they had was a run-of-the-mill thing. They were older than me, and because of our family circumstances and my illness they had much control over my thoughts. When I grew up, however, I came to see these unearthly flittings across the hall, and the deep silence which ensued, as something I had feared without being aware of it at the time. They did not mesh or unite. It was as if, for them, their relationship was already an absolute: nothing that had to be achieved by words, or avowals. To say that they loved each other might imply some distance between them that needed crossing. That they slept in separate rooms seemed, at times, almost unnatural.

Last night, just as I was finally dropping off to sleep, there was a screech of tires, a slammed door, a shout in a neighbour's hall. I woke with complete alert expectation of Durrand's heavy, angry tread upon the stairs. During their adolescence, hostilities broke out between them, hostilities

17

that had a different tone to the skirmish I remember in the kitchen. Mathilde was beautiful, popular with boys. Of the two, she was far the more outgoing. He would wait up for her, sometimes sitting in the dark drawing room for hours. I remember coming down for a glass of water one night only to find them both in silent confrontation in the hall. Mathilde's hair was mussed, her lipstick smeared. Durrand said, 'Good.' Then he wiped the lipstick off her face with a clean handkerchief. The next day, there was an ungodly row between them. On other occasions, he would simply storm about the house until late at night, and Mother never had the courage to stop him. Like a spider, he crouched over her love-life, vetting suitors, a pathological chaperone – or pander. For the few who braved the house for me, Durrand showed nothing but contempt.

But it is daylight now, and the daylight always seemed to draw from them, in past times, a curious change, subtle in its mood. Of course, they went to separate schools, and if neither of them invited anyone home to play, it may have been out of shame of the house rather than any feeling of exclusiveness they had about each other: on Ashby Street, when they were about eight or nine, they messed about with the other children. In fact, I remember some complaint being lodged against them for having led a group over towards the slums that once abutted our neighbourhood. It was something in the order of a raiding party in which Durrand challenged the poorer children to a battle with staves.

A thing I find strange about the two, now that I have had a wide experience of schoolchildren, is the fascination each had with his or her own gender. As a little girl, Mathilde had a tasteless fixation on the colour pink. She insisted upon her room being done in flanks of ruffles, and though Mother encouraged all kinds of arch, Southern femininity, even she was put out by the banks and swathes of pom-poms and puffs, sugary feathers and kewpie dolls that Matty favoured. She worshipped dolls, but never allowed a baby among them. They all had to be grown-up looking, and she showered them with little bits of fluff and bead. Until she was quite old, even when she was becoming learned and when nothing seemed to matter to her more than art, she kept this strangely girlish boudoir – out of kilter with her tastes and thoughts.

Durrand's passion for soldiers was not the only thing about him that seemed to reach out in a kind of hunger for the masculine. He had a punching bag, a set of weights, and an almost insatiable appetite for firearms and all information pertaining to them. The two of them seemed to mime and almost mock an image each had of what girls and boys ought to want to feel and do. In itself, and given the time and context in which we all grew up, there is nothing so remarkable about their personal predilections as children. It was the single-mindedness of pursuit that marked them out as different, the single-mindedness and the isolation in which both Mathilde and Durrand played out their separate roles.

As a child, I caught only glimpses of the sort of thing I mean. Walking out onto the upstairs porch this morning for some air after the stifling night, I had a vivid recollection of a moment I had buried in my memory; and yet, it was a trivial thing. The porch overlooks the backyard, and I was not allowed to go out there in case I had a fit and lurched through the barrier of screen and rail onto the ground below. My whole life then was padded and strapped by rules. Although I was seven years old, I was not even allowed to go to school, and I was rarely left alone. I have a shadowy memory of my elegant grandmother coming to mind me once for a while when my mother and Lettie were out. Whether she had no appetite for the task or thought too much of a fuss was made of my illness I do not know, for we had no contact between us. She left me to my own devices and I must have given her the slip. I remember the porch having some mystique for me, and I found my way there, and stood breathless with shame and fascination at having achieved the forbidden but beautiful zone where the lovely creepers twined in the dark and intricate wrought iron. What were they doing down there, Durrand and Mathilde, in the harsh sunlight? They stood back to back on the frazzled grass. They were exactly the same height, weight and build, slender and wiry both. They were not touching, but all at once in unison, they lifted up their arms to shoulder height and held their palms outward in a gesture that reminded me of the priest at Mass. With one accord, they turned, wordless, and faced each other exactly. It was as if nothing could move in the garden and I could not breathe until they had accomplished whatever strange ceremony it was. A dying, purple rose lost a petal. It seemed apt and only underlined the stillness of the moment. Their palms still outstretched, they came together, held their rigid hands out, and with complete precision, touched so that the measure was exact. It looked like one individual placing his hands on a mirror, until slowly, they intertwined their fingers, interlocking them tightly. Abruptly, they then separated and went into the house.

I remember now being horrified and frightened for no reason at all. I felt guilty and feared they must have seen me, and I quickly left the porch, only to find them both, marching up the stairs side by side, oblivious to my presence. They went into their separate rooms and for the rest of the day each played alone, Mathilde talking in a high, exaggerated voice to her dolls, Durrand gunning down the enemy.

When I remember all of this, I do not know how the rift finally came between them, or whether, indeed, it was a rift at all, but this is how my mother and I understood it: the two of them in early adulthood seemed totally estranged.

That estrangement and its reasons are terribly obscure still, though there were elements in their relationship throughout our childhood which, having a hairline insignificance at the time, can only now be said to have held the seeds of ruin. I do not count the battles as being signs of the final split, although after the split had occurred, their fights signified it. Like a partitioned country, north and south, their decision to loathe each other and to live under two separate regimes made raids and propaganda wars, intrigue and defamation a necessary evil. It was on their eighteenth birthday that the rift opened wide. On the surface, and perhaps very much below it, their quarrel had to do with religion; from the bitterness of their feeling, I can comprehend with painful understanding the Irish question or the Spanish Inquisition or the passionate fury between Iraq and Iran.

For just a moment I can see the dining room set up as it was on that September day: candles smouldering in the hot dusk, silver gleaming on the table, and a divided cake; and can hear Durrand's cold denunciation of my sister as a heretic. Mathilde's bitter voice comes back too – not in argument, because to argue would have been to stoop, but in controlled, articulate outrage at the Church.

'Surely there must have been some reason for that row. The row could not have been the cause, not in itself,' John said when I tried to explain to him why Durrand and Mathilde had flown so far apart. 'Perhaps there was some incestuous relationship between them, perhaps the games between them went too far for one but not the other. No one breaks a union that close over a difference of opinion.'

It has been hard to explain to him how cerebral Durrand and Mathilde both were, how obsessed they became, as they grew older, with ideas, and how rarefied the atmosphere was in which we lived. Arguments about free will and predestination, about salvation and eternal hell flashed like heat-lightning from their dark and humid relationship. It was as if their quarrels stood for an unfathomable anger they had at something else. Mathilde, however, told me that she had split with Durrand on ethical grounds – and whatever Mathilde told me at that time, I was tempted to believe.

I have found a card table in the cellar and am eating on that in the living room. This is the safest place and is where we used to put the Christmas tree, or entertain rare company. Everyone behaved as they ought here. What did they do with my memory? What *was* the rift between my sister and my brother? The night of their birthday party I had an engulfing fit.

I was very epileptic until the age of twenty when *suddenly* I wasn't anymore. The illness, which had always seemed to have a life of its own, vanished only to secrete itself without my knowledge in the interstices of my brain and slumber there until Durrand died. It is only now, in early middle age, that I am beginning to comprehend that things may have been different in actuality from what they seemed to be. As epilepsy has the peculiar capability to erase memory, I was extremely dependent on any scraps of information my family could give me as to what was real and what was not. Without a memory, one is crippled by a bizarre form of helplessness. Even now, my mind throws up high-pitched, vivid images set out like a collage upon a field of black, so that making continuous sense of events takes sweated labour. When I was young, I used to be amused when people told me not to cross my bridges until I came to them. With me, it was literally true that I could stand on one side of a bridge and watch myself coming across it from the other side. Heading towards myself, I watched myself, traverse myself in the middle of the arch. Which side my physical being was on had to be ascertained, in childhood, from Durrand or Mathilde.

If Mathilde or Durrand told me that:

I had not brushed my teeth
I had already said my prayers
I had set the curtains on fire
I had stolen something that Durrand had stolen
I owed Mathilde allegiance for the love and protection she gave me

I believed it.

The rock of my life was founded on this deep axiom: that my experience of reality had no reality. This was constantly proven by quotidian things. I would walk out of the house without any shoes. I would knock a glass and smash it and have no recollection of this. My hair would be a horrible snarl even when I had a distinct memory of combing it; or, I would set myself the task of combing it and find it already untangled. So when I was little, Mathilde and Durrand would have quite a lot of fun out of me, saying and unsaying things. *You were there.* 'Where?' *There. No, she was there.* 'It's my pie.' *No, you've already eaten your pie.* It came and then went like a conjuring trick. My pie, your pie, Durrand's pie. *Eat up, children! You've lost your pie! You've lost your pie!* They would shriek and dance like hobgoblins, and I was left with the abyss.

Pig in the Middle – they loved to play it in the yard. She would hold the ball like magic above my head and snap it across to Durrand, and Durrand was a good catch. He would graze me with it in the middle. It would go past me. I was a fumbly, awkward child and he would laugh as I missed it. Mathilde caught things well too. Nothing was out of bounds for them, but even if I did catch the ball, I was out of bounds. Catch, catch. They would go on until I was reduced to tears. *Baby, baby, baby!* Did they shriek in unison or was it only Durrand, or was it only Mathilde?

My mind was made up it was Durrand because Mathilde had told me so.

Was it? Wasn't it? Was it? Wasn't it? The argument no longer reduces me to weeping in the church down the road where I would take sanctuary. It is the Sanctuary itself that makes me cry, and for some unintelligible reason, with relief. The old questions themselves have a kind of odiousness for me which is perhaps born out of the fear of their being answered.

# Chapter Three

Durrand and Mathilde. Mathilde and Durrand. Even the neighbours treated them as if they were one. When they were little, Mother liked to dress them in ways which would emphasize the cuteness of their striking resemblance. They had identical blue tweed coats with velvet collars, and she bought them shirts to match with a corduroy skirt for Matty and corduroy shorts for Durrand made of the same material. People on the street would turn their heads. I remember old Miss Blaine across the street used to be fond of saying that they were just like a couple of dolls, and whenever she saw them dressed alike, she would give them a little reward — cookies or nickels. Mother was pleased with a comparison to dolls, and one Hallowe'en she decked them out as a little Dutch boy and girl and sent them out trick-or-treating. 'Double Dutch!' she said at the door, shaking her head and laughing. 'Double Dutch.' An hour later they were back, marched home by the Episcopal minister's wife. She told our mother that they had broken into the church and she had caught them just as they were about to daub the walls with whitewash.

'They've been reading *Tom Sawyer*,' said Mother. 'It's just like *Tom Sawyer*.'

'It's not,' said the minister's wife. 'No, it is not.' And I remember being conscious of a change in her tone from well-bred outrage to a pitch more quiet and decisive. She looked at my mother with troubled eyes. 'Silly woman,' Mother said when she had left. And she never left off dressing them alike until it could no longer be avoided and when they were quite a way past puberty. She loved their beauty, their long-limbed, blond distinction. I remember, in the drawing room, my mother over tea saying *sotto* voce to some relation that she had, at least, the *two* lovely ones. 'But even with *that*, she's quite p-r-e-t-t-y . . .,' the charitable female cousin replied, indicating me. 'Well,' said Mother, 'some might say so, I suppose, but will she ever . . .?' I knew the word she wanted to supply was 'marry'.

Every Hallowe'en, Durrand said, 'You don't need a costume, Reen. Freak. They'll run screaming.' And I remember trying to tear my face off in front of the mirror. Even when I was older and boys took an interest in me, notwithstanding the encumbrance of epilepsy, I could only believe that some side-show element in me drew them, and I came to ward off their attentions.

In the fight we had over my coming to Baltimore alone without him, John said, 'It's the lion's mouth for you, that old house, isn't it? A personal way of self-martyrdom, going back there and risking your feelings about me with memories of Durrand and Mathilde. At the end of it, you won't believe I love you. In some obscure way I think you *want* to see yourself through their eyes, feel those old humiliations and believe they are true. That way you can convince yourself I will reject you, when all the time you are rejecting me.'

And I suppose it is true that this morning, coming upon the mirror in the bathroom, I deflected my eyes from my own image as I used to in the past, then looking, perceived the arrangement of brown hair, pale skin and slightness of form burgeoning from the glass hideous, unloveable. I remember in childhood squeezing shut my eyes, swaying to and fro, and saying like a chant, 'No one will ever, ever, ever, love me. No one, ever, ever.'

My later discovery that men did fall in love with me – boys in college, a colleague at my school in Maine – made me feel that I had broken laws, laws which secretly governed a place in life to which I was bound until the death of Durrand. I am calling John tonight. Tonight.

Now I think about it, it was really Mother who obsessed us with appearance. Her every observation had to do in some way or another with how people looked or what people saw when they looked at us. If she were to assess a stranger in our midst, she would begin her critique with the clothes they wore, their facial characteristics, their manners. But of course, she had been a beauty herself, and Father, in his own way, was beautiful too. But if Mother liked the outward pattern of the two enchanting rigged-up twins – this perfectly congruous pair – she disliked, and even, I think, feared, their indivisibility behind closed doors. At least, she feared Matty. I really think she did. And she envied my sister's closeness with Durrand. This led her to make distinctions between them at home. Whenever Durrand showed her the slightest courtesy, Mother would swoop down on him and hug him, and call him 'my best beau'. I have a poignant memory of Matty rushing up to Mother and embracing her with that huge, pure spontaneity children have, and Mother shrinking back with an unguarded look of cold distaste. In fact, this episode and my reaction to it struck the bond which was to exist between my sister and me until she died. I myself knew better than to attempt such an embrace, and when I saw Mathilde's shoulders hunch and freeze, I can recall that first feeling of compassion I had ever had for anyone else. I clutched her hand and she squeezed mine back. There was a wordless dignity in the moment and it led to other things.

Mother always liked to dive between them if ever she saw a crack in that singleness of spirit that they shared. If they fought, she would take Durrand's side; if they were naughty, she would find reasons why Mathilde had put Durrand up to it. A thing they had in common was a tendency to lie, but Mother always believed Durrand. There was a rhyme from Hilaire Belloc she often spoke. It was written to be funny, but the way Mother said it extracted all the humour from it:

> *Mathilda told such awful lies,*
> *It made one gasp and stretch one's eyes.*

*Her aunt, who from her earliest youth,*
*Had had a strict regard for truth*
*Attempted to believe Mathilda.*
*The effort very nearly killed her.*

The emphasis she would put on the word 'killed' still makes me uncomfortable. It was I, too, who killed Mother daily with episodes and fits, but epilepsy was beyond her literary range, and she had no verse for me.

It is true that I myself could never listen to Mathilde with conviction. She was not a reliable guide to the uncertain terrain of the universe as I perceived it. I do not think she realized it was cruel to give me misinformation. I think she simply enjoyed seeing the effect that it had. As for Durrand, he lied about and around me with purpose. His deceits always had an end in mind and always had to do with justifying himself in some way. Mathilde herself exploded one elaborate plot he made against me, and to this day I cannot figure out why.

He took it into his head that my fits of absence were a good excuse to discredit me, and, evidently, he decided a way to do this was to steal money out of Mother's purse, spend some of it, then plant the change on me. My mother went absolutely out of her mind about this and called me a thief and made me go to confession. I could remember nothing at all about taking Mother's money, but I supposed I had done it. I went to Father Mowbray and talked as if I had robbed Fort Knox. He seemed somewhat unconvinced that I had committed any sin, but he told me to pay the money back out of my allowance and I did. It happened again, and then another time after that, and I became convinced that I was a monster of moral depravity. Then, suddenly, Mathilde revealed the truth – out of some revenge, I suppose, she wanted to wreak against Durrand. In a blaze of love, I was her slave for weeks, even though she had collected evidence for a long time against Durrand and had clearly known that I had been accused unjustly.

The thing that bothered Mother more than anything else

about Mathilde was that artistic nature which caused her most innocent inventions. The great distinction between Durrand and Mathilde was this: she was born with an unusual artistic ability, which she could translate to paper with sure strokes. Durrand had a very limited imagination and could no more draw than fly. Coupled with Matty's uncanny grasp of the material essence of an object, was her fascination with tales and myths and legends. She wanted to be a book illustrator when she grew up. Oh, she would come home from school with wild tales of her own personal exploits, things that were clearly drawn from her voracious and fertile mind, and if they were later confounded by a revised version from a more authoritative source, such as a teacher, Mother would hit the ceiling. She was far angrier at these inventions than at simpler, cruder lies, the sort that Durrand told. 'You're just like your father,' she would say. 'Just like him!' Father. Artist and deceiver both.

For many years, Mathilde and Durrand seemed to me like royalty or stars. Indeed, people sometimes called them 'the Heavenly Twins', or 'the Terrible Twins', and these appellations stuck in my mind as the right ordering of things. So when the day came that Mathilde stooped to notice me, it seemed that a goddess had entered a shepherd's hut, thrown off her veil and revealed herself as human.

The first time she came into my room, there had been a terrible quarrel with Mother. I remember her standing in the doorway, cool after the hot, flashing fight. She had her arms folded, her head was cocked, her eyes observant. I remember being very much afraid of her, especially when she entered. She sauntered in and flicked the table top. It was always padded in case I had a fit and cut my head. She flicked the pads and heaved herself down in a little chair. I remember her eyeing the crucifix on my wall, then me. I was trying to draw a picture with crayons.

'I have read an interesting story. Let me tell you, Reenie,' she said. 'May I borrow this?' she asked, indicating the crayon with what struck me as wonderful courtesy and condescension. 'I found a book of Father's,' she said. My eyes got big and round because it was more than our lives were worth to mention his name. She smiled. 'Yes,' she said. 'Here is the story. It is about a Greek man called Perseus and a Greek lady called Andromeda, and it has a monster called the Medusa. Really, there are two monsters. Let me show you.' She took all the crayons, and, after a moment's awkward start, she filled the paper and my room with antique struggles until the afternoon waned and I was caught up in wonder.

'It's stupid you don't go to school,' she said afterwards. 'It's really stupid.' And I went pink with pleasure. Suddenly, I sensed Durrand waiting outside the door, which Mathilde had closed with velvety tact. She evidently sensed him too, for she wrapped the pictures away, stood, and went to join him without a word.

I sat for a long time puzzling out whether she had been fooling with me or not. I did not know whether she had meant to be nice or not, but I had the pictures as proof of her interest.

'I want to go to school! I want to go to school! I want to go to school!' I remember the first temper tantrum I ever dared to have erupting from me shortly after this. I kicked and screamed in the kitchen in front of everyone. 'I need to, I want to read and write! I want to go to school and I want to go tomorrow!'

Behind muffled doors later, I heard Mother on the telephone to someone. It might have been Aunt Bethune or Father Mowbray, for Grandmother was dead by that time. 'But she'll injure herself. She'll get teased. Everyone will *know*. Do you think the school can handle it? Well, I know Sister said . . . well, I know he has . . . well, I hope you're right.'

Later that night there was her stumbling and the smell. I knew it was not my sort of stumbling. Poor Mother drank.

In September, I started the first grade and I'm sure my sheer love of school got me through the teasing. I had come, through Mathilde, to associate learning with secrets and power. To my surprise, the other children came to like me and I made a number of friends.

Mathilde admired the tantrum hugely. She said so on her next visitation to my room. 'Tell me another story, Matty,' I said shyly. She looked imperiously at *Dick and Jane* which lay upon my table. 'I have a story,' she said, lowering her voice, 'that isn't very nice. It is about a king who gets torn apart, limb from limb, by his own mother, but she doesn't know she's doing it because the god Dionysus has put a spell on her.' (She pronounced it 'Dion-wis-is'.) Mathilde tossed the reader to one side and we had a grisly evening of it as her hand flew over the paper beyond things dreamt of in Arcadia. Having seen that I had an aptitude for something else besides falling down and foaming at the mouth, my sister added words. I suppose it is no accident that I became a teacher. Mathilde herself decided I should be one when we were older. Somehow, I was always carried away by her wishes, and when I was with her felt I had almost no will of my own.

'Why do you say "gods" when there is only one God?' I asked her then in childhood.

For a moment, she looked uncomfortable, even frightened. 'Well, that's for church,' she said.

I wasn't at all convinced by this, the finished story of the Bacchae notwithstanding.

'You say your prayers,' she said.

I nodded. I always did. I always wanted to.

She turned to me as if imparting a valuable and almost unconscious secret. 'Durrand has the Egyptian ones,' she said in a low voice. 'They're very strong.'

I remember this well, because the phrase, 'Egyptian ones,' ᵗuck in my mind. It had something to do, I was sure, with ᵗhe Masonic Temple at the top of Sewell Avenue. Mother had forbidden us to go near it because it had something to do with black magic and Egypt. That Durrand possessed the 'Egyptian ones' made perfect sense to me at the time and had to do with death and power.

I am brought again to why they split. I cannot know it. Cannot ever know it. I am sure it did have to do with their odd games. They might have touched on something which exploded them apart. All I do know was that Durrand turned to the extreme form of piety and legalism which was always latent in his nature and that Matty turned to the life of the mind.

Maybe it is useless to look back, useless to evaluate the strength of Mathilde's character. It was always as if she drew on a source connected in her mind with unconsecrated mystery. She was the brightest girl in her class, but this was not entirely enough to liberate her from the humid atmosphere of Baltimore. Mother made every kind of objection to her continuing her education past high school, even though Reverend Mother said she could go to Radcliffe if she wanted to. What? We did not have enough money. Boys never fell for girls with brains. She could go to finishing school if we could afford it. Mathilde lit off for New York without asking a by-your-leave from anyone, contacted Father and made him pay her way through college. I could never understand why it was unthinkable to Mathilde that she should not do completely what she wanted. Mother could cry and carry on as much as she liked, Mathilde was deaf to it. Even (and, in her youth, especially) Durrand was unable to find any threat good enough to stop Mathilde proving, for instance, that boys lined up to take her out, no matter how intelligent she was. I never had it in me to rebel like that or stand out on my own.

It is perhaps for this reason that I got fooled by Mathilde like everybody else. I assumed that in the general burning of boats, her torch was her own, and that, fascinating creature that she was, she had found and forged an identity for herself that gave her all the permission that she needed to throw over every trace of origin.

She jettisoned the Church first of all.

'It makes me squirm,' she said.

'Then why do you go to Communion, Matty?' I asked

her when we were both in school together and she was in her senior year.

She shrugged. 'Well, I want a good recommendation from Reverend Mother, don't I?'

'Mathilde!'

'Agh, creeping and crawling on your knees. You're just like Durrand!'

'I'm not!'

'Oh well, you're sick! It doesn't matter.'

I was too much in awe of her to call her a hypocrite and too frightened of her to cry.

She took to drinking and smoking in front of Mother.

'Mathilde!'

'You're a great one to talk. You drink alone, why not with me, your own daughter?'

This had never been admitted. I could hear Mother being sick at night in the toilet. It was the first time I ever tackled Mathilde. I went into her room, 'Matty, haven't you got any mercy at all?'

'You hate it just as much as I do.'

'That doesn't matter. You shouldn't have exposed her. If you don't like it, you should talk to her about it in private and ask her to stop.'

'Oh, St Theresa!' she said, mocking me with a roll of her eyes to heaven. 'It's St Theresa herself come to admonish me.' And she gave me a queer, sick little smile she sometimes had – a knowing look.

When, much later, Mathilde got her scholarship to the Courtauld Institute in London and decided to move abroad, Mother acted like Dido on the walls of Carthage.

'Mother, calm down,' I said. 'Why shouldn't Matty go away?'

To Mathilde, she said, 'Why do you have to go and live in Europe? What's wrong with this country? Your brother is prepared to die for it. I'm proud of it even if you aren't!' At that time, Durrand was on his way to Vietnam.

'I don't like it here,' she said.

'I will never understand you,' cried Mother. 'Never!'

'I don't want to be understood,' replied Mathilde.

And she never was understood, never, not by anyone except, perhaps, Durrand. This was the thing that no one ever knew, not even Mathilde herself knew it until she had gone so far along the road of self-deceit that it was too late to resist him.

# Chapter Four

I am not sure that I want to remember everything.

In the A & P this morning, I remembered everything I had to buy, and was hit by more of an irony than I chose to think about. I remember the struggle I had to remember when I was a child here in this city. Now I have returned, the whole battle is reversed. I would like to build an inner dam to block out all that floods back to me about my sister.

The groceries did not work as a barricade against that sharp intake of mind I had last night as I was on the verge of sleep. It opened up the breach, leaving me in a pool of insomniac thought and wretched feeling. I thought shopping would help, but it did not.

Everything that had to do with my disease fascinated Mathilde. It was the one thing about me that drew her, as if she possessed an infallible magnet that searched the centre of my chaos. To Durrand, epilepsy was repellent; to Mathilde it was attractive.

'How do you see? How do you see? What do you mean, you see things backwards?' she would ask with the passion of a scientist. 'What do you mean you see things that aren't there? What do you mean by "there"? What things are they? Round? Flat? Do you believe in them when you see them or not? Do they move? Do they scare you?'

I would get these inquisitions from time to time, but

never when Durrand was around – only if he were at Scouts or something. She would slip into my room. Sometimes, even in the dark, she would materialize at the foot of my bed, wake me up and get me out. She thought best with a pencil in her hand.

The neighbourhood children chanted under the direction of Durrand:

> Irene is a moron
> She acts just like a fool.
> She wears a bib and diapers,
> And doesn't go to school.

Even after I went to school, they still sang it.

In contrast, Mathilde said, 'You see these? They are two parallel lines and they can only meet in infinity.' I remember her saying this with the deep, expectant, still look of a fisherman watching water. She had to explain infinity. Mathilde always read books too old for her. If I had had a girl like her in my class, I would have sent her to a school for gifted children. It appalls me now to think what Mathilde's frustrations must have been. Having devoured a book on geometry, she devoured me with questions about the visions that went with psychomotor seizures. 'The lines seem to converge at a vanishing point, but they don't really. If our eyes did not see them this way we would go insane. Do you see them going on and on? Going on and not meeting beyond the horizon? Or do they meet? Maybe you see something that is really there. Do you see something that I can't see?'

For some reason, she made me suffer when she impaled me with that look and questioned me, but at the same time I was flattered and a little amazed that Mathilde took me so seriously. Later on in life, she told me that her interest in icons stemmed from the insights I had given her into 'the unreal and altered proportions of eternity'. She published a paper on the bizarre perspectives and inverted sight-lines with which icon painters depict ecclesiastical buildings. Concentrating on her favourite theme of the Annunciation, she argued beyond my understanding; but to my overwhelming pleasure, she dedicated the work to me.

From an early age, Mathilde would pester Lettie to take her down to the station for our walk. She and Durrand loved trains, especially one called the Royal Blue. They loved the grinding power of the diesel engine and used to stand in awe of it as it slowly approached the platform. As she grew older, Matty would go to the station alone with her sketchbook and draw obsessively the tracks and overhead lines. Oh, Durrand, oh. He had a great devotion to St Sebastian. Mathilde took me to see a painting of his martyrdom which hangs in London. What really interested her was the angle the arrows went in.

I could see the parallel lines last night in my mind's eye, converging and converging on the place of my sister's death. The memory I did not want to have forced itself on me. Once, coming out of a fit of absence, I found myself in front of the bathroom mirror. Mathilde was gloating behind me. She had dressed me in an old sheet and stuck Mother's gold filigree necklace to my head with hairpins. It looked like a tiara. 'There!' she said. 'You are the Sybil and anything you say will come true.'

I said, 'The railroad track.' It was the first thing that came into my head. And then, for no reason at all, I was overwhelmed by panic. As if I were drowning, I clutched and fought until I could tear the headdress off. I fled to my room and lay trembling in the dark a long time.

Sometimes I shake myself and say, 'In this day and age, how . . .?' Yet sitting in this house, I have to make a mental effort to believe, rather, in shopping malls and jumbo jets. How was it that Mathilde managed to evade the modern world? She gave it the slip, and only part of her, as she grew older, used scientific methods in her work. She drank gin, paid taxes, slept around. Deep in herself (and it is hard to be convincing about what is really true) she believed in a terrible source of power that slumbered beneath concrete pylons and waited to be awakened.

It is my experience of Mathilde that alerts my instinct to

her true disposition at the time she wrote to me about Durrand's death. On the one hand, of course, she was really interested in giving me information and airing her views. She would have paced her London flat, thought, formulated theories, yet, in the measure that her strong intellect was dissociated from her real self, Mathilde would have been involved in other, very pressing preoccupations. It would have been her memory of what I had said that day about the railroad track that really prompted her to tell the story of Durrand's death in such minute detail. It would have been her belief that somehow I did *know* the truth of the story in advance that impelled her to falsify two facts. The first falsehood was a simple one; she merely changed the name of the organization Durrand belonged to. I think she did this so that I would not make any inquiry myself. She would have wished to have control over the whole story so that she could invent or delete what was necessary. The second falsehood was a deeper one as it had to do with the reasons for Durrand's death. In fact, I am not entirely sure it was a deliberate lie. When it comes right down to it, I do not think that Matty could endure the truth, so she put it up for auction. Whatever her motives, my sister would have been pressed, by the august presence of death, to turn to someone she thought possessed an arcane key to its secret: and that person, in Mathilde's mind, would have been myself.

I wish I had the letter to hand if only to salvage some spirit of Mathilde's vivid style and to remind myself why I believed, at least in some essentials, the story of Durrand's death as she told it to me. It was one of my sister's lesser gifts to produce pictures in the mind. From time to time, during her long absence abroad, she would send me letters I devoured almost against my will. She could summon up the whole geography of a scene in a sentence, and place a character in a word. Now she is dead, I realize with a wince that I was virtually the only audience she had, her sole correspondent, and the chief repository for her fantasies of love and danger.

The letter, virtually a parcel for its weight and thickness, arrived in May a few weeks after I had returned from the hospital. I could barely open it, my hands trembled so, and when I had read the first few sentences, I put it down on the kitchen table. Her tone was one of outrage. Why hadn't I called her? Why hadn't I written her with details of the fit? Surely I could see the significance of its happening at the hour of Durrand's death. Of course, she had heard that I had nearly died myself, and of course was very sorry I had been so indisposed, but the fact remained that I was still alive – thriving, in fact, she had heard from my neurologist. She had written him for details of the seizure and to the hospital chaplain whom she had also spoken to on the telephone. I could hardly accuse her of a lack of concern. She had gone to great lengths to establish how I was and had even offered to fly to the United States to be with me. She was sure that I had instructed them to put her off.

As it happened, I had had no idea that Mathilde had wanted to come. I put my head in my hands, at once feeling guilt that I had not contacted her. It was only on later reflection that I caught what she had written about Durrand. The beginning of the letter whirled and spiralled with indignation. Surely I could see how she felt, having nearly lost her entire family on a single night. Surely I knew she would have dropped everything for me. Why had I got the chaplain and the doctor to connive against her? Did I trust her so little?

I got up and put on the kettle. My motives seemed laid bare. Poor Mathilde would have been the last person on earth I would have wanted to tend me. It had never occurred to me how miserably alone she must have felt after Durrand's death, and it would have been terrible for her to have been rebuffed by both doctor and chaplain, terrible because they must have made it clear she was unfit to nurse me. I filled a cup I could hardly drink from, my hands shook so. I picked up the letter again and splashed hot coffee on the page.

Now that I was well, she continued, she felt bound to tell me, despite my snub, about the death of Durrand. He, after all, was my brother too, and if I had had a fit on the night he died, I must have been closer to him than she had reckoned.

At this point, she started to ramble on about twins and the psychic bond between them, about how she had read up on it and had even written to some scientific institute to tell them how she and Durrand as children had experienced thought transference on numerous occasions. She reminded me of the time that Durrand had broken his arm at Scout camp and how she had screamed with pain at the very same moment although she had been at school. She told me how interested the scientists had been in this fact, seeing that she and Durrand had not been identical twins, but brother and sister.

It took me quite a few moments to unravel all of this. Matty's handwriting had become quite illegible. At times, her pen had dug right through the page to the other side. It began to dawn on me as she went on that Mathilde was jealous of my experience, and I remembered what the chaplain had told me about her having been obsessed with the coincidence of Durrand's death and my seizure.

Eventually, she reached the story of what had happened. Durrand, it seemed, had years ago joined a religious order called The Holy Companionate. In anybody's books, she said, they could be termed fanatical. Even I, with all my bead-tellings and missal thumbings, would regard them as extreme. Indeed, she had half a mind to write to the Curia in Rome and instigate an investigation into their practices.

I was used to Mathilde's jibes at my religious beliefs, but somehow I felt reduced when she went on to describe the activities of the 'Companionate'. She made me feel as if my continued subscription to the tenets of the Faith was a kind of collusion with the Nazi Party. They were fascists, she said – not out and out fascists, because they were too wily to be caught out; but they were fascists nonetheless, preoccupied with discipline and order to the exclusion of all else. 'Christ is a Fuhrer to them,' I remember her writing, 'not king, but Duce, an improbable, tasselled coxcomb of a God, whose chosen ones obey him with a wriggling, joyous slavishness.' She added, 'I wonder if they would appeal to you. I suppose you are too much of a dreamer to be drawn to anything so collective as the Companionate – that swaying chorus line of Olympic thrusters. But would you condone them on the grounds that they say "Hail Mary" instead of "Heil Hitler"? I wonder.'

Oh, she went on, denouncing them in general and their leader in particular. Apparently, his name was Victor. He had founded the order with his own money, having been a rich man from a noble French family. It was like a monastic order, except all of its members worked in the world. 'Their mission is to the rich,' said Mathilde, 'and it is preferable to have a large bank account before you join. This is why Durrand must have appealed to them. I don't know whether any of them actually believes in God.'

Victor, she said, reminded her exactly of Dostoyevsky's Grand Inquisitor. 'Oh, Durrand walked in an interminable night of doubt,' she said. For a moment I considered that, and realized, with a shock, that it was true. Victor, Mathilde said, played on people's covert disbelief by scheduling a programme of thought-control. Members of the Companionate spent every waking moment drilling for spiritual improvement. One could set one's watch by their timetable for fasts and mortifications. Built into the package deal, she said, was a tangible, visible insurance policy. 'They sell the way to heaven, and they market it with Madison Avenue technique. Like toilet paper, the true function of the Companionate's tissue of assurances is airbrushed and packaged winsomely. When you meet members of the Companionate, you meet toothpaste teeth, filmic smiles. Victor and his subordinates have a regulation twinkle in the eye. It is as if the fountain of grace were easily got at by muscular action of the will. It is as if the water of life had additives and had been incorporated by Disneyland. Victor sells God under his own brand name.'

Curiously, that is an almost exact quotation from Mathilde's letter. I remember it because it struck me forcibly at the time and because when I later met the people she was writing about, her words came back to me.

Apparently, it was Victor who had called Mathilde from

Paris with the news of Durrand's death. According to him, Durrand, who had had much to do with the finances of the Companionate, had been attending a meeting at the home of an important banker. During the course of the evening, the light snow, unusual for the time of year, had begun to thicken and threatened to become an all-out blizzard. Although they had pressed him to spend the night, Durrand had decided to take his chances with the snow because he had an important meeting in Paris the next morning. But the fierceness of the blizzard forced him to abandon his car. According to Victor, Mathilde said, Durrand must have stopped to find a telephone or a mechanic, and stumbling onto the embankment of the railway line, he saw and took a chance at final redemption. A little boy was sliding downwards towards the headlights of the oncoming train from Paris. Without a second's thought, Durrand had hurled himself down the slope, rescued the child, but himself had fallen onto the tracks where he was killed.

'But it is a lie, a lie, a lie,' Mathilde wrote, underscoring the sentence several times, 'and I don't know why Victor told me such a lie when he knew how much of the truth *I* knew.' She said she could just see him smirking on the other end of the telephone. At that time, Mathilde had not known how difficult it would be to get to the truth and it was only later that she realized how pleased Victor had been with himself for covering the tracks 'with more fiction than snow'.

Victor had invited Mathilde to the funeral, but by the time she had made it to Paris through the weather, an inquest had been held, the case had been closed, and all material concerning Durrand's death was now out of Mathilde's reach. Apparently, the child had been found to testify and the verdict had been accidental death.

'Knowing what I do, knowing things I cannot put into this letter, it is my belief that they had Durrand murdered.'

I had put her letter down and shoved it away from me with a sudden impulse. Mathilde had carried me thus far without my catching the scent of unreality. It was not so much that I thought the murder of Durrand was preposterous. Somehow the shape of his life had suggested a violent end. It was more that her story had something of craft in it, and the shock of her accusation that Durrand had been murdered brought out a line she had been taking. I left the table and made for the orchard below my house clutching the letter. All the blossoms and the hawthorns were out. I tried to be grateful that I was alive, and I tried to cast out the contents of her letter on the fresh May breeze. Well, what line was she taking, I asked myself? Her letter might have been a sensational short story for all its breadth of description and detail, but it pulled my mind into strange, dark shapes that no amount of hawthorn, pear or violet underfoot could dispel. I could not imagine writing such a treatise myself if I were in deepest mourning. On the other hand, I persuaded myself that my sister's obsession with Durrand might cause her to exorcize his death in this way. I picked up the script I had crunched in my hand, and continued to read.

'Seeing his body – that was the worst,' she went on. 'They had it laid out in their headquarters in Paris before the funeral took place the next day in Notre Dame Cathedral.'

A young man, whom she described as 'vulpine', had let her in when she arrived and led her up a long carpeted flight of stairs to a palatial reception room where he left her alone. All at once, her eye lit on a door flanked by two Louis Quinze chairs. She remembered this detail particularly and that there was a holy water stoup outside it. At that moment, she knew that Durrand was on the other side of the door. She knew, but could not move. She knew he was there and she could not believe he was dead. Almost without knowing she was doing it, she found herself calling out loud to him, 'Durrand, get up. Durrand, this isn't true.' She called his name over and over again until she was almost in a trance, reciting it like a mantra. As she did so, she felt herself at one with the stench of lilies which permeated the cracks in the door. Outside, she noticed with a heightened keenness of perception that the snow was melting in the now fierce sun and the sky was unbearably blue. She kept on calling his name and telling him she did not believe he was dead.

Now I look back on it, I can see why Mathilde took such great pains to get this narrative right. At the time, it did not fully strike me. 'Suddenly,' she wrote, just as in a story, 'Victor was by my side.' She described the scent of his eau de cologne and how it mingled with the lilies; how well-dressed he was. 'His hair was cut "en brosse", and he wore expensive linen.' She almost gloated over his appearance so that I could see him in my mind's eye: a heavy set man with a faint goatishness about the mouth, notwithstanding his devotion to matters of the spirit. I could see him looking at her, the very picture of a hypocrite, as if tears had watered some tropic part of his soul and had given it leave to flourish. She managed to suggest a man who wore chunky jewellery – medallions inscribed with saints and religious exhortations. I could see him flourish his hand and wave Mathilde into the little chapel where Durrand lay exposed. 'He is the sort of man who genuflects more deeply than anyone else,' she said. 'He noticed that I did not genuflect at all.'

It stands to reason that if Durrand had been crushed by a train, there would not be much left of him. It took me several days to shake off the impression of what she had written and question it. It was as if she had to write it. Her handwriting, which had been so muddled, straightened itself. I followed her as if blindfold, seeing on my inner eye the picture of Durrand, mounted in sateen, stuffed and sewn together. With her, I stood and looked upon the scene, saw her hair falling over his face, saw her being unable to bear it. And there he was beside her, Victor, pawing the corpse's cold hands and wiping her tears from its face with a clean pocket handkerchief. I could see Victor groping around with his eyes for the latch to Mathilde's soul, and I could see her hatred for him – a sudden will to revenge. I had the sense that something had gone on between Mathilde and Victor that I could never fathom, that all she had hated about Durrand when alive was somehow now embodied in this man. Try as I might, I could not rip myself from this story. I saw worse things too, things she never described. I saw Durrand's nose as angular, more angular than it should have been, as if it had been straightened by an undertaker's wire. I saw where they had rouged his bruises.

She went on and on, not dropping her momentum. It was as if her pen could not take pause. There we were in Notre Dame where Durrand was shut in his coffin. I could almost hear the Requiem, opulently Latin. She wrote that she had thought of teeth in a reliquary and that everything had had a peculiar blue sheen about it. 'Even the pall seemed grubby,' she wrote, 'grubby and awaiting flies.' And so I flew over the church as if I hovered from the ceiling, the church packed with sleek-looking mourners; I could almost smell the lilies and mingled perfume masking the odour of corruption. How forcefully she made them real to me: the reptilean celebrant in a black biretta, the league of Companions who rose, fell and knelt in unison. The sermon, she said, had had to do with Durrand's exact corner in Paradise. The Gospel text was from the raising of Lazarus. She said there had been scaffolding up in the Cathedral. My mind went up the looming rods, and bent then to Mathilde whose heart I saw as being full of frenzied, shattered syllables that would not join, almost as though she were trying to pray but could not. She said someone had engaged a choir and that in the volume of ether above the nave their voices had sounded with the sterile purity of castrati. At least, she mentioned 'castrati'. I imagined the rest. I could see my sister standing detached from the group, icy and packed in mourning.

When the funeral was over, they had assembled on the pavement outside the cathedral, Victor, Mathilde, and all the 'bon-ton mourners', as she called them. Apparently, Victor approached my sister, took her to one side, and told her what I thought at the time I read it was almost the most shocking part of the story. He barred Mathilde from Durrand's interment. According to her, he produced a notorized will which showed that Durrand had left every book, gym shoe, every cufflink and article of clothing to the Companionate. In addition to this, Durrand had requested that his body be buried on Victor's estate in the Loire Valley.

'I told him over and over I was Durrand's twin,' she wrote, 'but he insisted that I had no right to enter his private property and that he could have me turned away.'

Suddenly, I felt desperately sorry for Mathilde. I could see her weaken before this prince of the Church, if that, indeed, was what he was. I could see she had been weaker than him, no matter how strong she was and terrifying to me. When she looked around, the cortège had gone, and when she jumped into a taxi and followed Victor's car, she had lost him in the streets of Paris.

The rest of the letter was almost incoherent, stained with tears. When I was finished, I walked back to the house and lay down on my bed. I was exhausted and I slept. Fitful dreams disturbed me, but when I woke I could not remember them.

Durrand was indeed crushed by a train leaving the Gare St Lazare, but he was not murdered.

Lazarus, come forth in all of your corruption. You more than anyone perhaps deserved the tears of Christ – no, needed them.


# Chapter Five


It is Sunday. I decided to visit the Cathedral this morning. It's the first time I have been in there since Mother's funeral – a dismal and touching occasion. No one cried but me, and even I cried because she wouldn't let anyone love her and died not ever knowing that she had wasted her life in fantasy. It was a typical Southern end, but one specific to her, nonetheless. She never went beyond her culture nor exceeded her context. She thought *Gone With the Wind* was a classic but our house was never Tara.

Mother used to take us to Mass in the Cathedral every Sunday when we were children. As I mounted the steps this morning, I could almost feel her hand in the small of my back, pressing and uncreasing me like an iron. 'A lady always has good carriage, Irene, no matter what!' Today, high singing was going on, but I do not think the somewhat wobbly soprano had been castrated, nor did the flowers reek. All the same, since my return I have preferred the simpler, Victorian church down the road with its old oak stalls. I can sit for hours there, rapt in its cool hush. The Cathedral, on the other hand, is the oldest Catholic church in America, and its columns somehow proclaim the consciousness of that. Mother treated it as our own, personal chapel. Although we were not related in any way to the founding Calverts, she felt a deep spiritual connection with them. She was stirred by them. Hatted in pale straw, or draped in a mantilla, always gloved, she flowed to the ceremony, a human antiphon. Watching her worship, you could almost think of Grace Kelly. My mother loved Grace Kelly. It was with a twinge I read she died.

At first light, before I rose, there was the sense of John. Like his letters, written on flimsy paper and coming from so far away, there was something tentative about my waking to an evocation of him; but it deepened, so that, like the smoke from burning leaves, he was almost embodied here, taking the place of Matty and Durrand. I went to the screen of the sleeping porch and rested my head on its cool mesh. It was as if, through the grain of the screen, I divined his presence – his hands, his voice, his burnished hair. I never expected love in life, yet now I can feel its expression even in absence and parting: waiting. Later, this strong preoccupation with him was engulfed by my visit to the Cathedral. As I knelt, tears were pulled from my eyes by the past's gravity, and I was once more a child – though not. It was like looking through a telescope backwards. Everything seemed smaller until I realized I was larger. The smell remained of wax and incense, and something insubstantial too. Motes danced in the filtered light. The too-rich soprano sang on: Ave Verum.

Overcoming the nausea produced by such emotion, I sat and tried to raise my thoughts to God, but memories clashed with this intention until I thought to myself that God, too, is in my memory, and I decided to allow Him access to it. First of all, there was Mother's coffin, and Mathilde and Durrand, returned from abroad, standing as rigid as a pair of statues next to each other, all but touching each other, stiff with guilt at having left her to die alone with no one else but me. Mother never forgave herself for never forgiving me that her giving birth to me had caused me to be an epileptic. I existed as a perpetual accusation to her. Accusation and expeller of Father, who left us when it looked as if I was going to be much more severely disabled than I am. I do not know when Mother started to drink; she tried to keep it secret. For days on end, she would have acute patches of sobriety where she would touch base with such grimness of feeling that a fugal binge was necessary to erase what she acknowledged: that Father did not and *could* not love her. In her cups, though, she would tell me I drove him away, and I think that Durrand believed this.

In the varnished parlour of the nuns, she would weep for her sins. In panicked tears before her crucifix, she would beg God to forgive her. She got it into her head that she had turned down a vocation to be a Carmelite and that I had been visited upon her as a punishment. And so she would beg God's pardon for His not making her into the person she wanted Him to want her to be.

In her airless room, she turned to me and said, 'How did I ever get into this mess?' I had to sponge her mouth out. She was thirsty, but she could barely swallow. Then she said, 'This *is* the mess.' And died.

Then, in a blur of white, I remembered my First Communion. For some reason, Mathilde giggled helplessly throughout the service; tears poured and squirted from her eyes. Our parents had been married in the Cathedral, and we had all been baptized there. So, the reel of commonplace, the redolent spool of experience vindicated by ritual ran on, until, like a projector run amok, my mind clicked and stopped – then saw. I was alone with my sister one night in the Cathedral. We were children. There was a coffin on a bier covered with a pall and flowers and surrounded by candles. Mathilde turned white and shook with revulsion. It is only now as I write that I remember why we were in there so late. Mathilde hated death and was terrified of anything that had to do with it. She had a complicated set of superstitions for dealing with funeral parlours and hearses. We saw the catafalque at night because she dared me. We had come with Mother who was talking to Father Mowbray, and Mathilde had found a bunch of keys belonging to the organist. She said I would not dare go in with a dead body, and I, who would have done almost anything to impress her, dared. She slid in to fetch me because she heard someone coming. I remember her eyes, first blank with fear, then yellow with fury that I had not been scared.

After Mass this morning, I helped myself to a leaflet promulgating the attempt to canonize a young Red Indian virgin martyr. Her modest portrait overwhelmed me with pity.

On the portico, there was an old black man fussing around with keys and buckets. 'Joseph!' I cried. 'Do you remember me? Irene Ward.'

He did. We had a long talk and he was sad to hear that Mathilde and Durrand had both died in foreign parts.

I recognized old Miss Leadbetter trickling into the hot sunshine. I am amazed to see she is still alive. I knew she had seen me but pretended she had not. I left her in peace. My father's proclivities became public in Baltimore when some Maryland worthies, on a visit to New York, met

47

him in the Stork Club dining with the 'no 'count Count' (Matty's phrase) he had run off with. He blandly told them the truth. Thereafter, it was Miss Leadbetter who led the pack that closed the doors against my mother – though why my mother, of all people, I cannot imagine. She had failed in her Southern duty, perhaps, to be sufficiently alluring to Father. Whenever we played 'Old Maid', Miss Leadbetter used to fill the role. That was Mathilde's idea. As I watched her walking down the steps, I felt a deep, unChristian urge to tell her that I live on the Count's money. He left it all to Father when he died.

All right, this is what I remember of Durrand. Only, I remember him obliquely as if he were a nemesis and not a person, as if, with folded wings across his breast, he knew unspeakable truths about everybody, but bided his time in order the better to mete out doom. Durrand reminded me of God except that Durrand wasn't good. The harder I try to recollect him man and boy, the more he eludes me. Durrand.

Sunday was not a good day here. At dinner, we would explore the mysteries of genealogy until Mother got too drunk, with sly nips into the kitchen, to continue the saga of who had married and who had begotten whom in our family. Did I hear a noise at the door? I went into the vestibule, but there was no one there. This was a house of genteel poverty whose doors were closed against eyes that pried. Mother refused to take 'tainted' money from Father. How shabby it was, and I the chief disgrace! But I am avoiding Durrand, who used to play up and down these stairs. Up and down, he acted out the Civil War (or 'War Between the States' as Mother preferred it). With his Woolworth cutlass bound to his waist with her sash, he strode. He rarely drew the thing, as in his eyes commanders need not stoop to combat. He would pretend to pace the battlefield counting the dead. Alone in his room, he contemplated the Lost Cause.

Durrand had a strange, blunt mind. I can see him now as he was the year he took to baseball. He would stand in the backyard for what seemed to be hours on end swinging his bat in one hand, back and forth, back and forth. Occasionally, he would hold it in both hands and strike – in the air, and at nothing at all. Chiefly, he would swing the bat, swing, swing, thrashing the air, making it whistle. I remember standing at the back door looking through the screen afraid to go out because he was there; afraid he would come in. I would be rooted to the spot in fear, and, I suppose, a subtle longing for his approval. Somehow I thought that if I could make Durrand like me, everything would be all right.

Durrand had a blunt mind, but that did not make him stupid, not by any means. He was not as clever as Mathilde, but he had a force and attack that her more wide-ranging mentality lacked. Not for Durrand were leaps of imagination, flashes of insight. He was thorough and systematic. He did very well at school, but he was not particularly proud of his achievements. He liked geography because of the maps and had a strong preference for mathematics. But of all things he wanted to be valued for, it was athletic prowess. He would scrimp and save his allowance for tickets to the Baltimore Orioles' games. In winter, it was football. He was always in training. He had hero after hero and would project upon each one in turn his own peculiar cast of mind. Durrand was very envious of anyone who excelled him in this field. When Lettie's son won a cup in a state competition, she was so proud I thought, she would burst. 'Nigger,' said Durrand. 'It doesn't count,' He said it just out of her hearing, so that she heard and did not hear it.

He was continually disappointed in his ambitions as an athlete, and maybe would not have been so had he taken up some solitary sport like riding. But he was only drawn to team games and by some peculiar mechanism, Durrand would always get thrown off of any team he joined. 'It's because I'm a leader,' he would say. 'And they can't take it.' This was partly true. He had a dominating personality and was more intelligent than most of the boys he knew. I can imagine now what happened, in the light of my experience as a teacher. Durrand was the sort of boy around whom fights would erupt. A haggler and stickler, he would try to get things to go his way by causing division. His sheer physical courage kept him from being teased, and there was something, too, wild about him, for all his piety, that kept the others at a respectful distance. It was this – the bold streak of anarchy in his otherwise tightly buttoned personality – that constantly rebelled against his conscious wishes. He would push and bully teammates on to stronger, braver efforts, and would then himself, by some foolish miscalculation, lose a game by an erratic throw, hit, pitch or tackle. Through the net and cage of a school playground once I saw him playing football. Even through all the shoulder pads and helmets, I knew Durrand was the one who seemed to occupy his space without regard to where the others were. Bulleting down the field he coursed, a directionless being expressing his own momentum, fulfilling his own ambit for his own motiveless sake. I do not know why I always thought he was oddly gratified by his rejections. Coach after coach said he lacked team spirit, said he was a disruptive element. One of them even came to see my mother in an attempt to suggest he needed psychiatric help. Trying to be kind, the poor, befuddled, inarticulate man struggled to explain his inexplicable instinct about Durrand, whom he thought a talented athlete and whose ambitions he did not want wholly to discourage. Mother was outraged, but Durrand was obscurely pleased. He smiled at the coach's back as he left the house, as if the man, fool though he was, had vindicated Durrand in some way, as if he had pointed out some aspect of Durrand's character that made him feel superior. For like Mathilde, and perhaps because of her, Durrand had an inner sense that he was special – special and invincible.

It is hard to say when Durrand formed the idea that he had a vocation to the priesthood or what he formed it from. His chief wish had always been to be a soldier. From the moment he heard about it, his greatest desire was to be accepted at the Virginia Military Institute, and as he got older, he subsumed everything into this ambition. Everything about the life fascinated him: the drills, the discipline, the uniform, brave with its buttons and sashes. He had visions of glory, of flags and of marching. Indeed, there is some pain in my memory of his touching love of valour. He saw the military life as a selfless pursuit, a sacrificial vocation. His lips were full of abstract words like 'truth', 'freedom', and 'honour', which he never sought to define with much precision. He saw the world in terms of 'them' and 'us' and wanted to make it 'safe from Communism'. By the time Mathilde began to study Russian, Durrand and she had already become engaged in their own private war, but he saw in her passion for the language a larger treachery than to himself alone. His was a monolithic patriotism in which there was no room for dissent; yet, insofar as he could never get America to behave as he wanted it to, he found it disappointing to defend.

Perhaps it was this feeling that he could not give himself wholly to such a diverse nation that caused Durrand, when he had been at VMI for several months, to become aware that something was struggling within him to be expressed. The Institute, for all that it was military, was full of actual boys who have become adults by now, adults who move around from base to base, marry, beget children, grow begonias. For Durrand, as for Mathilde, life had meaning only if it was lived to a pitch and intensity beyond the normal bounds.

At any rate, he let Mother know that he intended to descend upon the Jesuits during the Thanksgiving vacation with a view to looking them over. It was not in Durrand's make-up to consider he might be refused or redirected. Mother got all excited and confused; she laughed and cried a lot. She saw no border between herself and Durrand. To her, he was all she wanted him to be and more.

Weeks went by after Thanksgiving and we had no word about how his retreat had gone, and by this time Mother had told all of her friends he was destined, as she had always prayed, for the priesthood. At Christmas time he strolled in, flipped himself down and lit a cigarette. 'I wouldn't give them the time of day,' he said, 'much less my life.' And he spent the busy season of the Incarnation picking holes in what he called their watered-down religion.

'They didn't want you,' said Mathilde with malice under the tree on Christmas Eve. 'You have nothing to do with them and I could have told you so.' Durrand, giving, perhaps, a single gift, burst into tears. I had never seen him cry, and much to my own astonishment, I instinctively went to comfort him; but his shoulders froze at my touch.

'That's ridiculous,' said Mother. 'Of course they wanted him. A straight-A student?'

Although I knew they had not been able to consider him for more than perhaps a day or two, I kept my own counsel. It was Mathilde who, having wounded him, bucketed down next to him, and with her own sobs frightened him into looking at her. Her face contorted, she heaved back and forward with rage. The lights of the tree gleamed in their eyes, and they rocked together soundless into the night. From that time on, except for me, the Order became in our household an unmentionable symbol of apostasy: and, though I expected the breach between Mathilde and Durrand to be healed upon that night, nothing like that occurred.

I sometimes try to imagine the sort of priest he would have been, but it evades me. He was too troubled and withdrawn to be a mediator or a friend to man. As for God, Durrand seemed to see Him as a boundless autocrat, who brooded over a dark world in whose folds He poked His finger to condemn, disrupt and destroy. Not in Durrand was the capacity to imagine the Sabbath made for man. As far as he was concerned, man was made for the Sabbath. He hated life. All that was legal appealed to him, and when the Church burst past its old structure in the sixties, he found nothing left that could contain his wish to impose upon himself and others the rules and regulations that so preoccupied him. In the sense that he was one of nature's celibates, it could be said that Durrand might have found a place to hide from the demands of a world too taken up with pleasures of the flesh. Much that Durrand saw, smelt, touched or sat upon seemed to him rank with impurity. He had the notion that certain things defiled him: an immodest picture of a woman, a ribald song, the sight of a box of sanitary napkins on the drugstore shelf – these things seemed unclean to him, cancelled him out, made him feel meaningless, helpless and afraid. As Matty had a fear of death, so Durrand had a kind of revulsion from women. I remember he seared my sister with a look when once she mentioned her bra. 'Bra, bra, bra, bra,' she said. 'Ha ha ha ha,' she said. But even Matty could not sustain it long before his white-faced, genuine disgust.

It was this aptitude, perhaps, for an hysterical chastity that might have made them wonder if his vocation was quite the thing it seemed. To say that Durrand lacked desire is hardly accurate. This is nothing I can look at squarely, because at odd, dark intervals I then could sense an emanation from Durrand that makes me think now what a hot, tormenting thing his sexual nature must have been for him. Like an element, it must have boiled up from time to time and burnt him. What would he want? Whom? Men, women, children? Who knows? What he could not ever really do, no more than Matty could, I think, was fall in love. In other words, his lack of any notion that one person could reach out to another made him see the sentient world as animal, and thus he himself could not be transformed, albeit painfully, into a man who could give to others his whole self. For Durrand, the priesthood was an access to power. There was no sadness in him, no day or night. He could not love and he could not suffer except in the agony of isolation. He cast no shadow.

Physically, he did. Cast a shadow, I mean. I remember with dread its coming upon me – lengthening. My mind. I cannot. Fits. There were fits. Mother refused to believe he brought them on. 'Fiddle-de-dee!' she would say. She would cut dead any word against him. What I cannot remember, I cannot. I must not try. There were heavy things and pain. I cannot. I will not and I am not going to.

Durrand knew the ranks of angels and all hierarchies. He loved the structure of the world invisible. In a book, he read of unclean spirits, and one day, swelling in disgust at me, he told me I was possessed of the devil. I must have been quite young, about eight or nine. 'There!' he said, afterwards. 'That'll fix you! And shut you up.'

But I did not know what he wanted me to shut up about. I could not remember what he did. I could never remember it. 'You . . .,' he said, leaning close, '. . . are possessed. By the fiend, by the tempter.' I remember his neck swaying. 'You are the devil. Devil! I cast you out *in nomine Patris, et Filii, et Spiritus Sancti, Amen!*' I shrieked and screamed all night with terrors, but no one came. And so I talked to God all by myself.

Durrand was insatiably neat and clean. He always held himself stiffly as if in preparation for ceremonial dress. He hated mess and dirt. Once, he caught me in the backyard making mud pies. 'Devil! Dirty devil!' he said. 'Look at you! No man will ever want you.'

Something in me blindly feels that Durrand wanted to ensure this.

One day, I tried to dig to China in the backyard with Nathalie from next door. She sometimes stooped to play with me. Her mother had told her that Jesus had compassion on the sick. 'I'm only playing with you because Jesus has compassion on the sick,' Nathalie said. She had no idea what theological relief she had given me: and, even though she acted superior, I knew she really did enjoy our games. Nathalie and I hit a white mineral on our voyage to the centre of the earth. 'Look! It's the devil's nightshirt!' she cried. 'We sure are getting close!'

All at once, Durrand's shadow fell over the hole. 'That's because you've got Irene with you. She's going on a visit to her father in hell,' he said. 'That's where she goes when she has her fits. To hell.'

'*Do* you?' Nathalie asked. She was impressed.

I asked Father Mowbray if I was a child of the devil and if I went to visit him. I had it in mind that Satan maybe gave me a magic drug – a shot or something – so that I forgot where I went whenever I had a seizure. He was very serious with me and assured me that I was a child of God afflicted. I did not know what that meant until I looked it up, but when I did, it slowly dawned on me that by 'afflicted' he had meant that I was suffering. I had had the impression that it was I who made everybody else suffer. I was amazed and pleased. Father Mowbray said that if I bore my affliction patiently, it was a sure sign of God's favour. 'A sign that God loves you especially because He has sent you a great trial.'

And so I learned patience; or it grew from the rod and the stem of God, and it circled the affliction like a vine, holding and choking the devil.

It is Sunday, as I said . . . an honest day when the tomb was broken and life split the chasm of the grave, when the fearful custom of decay was broached by resurrection. It is a day when ointments, scents and salves, brought to mask the stench of putrefaction, could be put aside and had no further value, and the verge of light rising made chaos of a former order.

What did Durrand and Mathilde want of me? And what did death do to him that made her want to write that letter? I, who received it then, and I, who think of it now, are by no means separate beings; but I, who received it then, heard messages borne upon the text which snatched away my judgment and made me feel a child again, guilty about Durrand.

I brooded. I sat a long time in the orchard with the dog, unable to feel the authority of white trees and black branch or to live by the consequence of spring and my own revival from the grip of seizure. It had happened that Durrand had catapulted. He had been severed. 'Don't touch me,' I said to the dog when she brought me her ball. And I became afraid of myself. Where had I gone in my unconscious state the night he died? Had I flown, a dybbuk, spirit of malice, to the pinnacle of a French railroad embankment and pushed? Stern with myself, I marched myself around the country lanes, breathing the air and courting reason. Unable to find it anywhere, the full weight of Mathilde's confidences leaned upon the wild irrational part of me so that I was flattened before her. What she had been through! It filled me with an awful pity that she had had to look upon her own image, likeness, her twin, sewn together in that coffin; and, though it had deeply enraged me that she had thought me capable of seeing any merit in the cruel order of men she had described, the Holy Companionate or whoever they were, I was aghast at the thought that Mathilde, of all people, had had it forced upon her in such a way and at such a time.

It *is* Sunday. Although I do not think they walk here, the eerie silence that used to characterize their play when they were long ago absorbed in each other drifts through the hall and pervades the rooms so that I can almost see them once again, profoundly locked together. It was that silence that finally . . . No. They shared precisely the same taste in food, the same unconscious thought and gesture made to the nape of the neck, the ear, the nose. Even when they split, the same minute devices would apply. I remember an argument at the table. 'That's axiomatic! That's axiomatic!' Durrand chopped away at Mathilde's agile arguments and I pictured an automatic axe coming down. In the silence afterwards, they each peeled an orange – each cutting skin and tearing segments – as one, as if to the rhythm of an inaudible tune.

As in a troubled dream where nothing is connected, I see myself and Matty at an earlier time sitting in the bay window. What was she doing? Telling the story of the Three Fates. 'Clothos spun, Lachesis threaded, and Atropos snipped. Atropos was the little one and carried the shears. She was more frightening than the rest.' And suddenly Durrand burst in, crying, 'Cut it out! Cut it out! It's heathen idols!' And he hit Mathilde for the first time, and she just swayed from side to side like a cobra.

Then she said, 'You never really confess your sins, do you? You tell my sins and change the gender.'

He recoiled. 'You listen! You listen, you toad!' I was horrified that anyone could listen or lie.

Mathilde shook her head just once. 'I don't. I just know. It is you who listens. I caught you listening to Reenie last week, and I've been saving it up.'

The sight of white skin stretching across Durrand's cheekbones terrified me.

'I don't care,' I said quickly. I could not bear to think about his reprisals.

'Don't believe her! Don't believe her, Reenie!' Durrand cried.

'Don't be a fool, Reen,' my sister said with crushing coldness. 'If you do it again,' she said, turning to him, 'I'll tell.'

There is that: and again, arriving whole amid the detritus of other half connected, fearful shadows, is one more thing from a long past June.

I hear myself piping:

> *Here comes the bride,*
> *All dressed in white.*
> *Here comes the groom*
> *With his britches too tight.*

'I'm going to wash your mouth out with soap, Irene!'

'What did I say?'

'She foams at the mouth anyway, so I wouldn't trouble yourself, Lettie,' said Durrand. It was evening and the magnolias were heavy in the dusk. Everyone sang the song in Baltimore because the girls played 'brides' in the cooler air along the sidewalk, trailing from Ashby to Key in dress-ups. I did not know there was anything shameful about the song and I blushed to tears, and the screen door banged and Durrand and Mathilde went out and I watched them from the front stoop. Mathilde had borrowed Mother's crystal rosary and a lace curtain. For some reason, Durrand wore cowboy boots. She descended the marble stoop, sweeping past me. They met on the pavement, the twins, each ten, and the others stopped playing and stood around watching, somehow breathless. I could almost see the altar, the ascending, vaulted ceiling, smell the incense.

'Why aren't you playing?' Nathalie asked me shrilly from her house next door. She, too, sat upon the steps and watched.

'I don't think epileptics are allowed to marry,' I said.

'Brothers and sisters aren't allowed to marry,' said Nathalie.

'Don't be literal-minded!' said Mathilde, breaking the ceremony off and drawing herself up to her full height. Nathalie's mother laughed from inside the door, and later emerged with roses from her garden which she gave to Mathilde.

'Nathalie *is* a little literal-minded,' said her mother with grave amusement to my sister.

What happened to my mother and my father that they were not there, able to protect us from each other in the reaches of the outer darkness that their absence caused us to know?

# Chapter Six

I met my father only once. At the time, I was a senior in high school, in New York with my class on a school trip. Much to everyone's surprise, I had won a scholarship to college. Feeling that this achievement vouched for me, I suppose, I decided in the blaze of a moment, as I stood in Washington Square, to call Father up. It seemed the right thing to do. Agitated with a sense of his mystery, I called from a phone booth, and when he answered, wave upon wave of nerves made my own voice unintelligible to me. There he was, the root of my being. I hung on his every word. The minute I hung up and realized that he had agreed to see me, I felt positively ill with terror. My mother saw him almost as an adjutant to the Prince of Darkness, and suddenly, I realized that I was going to betray her – just as Mathilde had – by making contact with him. I knew Mathilde spent weekends with him now she was an adult, and there was no stopping her. It was she who had told me he was a homosexual and explained what that meant. There was a raffish bravado in her voice whenever she spoke about him. In Matty's eyes, he could not be too rich, too impious or too bad. She took a positive pleasure in all that Mother hated him for. Above all, she admired his intelligence and his taste; these qualities had forced him into open rebellion against the conventions of society, she said.

What do you wear when you are going to meet Caligula? My wardrobe did not rise to the occasion. I made the guilty compromise of hiding my little gold crucifix under a high-necked blouse in order to meet the apostate, my father. The thought that I might have a fit and disgrace myself evolved into near mania. My birth, after all, had been the last straw for Father. I stood, perhaps, for that aghast angel at the gates of Eden, unwitting witness to his fall and barrier to return.

The girls in my class, under the watchful eye of Sister Josephine, trooped out in search of culture. I feigned illness, then fled the Barbazon Hotel to the wild shores of Riverside Drive where my father lived in pagan splendour.

'You must be Irene,' he said by way of greeting. 'You don't look anything like Mathilde.' My father was a dazzler. His apartment dazzled with unique pieces of furniture, wallpaper, flowers. It is hard to say how it was decorated because it presented a whole unity of excellence and looked like a room in a museum. On one wall, there hung a fine Quattrocento etching of the Virgin executed by some minor exquisite of that period. It oddly resembled Mathilde – and him.

He gave me a drink – dry sherry – and made a few nudging remarks about my beaux, as if I could not really have any. I felt the pain of my sister's having passed through the place as a familiar, her hands touching his bibelots with light assurance My father was so handsome, it made me want to cry. His hair was greying, swept up at the temples. He looked like a movie star and talked like a European, though he let a Southern phrase or two drop into his sentences as a graceful genuflection to his past. 'I've never been allowed to meet the boy, Durrand,' he said, making a little moue, but otherwise, he said little that alluded to anything real.

His gestures were light and glamorous rather than effeminate. I fingered the cross under my blouse out of acute nerves. It seemed almost easier to believe I was a child of hell than a child of his. But I was his child. Am. He wanted to know my plans. Did they have anything to do with the history of art like Mathilde? No? Well . . .

I said I planned to become a teacher. He said, 'Those who can, do. Those who can't, teach.' He did not mean to be unkind. His remark seemed to be a witticism, delivered in a tone which included me. He spoke as if there were someone else sitting beside me whom he meant to exclude.

'It was an idea of Mathilde's,' I said, blushing into my drink. I felt I should have a name to drop, so I dropped hers. I could see myself in twenty years time with clumpy shoes and a tight perm, married to my work and boring in my wholesomeness. The Quattrocento head seemed to give a knowing smile.

My father laughed uproariously. 'I would be scared *not* to take Mathilde's advice,' he said. 'If she sees you as a teacher, then you are.' My father, my oracle decided.

What shrewd advice had Matty given Father, I wondered? For some reason, I was alarmed at the thought of her having been with him so much, and I sensed her as having been dandled by a loveless one. A heartlessness became apparent in everything he did and said. I could see Mathilde becoming more and more amusing and bold in his presence, turning herself inside out to be outrageously funny and clever. In the end, I knew she pleased him, but he spoke of her with complete detachment.

His mind did not seem to be on our conversation, and he let it trail off. He left the room abruptly and returned with a small, grizzled, black poodle wrapped in a rug. He said it was unwell and he began to fuss around the creature like a mother with a child. 'Poor Baby,' he said. He looked at me with sudden, sharp hostility. 'Baby belongs to Mitya, but we're both very fond of him,' he said. I felt a shame and confusion because I did not know what he was talking about. It finally registered that Mitya was his current boyfriend. I later learned that the Count, whom Mother called 'that Beelzebub', had been a kind and sensitive man whose life had been made a torment by Father's promiscuity, but that is another story. By the time I met Father, the Count would have been dead for several years. My father fondled the dog and said how much Mathilde adored Mitya and Baby. He had a childish, pouting quality. It was as if it were up to me to give my seal of approval to his relationship with men. Mitya had got Mathilde to learn Russian, my father said. They had had some super times together, Matty, Mitya, Baby and Father. They had motored down to Connecticut and gone sailing, things like that.

As he stroked the dog, I saw in a sharp moment my father's awful dread of me. He watched my face as if it were the weather, as if some squall of emotion, some accusation, moral judgment or insurmountable heartbreak might arise in me and spill out over the carpet. I decided not to tell him about my scholarship because it might be looked upon as an obscure, personal remark, critical of him – I didn't know why. We shook hands at the door, but did not kiss. I patted Baby. On my return to the Barbazon, I was sick, and to this day, I cannot bear the smell of sherry. Afterwards, I wrote him lots of letters, but I tore them all up. How could I have put it, after all, that I did not judge him and had not wanted him to do anything for me but love me? When Mathilde heard of my visit, she was furious with me. She made sure Mother found out and Mother was furious too. Only Durrand wanted to know. He got me off into a corner. 'What's he like?' my brother hissed. But he refused, on moral principle, to visit him.

I mention Father now because he must have been a spiritual connection between Mathilde and her freedom. I often wonder if her rage at my discovery of Father did not stem from my having seen that he was not nice. I think she had built it up in her mind that he did have warmth of feeling for her, and although I never said he had not, my own disturbance at his coldness may have frightened Mathilde into seeing an unwelcome truth. Mathilde had an odd, complex, and almost bizarre attitude towards me as we grew up. She would blow hot and cold about me, drag me into her internecine wars with Durrand, flatter me with confidences and compliments. She would gush. I was the truthful one, the holy fool, the innocent, the one with eerie insight into all sorts of matters she did not herself understand. Maybe I was a mystic, and so on. At other times, she would reject me and push me aside. Losing her temper with me, she would scream at me that I looked hideous. My appearance bothered her a lot. She would compulsively fiddle with my hair. Once, she invited me up to Radcliffe for a weekend, then abandoned me for a party to which she refused to get me asked. She came back drunk, then spent the next day in bed with a hangover. Intermittently, she regaled me with stories of some Harvard boy and how she and he had made out, and so on.

She had often made pointed remarks about my lack of friends, but it irritated her if I made one. She expected I would end up in a convent, but would then say no decent order would take an epileptic. I was very much afraid of her. I always felt she was asking me to be a part of herself that she did not dare acknowledge – a part of herself she scorned but needed.

As I grew up, I felt it necessary to take Mathilde in small doses only. In any case, she moved to London, and after Mother died I went to Maine. There, I lost touch with Durrand entirely, but my sister and I kept up a sort of relationship in which she assumed the power in all of our dealings with one another. It is hard to say what I really felt about Mathilde. We were not close in the way that friends are; yet, I always thought that my inhibitions about making close friendships with men or women came from whatever was wrong in the bond between Mathilde and me.

The very idea of her beauty and brilliance made me feel awkward, and my own attainments seemed valueless next to hers. In every way, she overshadowed me. She thought me socially clumsy and often told me so. I half admired the easy, drawling manner she adopted in company, but it pointed up the shyness which would often freeze me even when people made undeniably friendly overtures towards me. Sometimes my heart would leap hugely after people, but I felt powerless to say so or put myself in the way of knowing them. The barrier was primarily, I suppose, a view I had formed that love between adults was almost invariably destructive, but there was something else. It was almost as if I were waiting for Mathilde's permission, her approval. If I bought a new dress, I would always wonder if Mathilde would like it. If I found a man attractive, the back of my mind would always tell me what Mathilde would think of him. When I furnished my house in Maine, I found myself buying furniture that Mathilde would approve of when she came to visit. And she did come to visit. Because of her work, she made fairly frequent trips to New York. She would call me up from the Algonquin Hotel, where she always stayed, and invite herself up. I would feel compelled to spend hours cleaning and baking, knowing all along that Mathilde disliked the women she admired acting like housewives or servants, and would then feel crushed when, blowing her smoke rings or rattling her bracelets, she would call me 'Mrs Tiggywinkle' or 'little rabbit' – her favourite epithet. She would say this like a boa on the prowl, and, having got myself into the situation in the first place, I would feel angry at feeling numbed by her disdainful, yet somewhat greedy regard. She found me terribly unsatisfactory. She was like a parent. She was like other people's mothers or mothers-in-law, and this, I am sure, is why I felt as I did about her. It was not that my mother had failed to love me so much as that she had had no real opinion of me at all. There was no contesting with her, competing with her, resolving with her. She had been too wounded, was too weak. Matty was a harsh, but real substitute. She found me terribly unsatisfactory, yes: but, she found me a good listening post, and sometimes I felt I focused something for her too. Mathilde liked gin. I learnt to make martinis and they lubricated sticky evenings. Her tongue loosed, she would regale me with stories of a life lived internationally and of lovers, mostly married men. She would wait, I think, for high Catholic opprobrium from me.

I remember one occasion of peculiar and livid awfulness which taught me to avoid such conversations with Mathilde. We were both in our late twenties, and Matty, then at the zenith of her beauty, came to stay with me over Thanksgiving. The weather that year was bad, I remember. There was a lot of snow, and Mathilde was anxious the whole time about getting back to London. I remember feeling a vague resentment, as I stuffed the turkey and baked the pumpkin pie, that my sister hardly helped me at all. She spent most of her time looking out of the window at the sky, and kept disappearing to make long-distance phone calls. When at last the feast was prepared, we sat in the living room with the pitcher of martinis she required before dinner every night. The fire blazed, the snow fell, but my sister seemed absent from the proceedings until the phone rang and she jumped up, quite galvanized by it. Returning to the fireplace, she stood and warmed herself, and, helping herself to more gin, began to divulge to me the secret of her agitation. Her lover in London, she told me, had just announced to her over the telephone that he had made up his mind to leave his wife and four children for Mathilde. More than anything, she looked fed up, nervous and threatened by the news. The man, she said, was fifteen years older than she was, an archaeologist, She had

64

been in Greece with him that summer. They had had a wonderful time oiling themselves and bathing in the sun naked. Mathilde started to give me lubricious details of the affair, watching my face the while for a reaction. As she continued the story of this relationship, it became clear that she was helping herself to the man. Like someone at a buffet supper, she had sort of heaped her plate with him, and now he wanted her for good she was perplexed to know what to do.

'But you never told him you'd marry him, Matty?' I asked. I was indeed truly shocked by her story, as it seemed she had played around with someone's emotions not bothering to weigh the heavy consequences of her actions. She shrugged. 'I don't know. I guess I felt I might,' she said.

'You're shocked,' she said over the turkey and in the candlelight. For all of her elegance, my sister had strange, gluttonous table manners. They seemed so inappropriate to her way of dress, her manner. In every other respect, she had made herself a carbon copy of Father. She had his languor exactly, yet the way she ate, chopping and wolfing and talking with her mouth full, gave away the superficiality of that resemblance. In the working of her jaws, the grabbing of her food, she was pure Durrand. As I watched her, the striking resemblance to Durrand, the shocking story, the ceremonial meal of Thanksgiving, all conspired to make me feel curiously light-headed and frightened – as if we had been transported back to childhood without any of the safety rails that somehow had existed even in that troubled past.

I said I was not sure I liked the word 'shocked' as it sounded judgmental.

Mathilde waved her fork and gulped a glass of wine. She banged it down, nearly breaking the stem. 'You're a prude,' she said. 'A prude and a simpleton. I'll tell you why you're so religious. You're religious because you're a coward. You think if you make enough sacrifices then God won't hit you with another fit. You're powerless and it's only because you feel powerless that you have to back yourself up with some almighty, invisible spectre. You won't stop the dark, and you won't atone for me. I won't let you!' She shrieked the last sentence at the top of her voice. 'You can't even cook,' she said more levelly. 'Look at this breast. It's dry.'

'It's dry,' I said, unwisely, 'because you decided to spend the evening on the phone to Matthew.'

At this point, my sister jacked herself up out of the chair and heaved the contents of the dinner table onto the floor. She stood, quivering with outrage, her eyes bugged out, and in the pitch of a singing voice, she started a tirade of almost inhuman intensity; and, like an aria, sung in a foreign language with which one is a little familiar, her choked and senseless words made out a peculiar threnody – a shape of accusation, betrayal and denial of all the Church taught, said, stood for. It was I, I, I who stood perfidious against all her freedom; then it was Mother, then, at the crescendo of her diatribe, came Durrand.

At the very mention of his name, she stopped, froze, paused for what seemed to be an infinite moment, and collapsed onto the floor. From her foetus-like body, there came a long, low wail, like the wind in the chimney, which grew and grew into a frightful abandoned keening. I had stood quite still throughout all of this, for I feared Mathilde might actually kill me, but once she was on the floor, in that ghastly, rocking misery, I was moved to an odd compassion for my sister. It is really hard to say why. She was sobbing in an uncontrollable frenzy, the name of Durrand bubbling to her lips every now and then as mucus and tears streamed down her face. Slowly, I moved towards her, and put my arms around her, and for a very long time, she refused to be comforted. When I finally got her to bed and had cleaned up, I sat for a long time in the dark before the embers of the fire shaking and trembling, unable to know what to think or do.

The next day, Mathilde was calm and cheerful. Although she apologized to me in a cursory fashion, it was clear to see that she was not really sorry. In fact, she looked grateful to me – and oddly relieved. She returned to London, I heard nothing more about Matthew, and to all intents and purposes it was as if the scene had never occurred. If I had not had the proof of gravy stains on my carpet, I would have thought I had imagined the whole thing. Indeed, I had the instinct that if I mentioned the episode again to Mathilde she would have dismissed it as pure fantasy. In childhood, she had often denied me access to reality in this way, telling me that things I saw were only fits or dreams.

What was it about me that seemed to connect Mathilde to absent Durrand? I am sure this is the key to the whole story which follows. The answer still eludes me, no matter how much I puzzle over it. It may very well be that Mathilde was unconscious of her need for him. Again and again, I felt during our adult years that Durrand was lacking from Mathilde and she did not know it. Most of the time, she behaved as if she had flown, in wizardly fashion, on Father's wings past all the trammels of our childhood, quite beyond the influence of Durrand. Then suddenly, without thinking it, she would *be* him in the flesh. In a disquieting way, Mathilde would arch herself as she sat or as she stood, and embody him, head-hung and smouldering, her eyes blazing with some expression of his. I never felt this more than on one occasion I went to visit her in London – it would have been a few years ago – when she and Durrand were approaching forty.

I have recently been through the soul-numbing task of clearing out my sister's flat in Bayswater, which is an expensive, polyglot part of London near Hyde Park. There is something peculiarly pathetic about the little bits and pieces left by the once-powerful dead. What was I to do with her ice-skates, for instance? She used to exercise regularly at a near-by rink, where she would ice-dance solemnly to Wurlitzer tunes. Mute, with a mute partner she hired by the session, she would waltz, rhumba and tango, her face contemplative and indifferent. What to do with her old icebox? Her scented underclothes?

That first and only time I visited Mathilde in London,

her home filled me with awe. Perhaps her American self was flatter, for I never quite expected the dark and opulent grandeur of her rooms. Her European mode had more inflexion, as if she had pulled shadows around her to stress a vision of herself as complex. Her flat was almost like a cave, full of jewelled treasures from the East, as though, tyrant or pirate, she had retreated from sallies into a dark and almost womb-like cavern, carpeted sumptuously with Oriental rugs, hung with heavy curtains which excluded daylight. Paisley shawls, antique and picked up in market places, swathed the furniture. The place was full of stuffs. Mathilde had spent no money to speak of on mundane things. Her kitchen and bathroom lacked convenience; but the living room had the aspect of a small chamber belonging to Catherine the Great, or some other brilliant solitary. The room was lit with cunning and artifice so that her few marvellous icons glowed from the walls; yet she herself seemed more central to the place than they did. She would sit for long hours in a large, bright wing chair set boldly forward towards the centre of the room: in her sitting and in the chair's placement, she conveyed the idea that she ruled absolute over her life. My eye swerved naturally from the sombre icons – of bishops in chequered stoles, of saints, of an hieratic Virgin stiff with the consciousness of her calling – to Mathilde. The paintings almost seemed to be her servants, stuck around the room in varying attitudes of Byzantine courtliness. A photograph of Father on the mantlepiece somehow spoilt the whole effect; yet, his tilted hat, his angled face revealed much to me about my sister. From time to time, she gave swift glances at the silver frame, depending, perhaps, on his continuing patronage.

She had, indeed, taken something from Father. The room, though dark dyed, resembled his. Somehow I felt she had inherited his love of Renaissance painting – and stripped away whatever humanism there was in it. With all of his Madonnas, Crucifixions, and Nativities, one had had no thought of God; yet the sense of human beauty had been inescapable in his apartment. Mathilde's presence amongst her icons somehow robbed them of religious meaning too, and one was left only with an idea of in-human strangeness over which my sister exercised some peculiar authority.

Yet if Mathilde was in command there, she also seemed restless. I could not help feeling that she waited for some unspecified event to alleviate her boredom or unease.

Immediately on my arrival, I began to wonder what she expected from it. Even as I had packed my suitcase in Maine, I had felt myself torn between an absurd pride that Mathilde had asked me to stay with her and that caution I had grown against her, particularly at times when she left me in the dark about her motives. There seemed to be no reason for my trip other than her insistence that I should make it. I remember entering her flat, breathless and banging luggage, creased by flight, pleased with myself for having managed, exhilarated at being abroad for the first time, only to stop when I saw her face in the doorway. Mathilde rarely smiled, and this time she greeted me with a curt nod which intimated to me that my visit had some kind of use for her. All the same, I was drawn into a helpless admiration for her and it scared me. During my first hours there, I became slowly aware of something brooding, lashing and agitated in her, an immense force of feeling which she yearned to release.

I remember now Mathilde as a child, walking on stilts along the frying August sidewalk. I was never allowed to use the wonderful toy, although I longed to. It was feared that I would have a seizure and fall. Mathilde, as a grown woman in her own milieu, seemed to stagger psy-chologically along without, somehow, the knowledge of the drop. It was as if she went stilted across the wild, un-structured marsh of her inner thoughts, unaware that she had them. Sitting in her red chair, observing her hands, she told me some story or other about a setback she had ex-perienced in her work. Apparently, she had published a paper in a learned journal about archetypal, pagan images of women and their relation to the various types of icon which the Orthodox Church allows to be used in the veneration of the Mother of God. Before I had even had a shower, she gave me her strange, and uncharacteristically tangled article to read. I could not quite understand it. Mathilde was hugging herself as if she had been bruised. She then erupted into a bitterly angry attack against a feminist art critic, who had 'attacked' her paper in riposte. She said she had expected the Church to rise up against her, but not her own sex. Really quite out of the blue, she went on to talk about how badly she had been treated by men and how she would never be subservient to anyone. She was obviously goaded beyond measure into a fury against the woman who had disagreed with her. 'Imagine! Imagine!' she cried. 'When I have resisted all – everything! All the trappings of bourgeois existence in order to live an independent life, and she says that my very work itself shows how enthralled I am to a false image of woman!'

She carried on well past the point where my jet-lag could take it about sisterhoods and covens and how the universities were eaten up by it all now, and what did I know about it? And what was my opinion? At last, she let the matter drop and I fell into the bed in her augustly furnished guest room not knowing what to think. Lying down, however, I was overwhelmed by a sense of emptiness and fear emanating from Mathilde. Above all, there was that feeling I always had, queer and prickling, that Mathilde wanted something from me.

It was like Mathilde – indeed, it was her pattern – to drop in on me without notice. From our earliest times together, I was the one for whom she had a curious need, like an appetite for an obscure but vital substance to her diet. I never knew what it was I supplied, and I never knew when she was going to want it, whatever it was. In this matter, I was hardly a cold observer, and, even now, it takes me the greatest effort even to attempt to objectify the subtle way in which I felt compelled by Mathilde. Our encounters always left me exhausted and demoralized. This was an incurable condition of our relationship, because in her presence I found myself unable to assert my own thoughts. When I look back on it, I can see that she did this by revealing nothing to me except the pain or predicament of what was present to her. It always looked like a kind of gift to me that she would arrive, and confide, and then go away. But the very Trojan horse – of her misery at a broken love affair, her happiness at achievement won, the bizarre emotional agony which she showed me that Thanksgiving – concealed a huge number of expectations and demands that I never recognized until they were upon me. I think what worried me most of all about being summoned by Mathilde to see her in London was the eccentricity of the invitation in itself. It broke the pattern which I understood, left me without the ground of home territory under my feet, and put me in the way of confronting something unfamiliar.

Every time I think of that sojourn with Mathilde, my mind closes like a door with a spring-loaded lock. I do not think I could approach that mental door at all if John had not been with me, at the end, in the flat itself. After all, we had met on the journey which was to be Mathilde's final one, and he had seen me through her death. Together he and I heaved books and stacked papers. Together, we drank instant coffee and looked about the bare walls, silent but unified still in our mutual astonishment that we had found each other. It seems so unasked for, so unlooked for, that it verges on miracle, I thought. 'It's like a miracle,' he said, 'or something we've got away with. It seems unfair to other people, who cannot be so happy.' I said, 'It's utterly ridiculous!' and I started to laugh so that tears of relief came to my eyes. 'How did you ever see? I could never see.' He said, 'I *saw* only you. It is either a limitation or a gift, and I choose to think of it as a gift. Seeing her would have done no good at all, even if someone as opaque as Mathilde could have been seen. Irene! What was she doing with *icons*? How did she involve herself with images of real substance?'

My real perplexity on this question is perhaps the basis

of my motive for giving the beautiful things away. Like columns in a stage-set temple, they somehow framed Mathilde's denial of their meaning. It was as if she allowed them to evoke a universe for her in order to contain her inner necessity to flout its laws. She was as bound to religion as Catherine on her wheel, or, as Ixion-bound. In it, she could find no solace and its purposes were hidden from her; yet, she was automatically compelled to scrape, tweeze flakes of tempera from the face of the saints, study them, reset their jewels and burnish their crowns with gold leaf. She loved the physiognomy of virgins, martyrs and apostles. The Saviour's face could rivet her attention for hours. She explained to me with rapturous seriousness how from the dark 'oklad' of the background, the painter built the features, reversing the method used in the West of creating shadow with 'chiaroscuro'. It was as if the images themselves were called from chaos into form, born into their light from shadow. Above all, Mathilde was preoccupied with the image of the Mother of God. There are certain typical patterns that are used for her icons, and Mathilde had made them an especial field for study. It was as if she were consumed with a passionate longing to embrace her own femininity through the obscure mystery of these paintings, yet constantly she turned aside the messages contained within them of how to do it. She could make a dissertation on the Mother of God of Compassion, but she could not embrace other people with any feeling; she could write a monograph on the Mother of the Sign, but could find no significance; she would work on the Mother Who is Indicator of the Way until her fingers ached, the Annunciation until dawn, yet she remained directionless and unfulfilled. To Mathilde, these images were powerful rather than sacred, but underneath it all I think she lived in constant terror that her icons might betray her with a revelation of their source. It was as if Mathilde played with fire all the time as the best means of preventing herself catching light.

Ultimately, I do not know why my sister involved

herself so deeply yet so faithlessly in the purest and most orthodox form of Christian art, but my instinct always was that it contained a vision of womanhood that Matty both hungered for and abhorred. Indeed, this is the only theory I can muster which can contain the contradictory facts which have so tormented my reason. Now I look back on it, I think that her passionate, obsessive need for a mother who was consecrated, wise, dignified and effective compelled her towards the truest image she could find of a woman; yet, the truer it was for her, the more Matty felt the dichotomy between it and herself; and the more she felt that, the more she sensed its rejection of her, and so she ended up by rejecting it until compelled again to further pursuit. It was not until Mathilde's connection with this chaste, incarnating woman, strong and profound, was exploded by another woman, the feminist art critic who was probably much less intelligent and capable than my sister, that she had any doubt at all about the value of what she was doing. It never struck Mathilde that she had written an emotional and garbled account of feminine archetypes, nor that she had given her attacker some justification for misunderstanding her. All Mathilde saw in this woman's riposte was a kind of desecration of her life's work. The woman had said that Mathilde's images, upon which she had lavished such thought, were nothing more than symbols of the subjugation of women to the paternalistic ideals inherent in all Christianity. For some reason, it was this argument and this argument alone that set my sister into an almost incoherent frenzy. It seems odd to say it, but I did not know Mathilde well enough to ascertain just how far this incident had penetrated her: my feeling now is that, for reasons that were hidden to me, Mathilde had reached the very limit, had gone about as far with her pretended self as it was possible to go, and, offering her throat to the knife of her opponent's analysis, had mysteriously allowed it to plunge. The truth was that my sister lived the most awful, lonely, isolated life. She had failed to make any abiding relationship with anyone. She had stretched and stretched and stretched herself out towards an identification of herself with an absolute feminine self which was essential and blessed, and when this image was confused with its very opposite, the elastic of my sister broke, and she was propelled, I am now convinced, towards her ultimate doom in Durrand.

For it was he she continually, unconsciously evoked during my stay with her. Sitting on the bus with her, going to Regent's Park, I turned to find her face set in a rigid, insolent stare. She was looking at me, and when she caught my eye, she gave his thin-lipped little laugh. At Buckingham Palace, I caught her standing fixedly in a rooted fascination with the ceremonial changing of the guard. She stood completely still except for one strange motion of her arm, which swung lightly back and forth with clenched hand. This he used to do when preoccupied with watching a game or parade. She took me to the Victoria and Albert Museum. Without appearing to think about it, she strode through hall after hall, examining the exhibits with a shadow of the casual contempt he had in his eyes. It disturbed and worried me. I felt helplessly that I walked now with him, now with her. She slowed her pace, stopped, stood and looked confused, then, as if in a dream, she led me to the costume hall where she seemed to be seeking something important. We moved amongst the mannequins in bustles, beaded gowns, until at last she stopped in front of a case which contained a headless Infanta. I looked at the dummy draped in egregious paniers and stiff brocade, its bald neck jutting out of a square collar. Suddenly, I became aware that Mathilde was crying. 'What's the matter? What's the trouble, Matty?' But she would not say.

It was these odd lapses in her otherwise controlled behaviour which frightened me. My nights were filled with restless dreams. Day after day my anxiety grew. At this point I had no idea where Durrand was or what he was doing, but I could not stop thinking about him. I had an odd notion he was going to turn up. It was wholly irrational, but I could not get it out of my head that Durrand was expected.

It seems very strange to John, although I always took it for granted, that Mathilde and I had grown into the habit of never discussing Durrand directly; this was, of course, before he died. After that, everything changed. But during his lifetime, she and I would only allude to him. I always felt that his dark spirit belonged to her alone, not withstanding their rift. Matty had a weird, passionate ambivalence about Durrand. I never knew whether they communicated with one another or not. Although I had a sketchy idea of what had happened to him after our parents died, I soon stopped inquiring of Mathilde. Her face would distort with anger and I knew it was more at me for prying than at Durrand against whom she would rail on these occasions. With one side of herself, she seemed jealous of anyone who had anything to do with him, even God. In another way, she violently disapproved of him. So we did not speak of him.

One night, however, just as my visit was drawing to a close, Mathilde and I were sitting in her yellowed kitchen eating an omelette she had hastily prepared on her rickety old gas stove, which looked as if it might explode at any moment. She seemed in a terrible hurry to get through the meal, and throughout it, she kept looking at me oddly as if something were going on in her mind and she was not sure whether to tell me about it or not. At length, she pushed back her plate, lit a cigarette and dipped the ash in the egg, immediately putting it out. Evidently, she had succumbed to her impulse. She told me she would value my opinion on an icon she was restoring, as it had given her a lot of trouble, preoccupied her a lot. I said I did not think it was possible that I could give her any advice, but she brushed this aside. She suddenly seemed very breathy and taken with the idea. 'You can see things that I can't see,' she said. 'You have gifts that I lack.' She had a sort of childish, addled look on her face. I felt uncomfortable with this remark. Mathilde often made me feel as if there were some rudimentary quality in my psyche which had not been ironed out by the press of civilization. When she considered me in this light, her expression would become credulous and naive. 'Yes, you have gifts, powers,' she said. 'You don't know what you're sometimes capable of saying, and you're totally unaware of it. You will mention something I have been thinking about, make allusions to things you could not possibly know that affect me deeply. It's as if you were endowed with second sight.'

'Mathilde!' I cried. 'I have nothing of the kind! And I refuse to look at any painting of yours if you intend some kind of witchcraft!'

She became very agitated. 'No, Irene, no. I don't. I'm sorry. I just want you to look at the thing, that's all – just to tell me exactly what you see, no more. Please. It's very important to me!'

'Matty! Leave me alone!'

But she started to reason with me. How, she asked me, could looking at a holy picture do anyone harm? As I was a Catholic in a state of grace what evil could it possibly do to help her restore a badly damaged icon so that it would better enunciate the truth of its theology? She started a long explanation about the place icons had in Orthodox teaching, about how the Eastern and Western churches had both lifted their anathemas on each other so that it was quite proper for me to regard what she was about to show me as an object of veneration. Indeed, she told me, the process of making an icon was undertaken only by those who embraced a rigorously holy life. On she rambled about Byzantine wars and the real intercessory power icons were supposed to have, how they affirmed the Incarnation and how the Incarnation of Christ in a human mother made them desirable objects of devotion. I could not understand what she was getting at. As she delivered her obfuscating lecture, the nerve ends in my hands and arms began to tingle and prickle. Stifling memories of childhood came back to me, moments when I had felt powerless against her hidden wishes. In the end, I could not resist her.

Mathilde's studio looked more than anything like an expensive operating room. There were racks of jars with chemicals and the place was antiseptically clean. She kept it at a special temperature. There were drawers and drawers of special instruments and optical devices. She had huge tomes in Greek and Russian. Hidden not entirely from sight were wonderful pigments, gold leaf, jewels worth a fortune. There was even an X-ray machine. The room made one feel as if somewhere in the background, a wealthy woman was being prepared for cosmetic surgery which involved Mathilde's lining her eyelids with tiny diamonds.

At the back of the studio, there stood an easel shrouded with a cloth. Mathilde went to it. Slowly, with either a show of reverence or a desire to create suspense, she unveiled it.

At first, it was difficult to see the icon. It was very dark, caked over by centuries of pious abuse, and the faces had been all but occluded by incense, smoke and kisses. Through the gloom, it was just possible to see glints of beauty. It was a representation of the Mother of Christ, and as I looked at it more closely, her brooding, passionate regard caught and held me in an oddly human way, almost as if she were alive. I had somehow not expected her. What was she doing? I had to move closer to see through the damage. The infant Christ sat on her lap, his hands clasped in hers. He was looking over his shoulder at something I finally identified as the Cross. When I at last had made out what the whole picture was, I felt a little ashamed of my earlier wariness. The more I looked into the painting, the more I became held in the bond between the two figures. A nexus of cloth and a similarity of radiant expression in the eyes seemed to hold them together in a vision of destiny which might have been tragic but for the profound intimacy and humility the two figures had. All of a sudden, and quite beyond my ability to account for it, I felt a deep compassion for my sister.

'Why are you crying?' I heard her exclaim sharply. I did not realize I had been. I turned and looked at her, but knew I could never explain to her the cause of my weeping, which was quite beyond my control. How could I tell her that she seemed infinitely touching to me? 'I don't know,' I said. I reached out and tried to embrace her, but she shrank away from that. 'I suppose,' I said, 'because it is very beautiful.'

It was clear that she was utterly confused by my reaction. 'It's supposed to have been miraculous,' Mathilde said. 'That's why I wanted you to see it. I can't bear to work on it. It drives me crazy.'

I said nothing, but looked back at the gentle, occluded figures in the painting.

'Do you think you could ask it something?' she said after a long pause, 'For me.'

'I think I already have,' I ventured.

'I want to see Durrand,' Mathilde said.

I looked away from the icon. Outside, from the window, I could see the trees swaying, their leaves blown backwards so that they had a whitish appearance in the windy dusk. It was beginning to rain.

'Matty! Look at me! No!' I said. 'You must ask yourself that – not me.' There was a wizened look on my sister's face. Like a small child, she started fretfully to cry. 'But I want to see him,' she said. 'I just do. I must see Durrand.'


# Chapter Seven


He needed her too; Durrand needed Mathilde; or rather, I think he required her. It was not in Durrand's character to lose his head over a woman, even if that woman was Mathilde, nor do I think he would have allowed nostalgia to invade his breast. More to the point, when her time came, when her re-entry into his life became necessary to him, there was bound to be a functional rather than an emotional aspect to it. Like a diabetic, he would have craved her as sugar, or sought to balance himself with her as if she provided insulin.

It has taken me a long time to discover how his life actually matched with hers from the time he left the army up to the time of his reunion with Mathilde, which took place shortly after my visit to London. My first difficulty was that Mathilde had disguised the name of the organization to which Durrand belonged, and for reasons which will eventually become evident. To my surprise, I found that Durrand had been a member of 'Fraternitas', a legitimate and even respectable religious order, which does, in fact, have its headquarters in Paris.

The second difficulty was posed by Fraternitas itself. Every attempt I made to get a straightforward explanation for the circumstances of Durrand's life within it, and their side of the story which might counterbalance Mathilde's lurid speculations about his death, was met with bland, high-toned discretion. I felt I was playing with Chinese boxes. First one picture of Durrand emerged, then another. I found my queries being turned around and answered obliquely so that I followed them to far-gone conclusions, only to find that these had no basis. The bare facts I did glean were that Durrand had renounced his army career after he had met up with Fraternitas workers in Saigon; some years later, after his vocation had been tested, he became a full member, taking vows of poverty, chastity and obedience. They taught him Spanish, then sent him to one of their houses in Argentina, where he lived at home under their severe rule and worked in a large multinational corporation in Buenos Aires. When he was forty years old, he was returned to the mother house in Paris, and, until his death, worked at the Banque Occidentale de Crédit, just as Mathilde later told me. Whether or not they had told my sister that he had died saving a child, I will never know. They told me his death had been accidental. Their courtesy to me very quickly wore thin, and when it became clear to me that they did not welcome my inquiries, I was at a loss to know what to do.

Finally, I took the course that I believe Mathilde herself should have taken. After really not too long a struggle, I found a priest at the cathedral who spoke good English. I submitted to him all the worries I had about Fraternitas and about everything there was to do with both Durrand's and Mathilde's deaths. I was lucky in finding a very strong friend in him. Eventually, he directed me to an ex-member of Fraternitas who is now studying for the priesthood in London, where of course I had much to do in getting rid of Matty's things anyway. He said this man had probably been a contemporary of Durrand's and might be able to throw light on my perplexities. The French priest had little sympathy with the aims of Fraternitas, and used the word 'mauled' to describe the state of mind its defectors had on leaving it.

Durrand's ex-colleague refused to be identified and I wholeheartedly respect his wishes. He is nervous, pale, a deeply religious man who entered Fraternitas because it seemed to ask everything of him for God. His reasons for leaving it I will not go into, but he did know Durrand, who had been alive at the time he left the organization. He was shocked to hear the story of Durrand and Mathilde – the story I am coming to – and I am afraid I disturbed him.

His memory of Durrand, nevertheless, had some correlation with mine. Fraternitas had spoken of him to me as buoyant, optimistic, full of boundless energy in the service of God, tireless in his devotions, sadly missed by all of his brothers and sisters. My informant thought Durrand had been mentally ill, and had always thought so, though for years he had suppressed his thoughts because he felt guilty about his dislike for Durrand. No one, he said, could have matched Durrand's frantic zeal for the numerous rules and regulations which govern even the most intimate and trivial details of the lives of Fraternitas members. There is a rule, he said, about the manner of opening and shutting doors, a rule about the temperature of baths, a rule for the exact length of time to be spent daily in mental prayer, and so on.

'But,' I said, 'that's the sort of thing many religious

people require. Some monastic orders have stringent rules about daily life. So do Orthodox Jews.'

My informant shrugged. 'It's not the same,' he said. 'There is a different spirit. In any case, they wouldn't appreciate your analogy with the Jews because they are almost uniformly anti-semitic. So, I'm afraid, was your brother. He once told me as a matter of fact that the number of Jews slaughtered in the holocaust was a great exaggeration.'

I thought about this for a while. We were sitting by a large window which overlooked a leafy square. A fine autumn rain needled onto the changing trees. I shivered to think of Durrand saying that – he with his engine mind, his oven mouth, 'Mathilde said they were fascists,' I replied.

'Oh, they're very careful about that. I wouldn't say there was anything overt; an approach to life, an attitude of mind is similar. They don't leave anything to the individual, and they do try to recruit from society's elite. Mostly, they're against Marxism in any form, even if that form may look sometimes like a mild kind of parliamentary democracy. I mean to say – some of the things they're against are just liberal. They don't like diversity. It bothers them if people think for themselves. They have a very strict index and you would be surprised to learn what one isn't allowed to read: Kierkegaard, for instance.

'Anyway, Durrand looked very good to them for a while – a good candidate for the thought-police. He's bright, of course – was. I still can't get over the idea that he's dead. The big challenge to them is South America. They have no opinion at all of liberation theology. "Look what happened to Cuba," they say, in support of any argument against their cosiness with regimes that torture people and extort money from the poor. You get an end justifies the means situation without even trying. Durrand was dead keen on this. He often led group discussions on the Vietnam War and its implications. Durrand seemed to have guts. He was not squeamish. He seemed to have found his haven in Fraternitas. He was so *competitive*. If one man went without meat, Durrand would go without food altogether. No one could prostrate himself as low as Durrand, but no one aspired higher in a way.

'The real secret, I think, of his life – the mainspring – was his adoration of Victor. Victor's a strange man, very idiosyncratic, very prayerful. He has a compelling personality. It's as if you are sucked right into it. You can't say no to him, and this is more so because the people who are attracted to Fraternitas in the first place are generally insecure. I know I was. I mean, why not join the Benedictines, the Carmelites? They have rules too, as you say. But those rules only do some of the work for you, not all of it. The rules are meant to exclude distraction from God. With Fraternitas, you get a total package. Heaven is a place you go to en bloc, and . . . well, I mustn't be bitter.

'Your brother was sent to Argentina, and that was a bit of a compliment at the time. Oh, he polished his boots. There I go again. And I don't know what happened there, but time passed, and we at the main house heard less and less about Durrand. I'm afraid I can't fill you in with all of the details, but all of the sudden, a great shock wave went through everybody. Durrand had fallen foul of the law, but no one said why. Not, I may say, that anyone at Fraternitas ever questioned anything much. I mean to say that no one said how he had fallen. My guess, from the nature of their reaction, is that Durrand at forty and in a hot climate might have cracked up sexually. What could he have done, after all, that the Galtieri regime at that time would have minded so awfully much but that? Was it someone's son, someone's daughter? I always thought Durrand was a little ambivalent. When I knew him in Paris, he used to stare at people on the streets, then look away with scorn. I always sensed a hidden voluptuousness in him. I'm not blaming him for that, because it is very hard to lead a celibate life. No, it was somehow disturbing. He was deeply wounded. That's what I think now of him. Somehow, he never got to the point of having a heart.

'At any rate, he returned to Paris after a while under a

cloud. Few things would have upset him more than to merit Victor's disapproval.'

I thought about Durrand's escapade in Argentina, and about the wounds he had inflicted on himself as a child – the fleeting, intense expression on his face when he had done something that really hurt him. What if, the mortifications my informant told me were encouraged by Fraternitas were insufficient to Durrand? What if, after a while, the sensation of pain itself had not suggested another victim? I said nothing about this. 'Do you remember when Durrand returned? Do you remember seeing his twin turn up at the door?' Somehow I myself had to think about Mathilde, and the story she told me on our journey to the East in order to stop the other memories.

'I remember the return. Durrand came back to the house one day – I think we were going into lunch. I'll never forget his face. You talk about your sister's icons ... Durrand's face was like a sign to me that I had to leave, no matter what the cost. I was beginning to lose my mind, but Durrand seemed to have gone all the way. Not that I think he was crazy, exactly. It's just that he had the look of a man who finally had no soul at all. You know, eyes – like the Moonies, I think they are called. The funny thing about Fraternitas, is that everyone is much too well bred to countenance ... how can I call it ... the natural consequences of their philosophy. As for seeing your sister, I never did, but if she did turn up, they would have been only too glad. Durrand troubled everyone. They would have seen your sister as a utensil, and might have tried to get her to help out.'

I felt it almost immoral to probe more. My informant was becoming more and more exercised. A great tiredness around his eyes and mouth, his sitting back, his exhaustion, made me feel that it was time to stop, but I had only one question more. 'Do you think they murdered Durrand?' I asked him, for at that point I did not know how Durrand had died.

He shook his head slowly. 'No,' he said. 'I don't think

they would have done that. In the first place, it wouldn't have served any purpose. In the second place, it isn't the Mafia, you know. No, your sister sounds as paranoid as Durrand was, maybe more. People do get ludicrous notions about Fraternitas. The important thing is to stick to the truth.'

Hindsight, foresight, insight, second sight.

Suppose I had known instead of merely sensed that Durrand was in desperate straits at the time I left Mathilde in London. Would it have made any difference even if I could have plumbed his motives to the depths?

What insight should I have gleaned from the seizure I had the night that Durrand died? Was it so wrong to consider it a coincidence? Should I have taken it as warning, rather, never to see Mathilde again?

And if it is true that I was granted the dubious gift of second sight on the journey I took with Mathilde, why was I unable to see the dreadful consequences – the meaning of vision – until it was too late?

The only truth is the hidden dignity of each present moment in which all wisdom is contained. I am not my own God.

All things went contrary to my knowing about what was in store for me. As the months went by after the death of Durrand, my health improved. In fact, the whole episode of those convulsions associated with Durrand's so-called martyrdom puzzled my doctors, who had expected the seizure to be a prelude to a complete reversal of things as they had been for fifteen years. Once the electrical tide of the major seizure had receded, my EEG showed an oddly settled state of affairs. At the best of times, epilepsy is a strange disease. We all waited for more. It is well known that the encroachment of middle age can bring back a childhood tendency to convulsion, and I despaired of ever regaining my health. Nothing was wrong with my health.

A barrage of questions came regarding what they increasingly thought was an isolated episode: Did you oversleep? Look too long at a flashing light? Were you at a school disco, perhaps? Did you sit too close to the television? Bang your head? Were you emotionally upset? Overtired? And so on. When I told them about Durrand's death, they pounced on it. 'But I didn't know until afterwards,' I told them. 'Déjà vu!' they cried, as if this proved it. Back I checked, re-checked and double checked. Although it seemed quite impossible for me to have found out about Durrand until after I had recovered, they refused to believe me. 'Did your sister perhaps reach you on the telephone? How could you remember anything after such a convulsion? Couldn't it have obliterated your memory of her call?'

And this, I think, was my first mistake. I rang up Matty in London to check.

What had been on her mind all those months? Now I have heard her story, and pieced together the rest of what really happened to Durrand, now I have returned from the ends of the earth with her bones, the central pieces of the puzzle must be rearranged. At the time, I was so terrified of becoming once again a prey to the disease that the danger in my query escaped me utterly.

'How interesting,' said my sister's voice, 'that you should ask me that question now. I was only thinking this morning about the coincidence.'

'You're sure it was a coincidence, Matty? Are you sure you didn't get me after all – and then forget, in your grief, that you had spoken with me? Are you positive? It makes a tremendous difference, you see.'

She was silent, but attentive on the other end of the phone.

'Mathilde,' I said, 'no one can figure out what set this thing off. I was in perfect health. I know you think my life is bound to routine, but the routine has always kept things stable, and the day I had the seizure, I followed the routine completely. Nothing else could have set me off. I'm sure of it. Don't you understand? If you did tell me about Durrand before the seizure, it's almost certain that I'll get better again. If you didn't tell me, it's likely that something has gone haywire and I'm in for it. It's a bit of a life sentence, Matty.' I was near tears. She was still silent. 'Mathilde,' I said, 'I'm living on Valium and Dilantin. I think I may lose my job.'

'I'm afraid to disappoint you,' she said at last. 'It was because I couldn't reach you that I called your neighbours. I'm afraid you are going to have to admit to having a psychic experience. Maybe that is what it was, and maybe that is why you are better. Why talk about a life sentence?'

Unless my memory heals completely I will never know if she was lying.

The tests may have proved negative, but what was I to do with my shaken confidence? The fearful return to living each moment in dread of spasm and collapse, antic vision, enuresis, humiliation and pain? My Judas brain, linked in my mind with the father of lies, had sold me out when I least expected it and at the worst possible moment. Of all times to be afflicted, the occasion of Durrand's death was worst. It was like the device of some fiend. The harder I tried to struggle out of the notion that the accident was my fault, the more I was sucked into guilt. The guiltier I felt, the more desperate became the need to expiate. When I reasoned with myself that I could not possibly be responsible for Durrand's death, another plausibility asserted itself: that I was truly unclean and possessed of the devil and that a malign clairvoyant experience had caused me to lose what fifteen years of hard work had built up for me.

Almost as an answer to these black suspicions, a confirmation of them, came the gradual but measurable loss of my autonomy. I was forced to surrender my driver's licence until I could prove that the disease had gone for good. 'Well, supposing you'd been in the car at the time. You'd have crashed into a tree, or even killed someone,' said the helpful woman bureaucrat at my tearful surrender. I had to rely on an erratic bus to get to school. This made me late

86

from time to time. 'Are you sure you're well enough?' my principal asked. He called me into his office and showed me letters he had received from parents who objected to an epileptic teaching their children, for word had gone round our small town. Did I notice people avoiding me or not? I began to wonder if I were really fit to teach the fifth grade. I began to wonder if I should not resign. The inherited money I had made me feel guilty. It seemed squalid, filthy lucre, yet there to make the sacrifice of something I loved doing both possible and desirable.

What if I did disturb the children I taught? What if I were unconscious of my true behaviour? What if, through the lattice of my conscious behaviour there appeared lacunae? How did I know, for instance, whether or not I stopped midstream in tracing the Amazon River, smacked my lips and drooled? In marking an English test, did my nostrils pinch? Did my hand go flat upon the page? As I walked through the town, a snatch of music heard through an open window could freeze me on the street until I established it was not an auditory hallucination. I became obsessed with the appearance of my clothes. Had I put on a stained skirt in a fit of absence? Put things on backwards or inside out? Had I locked the house? Fed the dog? Left the iron on? I started making scrupulous lists, checking off each figment of detail. Had I taken my drugs? Had I taken too many? Did my speech slur because of them? Did people think I was drunk? Or insane? Worst of all, my memory started playing tricks again, as if it bucked against my careful lists. Time seemed to bulge. It warped itself. Odd conglomerations of events glutted my mind, then blanks would occur. It was as if my own personal history became distorted. All seemliness and dignity and purity of line became muddied, and everything trailed off into a flat misery.

About a week after I had spoken to Mathilde on the telephone, she rang me in a state of high excitement. Her voice sounded airy, almost positive. For a moment in which I turned over inside, I thought she was going to tell me she had recalled having spoken with me about Durrand's death before my seizure, but she made no reference to this at all.

'I've been doing a lot of reading and thinking,' she said. 'There's the prospect of being included on a very interesting trip through Central Asia this August. I've decided it would be best for you to come along.'

I could see her in my mind's eye as a little girl again, erupting into my room with her gifts of friendship. Her voice had the same tone, cast the same spell.

'Mathilde, I don't know that I'm well enough to travel,' I said.

'Oh, you'll only sit there and brood. Probably pick blueberries with a lot of girl scouts, and go on expeditions to scenic places crammed with summer people. Besides, I want to see you. I want to talk with you.'

'I'll have to think about it,' I said.

'Listen, Irene, this is a big opportunity. I've been invited to do this trip with Vinnie Winston.'

I drew a blank on Vinnie Winston.

'You know about Vinnie Winston, don't you? I mean, his books are published in America too. He's opened up a terrific route to China, and I want to go. We go all the way across Europe to Moscow, then travel to Irkutsk in Siberia, through Outer Mongolia, and then to Peking.'

'Mathilde,' I said, 'I don't want to do this, because I don't feel safe.'

'You're safe,' she said.

'Mathilde,' I said. 'What put this into your head?'

She was silent for a long time. Then she said, 'If you knew what I'd been through, you wouldn't ask such a question. Reenie, I need you. I need you,' and with that, she collapsed in tears.

What should I do? Oh God, what should I do? Which? Give myself to her? Help her? Help myself? Which way?

There was silence in the church and silence in the courtyard, silence in the garden and silence in the orchard where the trees seemed to thrust beauty away from themselves. There are two kinds of silence, one of which would be profaned by even holy thought, and the other which horrifies the soul with black absence. I seemed to be between dream and waking, cluttered, confused with dark and ineffable terrors. What I dreamed of seemed sharp and real; my waking was fogged and thought seemed untenable. It was as if my unconscious mind had been laid bare by the seizure so many months before, and as if Mathilde's request had set a spotlight on it. Waking or dreaming, there were visions of Mathilde and sateen coffins, Mathilde in trains. As if in a whisk of smoke, I saw wild, velvety expanses of corruption in high places, gargoyles sitting on church roofs. Febrile and unconscious, I met dream men in heavy dresses waltzing over parquet floors. Thrones and dominations appeared in snatched moments between sleep and waking. 'Get up! Get up!' I heard Mathilde call to a sealed coffin.

I decided not to go. I wrote to Mathilde, not trusting to her coaxing on the phone. Time went by and she wrote to me furiously that I had made a nonsense of her plans. We had missed the train journ  from London but Vinnie had given her one last chance. We could fly from London to Moscow, and thence to Irkutsk, joining the party for Mongolia there. She had taken the liberty of booking me and obtaining visas, which she had filled out but I would have to sign. She enclosed these with a deadline for mailing them back to her. Mathilde never did say please. Helplessly, I went on a round of priests and doctors hoping for some alibi. 'It will do you good,' said Father Walak. 'Change of scene.'

Painfully, I told him of the darkness of my spirit. 'Don't give yourself airs,' he said.

The doctor has much fondness for psychology, but is not in my view a brilliant amateur. 'You'll be perfectly all right if you take your medication with you,' he said. 'Don't you think you should confront your sister?'

I did not think so. But when the month of June drew to a close, the thing I really dreaded happened. The school board reached a decision that I was no longer fit to teach. A letter wished me all the best and hoped I would see that they had acted in my best interests. Quietly, and slowly, the news got round the roots of me and pulled.

'All right, Mathilde,' I said, 'all right.' And I sent her forms, and made my mind prepare for the boundaries of my better judgment to be crossed.

That night, I dreamed a strange, sustaining dream. It was winter, very cold. In my hand, I held a letter from Mathilde, but I did not know its contents. I knew it was pointless to open the letter, for it contained something in a language I could not understand.

Suddenly, I was walking alone, dressed in boots and coat down icy roads and into the woods above the fields. Below me, I heard driven beasts through the country snowstorm making silence in it with their muffled step and lowing. I reached a copse in the wood which encircled me. I stood with the trees around me and heard the ice rattle. The branches sheathed in ice rattled against each other in gust upon gust. With the blind intelligence of dreams, I knew. What did I know? The snow blew off the branches in tall eddies; little cyclones of snow flew in glitterless, pale order. I knew that we are in Heaven which is in and around us, but we cannot see it – except in these bright flashes through the dark, which leap like fish from a cold pond, and then are gone.

# Chapter Eight

John was standing by the window in the departure lounge at Heathrow Airport when I first noticed him; and he might have been going anywhere at all. I may have remarked him because he bore so little resemblance to the other travellers, who milled about with trolleys, plastic bags full of duty-free goods, heavy hand luggage. He carried nothing but a small case, and stood at ease with the rest of his surroundings. He was dressed without idiosyncrasy or ostentation, and next to him the surging tourists with florid clothes and the starched businessmen with their briefcases and air of self-importance looked, perhaps, a little foolish. He seemed to need no camera, no book, no newspaper. He appeared to be absorbed in what was going on around him without being too much caught up in it. He is neither tall nor short, young nor old. He is slightly built and has pleasant features, but is not particularly good-looking. I at once found him so, however, and blushed slightly when I saw that he returned my glance. For the merest fraction of a second, there was that small spark of contact that sometimes passes between strangers, and they become precariously knowable to one another. Looking again at his case, I saw it had identical tags to mine. It was a discreet purple logo that proclaimed us both to be members of Vinnie Winston's Tours. I sighed because the flight to Moscow was late. He smiled. Although I let my eyes trail past him to the sky, I was pleasantly struck by his most distinct feature: a head of curiously irradiated red-gold hair. It is turning grey, but the luxuriance of its mass and colour charmed me. He looked out of the window too.

I was extremely tired and fed up. I had disembarked expecting to find Mathilde waiting for me in London. We had planned to meet there and travel to Moscow together. Instead there was a message waiting for me at the Aeroflot desk telling me that Mathilde had flown to Russia three days earlier and would meet me at the airport there. I could not understand why this was when she had pressed me so hard to accompany her, but it made me feel very uneasy. My sister was at home in the Soviet Union – a place, to my mind, of irreducible foreignness. As I waited for the flight, a flow of meaninglessness seemed to pass me by, as if it actually walked the polished floor of the airport lounge. A Russian couple sat next to me, arguing without rancour. I realized that I was going to a place where I did not understand a word of the language, and I had never travelled before to any place where English was not spoken. Indeed, I had spent my whole life staying as still as possible. What I could not understand, as I sat through the interminable hours of boredom, was why I was sitting there at all. If the light of inner certainty had been given to me the night I had accepted Mathilde's invitation, it was soon eclipsed by the wrenching feeling of disorientation. Without my sister there to mediate the experience of flight and displacement, I felt dazed at the prospect of being ejected like an untrained cosmonaut into areas I did not understand. A song, popular at the time, jangled idiotically through my head. 'Rah, Rah, Rasputin, Lover of the Russian Queen.' I could not imagine the land of Chekhov or Dostoyevsky.

By the simple chance, I suppose, of our being booked on the same tour, John and I were allocated seats together on the airplane. We bowed and smiled, exchanged a few courtesies. As the plane bowled out along the tarmac and lunged into the air, I surreptitiously fingered my rosary. For days before the journey, I had been preoccupied with irrational fears of dying. Although my doctor had reassured me that I could withstand the journey, I was morbidly concerned that the pressure in the cabin would drop and cause me to have another convulsion. Then, I began to think the plane would crash. All of these dreads took place in the odd inner framework of a sense of guilt that did not seem truly to belong to me or have any direct purpose. I had been to confession the day before I flew, yet it had not rested or eased me. Above all, I had the strange, unbalanced feeling that I knew something or possessed something that did not belong to me. I searched my mind, but could not think what it was. I bent backwards to forgive those who had taken away my job, and had, in a last urgent moment, packed my Bible.

'Are you frightened of flying?' John asked me. We were given Russian salad and drinks by a stern looking stewardess.

'I feel uneasy about it.'

'I love it,' he said. He ate a bit of the salad, then stopped. 'Of course, that doesn't mean that *you* have to enjoy it, does it?' I got the impression that he wanted to start a conversation but did not know exactly how to do it. This in itself was reassuring, but I found that I myself did not have an idea of how to carry on with the topic of flying in general, so I looked out of the window at the brilliant atmosphere above the cloud and the shade of violet in its upper reaches. I, too, nibbled at the salad and looked back at him.

'I see you are in the same group as I am – with the fabulous Vinnie Winston. I understand we don't get to meet up with him until Irkutsk, though. I decided to come at the last moment.'

'So did I,' I said. 'I nearly didn't come at all. My sister booked me in. I'm meeting her in Moscow.'

'What's your subject?' he asked.

'Subject?'

'Everyone is supposed to have a subject – a special interest in something to do with the places we are visiting.'

'Oh no!' I said. 'I don't know anything! My sister is an icon restorer . . .'

'Don't worry,' he said. 'I've really just come along for the ride myself.'

'I'll bet that isn't true,' I said. 'You're just trying to cheer me up.'

'Travel,' he said, 'is my whole way of life. I even spend my free time going to odd places. Last year, I went to Tibet. Fascinating, Tibet.'

'What do you do?'

'Oh, something-or-other for the Royal Geographical Society. I get about a lot, at any rate,' he said modestly.

I do not know why I did not realize until then that he was an Englishman, even though his accent and his manner of speech were marked. From the very beginning, I did not think of our being alien to each other in any way. As he himself later said, it was 'most remarkable'. 'My sister lives in England,' I said. 'That's the only place I have ever been outside the United States. I wish I knew something, but I was hardly aware of Outer Mongolia until the other day.'

'I wouldn't let it worry you – honestly,' he said. 'The best way to travel is to go with a mind empty of all pre-conceptions. When you go with acquisitions, you become a trader or colonialist. When you go to acquire things, you become a tourist. A real journey,' he said, describing something vague in the air with his hand, 'is a hard thing to make these days.' He stopped and laughed a little ruefully. 'You probably have your own theories.'

I swallowed a bit of salami the wrong way, choked, and felt awful that yet again I had proved that I could not negotiate the simplest conversation with a man who attracted me without doing something stupid. He looked as if he wanted to pat my back, but he didn't. He gave me a bright, direct look instead. 'I'm not the sort of person who makes theories – unless I have to,' I finally wheezed.

'Then you lead a blameless life,' he said. I sipped at air-plane coffee. We found we were smiling at each other with more warmth than we had intended.

'I wish that were true,' I said.

He made no reply to this remark, but I saw that he had registered it. I felt I had revealed something about myself without really meaning to. Unlike other acute people, he did not seem to make observations in a guileful way. From the start, I sensed in him a kind of innocence and I imagined he often gave people the impression that he was less intel-ligent than he was.

'What an interesting life you must lead,' I said, re-membering to talk stupidly as at dances.

He heard the self-consciousness in my shift of tone. 'Travel broadens the mind?' I looked sharply at him, but he laughed. 'Oh, yes, it's a very odd life. I have an irresist-ible urge to transverse the globe. Going to a place for a reason wrecks the whole thing for me. To me the journey is the art and I never deliberate what is going to happen. You'll never guess why I decided to come on this trip . . .' Then he stopped.

'Tell me!'

He looked from side to side, as if deliberating whether to go on or not.

'Well, it's silly. I was in a Chinese restaurant near the British Museum ordering a take-away, and suddenly, a greasy photograph above the counter caught my eye. It was the Temple of Heaven in Peking. I've seen hundreds of pictures of it, as I'm sure you have . . .'

My class had once done a project on China, and I remembered the temple with its geometrical perfection: one circular pagoda hovering in absolute proportion to another so that the three tiers seemed both to float and aspire. I did not want him to know that I was a schoolteacher, yet I found myself talking with unusual ease about impressions I had gained from the pictures I had seen.

'It had never struck me before,' he said, 'as having any meaning, yet suddenly it did. I had no idea I was going to make a journey to China. I don't know if I'm explaining myself properly. I've never really chosen where I go. You'll think I'm utterly ridiculous, I guess, if I tell you that the places I go to choose me.'

'I don't think that's ridiculous at all,' I said, but he checked my eyes for the truth of my statement before he went on.

'I suppose I have determined the rest of my life too consciously,' he continued. It gave me a kind of delight to watch him warm and expand. 'I studied and studied, then worked and worked. My work has to be so precise. The journeys are the obverse. What I mean to say is that I am not going exactly to see the Temple of Heaven. We might not even get there, who knows? It isn't even a goal . . .' He floundered and stopped, looking a bit embarrassed.

'Maybe,' I said, clearing my throat, 'it describes the shape of the journey itself. To you. Perhaps.'

'How extraordinary,' he said. 'That is what it is. I become absorbed in the journey itself.'

'You're a sort of explorer,' I said. I thought he flushed slightly.

'Not really, no, not at all,' he replied, but he was smiling. 'That's what I wanted to be in childhood. For various reasons, I ended up being a cartographer.'

'You make maps?'

'I have a lot to do with them.' He paused. 'I don't usually ramble on about myself like this,' he said.

'It's interesting.'

'What about you?' he asked.

He tells me now that my expression changed so that he wondered if he had offended me. More than that, he perceived an element of fear in my eyes which he found hard to connect with anything that had taken place in the conversation up to that point.

My previous and unconsummated relationships with men had always been hedged about with my mistrust. At some point, I would always take flight – stop answering the telephone, pretend I had not heard a remark which was meant to advance the situation. It was as if I had a cave prepared inside me where I would fall, and in which I would lie panicked and reclusive, until the whole thing passed. I would think about epilepsy or the demands of my religion. Looking back on it, I can see that the whole pattern with John was reversed from the very outset. I felt afraid, that is true, but afraid to be suspended in mid-air with him where I thought I might make the reckless error of telling him what there was about me to tell. Sitting there and belted up, I felt the compulsion to talk to a stranger about things I had not been able to talk about with friends. He did not frighten me. I frightened myself with a sudden emotional urgency to make myself safe from the coming meeting with Mathilde by talking to him. It was, perhaps, his openness which made me feel as I had not felt with other men – men who had closed me up in a horror of revealing anything about myself at all.

He bore my silence. 'It's not far,' he said. 'We're not too far now from Moscow.'

I felt ashamed that I had been unable to offer him an easy social assurance which would have made the flight more agreeable. My sense of awkwardness clouded the windowpane for me and I only pretended to look out at the sky. At the same time, I sensed that he really did not mind my reserve. I gave him a little glance and he gave me the shade of a smile, as if to indicate an understanding of my sudden retreat. I wondered if he too had known a dread at being too quickly revealed.

I pretended to sleep. I thought now of my sister, now of Durrand, until the airplane began its slow descent. I opened my eyes and looked out of the window. Large forests emerged beneath us, and breadths of uninhabited land stretched out. The sun was beginning to set. In its chill and roseate light, shadows deepened everywhere. I saw in the landscape that featureless depth, fraught erratically with gold, of icons – of the icons belonging to Mathilde.

The Russian customs shed was confining and dingily ochre. While I filled in long forms about how much currency I had, what jewellery I was bringing in, I kept on imagining Mathilde waiting for me on the other side of the barrier – then I wondered if she would be there at all. She both beckoned and repelled me. I both yearned for and resisted her. By the time my suitcase had debouched from the plane and I had taken it to the customs table, I was in an acute state of nerves regarding our meeting. It was thus that I came down with a grim thump as the blond, heavy-set man who inspect my luggage pulled triumphantly at my Bible and waved it in front of my nose with mild outrage on his face. 'Chto eta?' he asked. I could not think what he was talking about. Again and again, he asked the question. With his heavy hands, he began to peel the Bible, leaf from leaf, going from prophets to psalms to Gospels as if each page was written in a secret code, as if the words threatened his safety and undermined his life. He removed my pocketbook for a similar inspection, found the rosary, fished it out. He dangled the crucifix on it from his fingers and gave me a look of amazement that I had been so bold as to bring such a thing. John arrived with his bags. I floundered around not knowing what to say, but he spoke to the official in halting Russian, and the man went away.

'What's he going to do? Is he going to send me back?' My mind crazily thought of labour camps.

'I asked him to fetch his superior.' Sure enough, the official stormed back with a greater official still, and he spoke English.

'Give this woman back her things,' John said. 'They belong to her.'

The older official had brown eyes and a sad moustache. He held the religious articles uncertainly. 'Are these for your own personal use?' he asked. His subordinate with the heavy, Slavic looks pawed through all my underwear. I felt exposed and humiliated. Close to tears, I said 'Yes. Please let me have them back.' But although John argued patiently and cogently with the man, they took my things away, and I was left beside myself for a moment, seized by a sickening fear.

'What's the matter?' John asked.

'I don't think I can explain it.'

'It's all right. They can't take away the substance of it – whatever it is you believe in and live by. Can they? They really can't, you know.' I noticed that he too was trembling slightly, his jaw working in rage at the retreating backs of the customs men. 'It only shows their colossal ignorance that they think they can.'

Together, we went out into the body of the airport.

For a moment, I did not recognize Mathilde, she had altered so. She had lost weight, but looked both gaunt and puffy. In the main body of the airport, she was awaiting me with the Intourist guide, and they were conversing in a casual manner. Her dress was creased, and her hair had turned a little grey around her temples. As I approached, she looked up, then looked down again as if to assemble her feelings. She waved stiffly, then came forward to embrace me. 'Irene, so at last you are here,' she said. 'You see, it didn't kill you.' Her breath smelt stale with alcohol and cigarettes. I was so startled by her appearance, that I turned to John, who stood in the deep background, and then to the guide as if to verify my experience, then, realizing it was impossible to verify, felt uncomfortable at being alone with her. Like an avoided room, opened by an unwitting hand, Mathilde seemed to exude chill.

We evaded the emotion of reunion. 'It's wonderful to see Moscow again,' she said. 'I decided I needed a few days on my own here before we met. If I were a Marxist, I would live here, but I'm not. Don't you think it is exciting? It is.'

The guide was a girl with bubbly hair called Vera. She held a clipboard and was processing papers. I wondered if it were my imagination that I saw her shoot a doubtful look at Mathilde. As we walked to the car, I told Matty what had happened in the customs shed and how John had tried to help me.

'You're an idiot,' she said, 'bringing things like that here.'

I said nothing.

'It doesn't matter,' she said, as if talking to someone else. 'I guess I'll just have to put up with it.' She said something to Vera incisively, in Russian.

The guide did not respond. She got us all settled in a black limousine, and sat herself in the front. Outside the terminal, two Russian friends embraced. We disappeared into the darkening countryside. Mathilde tried frantically to strike up a conversation with the guide. I fell into the dark car beside John who sat between Mathilde and me.

The car had gone some distance down the lonely road to Moscow, past long stretches of pine forest, twilit and silent, when all at once, and without any warning, the primary thing, the thing that has compelled me to tell this story, happened:

There was Durrand. It's not that I saw him, precisely. It was only after I knew he was there that I formed a picture of him in my mind. It was as if he were really outside of me, actually sitting on the jump seat of the limousine. I sensed his whole presence, as if he were another member of the party, but he was not formed before my actual eyes. Like a laser image on my inner eye, however, my brother was vivid. His cold, geometric face was angled at my sister, and, shed from manacle of flesh and bone, he seemed to enjoy enormous freedom. The vision flooded me, and then was gone.

I was truly terrified, and made for my reason as fast as I could. 'It's a fit,' I thought, crazily aware that this had hithertofore seemed the most awful thing that could happen to me. 'I am not going to, not here, not now . . .' I did my counting trick, counting slow numbers in complex combinations. It had warded off convulsions in childhood sometimes. I tried to breathe slowly. No. Then, in an ulterior sense, I felt Durrand deeper, like a comet or some fallen star, dense with unintelligible meaning, heavy with desire.

Briskly, I tried to construct a grid of something rational on top of this. I was tired by the long journey, upset by seeing Mathilde; I had felt more violated by the Russian guards than I gave myself credit for. I thought these things, but all obvious conclusions were attenuated by Durrand's salutation to my inner being, his grim annunciation. I began to pray, and slowly the fear of him vanished.

'. . . went to Bokhara a few years ago and found it very interesting,' John said.

Like someone coming to the surface of a pool, I heard him and knew I had missed a part of the conversation. I drew upon this evidence of a fit of absence with great relief. What I was doing remembering the contents of one, I did not care to think about.

'Is this your first visit to the Soviet Union?' the guide asked. I realized that she was addressing me and I prayed she had not asked me the question several times before.

'Oh, yes, yes,' I said.

An old black woman is singing mirthlessly on the corner of Ashby Street across the road from this house. I sit by the bay window and watch her sway to her song of degrees. She is swaying next to the Episcopal Church where Nathalie and her mother used to go on Sunday. They wore hats and gloves and carried little prayerbooks with gold crosses on them. The apse above the altar used to be painted dark blue with stars and angels. Nathalie took me in there once. I was afraid to go because it was Protestant. The black woman's name is Meredith, and she thinks God has sent her to save white people. Yesterday, she stopped me on the street, put her hands across my eyes, and drew my eyelids downwards. 'I want to see your lashes,' she said. She asked me to say the Lord's Prayer with her, so I did. She is absent from herself too. Now, they have painted the Episcopal Church Nile green inside and there are no more angels. It is also all right for me to go in there. People do not mention angels now, for fear, perhaps, of falling into their grip.

*A nasty business, Irene*, said the presence of Durrand to my inner ear in the Muscovite dark.

'. . . hope you will enjoy your stay,' said the guide. I had the impression of Durrand smoking just as he always used to. He had the habit of letting large, white puffs exude from his mouth, and he would then inhale them backwards through his nostrils. I had the impression of Durrand smoking and watching Mathilde. I smiled at the guide unevenly.

'It was a good thing to get on Vinnie Winston's tour,' Vera remarked. 'It is very serious. At every stage, you will be informed. Of course, you do not meet them until Irkutsk, but I will try to make it up for you in Moscow if I can.'

'My sister will find you very helpful, I am sure,' said Mathilde in a faintly superior tone.

'You are sisters? You did not say she was a sister. I thought you were friends. You do not resemble each other.'

'Life makes people look different,' said John. 'My sister and I looked so much alike as children that people used to call us twins, but it's all changed now. The only thing we have in common now are parents and they are both dead.'

'I had a twin called Durrand,' Mathilde said, 'and he is dead.'

There was a moment of unease in the car. The tone in Mathilde's voice was shocking in its raw and angry intensity. Everyone was silent for a moment, but another silence hung around the car, active and peculiar. I had an impulse to tell the driver to stop – to get out and run; but where to in the Russian woodland? And why run when I sensed Durrand as an interior threat, scratching at my consciousness like a cat at a pane of glass? With a large effort, I concentrated on John, focused on John as the dark landscape whizzed past.

'Where is your sister now?' I asked.

'Oh, she invents knitting patterns. We have a family firm in Yorkshire, but I sold my share in it and moved away.'

'My sister knits,' said Mathilde. 'She knits and she is a schoolteacher.'

*Death is an interesting teacher*, said Durrand. *Go away!* my mind cried, and he did.

I am going insane, I thought. Most epileptics dread this more than anything. Schizophrenia sometimes becomes tangled with the disease, can enter it and split the mind. The voice of Durrand was so lucid and I was so conscious. I wanted to take someone's hand. I wanted to take John's hand.

At last, the car stopped in front of an enormous hotel. Part of it was panelled with bright blue tiles. Other tall, block-like buildings surrounded the hotel, and raw earth was dug up everywhere. Vera explained that a large conference was going on in the centre of Moscow, making it necessary for us to stay some way out.

As we struggled with our baggage, the driver of the limousine turned to me, smiling sheepishly. After moments of gesticulation and misunderstanding, I realized that he wanted to have my pen for which he was willing to exchange a badge of some sort. I rummaged through my bag, found the pen and gave it to him. To my intense relief, I saw that the ink had squirted out of the pen – a ball point – so that it smeared my hands. This had clearly been caused by the pressure on the airplane. What it had done to the pen, it could do to my brain, I thought, forced through me a leak of electrical disturbance. I argued to myself that I had plenty of medication and that Russia was a civilized country with hospitals and doctors, nurses and epileptics aplenty. I refused to enter into any idea that I was mad.

Mathilde was standing in front of the ugly hotel, looking up at it as if it were a monument to an outrage. I could not understand why she seemed so generally angry. 'When you think about it,' she said to me, 'all totalitarian architecture is insulting. It gives you the feeling of being dwarfed and powerless. You should see Stalin's university tower. It relieves you of your belief in freedom . . . What's the matter with you?' She tapped her foot impatiently.

An instinct told me not to say anything about the episode in the car. 'Nothing is the matter,' I said.

'I don't know, you get a judgmental look on your face.'

'What are you talking about?'

'I suppose it shocks you that I've been drinking. But that's too bad. In fact, I would like to go on drinking, but I shan't. I'll go to bed instead. Isn't that good of me?' She grabbed hold of my luggage and vehemently pulled it through the lobby into the elevator. When I made an attempt to follow her, she shook her head. The doors closed and she was gone.

I stood there utterly mystified. John and Vera fiddled around with documents at the reception desk. I kept dropping my papers. Everyone seemed to avert their eyes. At last, the guide took my arm and led me down a polished hall at the end of which there was a bar. Over it hung a large, plastic, orange sculpture, lit from within. It represented nothing I could identify. 'Look, Irina,' Vera said. She grasped my arm like a friend. 'She has been in here all afternoon and she has been saying very tactless things, which is not good.' She paused, and grasped my arm with further urgency. Her eyes showed great sense and warmth.

'She has been a welcome visitor to the Soviet Union many times before, but icons are . . . sensitive, and maybe, if she goes on acting like she has been today . . .' She threw up her hands and shook her head. 'Maybe it's this death in the family she spoke of, but please look after her. Don't let her say stupid things. And vodka! Please, no vodka!'

'I think it was my coming that bothered her,' I said.

'No, she was looking forward all day. But you are not really sisters?'

'Oh, we are.'

I sat with John in a dining room the size of a football stadium. I played around with my soup. It was made of cabbage and tasted good, but I was not hungry. The episode in the taxi had left me sick and cold, no matter how much I reasoned with myself. I struggled within myself to remember any similar event from my childhood, any time I had been subjected to an illusion of haunting, but the effort of memory itself disturbed me. I decided that the only course open to me was to relax my will and loosen my grip, for experience had taught me that I invariably lost any battle with my memory when I tried too zealously to find it. I looked up from my soup at John and found that John was looking at me. There was a focus in his look that led me back through the thickets of distress and confusion to the edge, as it were, of that inner forest: it was a vantage point for me, a place from which I could see him.

'You have been warned? Because of your Bible?' he asked.

I noticed a stillness in his hands, the sturdiness of his palms, the length of his fingers, the cusps of his fingernails, his flexible wrists, and fixed on them. I realized that his voice had a particular resonance that I associated with – music. Calm? Certain frequencies of sound can split and fracture the brain's stability; others are curiously healing. John.

'It wasn't about the Bible.' Without meaning to, I leaned towards him and confided. 'It was about Mathilde.'

'She's in trouble with them, is she?'

'Not exactly. Apparently, she has been "tactless".'

A large party of British tourists was sitting at long tables in the dining room, which was otherwise practically empty. A bull-necked man rose from time to time from his chair, and baited the waiter with hostile remarks about the Soviet Union – remarks the waiter clearly could not understand. I wondered what Mathilde had done worse than this. 'I'm sure I set her off in some way,' I added.

'Why should you think that?'

I had a sudden, urgent desire to tell him about Durrand, but I checked myself. 'I don't know why. My sister is very sensitive. Sometimes I say the wrong thing without knowing it, or even give the wrong sort of look. She got it into her head that I was making some moral judgment on her tonight, but I wasn't. To tell you the truth, I'm more afraid of her than anything else . . . though, of course, I love her.'

'I have a sister like that,' he said. 'She's the one who knits. She is very easily offended. She's always trying to get me to settle down, which is odd because she's managed to ditch two husbands herself. My sister is very tidy and I think she thinks of me rather as an odd sock. I hang around unmatched in the drawer of her imagination.'

I looked at him, attempting to veil my surprisingly intense wish to see if he had meant to communicate to me in particular that he was not married.

'That's a little different from Mathilde,' I said. 'Mathilde . . .', but I realized that if I said Mathilde always treated me as if I had no qualities at all that could attract anyone, it would sound embarrassing.

'What?' he asked.

'Oh, she just treats me like a child,' I said. Then, more bravely, 'She thinks of me as an old maid schoolteacher.'

'Ah,' he said, and smiled.

Suddenly, the lights in the dining room went low and a spotlight appeared on a little stage. A glittering MC bounded on and announced a chanteuse in sequins. With a lot of banging and microphone scraping, she began to sing a very sad song to a recorded background.

'When did you start?' I asked. 'When did you start to travel?'

'In the army,' he said.

'My brother Durrand was a soldier,' I said, grazing on the subject that still perturbed me.

'Oh, I wasn't a soldier. Not in the sense of being a professional. I was called up during Cyprus, but I suppose you are too young to remember that.'

'I'm thirty-five,' I said.

'I go back farther than that,' he said wistfully.

'You don't look . . .'

'I travelled a lot then – I mean, got a taste for strange places. Leeds was somewhat confining.'

'Leeds?'

'I live in London now. I have a flat near the Portobello Road. Do you know that?'

The chanteuse was not very good.

'Isn't there a market there? Mathilde shops there. She gets antique things.'

'Yes, it's a famous market.' He looked very sad. 'I'm not there often. Always moving, always going. "You come and go so much, you'll meet yourself on the way, John!" my sister says.'

Ruefully, I remembered how often I had actually met myself on the street. I felt so at ease with him, that I nearly told him about my false image, thinking that it might interest him.

All at once, the music blared and an energetic couple on roller skates blazed into the spotlight and began to dance. They whirled around to the tune of 'Moscow Nights'. They reeled in and out in complicated formation.

'Do you have to see her if she's so bossy?' I asked him.

'She's the only family I have. I'm beginning to feel that now.'

'So is Mathilde, my only family.'

106

Another tune was struck; a wild gypsy song. The skaters joined hands and began going round and round until they achieved demonic speed. It was impossible to tell the man from the woman, they went with such dervish whirling.

I began to think of Mathilde and was suddenly filled with remorse that I had left her on her own, and, indeed, forgotten about her entirely while I had been talking with John.

'I must go see if she's all right,' I said.

'I think she would be sleeping,' he said dryly.

I stood, hovered, reluctant to go. He rose. 'If you must go . . .'

'We'll meet in the morning,' I said. 'Good night.'

This is ridiculous, I thought to myself as my spirit soared from the warmth in his smile.

# Chapter Nine

I knew from the shadow she had become that my sister had substantially changed. She lay curled up on a bed in the Russian hotel room. She looked half-submerged. Although she had become thin, she moved heavily on her pillow like an elephant rolling over, as if all her limbs were too much to bear. She looked heavy, frozen. She had left the light on, but she had her eyes shut. The dim bulb gave her a leprous look, as though she needed a bath – Mathilde, so fastidious, so scrupulously clean.

What have you done, Matty? I thought. And why are you accusing yourself through me? She turned again fitfully, then snored, but I knew she was awake.

Our Aunt Bethune had a house in Charleston. I have, on the whole, happy memories of the place, because Mother went there whenever she felt like being rescued. My aunt was a tall person who often wore blue. Her hair had gone prematurely grey, and she wore it in a cloud around her head, which gave her the aspect of a holy statue or a wraith. She had married well, better than Mother, and when Father left us, this had been admitted. Aunt Bethune's house had shutters and it was surrounded by palmettos. When we went to church, there were palmetto fans in the pews. Everything in my aunt's house was polished. She was fond of peonies and had a standing order with the local florist. She played the piano and sang Schubert lieder. 'She's what's known as "gracious",' Matty said.

I always thought Mathilde was obscurely jealous of Aunt Bethune, who was a Christian woman if there ever was one and on whom Mother sagged whenever we got to Charleston. My mother, a former debutante, had been launched, but she had sunk. Aunt Bethune had sailed on.

We rarely got to Charleston, though, because we did not have any money, and Mother was too proud to ask. Besides, she felt obliged to dress us up for our visits, so money had to be found for wardrobes too. We had dresses with sashes, hats and gloves. Durrand had a suit. Once I had a peach-coloured organdie dress which I spoiled the look of by having a fit at a party held in an heirloom of a place on the outskirts of town. That was the party where I realized that Matty necked with boys. She disappeared from the dance and went down to the swamp with a strange looking boy with big ears. Durrand got drunk. We did not make a very good impression.

My mother wanted my sister to be popular, yet on her own terms. Matty was too intelligent to be a belle, but she tried. In an attempt at belle-dom, she giggled and frittered away the summer days with our cousins on Pawley's Island. She wore shorts, and hacked about, enveloped in the endless bounty of the calm sea and sky. In town, she wore crinoline skirts and cinch-belts and make-up, and Mother allowed it because of belle-dom and because Aunt Bethune allowed Cousin Eva to wear it.

The summer she was sixteen, Mathilde did a dreadful

thing. She and I shared a room, and she asked me if I would leave her alone one evening because she had a headache. I went down the road to see my cousin Sally, who was younger than me. For some reason, she looked up to me and I treasured this knowledge. When I returned, Mathilde was lying in blood. A boy called Ted stood by her. He was a big, dumb boy, strong and blond. He kept wringing his hands and saying, 'Oh no, oh no!' Mathilde's nightgown was all askew. For a moment, I thought he had hurt her, hit her; then, I thought she had got her period; then, I knew, young as I was, what had happened. She made me go downstairs in the middle of the night to wash the sheets in our Aunt's machine in the cellar. I remember standing there, listening to the cycles changing, my teeth chattering and clacking together in mid-July. When I had hidden the evidence and returned, she was lying there in that same, unusual position she lay in on her bed in Moscow. Her knees were drawn up, and she was swollen-looking, dead, almost. I could not believe that night in Charleston that she would tell Durrand, but she did. He had heard her crying and come in. He said he would challenge Ted to a duel. 'Don't be a fool, Durrand,' she said. 'I wanted him to. Now it's over with.'

The very next day, Mathilde sashayed up and down the floor at a square dance as if nothing had happened.

'You'll go to hell,' said Durrand.

'Oh pooh,' said Matty and snapped her fingers. She might as well have been Scarlett and said, 'Fiddle de dee.'

When Matty wanted to make Durrand suffer, she usually did not have to try as hard as that. At the time, I thought it had been a reprisal, but I never found out for what.


'Well, there you are, same as ever,' said Mathilde upon waking. The sunlight on her face and hair bleached the rumpled sheets she drew up to her neck; the light accentuated her features, so that for a moment, she looked like Mother herself.

I had been up for some time, and was looking out the

window. Across the road from the hotel was a small church with cross-hatched decorations and onion domes. Near it, the earth was dug up. A raw, red pit lay waiting for the foundations of some new development. I had not seen the church the night before.

'We'll miss breakfast and our tour if you don't get up,' I said.

'Oh God! Is that the time?' She blundered up. 'Reenie, darling, it was so good of you to come!' She leaned over and kissed my brow. She smoothed my hair. 'What are you looking at? The church? It is not a "working church", as they say here. Vera told me it's used as a warehouse. Would you like to go to church? I'll make sure you can go. Have you ever been to an Orthodox service? Very impressive. I know you'll find it interesting.' She skittered to the bathroom girlishly. 'Oh, goodness! Look at my hair!' she cried. With her running the taps and splashing, with her energetic flow of trivia, she blocked all discussion of the unpleasantness of the previous night.

'Did you talk to that man last night? What's his name? He's taken a shine to you, I can tell. I don't know, but *I*, at least, thought we'd be alone together in Moscow. I didn't see how we could talk, really talk, last night.'

'We could have talked in here,' I said.

She was applying mascara and stopped. I felt my tone had been too hard, and I was surprised at her beseeching, placatory look. Mathilde never found it easy to be sorry, yet I felt she regretted the way she had behaved to me. She put the wand of mascara down and her finger to her lips. 'Bugs,' she mimed, gesturing about her. 'The rooms are bugged,' she mouthed. 'Well, we have all the time in the world,' she said quite loudly.

I wondered who could possibly care about the little details of our lives. She ran the water again and beckoned me. 'If you think I'm paranoid,' she whispered, 'look under the bedside table. Just run your finger along gently and do not tap the device.' I did as I was bidden, and at once found a little metal object. Immediately, the pleasantly furnished room was turned into a cage. Mathilde shook her head, rolled her eyes and shrugged. In a few minutes, she was dressed, transformed into some semblance of her former self.

On the way down the corridor towards the woman who kept the keys, my sister gave me an affectionate hug, and, linking her arm with mine, started to speak in fluent Russian to the solid-looking character in braids, who smiled widely at hearing her language so well expressed by a foreigner.

Mathilde did have a way with Russians. She seemed to have found the right direction with them. I remember her saying once how split they were in themselves, about how the Oriental and European strains in them battled, that unable to achieve a resolution of the conflict this produced, they were forced to suffer towards a transcendence of it. Mother thought she was a Communist.

'Is it all right to talk in here?' I whispered to Mathilde in the elevator. She nodded.

'The guide told me she was worried about you,' I said, 'and you would be able to interpret that better than I can.'

'Pah!' she said, bursting out of the elevator when it stopped and opened. 'She's a young girl and knows nothing. I've always said exactly what I pleased here, and this is how they know to trust me. Nothing hidden. See?' She spread out her hands like a conjurer.

'What did you say last night before I came?'

'I said Marx had a vulgar mind.' Then she looked very ashamed. 'I also said something extremely vulgar myself. I shall have to apologize.'

And apparently she did. After a breakfast of cold meat and rye bread, we launched off with John and Vera in a new mood. In the large, black car we took to the centre of Moscow, there was talk and laughter. There were little swaps of confidences and badinage between Mathilde and the guide.

Vera told a story about a scientologist who had tried to convert her to his esoteric faith the previous year. Mathilde told a tasteless story about a lecherous monk in Leningrad, who had tried to convince her he knew where she could buy an icon by Andrey Rublyov.

As I listened to her, I became aware that John was listening too. In a swift and unintelligible moment, I caught an intimation of how he heard. The archness with which she told the story made it sound both blasphemous and foolish, as if she had invented it to show off. In my inner eye, I saw him weighing something in his hand, as if to divine what was really going on; but, by the time we had reached the Kremlin, I lost sight of this preternaturally vivid image. We left the car and stood in Red Square.

The square is smaller than I imagined. In the morning sun, St Basil's Cathedral dazzled me with its chequered, zigzagged walls, its lofty onion domes. Vera told us it was now a museum. Robbed of the aspiration to God that had inspired them, the cupolas looked flat, the walls bizarre. The church looked like a plain girl to whom a vain mother has given an exotic name that mocks her throughout life. Mathilde apologized for the building as if she had had some hand in designing it. She kept saying we must see the churches inside the Kremlin walls or the Novodyevichy Convent where, she said, the architecture was truly inspiring. 'Did you know,' she asked, 'that St Basil's was commissioned by Ivan the Terrible, and that he *blinded* the architects when they had finished?'

At the bottom of Red Square, at right angles to the frowning History Museum, a long line of people waited to visit Lenin's corpse in his tidy, ugly ziggurat of a tomb.

'I'm not going in there,' my sister said, indicating the tomb. From the way she spoke, I could sense fear whistling up her nose.

'It's all right, you don't have to,' said Vera. Neither John nor I took an interest in the dead leader, so we moved on to tour the fortress of the Kremlin itself, which lay behind the high walls. Mathilde tittered nervously. 'Lenin threatens to spoil from time to time,' she said in a whisper. 'They have to take him out and clean him up.' Indeed, I myself felt that the tomb emanated something unclean, unfinished or unburied and I wanted to shun it.

'An empty cathedral but a full tomb for old Pharoah,' said John.

My sister seemed so tense in the Kremlin Museum that I found it difficult to look at the exhibits without referring to her with my eyes. We stood in front of the furred crown of Boris Godunov; its golden dome was jewelled as if the Czar, cathedral in his own person, had moved hieratically about under it. 'He killed a little prince in order to ascend the throne, didn't he?' John asked.

'There's no historical evidence to support that,' Mathilde snapped. 'In many ways, he was a good king.'

'I only know the opera,' John said meekly. The air was full of embarrassment and nerves. Mathilde lingered behind to look at a dinner service of Catherine the Great. We waited for her below. At length, she appeared and started to descend the staircase.

'Your sister thinks she is the Czarina!' Vera said. Russians seem to have a solemn way about them until suddenly they laugh and a whole climate is reversed. Indeed, Mathilde held onto the banister with regal disdain for its support. She trailed her oval nails down; her almond eyes shed a slanted gaze, and her coiled-up hair seemed to suggest that it might very well support a diadem; her graceful neck seemed to ask for a choker of pearls.

There he was again: Durrand. It was as if he battled against extinction and scratched with desperate nails to be made visible. It's their resemblance, only their resemblance, I said to myself. Then thought, he would do anything, anything at all to get back to her.

'They shot the Czarina,' John said.

'You people do not understand this,' Vera said. 'She was a dreadful woman. It's not just the party line. She was consumed with desire for her son to be czar. She polluted the country with Rasputin, and betrayed her husband and the Russian people. Of all, I think she deserved death the most.'

I saw them in my mind's eye, the Romanovs, perched on little gilt chairs, smiling and waiting to be shot; trembling inwardly, but outwardly alert to a final duty to be dignified. Did one of the children scream with terror? Who shot them? Who shot the Czarina? What was his name and what did he feel about it? Was she merely murdered, or had she arranged her destruction well in advance of it, so that it simply arrived at its ultimate destination like a train? Was Rasputin her henchman in a kind of suicide? How did he penetrate the world of little white sashes and trying-to-be-nice? The glittering, Edwardian order? Did she open the door and let him in? Or did he appear horned and complete in their midst?

'Maybe I am wrong,' said Vera. 'Maybe she wasn't really wicked, only stupid.'

In Moscow, there are churches, churches, churches. We found ourselves in a whole square full of churches all nullified and silent. Going behind a dead cathedral, I looked through the window. The walls were solid with icons which seemed to grow organically from floor to ceiling. They glowed like dying stars. And there were other churches too, crisply white and topped with golden cupolas burnished in the sun. With effortless dignity, they stood like monuments to an ancient order whose thrust and meaning had gone awry. The square itself was thronged with Uzbeks with Muslim hats on, and we saw the great bell of Ivan the Terrible. Walking past the hall where the Politburo meets, I stepped into the road. Vera shouted at me, then apologized. It was against the law, she said, to walk in the street. Chagrined by this, she went ahead, and Mathilde fell in beside me. 'We are being followed,' she said. 'I stayed behind in the museum to make sure.'

'Why? Why would anyone follow us?' I asked.

'Suspicion is an industry in Eastern Europe,' she replied. 'The nature of trust as we understand it has been systematically undermined. Relationships are conceived of in a different way. The system seems to draw paranoia out of people just as fascism touched a buried sadism.' She gave a little shudder.

Wherever we went, she seemed to sense this shadowing pursuit. I often looked behind myself, but I could not identify her pursuer. 'He's a lightly built man in a black coat,' she said, 'but every time I look around, he's gone. You can see him, just out of the corner of your eye. They're always doing this. They're such blockheads.'

I could tell that her distress was genuine, however, no matter how much she tried to conceal it. 'Are you all right, Mathilde?' I kept asking her, but she shrugged off my questions.

It's absurd to think it's Durrand, I said to myself. It couldn't be.

We stumbled with fatigue into the Tretyakov Gallery at the very end of the afternoon, having been to the metro and gone to a park full of Soviet achievements.

'I don't want to go downstairs,' said Mathilde sharply to Vera in the hall of the museum.

I could not understand what was going on. 'Perhaps the others . . .,' Vera said.

'The others can do what they like,' she said. 'I'll rest here.' And she sat on a chair, her arms folded.

To my surprise, the basement was filled with icons.

'This is a very historical one,' Vera said, pointing to a majestic image of the Virgin and Child. She looked over her shoulder as if still puzzled by Mathilde's refusal to visit the place most closely associated with her work. 'It is the famous Vladimir Mother of God.' Vera stood apart from the dark image fraught with webs of gold as if to avoid looking too closely at it. 'There is a superstition that it defended Moscow from the Mongol hordes,' she said. The deep eyes of the Mother seemed to penetrate both motive and desire, so that, peeled like an onion by it, I felt unlayered and alone before it. I was aware that John watched me looking at the painting.

'It's important to you, religion, isn't it?' he said, rather than asked.

'Yes. Yes, it is,' I replied. 'Yes. It's of great importance.' I did not dare look at him in case he did not like this.

When we joined Mathilde, she was crying. 'Mathilde!' I said, and put my arm around her. John looked studiedly at an historical pageant on the wall, a triumph of Peter the Great.

She refused to say what had bothered her.

That night at dinner, Mathilde set out, perfumed and beautifully dressed, to display how little she had meant by bursting into tears. She chattered away to Vera and John about her previous visits to Russia, put forward theories, made allusions, while I stirred at my borscht, patient with a feeling of madness I had that I sat in a glass booth completely removed from the proceedings.

At the Bolshoi Ballet, where Vera took us afterwards, we sat far from the stage and watched *Swan Lake*, and I felt even more detached from what went on – the surge of music, the oceans of tulle. Odette and the Prince yearned, but I had to pinch myself to stay conscious of all that was going on outside of me. The swan soared wonderfully in the arms of the prince. I was tightly aware that I had wanted to talk to John all day. Against the fluent ardour of the music I bent, trying to stop myself caring about what he thought of me. I glanced at him; he seemed wholly intent on the ballet.

In the dark, the burden of the past few days descended on me, and there again, seeming to pierce through a sharp crescendo, was my sense of Durrand. It shot through me that Durrand was somewhere in the audience, camouflaged by the plainly dressed Russians. I battled with myself as if for air, but the feeling would not go away, and when the lights went up, I nervously looked for him, despising myself for being reduced to such childish behaviour.

'What is it?' Mathilde asked sharply, as if she too were expectant.

'Nothing. You just made me worried that we were being followed. It's creepy.'

She herself looked around but shrugged and said nothing.

We barged into a long buffet and Mathilde ordered

champagne for everyone. Drinking our health, she winked at John over the glass. I felt a great 'Oh no!' surging from my heart, but pressed it down so hard that I spilt my champagne. John wiped it from my skirt with his handkerchief.

Mathilde began to flirt. I noticed that her hand was shaking a bit. She told a beguiling series of anecdotes about English life which only John and she could understand. She even spoke about cricket and knew the latest scores of an important match. I felt lost and started to eat some chocolate she had also bought.

*How* does *she do it?* my brother's voice inquired. *She sure is making tracks.* My thoughts cleaved, my heart thumped in panic. I made my way to the ladies' room and stood in the cubicle, banging my head quietly on the door until I felt all thought of Durrand had gone.

This is ridiculous. You are jealous of her and you always have been, I said to myself. An acute feeling argued back with a shudder at the clarity of the voice. I was late back to my seat, and spent the rest of the ballet drenched in shame at my own absurdity. John offered me a mint, reached out and clasped my hand, then let it rest, then quietly removed it. Odile spun blackly and I shut my eyes, still unable to shake the force of Durrand.

'Oh God, what a boring man!' said Mathilde when we were back in our room. 'Do we really have to spend the whole trip with him?' She slid out of her clothes and flung them on the floor.

I was stupidly crushed by this remark. 'I thought you liked him,' I replied.

'Oh well, I suppose he's all right,' she said, yawning.

'Mathilde,' I said, 'I think we ought to talk.'

'Not here, not now,' she said, and turning off her light, immediately slept.

# Chapter Ten

As a dam is first breached by an ooze trickling from a hole, and then a gush from the crack the ooze has made, so Moscow was saturated for me by the drenching presence of Durrand. There was nowhere he was not, yet there was no focus for him, unless Lenin's tomb can be counted.

We seemed to pass it, set off from it, return to it no matter where we went. The city is organized radially around it. Like the pivot of a clock, its life seems to march around the tomb, hour after hour. It could not be avoided. Across from it, we shopped at GUM and ate ice-cream in its yellowed halls. Mathilde bought caviar and scooped it up with her index finger. Some of the black eggs lodged between her teeth. There was Durrand, not visible, but powerful as a vacuum, sucking her into his absence.

By the time Sunday came, I longed to go to the Orthodox service which Vera had promised us that evening before our flight to Siberia. Mathilde refused to accompany me. She sat outside, talking in Russian to Vera in the churchyard while John and I went in. I was on the whole very glad that she had decided not to join us. In an elliptical apse at the entrance of the church, there was a corpse laid out for burial. At first, I took it for an effigy, but my breath caught and when I realized it was a dead body, I became still. The figure was that of a young man with a tawny beard. He was dressed in black and some folded linen or, perhaps, verses from the Bible had been placed across his forehead. I was very much struck with the peace of the church, and had an almost friendly feeling towards the dead young man, as if I had known him.

The light, exotic body of the church was filled with candles and singing women in black nylon dresses. I supposed that they were nuns. The congregation flowed in and around the church according, it seemed, to individual inclination. People would kneel or prostrate themselves from time to time on the cold stone floor.

Durrand. I clanged the thought shut, and found my way through the milling worshippers to the place where the ritual was occurring. Durrand? I joined the Russians, who seemed to take me in amongst them and absorb me as I absorbed their prayer and felt for its direction. Like prehensile animals we clung together to the dark atonement expressed within the rhythmic and atonal liturgy which seemed to pool around us and beyond.

Imperceptibly, the ceremony seemed to open onto a deeper urgency. The worshippers shifted, as if to enter something more compelling; unbuttoning themselves, uniting with me and including me, we abandoned ourselves as if partaking in a ceaseless, uncreated dance. It was as if we were a terrible army a long way off from ourselves; it was as if we heard our own hoofbeats from a distance although it was we who rode and appeared to make the approach. We were entered in a bond more intimate than love, and out of us was pulled a terrible, heard cry – heard because it was pulled from us by the hearer: and I was frightened of it and its consequences.

We prayed to the tune of dry words intoned from a thick book by a wry-looking priest in vestments. The ceremony flowed like an ocean or a cloth through fingers.

I thought, this is going to be a battle. A real battle, but even I at the time did not know what that meant.

I lit candles for Mathilde and Durrand in front of the icons in the church and fell to my knees before them. Even though it was August, I sensed something autumnal in the air. If only I had known how to prevent . . . If only I had known how to prevent . . .

What was won when only I survived it?

John stood at an angle to me and the choir of singing women in black. He mused to himself. It was as if he were all alone. The light from the tapers fell upon his cheek, deepening the shadows, the lines around his eyes.

'It's time to go. We'll miss our flight,' Mathilde said, tapping me on the shoulder. She had come into the church to fetch me.

We stepped into the evening light which filtered through the Russian churchyard. Vera sat on a gravestone inscribed with Cyrillic letters. The tomb was covered with moss and lichen. She was waiting for us, her arms folded under her neat bosom.

John picked up a pebble from the gravel walk, then tossed it away. He keeps nothing, I thought. Nothing at all. Yews and cypresses lined the walk. Vera inclined her head to us and smiled. The Russian chanting still reverberated on the summer air. 'Did you enjoy yourselves?' she asked. Her pretty hair and clothes were framed by the disagreeable trees. She swung her leg on which she wore a fine sandal. Mathilde had said earlier that Russian women always looked at foreigners' shoes, but we looked at Vera's instead. They seemed incongruous with Russia.

The airplane smelt of urine and unscented ₌ansing powder. In it, I thought that I might be able to get away from Durrand. As we were borne aloft, I began to wonder if a strange effect of Moscow had not produced my illusion of him. When we had left the church, I had been repossessed by a sense of him. Whatever 'he' was, I had the strongest urge to flee him; thus the take-off and the flight gave me positive pleasure.

John sat next to a Hungarian who said he was travelling to Japan by way of Irkutsk. 'Russian planes stink,' he said in perfectly articulated English. 'Russians are filthy.' His face looked exhausted, frightened, compromised and sad. He and John fell to talking quietly behind Mathilde and me.

The light in the airplane was harsh. As we travelled through the dark sky, I could see Mathilde's profile reflected in the grubby window. Surely, I thought, there could be no ghost when Durrand's twin could project his very image on a pane of glass. Nevertheless, I fixed my eyes on the seat in front of me, eschewing the pressing fantasy that Durrand had attached himself to the outside of the airplane like a gremlin. I shook my head to rid myself of the impression that the two of them sat by me, like photograph and negative.

'Well, they've stopped tailing us,' she said, 'or at least they've put on another man.'

'Mathilde,' I asked, 'why did you decide to bring me to this place? If we are being spied on and listened to all the time, there doesn't seem any point in talking. You could have come to my house as you've often done before. It isn't bugged. What is more, my health isn't in any danger there. Ever since I arrived in Moscow, you've done everything to avoid me, and I don't understand what is going on.' I was really very surprised at my courage. My sister had a store of blazing looks that silenced opposition. I armed myself against one of these, and decided to hold my ground. Instead, she melted me with another kind of expression. Like a dumb animal in pain, her eyes had a look of wretched incomprehension. I was moved towards her without being able to help myself.

'I'd explain it to you if I could,' she said. For a long time, we were both silent. Then she said, 'I suppose I never told you anything about my reunion with Durrand. It all happened some time after your visit to me in London. Or did you know?'

'No, Mathilde, you never told me. And I knew nothing.'

'It was very odd,' she said, 'very strange, coming after your intercession.'

I stared at her. 'Mathilde, what do you mean? I made no intercession!' She ignored my remark as if I had not made it.

'The whole thing was odd. In fact, at first, I thought Durrand was a burglar. One night, late in August, I woke, about two or three in the morning to a funny, clicking, scratching noise. You know how it is when you are in danger and you instinctively become wide awake? I lay rigid and listened. Again, I heard another noise, this time a bump. I can tell you, I was absolutely terrified. And through the terror, I began to think about the icons. You know, I have no insurance. It may sound silly, but it really would be too expensive with all that gold leaf and so on, and also, I don't know . . .'

Also, you like living with risk, I thought.

'Now I look back on it, I think I behaved very foolishly, but my reputation would have been ruined if other people's paintings had been stolen from my flat. I picked up a heavy ashtray from my bedside table, and crept into the studio.

'There was Durrand. I suppose I could have thought it was a burglar, for his back was turned to me and he was rifling through my drawers. He had taken out a valuable icon of the Transfiguration, too, and left it exposed on an easel. Still, beyond all of this evidence, I knew it was Durrand . . .' She let the sentence trail, was silent for a moment, then continued:

'I called to him, "Durrand!" and abruptly, he turned around. We looked each other in the eyes for the first time in seven years.

'It is odd,' she said, breaking into her story, 'how I always loved mirrors. Do you remember the old-fashioned kind they used to have in department stores? I remember Mother taking us to Hutzler's, and my looking in the glass which reflected the glass behind, which reflected the glass in front, and so on, infinitely. I used to think, if I allowed myself to be mesmerized for long enough, I might be able to reach into another world entirely.' She looked back, directly at me. 'So it always was with Durrand's eyes. Sometimes as children we would stare at each other for what seemed hours, his eyes, reflecting my eyes, reflecting his, and on and on and on. Seeing him there, standing in my studio, I had that odd sensation once again, and I think he had too. Neither of us spoke nor moved for what seemed ages.'

It made me shudder to think of Durrand rifling Matty's drawers. I remember him once going through mine. Although I was never allowed to enter his room, he entered mine whenever he felt like it. I watched him from the hall, not daring to interrupt him. He knew I was there, but he did not acknowledge me. He found a few of Mathilde's drawings, scrutinized them, checked them, but put them back. At last, he seemed to find what he wanted; he pocketed it, and left the room, brushing by me. When I could bring myself to do it, I looked to see what he had taken. It was a little doll I had which Mother had given me and it was dressed in nun's clothing; but I had no idea what he wanted with it, nor could I summon the courage to ask for it back.

'Finally,' Mathilde continued, 'I . . . sat down . . . still, I wasn't able . . . couldn't say, "What are you doing here?" I began to think I was dreaming.

'At last he spoke. He seemed to be interested in the X-ray machine. For some reason, he asked me about that, about why I had it. I had the impression his throat was sore or that his voice had deepened. His accent was more Southern than I remembered it. I told him I X-rayed paintings to see if there were more valuable ones underneath.

'He shrugged and said, "Oh, then there must be a lot of radium – radiation. You should watch it." Then his eyes moved from the machine to the paintings around my studio. Finally, he looked at me. Our eyes rested on each other. It was as if there was too much to say. He had barely aged, Irene, he had barely aged. I sat and shivered in my nightgown. I felt as though no time had passed at all.

'"What are you doing?" I asked him, meaning what was he doing there. I could still hardly believe he *was* there.

'His head twitched – and his hand. He said, "I was in mining in Argentina. I just got in from Buenos Aires. I'm on my way to Paris. I'm going to work at the Banque Occidentale de Crédit."

'I said, "How can you work in a French bank when you don't speak French?"

'He said, "I do speak French. I speak Spanish too. I've been around since I saw you last, Mathilde, so don't heave the cultured pearls at me."

'There it was – the old sarcasm in his voice, the sneer, you know, and that did it. The sneer put me into a kind of rage. I started to shake uncontrollably and said, over and over, "Why have you come to see me? Why have you broken into my flat?"

'Durrand's face gave nothing away at all. He just said, "I thought I'd give you a little scare."

'"You! Scare me!" I said. But he had scared me. He did scare me, standing there after so many years, after so long – the same. Even so, I gave him a hard stare – like when we were children.

'He gave a little shrug and told me it would teach me to get better security for the place. "These pictures must be worth a fortune," he said.

'It was that shrug he always gave when he was trying to wriggle out of something, so I knew I had him. I said, "Durrand, do you want me to turn you over to the police or do you want to tell me why you are here?"

'And I did have him! I did have him then, Irene,' Mathilde said, turning to me. Her face looked bruised in the bluish tinge of the airplane light. 'He started for me, his face full of menace and rage, but all at once, I remembered how to handle him. I always could handle him, couldn't I?' she said in triumph. 'When he reached me, I knew he couldn't, couldn't bring himself to – hurt me. We stood face to face for a long time. I said, "Durrand, you fool! What have you done?" He said nothing for a long time, then he breathed out slowly and said, "Matty. Matty, I'm all in."

'And that was all I needed to know for the moment. I led him into the kitchen and gave him some brandy. We never did have to talk much. We sat there for about an hour in the dark, smoking and drinking brandy, peering at each other's shadows, not speaking. At last, he said, "I got into a little trouble with the police in Argentina. It was nothing. But I don't want any more trouble because of my new job." We said nothing much else. There was nothing else to say.

'Finally, he went to sleep on the sofa in my living room. I suppose he had been travelling for the better part of two days. That and the brandy put him right out. I sat there with him for a long time in the dark, quite unable to go back to sleep myself.

'I don't know why I did this. I suppose it was an impulse, an intuition about him. I had the itch, the desire to watch him sleeping, so I got up softly and lit the candle on my mantelpiece, and carried it over to my brother and crouched there for a long time, breathing gently lest I should wake him. And then I knew, by instinct, that I must find something, that there was something for me to see, and so I opened his shirt, button by button, very carefully, waiting between each button so that he would not wake. And at last, I parted the whole shirt from his chest. He wore a heavy, iron crucifix, and his skin was covered with lacerations, some of them so deep that they should have had stitches . . . some of them quite fresh.

'So I knew. I knew if Durrand was hurting himself again that something was going on. I mean I knew what was going on inside him, and I blew the candle out and sat there crouched beside him for a long time.

'He used to do that sort of thing when we were children. When he got into that way, I'd quit playing with him and come to you until it blew over. It disgusted me to watch him hurt himself. He always wanted me to hurt myself too, but I could never bring myself to do it.'

*Cast your mind back, Irene, to the sticky blood.* The renewed onslaught of Durrand's voice crammed my head with terror.

'What's got into you, Irene? What's the matter?' Mathilde asked me. She was staring at me with a slightly addled look upon her face, staring at me with pleasure.

'It upset me! It upset me to remember how he used to treat himself,' I said. 'I didn't know he'd tried to get you to do it.' I said this while a memory, long buried, rose through my conscious will to suppress it and occurred before my inner eye. I knew then on the airplane, and I know now and remember what she told me that I hadn't seen and bribed me to forget with her red lamp. I am writing in the light of that lamp. Them – they – I came upon them, slicing and drinking, their lips covered, parted and merry, with cup and candle between them, and when my scream broke their communion, they told me Mother would have me locked up in a mental hospital for having such a crazy fit. 'Crazy! Crazy! Crazy!' Durrand cried, hopping up and down. After I had run into my room and buried my head in my pillows, Mathilde came in all soothing, as if I had actually had a fit, and she gave me her lamp, the one I liked, and she said she understood and how she had found me on the floor biting my tongue and how Mother would lock me up and have my brain cut if I told her I had seen something which I had not seen.

With every instinct, I knew not to give this sudden memory away. I searched wildly for anything I could say or do which would distract her gaze from me.

*You. You made me do it, devil!* cried the voice of Durrand.

'I think I am going to be sick,' I said. Mathilde found a bag and handed it to me, watching.

'He upset you too, poor baby,' she said.

'I am not a baby, Mathilde,' I said.

'Well, be like that!' she said huffily. 'I thought you would be interested to know that I bathed Durrand's wounds that night with my tears. Oh, they fell and fell, and I anointed him.'

'Mathilde,' I said, 'Why did you do that? Why didn't you just leave him alone.' And she withdrew into an angry silence until the airplane started to descend to Novosibirsk. I thought of Durrand sitting there, perhaps a few seats ahead.

# Chapter Eleven

While we refuelled at Novosibirsk Airport, we were forced to wait separately from the Russian passengers in a stuffy little room. My sister ignored me, and for this I was grateful. She made for the bar and bought a glass of vodka, drank it and bought another one. She sat down at a little table in the corner of the room, not exactly excluding me from sitting next to her, but following me with occasional hot looks to indicate her displeasure and pain at my failure to respond to her story the way she had expected me to. She lit a cigarette and looked off into space.

I went and stood by the window and attempted to control my feelings. I could not seem to gather them. Outside, a few planes taxied around the nearly empty tarmac. The airfield was so large, it could have accommodated three times the traffic. Durrand is dead, I said to myself, and all of this is merely unearthed memory. Someone was speaking to us. I turned and there was a girl with flaxen hair, welcoming us to Siberia in careful English. She seemed nervous, like an amateur actress who is not sure of her lines. On and on she went, piling fact upon fact about Novosibirsk. I made myself listen intently to this, trying to memorize every detail in order to calm my shaking apprehension of Durrand. The girl gave us figures – population figures, industry output figures. Had I really remembered all of that about the blood or not? She talked about chemicals. Agriculture. Or was Durrand in truth a kind of demon trying to misinform me for his own fell purposes? I tried to concentrate on the girl. 'Siberia is bigger in area than the United States or China,' she finally said, and stepped back, like a child who had recited a geography lesson.

Novosibirsk. The girl said it was very cold there in winter, sometimes — 40 degrees. It was hard to know what time it was as it kept changing while we travelled over Russia's vastness.

I made up my mind to take my pills and asked the flaxen girl for the bathroom. At first she seemed reluctant to let me go, but finally she relented and unlocked the door which led to the rest of the airport. The bathroom was across the hall. For a moment, I stood on the landing of a staircase that led down to a light, busy terminal full of people. I was possessed by a sudden, strong urge to make a run for it and escape into the throng. What would happen if I did? They would certainly catch up with me, and when they did, how could I explain my actions? To Russians, Americans, Mathilde, or even myself? I stood there fixed for quite a while, paralysed with the complexity of choice. Should I believe that the spirit of my dead brother was leading me on an expedition which would end in madness? Or should I believe that the evidence of his clear syllables only reflected a functional disturbance in my brain? Or should I believe that I heard him because Matty wanted him – that my mind had become a servant to her desires?

The door opened, and John stepped out upon the landing. I looked up and realized that I was already half way down the stairs. I saw him in the shadow at the top, and I saw the bustling Russians in the light beneath. The choice crystallized immediately in my mind. I knew that he would not betray me if I ran, for on his face was a kind of sympathy for my dilemma, even though he did not know what the dilemma was. He held back, as if to allow me to do whatever I intended freely, and in a flash, I realized I would probably be all right if I threw myself upon the mercy of whatever fate Novosibirsk might present to me. What I did not know was if this choice – escape – would take me beyond Durrand. For one way or the other, it occurred to me that I had been forced into extremes beyond which I must travel if I were to withstand this monstrous visitation.

For a moment, I held myself upon the banister and in my spirit clung to the holiness and blessing I had felt earlier that evening in the Russian church. For whatever Durrand had believed or Matty did not believe, I knew that quite beyond the use they made of symbols and of doctrines, there existed another world that neither of them had real access to; and, though I worried that it might be arrogant of me to think I had some better belief, it nonetheless persuaded me to find understanding, a kind of courage. I found a firm intention in myself, the only one I knew to make, never to tell my sister of the voice. Slowly, and with effort, I ascended.

'Are you all right?' John asked. 'I wondered if you were all right.' And in his face I sought and found a reassurance that, having made my decision, I would not pursue the course I had chosen without his help.

'Are you all right?' he repeated.

'I think so. I think I am now,' I said, and I looked back down the stairwell with a reeling sense that I would have escaped nothing if I had run down it into the crowd.

The Russian girl looked at me mistrustfully. She announced that the plane was ready for boarding. The Hungarian looked impatiently at John, as if eager to resume their conversation.

When we were again in the air, the stewardess brought us a light meal. Mathilde played with hers, but I ate mine although I was not hungry. Suddenly, she erupted – not loudly. I could feel her spirit heave and spill over her ability to control its boundary, so that it washed out over me.

'I loved him,' she said, and put her hand, aghast, across her mouth. 'I loved Durrand,' she said, and she rocked to and fro like a person on a television report of a war or earthquake. 'I don't care what he did! We were together from the moment of our conception . . . before you even existed, we were together!' And she looked at me bitterly for a moment.

I waited for her to calm herself. She put her head back

on the headrest of the seat. She spoke with her eyes closed, her voice low, like the growl and throb of the plane. 'I can't believe he's dead, not really dead. I keep thinking they buried him alive and that he clawed away at his coffin, and is still there, alive and waiting for me to find him and save him.'

Although that thought made me shudder, I said, 'Mathilde, this is not going to get you anywhere. It isn't. You just must let him go – eventually, you must let him go to God who is just and merciful, no matter what you may think.'

I think she made up her mind to ignore what I had said, because she was silent for quite a while. With her eyes still closed, she said, 'You see, I cannot get it out of my head that he is still alive somewhere – needing me.' Her voice droned almost in tune with the noise of the airplane so that I barely caught what she said. 'He would never have broken into my flat that night if he hadn't needed something, would he? He was too proud to return to me in any other way. He had to wrench things open by violence. He could only get back to the bond between us by violating something.' She opened her eyes and turned to me.

'Do you always have to give things to people just because they need them?' I asked, but thought, I should have run for it, I should have bolted.

'Why are your teeth chattering?' she asked. 'Are you cold? It's not cold.'

'I am cold all the same,' I said. She handed me her sweater from her lap, and I made willed efforts to pretend it warmed me. I hid my shaking jaw behind my hand.

'But he was my twin!' she exclaimed. 'How could you understand that I couldn't stop feeling what he felt? Even during the long years we were separated, I could never exclude Durrand's feelings from mine; and I think we did separate because it was all so strong we had to try to extricate ourselves . . .'

'Can't you extricate yourself now? You must.' Even though I spoke with a voice trembling with emotion, she did not seem to hear me. I could see from her face that she was quite obsessed with him, and there was no way of deflecting her.

'The thought of his need, the need he expressed in his nocturnal visit to my flat, preyed on my mind,' she continued. 'Although he had denied it, the more I thought about it, the more I began to wonder if Durrand had not actually meant to rob me that night. You know as well as I do what Durrand was capable of – or perhaps you don't. It was all very well his stuffing things into little drawers in his head and labelling them theocratically. He never could and never did meet any situation which required originality without panicking and doing something delinquent. If something did not correspond to a little card in his mental filing system, he was completely at a loss to know what to do. When he was confused he became utterly ruthless.' She uttered this last sentence in muted rage.

'Mathilde, why couldn't you just let him be?' I found myself imploring her. 'You knew the way he was . . .'

'You'll never understand what was between us,' she said contemptuously. 'How could you even think that I could let him be? Twenty years we were split and you can *never* know why. Never. I have not forgotten a word or look between us. I know all the secret gestures and the rules. You don't think that I ever for one moment *failed* to wait. And do you think that he could really ever have denied those deeper things we knew?'

I said nothing and stared fixedly at the seat in front of me. As she often had in childhood, Mathilde seemed to sense she had gone too far. After a moment, she began to speak again, but with a marked change of tone.

'Irene, Durrand wouldn't have turned up like that unless it meant something. How can I tell you what that was when I hardly know myself? Did you ever know we invented a language? I could tell you what his visit meant in that, but I could not translate it. The only explanation I can give you in plain English is that Durrand was showing that he wanted and needed something from me. I only later discovered how much he needed money. At the time, all I knew was that he had had half a mind to take one of my icons and sell it. To Durrand, it wouldn't be stealing to take from me. Even when he stole in the past from Mother or Woolworth's or you, he would talk about his acquisitions as if they were prizes from a game of skill. He would work out whole strategies. Most of the time, I would make him put things back — that is if I discovered them in time. I knew what happened to thieves. Oh, Reenie, no one ever knew how many times I held him in check. It was more than anyone ever appreciated.' She smiled thinly and I remembered how she used to call him off me — like a dog.

'At any rate,' she continued, 'whatever the reason, I made up my mind to go to Paris and find him because I could not stay in London alone with that overpowering feeling I had that Durrand was somehow calling me. The trouble he had spoken of — the trouble in Argentina — I knew, I *knew* it was only a fraction of the whole trouble he was in.

'What bothered me most of all was that Durrand had refused to give me his address. Or rather, he had not refused. I knew that he had lied when he told me he had not yet found an apartment and did not know what hotel he would be staying in until he got settled. And what is more, I knew that he knew I understood he was lying. When I got to thinking about it, I decided he had lied in just such a way that I should know he was, so that I should search him out and find him.

'Question after question tormented me. If he was in trouble (and he was), what was he hiding from me? Had he got himself tied up with some mercenary outfit? That would be plausible, given Durrand's personality. Had he even got sucked into the Mafia? I had the wildest fears for him, that his life was in danger.

'I set out for Paris with a careful plan in mind. The only clue I had to go on was the name of the bank he had told me he was going to work for, and though at the time I did not really believe that story entirely, I decided I had to start somewhere. I booked myself into a good hotel and had the switchboard operator there place a call to Durrand at the bank. I had decided that my voice over the telephone might alarm him into more evasions, and I could not risk that. Imagine my relief when the operator put me through and I heard his voice on the other end of the line. "Allo, Allo." I clapped my hand over the receiver so that I would not be tempted, but I listened to Durrand until he hung up, listened to the impatience and uncertainty and wondered if he guessed anything at all.

'When I learned that this part of his story was true, that he did indeed work at the Banque Occidentale de Crédit, I put my second plan into operation. If Durrand was not going to tell me where he lived, I was going to find out.

'I found a café just across the road from where he worked. Around five, I planted myself there and watched the doors of that large and very respectable place of business. Oh, it's the sort of bank where duchesses keep their pearls: not the sort of place where Durrand would have felt comfortable. When dusk fell, the bank workers started to stream out. I had neglected to notice a metro station nearby, and I was panicked by the thought I would miss him in the rush hour crowd. Eventually, however, he emerged, all alone, late. He was dressed in a black coat, and he moved sideways like a crab against the autumn wind.

'When I saw that he was obviously going to walk to wherever he was going I was relieved, for I realized that I would never have been able to tail him if he had taken a taxi or gone by metro. Not only did he walk, he walked very slowly, stopping from time to time like someone lost in thought. After a short while, I became confident that he would not look round and see me. Indeed, he looked at no one. He seemed completely isolated, and I realized I had never seen him look that way before. I had never observed Durrand, because when we were together, we were never alone. I felt like a ghost, frantically watching and powerless to help someone who had been of great importance but who was now beyond communication.

'At last, he stopped in front of a large, opulent house, took a key from his pocket, climbed the steps slowly – he trudged – then let himself in at the front door. For a long time, I stood on the sidewalk deliberating what to do. I had absolutely no idea what this place was. He obviously lived there; maybe it was a block of flats; maybe he was living with someone. Durrand finding romance at last? Finally, my urge to see him completely got the better of me. I mounted the steps, fully expecting to have to talk my way past a concièrge. I rang, and to my surprise the door was immediately opened by a young man whose correct dress and formal manner indicated his association with some profession – perhaps the law. Indeed, he struck me as being the very model of a successful young advocate, prosecutor. He summed me up with a cold, yet not impolite, scrutinizing stare.

'Looking past him, I could see I had stumbled upon some sort of residence, which I took at first to be an embassy. In fact, the imposing hall with its sweeping staircase and chandeliers, guarded as it was by this mistrustful looking bruiser from the upper middle classes, gave me the impression that I had wandered into a hostile foreign mission. The young man spoke French with a heavy accent. I began to wonder if someone was holding Durrand against his will.

'I was so utterly confused by this wholly unexpected turn of events that I completely lost the power of speech. The young man looked as if he were about to close the door, when suddenly Durrand himself appeared. He was walking slowly across the hall to the staircase, but he turned and saw me. He stood stock still. Trying to say my name, he could not.

'The young man at the door gave a start, as though the current of the shock of our seeing one another passed through him. He looked around at Durrand, then at me.

'He looked at Durrand as if to question what he was seeing, and Durrand confirmed it. I remember. I can hear it. He said, "C'est ma soeur." His voice was soft. I could see some puzzle had been solved. Of course, it had been my resemblance to Durrand which had struck the man who had opened the door. He looked relieved, and let me into the house with an excess of unctuous good manners.

'Durrand and I stood together in the hall. He was too flabbergasted to speak. I asked him what this place was, but he did not answer. I looked around me. There was a large crucifix over the mantlepiece, and a Gothic Madonna stood in a corner. These seemed baubles next to a blown-up portrait of a man whose face and eyes instantly grasped my attention. It was not even a very large photograph, but I could not stop looking at it. The tilt of the head, the jut of the jaw, the knit of the brow led me to assume that the man in the picture was a president, prince or general, perhaps of some banana republic to which Durrand now owed his allegiance.

'I almost did not hear Durrand's questions. Again and again, he asked me how I had found him. "I have ways," I said. And he shook his head over and over as if I had arrived by some perplexing chance or grace.

'I asked him what country he was working for, because I really did assume that this was an embassy, of some Catholic country, perhaps. He looked very puzzled. Suddenly, a door opened and two young men came into the hall. They were carrying squash rackets. They stared at me and at Durrand, then vanished up the stairs.

'He told me he did not work for any country. He kept looking nervously around. "I don't know how you found me," he kept saying. All at once, yet another door opened, and a priest in a black cassock entered the hall and approached us. I could not tell whether Durrand was relieved or upset to see him. He took Durrand to one side, and I could hear something murmured in French. The name Victor kept on cropping up. I was absurdly proud that Durrand had mastered the language so well.

'I don't understand the ins and outs of it, but from what I gathered, membership to the Companionate was not a thing you bandied about lightly to all and sundry. The priest slid over to me and started to ask delicate questions about how I had found what was, after all, my own brother.

'And this is where what was between Durrand and me *worked*, Irene,' she said, looking at me. 'With my eyes closed, I could have read Durrand's thoughts and instructions – and *did* without even looking at his face.

'I mentioned that I had stumbled across Durrand in Kensington Gardens quite by chance and he had told me he was on his way to Paris, having been employed for some time in South America. "He happened to mention the name of the bank where he was going to work," I said, "but I had no idea he lived here." I told him I was in Paris on business of my own and had decided to drop in on Durrand because I had some pressing family business which involved us both. I had missed him at the bank and had decided to follow him home in order to give him a surprise. God! You don't know how cool I was, and Durrand appreciated it. I could tell by the sidelong glance he gave me. He had taken in every detail of my story.

'I felt I was on firm ground at last, so I began a counterattack. I asked the priest what was so wrong about my seeing my own twin brother whom I hadn't seen in seven years.

'Looking back on it, I suppose he had no option but to receive me. I always got the feeling that the Companionate was secretive even about its own secrecy. The priest drew me aside, and at a nod of his head, Durrand fell back out of earshot. The whole thing was done with much smiling aplomb. He told me a bit about the Companionate and that Durrand had taken holy orders. These, he said, involved much sacrifice of family ties. It was reassuring to him, he told me, to know that Durrand had managed all these years to mortify himself so completely as to conceal his whereabouts from me; yet, he indicated, this had perhaps gone too far. He said Durrand had a way of being over-zealous, and he was sure their leader, Victor, had had no intention to deny him contact with me completely. It was not the Companionate's policy to make families suffer, only to strengthen the members' commitment. He began to wonder aloud if I had any interest in joining myself, for they had a sister order on the other side of Paris. Might I be interested in subscribing to the "Friends of the Companionate", which was a kind of third order? Perhaps he himself could help me with this family worry. Perhaps the Companionate could help out in some way.

'I wanted to talk to Durrand alone. He stood to one side, watching my conversation with the priest. His eyes were veiled and a muscle twitched in his cheek. I felt him willing me not to beg for an interview with him alone. He was willing it. I know.

'I also watched the priest with great care, for despite his soothing tone, his eyes worked around my face, appraising me. I, too, summed him up. I wondered what his weakness was, and decided that from the way his eyes moved from my bracelet to my necklace to my shoes, it was money. I caught the scent of his knowing I was rich.

'I said, very prettily, that I thought that I did not know how the Companionate could help me out with money matters. He said, "Oh?" He really did, Irene. Anyway, I signalled that Durrand must be in on this conversation because it involved him. He beckoned to Durrand, who came obedient as a dog.

'You would be amazed at my powers of invention, Irene,' Mathilde said. 'I told them that it was you, of all people. You, who had suddenly turned into a monster of avarice and had questioned Father's will.'

'Me?' I asked, interrupting her story. 'What have I got to do with this, Matty?' I felt sick that my name had been drawn into it.

'Oh, don't be so silly. For a moment, I thought that Durrand was going to give the game away and laugh. No, I made up a great big song and dance about lawsuits. I took care to reveal, meanwhile, the extent of my own fortune. It was really very amusing. Talk about avarice, the priest practically insisted that I give him my name and address so that he could send me brochures and pamphlets about the Companionate's activities. Durrand said nothing for a while, but his eyes glimmered. I had the feeling it was all an answer to prayer, albeit coming from me.

'But I could not take my eyes off the photograph on the wall. I said, "Who's that?", and here Durrand spoke, really spoke. He said, "That is Victor, our leader and the greatest man alive." Something about his eyes told me he really meant it, and I knew I would have to be very careful if I was ever to get him back.'

'What about this lawsuit, Matty?' I asked. 'What were you saying about me?'

'Oh, you won't like what Durrand said,' Mathilde laughed. 'He told me that your suit could be thrown out of court at once by reason of insanity.' She looked out of the window and peeked at her watch. 'We're about to land,' she said.

I could hear my voice giving a sob I meant to control. 'But I am not insane!' And whatever Durrand was gave an audible snicker.


# Chapter Twelve


Time goes slowly for me here in Baltimore, yet sometimes I am aware of a timeless present which holds within it elements of what has been, is now and will be. I am stretched out before this dark illumination painfully. It is active, and sharp as a laser.

We landed in Irkutsk at dawn. An almost hallowed light edged the trees and grass as we descended. As we left the plane and walked across the tarmac, Mathilde's face was caught in a look of stillness and innocence in the glory and light of the sun's ascent.

A portrait of Marx frowned out at us in Irkutzk airport.

Because of his beard, he seems to have no neck. Apparently confident of the destiny and weight of history, he frowns out his view of the inevitable. He's murdering time, he's murdering time, I thought. Off with his head! His head is off and his image is everywhere.

Depending on what is real, there are two separate histories of our sojourn in Irkutsk. What I saw and heard outwardly carries me to one conclusion: what I saw and heard inwardly drives me to another. The mystery is: what happened? Like a shuttle, the memory of Durrand, who is dead and therefore cannot have a memory, jabs through my own memory of what Mathilde told me of what she remembered. Who or what uttered the voice of Durrand which I heard against my own volition? Was I being haunted by the ghost of my dead brother? Some of the things I heard from him were true and some were not. Some of the things he said I could have known without him, some of the things he said I could not have known. Did he tempt me with lies or did he tempt me with truth? Or did he, like the witches in Macbeth, tell truthful lies, lying truths hatched out to be misleading? Was he a spirit or even an angel from the dark and negative rim? Or was he an insurrection of my own personality? I do not know, but can only give evidence of the battle I had against him.

Irkutsk is a handsome town situated on the River Angara. It was settled in the sixteenth century by the Stroganov family, who hoped to extend the fur trade into the then unexplored territory of Siberia. The Buriyat Mongols, who were indigenous to the area, fought fiercely for the possession of the land, but evidently lost. The city itself was founded in the seventeenth century when the conquest had been accomplished.

'Where are they now? The Mongols?' John asked Sonya, our new guide who had regaled us with this information as we were travelling to our hotel in a minibus. She was a European Russian, but her features were noticeably angular – chunky like an Eskimo – and with her heavy amplitude she carried an authority that seemed natural to her. 'Oh, they have their autonomous region, east of Baikal,' she replied. We passed lofty houses set back from broad boulevards lined with trees. On less exalted streets snug timber-framed cottages with gingerbread shutters give the town a fairytale appearance. Some of the little houses are buried in the ground up to their window ledges: the result, Sonya told us, of permafrost.

On she went about Peter the Great, who had sent missionaries to convert the Mongols; about the Decembrists who had finished their exile in Irkutsk; about Admiral Kolchak's last stand. She spoke of the mining of precious metals, the Trans-Siberian Railway, the industry, the universities of Irkutsk, and ended up telling us about something called the Institute for Terrestrial Magnetism, whereupon Mathilde, who had been unnaturally silent during the short trip, burst out laughing. She said something in Russian to Sonya, who smiled at her remark.

We arrived at the hotel where we were to meet up with the other tourists, and disentangled ourselves from the minibus. Mathilde went ahead and entered the building.

'Imagine! Terrestrial Magnetism,' John said to me.

All of the sudden, I was gripped by a keen sense of Durrand. There he was, like a featureless pillar of smoke.

It is *not* Durrand, I thought and I will not communicate, will not allow . . .

But vision was upon me, and I was translated back to this house in Baltimore. A party was going on and there was champagne. Mathilde in a little flowered dress was holding a baby in christening robes, and I realized the baby was myself. She was jogging the baby up and down. Tall, cloudy adult forms were not paying attention to her. She jogged the baby more frantically, then all at once, stole out of the room with it. The adults were laughing stupidly. Mathilde, both frightened and intent, was now in the bathroom, and Durrand, shadowy at the door in a suit with an Eton collar, watched as she took the baby and dropped it deliberately on the hard, tiled floor. She stood there, watching the head of the baby, and Durrand stood, watching her. They were both aware that this had happened, but made no communication with one another. She covered the baby's head with a bonnet, and returned to the party. The voice of Durrand, with horrible clarity, came into my head, perfectly articulated. His curious, nonchalant burr which he clipped when he came to the end of sentences, spoke of Mother's confusion about the cause of my epilepsy, and how he knew and never told on Matty. *You see now, don't you? See. See.*

I felt someone jogging my shoulder and asking me something, but it came from a long way off. The burning smell came and I was afraid of falling. The road started to stretch out towards the infinite horizon. Sick and jumpy, I was about to jerk and thrash, then suddenly it stopped and my mind was informed with immense clarity. There had been something insidious about the vision – like a propaganda film. I felt myself being guided to a bench.

'It isn't true,' I said.

'What? What isn't true?' John lurched into my view. He was sitting next to me, lightly slapping my hand.

I closed my eyes. Ridiculous pictures of St Theresa in ecstasy formed and unformed in my mind's eye. Vision. Bastard. Bastard vision, was all that I could think, words coming like pepper shot. I prayed to the saint. I opened my eyes. John looked distressed and fiddled with his tie. I was overcome with shame that he had seen me having a seizure. 'What's the matter?' he asked.

I sat for a long time, it must have been a long time, making the decision that, in fact, led to other decisions which were to alter the course of my life. Looking at his collar and his hair, his grey eyes, I thought the truth or nothing, the truth or nothing, and, making what I thought was a final renunciation of any chance with him, I said, 'I am an epileptic. And it's awful. I'm sorry.'

'Shh!' said John. 'It's all right. I don't mind.' His hand quivered on my shoulder, and with that acute sense given to the blind, I heard his touch with strange, ulterior joy, as if his fingers were harmonies. We sat for a long moment, then entered the hotel. As soon as I went into the dining room, I knew that the episode had not yet passed. Everything I saw seemed to fly up and down, as if on silvered rods.

I caught a glimpse of my sister eating sugared yoghurt, but the glint of her spoon carried me away past her to the vision of a flash in the dark. A sibilant Englishwoman was speaking to Mathilde in modulations that shivered my ear, so that she became the voice she was, and I saw the light flexibility of her inner person standing before me, although she remained seated. A bearded, male presence loomed out of this perplexity, smiling a competent, confident smile. He boomed out some greeting and I heard John answer for me, and I was grateful for this as I felt myself ascending from myself, and could only hold myself still so as not to vanish altogether. The man leaned and boomed at Mathilde. Snagged down for a moment by the reverberations of his bass voice, I heard him say that he was Vinnie Winston, and that the woman my sister was talking to was Alma Lakeland. She had a beautiful smile and wore a padded jacket. There was some garble about lamas and shamans. I am piecing together now what was fragmented at the time so that I can derive some coherence from an incoherent experience.

And then the descent into seizure came. I could not hold, and my nostrils were being sucked back into the vacuum. I thought I heard Mathilde scrape back her chair. Through muttering and murmuring, I felt her hand grasp my arm that had turned into breeze. I counted slowly in order to hold: '10, 9, 8, 7, 6, 5, 4, 3, 2, 1. 5, 10, 15, 20 . . .' Sequence of the dark. And I thought I was going to make it. Mathilde was holding my arm, but she was not supporting me. Her voice came dry and garrulous to me. She was not John and she was ashamed of me. Was she? At any rate, she hustled me away from the crowd, and eventually, we found ourselves upstairs in a long, polished loggia which led to our bedroom.

'What set it off?' she asked. 'I thought you were going to be all right.'

I felt better in the lighter atmosphere. I thought, I must get to my medicine. Mathilde continued to question me in a harsh, dry voice. We passed a case full of souvenirs: dolls in Siberian dress, and jewellery. My eye caught an earthy, purple stone with streaks of marble in it. I set my eye fixedly on the complexities of the gem. 'It was the flashing of a bird's wings in the sun,' I said. Sometimes this sort of thing can set off an episode, as Mathilde well knew.

*Liar!* said the voice. *Go on. Ask her what she did to you. You can prove me.*

I will not cooperate with this, I replied inwardly. Mother of God, help me.

At last we reached our room. 'All I need is rest,' I said to Mathilde. *Devil!* said Durrand. *Liar and Devil!*

Mathilde drew the curtains against the early morning sun. I felt as though she were walled up inside herself and crying, beating against the walls in silence.

I took my medicine. *Tell her!* said Durrand. *She wants to hear from me. Let me talk to my sister!*

I collapsed on the bed for a while, holding myself to myself.

Then, someone shook a plum tree. I saw a man in a black apron shaking a plum tree in a vision which was inside me. He shook the tree for fruit, but there were only flowers. In a rage, he tried to tear at the flowers, but he could not hurt the tree. Like a celestial being, the tree blossomed iridescently. The blossom could not be touched, but the man could not see this. It was Durrand.

The tree rose and grew so that everything was covered with majestic, obliterating white. It spread its branches, rejoicing in the Creator. No one could touch the bark or the flowers of the tree for fear of its great beauty. Although it was beyond the state of birth, growth or decay, it started to expand. The veins of its leaves and blossoms, its roots and its branches filled themselves with light. Everything was filled with light. The tree could not become, but it became – never-ending, expanding, increasing, creating. It gave itself as generosity, giving everything and replenishing everything it gave by giving all. Its splendour filled my mind with awe at the inexhaustible love of God, and I wept in an ecstasy at the plum blossom that could not be touched.

I don't know how long this extraordinary vision lasted, but when it was over, immediately I felt better, and in firm possession of my faculties. I went to the window and looked out. Mathilde was getting onto a coach with the other tourists, and it went off. I had not been aware of her leaving the room, yet I recalled every moment of the vision of the tree. I stood for a while and thought. What sort of epileptic episodes were these that I remembered them? The ruling principle of the past had been a chaos from which I had emerged with little or no recollection of what had happened to me.

Yet, what, after all, in the past had I been *allowed* to see, or to experience, or to remember? Hadn't a complicated set of wires around my head sent impulses to a jogging needle which defined me? A specialist would take the chart and muse upon its pits and crags as if it were a map of me. They had constructed limits for me, boundaries beyond which what I saw was not real, so that I was not real myself unless I saw what they saw too. Each Sunday, I had to declare my faith in the invisible, yet seeing the invisible made it visible, and if visible to me alone, not real. Not real enough, at any rate, for those who probed and prodded me in hospitals. I myself had grown up in a terror of the border between the seen and unseen things, and in the inner holocaust of my experience could only grasp a mystery, which I sensed blindly at the centre of myself like a pole or ladder connecting me to God who made me.

Then what of the tree and what of Durrand, I asked myself? And what of the uncharted territory beyond what was agreed as sane or factual to believe?

*So you think you're a mystic, do you?* Durrand's voice bit sharply. *Mescalin and acid can have the same effect.*

I made no reply.

*A mystic is only available to the will of God and counts his experience as nothing.*

I sat clamped in a refusal of Durrand. I began to wonder if he came from hell.

*Hell? It is you who have a devil. Unclean. It is I who have been sent to give you a last chance to redeem yourself. It is Mathilde who must be saved, and you are the instrument. Act humbly and let me speak through you, guide you.*

No, I said, inwardly. Go away.

*Pride goes before destruction and you are making yourself out to be exalted.*

Oh, Mathilde, I thought, whatever you did to me, I forgive you, and if I forgive you no one can blame you. And when I had said that, I felt a great deal better.

Today, I washed the bathroom floor in Ashby Street, making the tiles shine where she was supposed to have dropped me. I do not think she did. I rinsed and dried and polished the tiles. I would like to have a baby.

Then, in Irkutsk, I decided to go out if in the room I was to go on hearing my brother – or my own head. I had no idea where Mathilde had gone, but I was glad of a chance to be alone.

I bathed and dressed and went in search of fresh air. No one seemed concerned to prevent me. The early promise of a fine day had been broken by rain. The sky was overcast, and little stipples of shower burst upon me. Clearly, there had been a deluge earlier as huge puddles lay about. I made my way first of all to the imposing white church which dominated the town from a hill, but on arriving there, I found it was closed. An old woman clothed in black stood behind the iron gate and motioned me away, so I went down and explored the maze of alleys below, alleys flanked by the backs of wooden houses. A black mastiff leapt from its shelter, barking, and straining against a chain; its hackles rose, the stiffened fur silhouetted against white household linen which billowed from a washing line. I was frightened of the dog. I would have liked to pray in the church about Durrand and the plum tree. I would have done anything to drive away the dark memory of that voice.

Yet, as I found the embankment of the River Angara where I walked for a while musing, I began to see reason. Durrand's voice seemed to take on the psychiatric look of undigested mourning. Perhaps I had been more attached to him than I thought. I wondered if, perhaps, he had not taken the place of a father for me, and if, indeed, he had not been put in that position unfairly. His rejection of me had been painful, but at least he had been there, whereas what had signified my father chiefly was his complete indifference. It seemed ridiculous as I walked and looked at the swollen river that I had believed only a few moments earlier in an actual phantom. I began to feel sorry for myself that I had countenanced such pagan thoughts, such untenable mumbo-jumbo.

Some Russian boys of about eleven stopped me and asked for cigarettes. They had hard little faces. Their hair was cropped very close, and they looked tough. Surely, I thought, as I waved them on, Durrand had been only their age when I had been so frightened of him, and it was absurd of me to be frightened of him still. It began to rain heavily. I had reached an avenue lined with old trees and mansions set imperially from the road. Seeing a public building at one end, I took refuge in it. It was a museum.

A guard seemed to object to my going in, but I could not understand him. I thought he wanted money, so I gave him a few notes – I could not understand what they were – and he accepted them greedily. Putting his finger to his lips, he ushered me in. It took a while for me to realize that he'd thought I had bribed him and was mightily pleased.

I walked round the empty museum, which seemed devoted to anthropology. I passed exhibits of snowshoes and yurtas, tepees and jewellery that looked as if they had come from America.

I began to wonder if I should not after all tell Mathilde about Durrand's voice. Surely, there was something stupid about concealing something from her, something that might actually help her. If she knew that I too had a kind of obsession with him, we might be able to share our feelings. Why not come straight out with it?

I wandered into a light hall. Cases were ranged around the room, but one in particular caught my eye. A curious costume hung inside it. It was made of greenish leather tinged with age and was surmounted by a mask made of the same material. From the ear pieces of the mask hung many leather thongs, and these too decorated the apron-like shift underneath it. The costume was festooned with knotted leather ribbons, and little iron symbols hung from many of them and this gave the dress the appearance of a vestment. Around the navel, there was a round disc which was either a shield or a mirror. I knew that it was a mirror. In a separate case, there was a hat of iron and crowned with antlers. For a sudden moment, I thought the figure in the adjoining case, the one with the costume I had looked at, moved: but then I realized I had moved because I was frightened of the thing for no good reason and had jumped.

To the right of the cases, there was a photograph which hung upon the wall. I went and studied it closely. It was a picture of men in Mongolian dress surrounding the body of a horse flayed, its four legs stretched between two poles. One of the men was wearing a costume like the one in the case. Without being able to read the words under the picture, I realized that the horse had been sacrificed.

I did not know what to do with my ulterior knowledge of this picture, and the understanding that was born upon me through it that I must under no circumstances tell Mathilde about the voice.

I was bewildered almost to tears by the savage picture which I understood without being able to understand it. I did not know what to think about the carnage of the horse or of Durrand.

I fled out of the museum into the drenching rain.

'What are you doing wandering about?' Mathilde cried. She was jumping off the parked coach which had evidently just arrived back at the hotel. I straggled in with her, soaked to the skin.

# Chapter Thirteen

'So you're better,' Mathilde said over lunch. She dawdled with a piece of fish.

'Yes.' Looking at her, I could not stop thinking of my christening, my head, my bonnet. I again forced myself to think of my own stupidity at letting myself get away with taking the absurd locutions seriously. Surely, a more matter of fact explanation for the accusatory voice of Durrand lay in my own emotions; for, having been dependent as a child upon Mathilde, and frightened of her too, I must have buried anger against her. Now we were both adults and had lived our separate lives, I could see she was, and always had been, difficult, demanding. I was sure she had herself locked away resentment at me. My disablement must have been hard for her to bear.

'You never had fits like this when you were little,' she said. 'They were always very different. Once you went into one, it took you a long time to get out. It was like watching someone being thrown violently into a maze, and it was as if you needed a thread to get out safely. You looked different too, then, in childhood.' She leaned across the table. 'Tell me, why do you think they've come back? Why are they so different? Are you sure it's epilepsy?' Despite the mildness in her tone, I felt a little hook in Mathilde's question.

'Oh, medicine has advanced since then,' I said, maintaining a casual voice. Nonetheless, her questions had posed a threat to me, for the medication I had brought with me had no effect whatever on the voices in my head, which almost certainly it would have, had my attacks been straightforward. I added, in order to be truthful, 'and so have I – advanced since then. I've learnt to deal with the whole thing better.'

She shrugged, but I could see that she was annoyed at my answer.

'What sort of morning did you have?' I asked to fend off questions about mine.

She began to describe a geological museum and examples she had seen of ore unique to Siberia. 'Your friend John talked a lot about you on the bus,' she said. 'You seem to have intrigued him.' I blushed and she tittered. I had a bleak fantasy that he had quizzed her about the extent of my illness or that she had told him. I glanced across the dining room. John was eating with Vinnie Winston, who was holding forth with fulsome bravura on some topic or other. John's back was to me, but I felt he was aware of me all the same, and then I was ashamed at such a fantasy.

'Yes, he said you were the most unusual woman he'd ever met.'

'Did he?'

Suddenly, Mathilde gave a shudder of disgust. 'Do you see that woman over there?' she asked me. 'Those two women, I mean?' With a nod and a harsh look she indicated the half-concealed person of a woman in her early thirties who sat at an angle to us and who was talking with vehemence to her companion, a tall, angular woman of the same age. They were not quarrelling, but the dark woman was making statements in an over-definite tone – a tone, I observed, that probably came naturally to her as it does to lawyers or politicians. Her friend was listening with admiration.

Mathilde's voice was trembling. 'Do you think I really have to put up with them all the way to China?'

'What's the matter with them?'

'The dark one on the right is called Myra Bedrosian. The one on the left rejoices in the name of Happy Vavasour. They are proselytizing feminists from Ohio, and they wanted to know if you and I were lovers.'

'Goodness!' I said. 'Did they?'

'While I was out this morning with them, they spent the morning hacking away at me; that's why I ended up sitting with John on the bus home. If these women liked other women as they say they do they wouldn't spend all their time attacking. Do you remember that business about my monograph? That woman's piece virtually destroyed my career . . .'

'Mathilde, ignore them,' I said.

'It virtually destroyed me, being attacked like that.'

It suddenly occurred to me that Matty had never had a close woman friend. With the exception of me, her whole social world seemed to consist of relationships having to do with men in one way or other. I nearly answered that her career had in no way been destroyed, but thought the better of it.

'What is their interest in this trip?' I asked instead.

'Myra claims to know something of Chinese glazes. Isn't that wonderful? Porcelain and politics!'

'Do you think she might be more fragile than you give her credit for?'

'No!' cried Mathilde.

Myra stood up. She was shamelessly fat and had heavy, tough features. She sauntered over to the nearby table where the beautiful Alma sat and started to speak with her. Happy's face looked strained.

'I think she's been pestering Alma,' Mathilde hissed. 'Of course, Alma being an actress sort of riles Myra, but she can't work Alma out. Alma's too enigmatic.'

'It that the woman you were speaking to this morning?'

'Yes. Alma Lakeland. She's well known in England. It sounds extraordinary, but her great passion in life is Tibetan Buddhism. She got interested in it while doing a radio programme on the *Book of the Dead*.'

'The *Book of the Dead*,' I repeated. I began to wonder if anyone on the trip knew about the horse sacrifice photograph I had seen in the museum.

Chairs scraped and we were soon on the bus for more sightseeing around Irkutsk.

The weather became still, then broke. Sheets of rain engulfed the bus as it plied its way forward towards our destination, the War Memorial Square. Through swathes of water, which trickled down the bus window, it was just possible to make out the figures of a few damp children walking stiffly: they guarded an eternal flame, patrolling back and forth, even in that weather.

Sonya started to talk about Russia's participation in both wars.

'It's hard to think of war in this remote place,' said Alma to my sister across the aisle. My sister said nothing. During the bus ride, she had been staring at Myra, and now her eyes were wholly fixed on the unfettered woman who sat slightly in front of us. Something about Myra gnashed at her mind.

'Perhaps Mathilde could tell us something about the fresco on the church over there,' said Vinnie.

We all looked to where he was pointing. Through the streams of rain, we could see a large image of the face of Christ, painted high up on a wall. Because of the downpour, the painting had the strange appearance of something that hovered on its own. It hovered as if watching the disciplined, uniformed children who strutted around the eternal fire.

'It looks like the Cheshire cat,' said Myra.

Everyone waited for Mathilde to speak, but she said nothing. There was an embarrassed silence.

At last, Sonya spoke in desperation. 'It is the Mongol Christ. If you look at its features, you can see they are Mongolian. It was painted because of the mission to the Buriyats at the time of Peter the Great. If you look to the right, there is another icon of the Mongols being baptized.'

Anyone could see that the large triptych over the church porch depicted the Baptism of Christ. There was the river, the Lord, the Baptist, and the Holy Spirit like a dove descending. But Mathilde did not contradict Sonya and said nothing.

The fat woman started to chuckle.

'I don't know what she finds so funny about me!' said Mathilde through clenched teeth.

'Matty, I don't think she's laughing at you.'

'Oh, she is. She is laughing in triumph!' Mathilde's lips cringed from her teeth. I could not understand why Mathilde found the woman so objectionable.

It was getting later and wetter. Sonya told us we were driving off to see the tomb of a princess: the Princess Trubetskoy, who had followed her husband into exile after the Decembrist uprising, a woman whose courage and good works caused her to be honoured still.

'Who is that man there?' I asked Mathilde. I hoped to distract her from staring at Myra. She stared and glared at Myra. It was as if all her viscera were tangled up in Myra. I sharply indicated a man with protuberant black eyes. He sat alone and was engaged in some solitary meditation against the bleak Siberian perspective of rain.

Mathilde tore her engorged eyes from Myra. 'That is Dr Hartmann. He has something to do with animals.'

'Is he a zoologist?'

'I don't know,' Mathilde said. She shook her head as if to dislodge her stuck notion of Myra. 'Maybe he is a zoologist, maybe not. He was chatting me up earlier at the geological museum.'

Mathilde had a store of Anglicisms. I did not know what 'chatting up' meant, but I could guess from the way she rolled her eyes that Dr Hartmann had made some attempt to flirt with her.

'Are you sure?' I nearly asked her, but I checked myself. It annoyed me that Mathilde always had to think that men were paying court to her. Looking at Dr Hartmann, I thought I saw a seriousness, a sadness about him which would preclude the lechery her eyes suggested.

'He seems to be particularly interested in an animal called Przewalski's Horse which has either more or less chromosomes than other horses. I can't remember. He went into some long thing about how it could breed with horses with the normal number of chromosomes, and how their offspring could produce offspring in turn, "unlike a horse and donkey which produce only a sterile mule",' she said, pulling a face and mimicking the man. 'As he seemed so interested in genetics, I told him all about Durrand and me, looking so alike even when we were not identical twins. He seemed quite interested. He told me the horse was supposed to be extinct in the wild, but that he was going to Mongolia in order to find it. He says some people say that there may be a lost tribe there too – like yetis – the missing link. I became very absorbed in that,' Mathilde said. 'I like to think of a land where there might be strange and hidden things.'

I glanced at Mathilde, somehow alarmed that she had interjected Durrand into the conversation she had reported to me. I could not see how her being a twin could have been apposite to Dr Hartmann's remarks about Przewalski's Horse.

'He seems to have made friends with your beau, at any rate,' Mathilde said archly. 'What does he do for a living, your beau?' She spoke loudly enough for other people to hear, and I prayed that John could not hear her even though he was seated three rows away.

'He isn't my beau,' I said. 'He makes maps.'

'How dull,' said my sister. She glanced at me and saw my jaw tighten. 'I thought you said he wasn't your beau.'

'Mathilde,' I said, 'stop it.'

The bus had stopped, and the pneumatic doors opened. Sonya started to give a speech about the Decembrists and about the princess who was buried in the graveyard at the church where we had stopped. The rain was sluicing down on the roof of the coach.

'You know, Irene, for a sister you are hardly very sympathetic to me – after all I've been through. You snap at me every time I pull your leg or make a little joke. You just won't admit to yourself that you hated Durrand, and you take it out in other ways. I *need* you, Reenie, and you just seem to ignore that.'

The other members of the tour started to get off the bus. I hardly had the energy to move. 'Mathilde,' I said. Then I said, 'Look, let's go and see the church.'

'Seeing what religion has done for you and Durrand,' she said, 'I wouldn't darken the door!' and she sank into herself, folding her arms tightly across her chest like a small child in a rage.

I felt I needed to be inside the church and that if I did not get into it I would not be able to bear another minute of Mathilde. John stood in the bus as if to wait for me.

'I just don't see how you can call yourself a Christian if you are always losing your temper at me,' Mathilde called after me so that the remaining tourists heard. So that John heard.

He offered me his raincoat, and we shared the shelter of it up the pathway to the church. I was frightened of his pity, or of something else perhaps, and so I said nothing except to thank him. All the same, I had a strong sense of his physical presence. Under the wet raincoat, I caught a sharp scent of his being. In the dark church, I felt his eyes upon me, but I did not dare look round.

While Vinnie and Sonya instructed, I moved in the shadow along the wall towards the great doors which guarded the sanctuary. I had a large impulse to take refuge in the church. I could feel my toes curl in my shoes as if they clutched to hallowed ground. God, what am I going to do? I asked. What? There was such urgency in me that I would not have been surprised at manna if it had fallen as a sign. I cast my eyes around the tiered iconostasis which bore paintings of prophets and angels. Storey after storey built the familiar history of foretelling and fulfilling: Moses and Elias, Gabriel, the Virgin, Nativity and Resurrection. It was as if the weight of my expectation to be rescued towered over me in picture after picture. As if each illumined some hope I was supposed to have in God's deliverance at a time when my mind veered acutely towards a despair that I would ever get through this trip with my sister without damaging myself. You are right, Mathilde, I thought, there is no forgiveness in me of Durrand. God, I thought, she is right that I cannot fulfil her needs. At another end of the church there was a very large Crucifixion painted on an almost life-sized scale. The painted witnesses gathered round the dead Christ stood in shadow and I could only make out the large details of the sombre construction. Sonya had stopped talking and the tourists milled around, looking perfunctorily at the icons, which were, I suppose, of no artistic merit. At length, they meandered out into the rain to see the tombs of the noble exiles who had tried to free Russia from the tyranny of Czar Nicholas I. I stood there in the church alone, starkly pleading. There were no words I could think of to say.

Two middle-aged Russian women were selling candles and little, cheap copies of icons at a counter near the church door. They signalled to me and smiled, said some word I could not understand. I gestured largely at the Crucifixion in order, somehow, to express some common bond with them. I wondered how brave it was of them to be there at all. I made towards them with an idea in mind to buy some little article – the picture of a saint, perhaps, thinking that it might sustain both them and me if I did this, but a stronger instinct possessed me and I decided not to. It was as though I had understood that I had to go on darkly now without vision or image to distract me.

At the church door, John waited. 'You know what they were saying?' he asked.

I shook my head.

'"Molodyetz." It means "Well done", "good lad" or some such thing. They liked it that you prayed in their church.'

That evening, Mathilde seemed to have shrugged off her mood. We had dinner with John and a woman from Malibu called Alice Trumpington. She had written a book on the folk tales of Siberia, and she streamed on brightly about them all evening. She was about sixty and wore her grey hair cropped; her bulky form was swathed in Indian cotton. It was impossible not to be infected by her friend-liness, and everyone relaxed as she spoke. She was a keen amateur photographer and voyager. She showed us pictures of her house, of her daughter, and of her daughter's children. And so, the evening played itself out mildly, and we all retired to bed early; I was glad of a space of calm.

I pretended to sleep while Mathilde sat for a long time at the mirror, brushing and brushing her long, gold hair.

# Chapter Fourteen

The next morning, Vinnie and Sonya herded us all onto a coach, and we set off for Lake Baikal where we were to spend a night by the water's edge at another Intourist hotel. There were about twenty-five of us in all, but Mathilde and I sat apart from the group. John sat alone at the back of the bus. I thought, He only picks up human curios. I'm just part of the way to the Temple of Heaven – an oddity. Amongst the others, little friendships and antagonisms had already been formed before we had joined the party. There was a quiet buzz of conversation, and Mathilde and I were left to ourselves. The day was fine and bright. My sister had spent breakfast talking about the weather. She liked, she said, the clarity of light through the pure Siberian air. Once we were on our way, however, she continued her story about Durrand. I had anticipated this and had braced myself to receive it.

'The letters and phone calls began soon after my trip to Paris,' said Mathilde.

The coach took a narrow road which plied through a wilderness of birch and pine. Birch and aspen leaves shook and quivered in the morning light.

'At first,' she said, 'I thought it was one of those lunatics. The phone would ring, and the echo in the receiver made me aware that the call was from abroad. There would be a breath, or the sense that a breath was held. I would say "Hello", then there would be a click. Then I realized it must be Durrand.

'In the meantime, I received a large number of pamphlets from the priest I had met in Paris – pamphlets and a glossy brochure advertising a house for women run by the Companionate. It's hard to convey their tone. It was as if the path to salvation consisted entirely through the exercise of will, and most particularly in the conformity of the will to Victor's own theories of piety. This involved an odd combination of worldly aims with other-worldly attitudes. Each individual member of the Companionate was enjoined to pursue a rigorous course of prayer, mortification and obedience to Victor's highly itemized rule of life. Of course, you are a believer. Still, even you, I think, would find it difficult to place your spiritual weight so heavily on one foot – your will, or rather, Victor's. The essence of the matter, as it appeared to me, was that God, if he exists, has no regard for individuality. Indeed, I got the feeling as I read on and on through these leaflets, that the Procrustean bed of the Companionate's insistence on conformity was the model for Christ's cross, and not the other way around. I mean to say that one could almost see the instrument of torment, the cold legality, the ruthless logic of pain as having a supreme importance to them, quite to the exclusion of any real thought for the nature of the victim and the meaning of the sacrifice. It was almost as if the Romans had been *correct* in stretching Christ out and nailing him down to a gruesome death, instead of being inevitably bound to commit an obscenity against God.'

'If you can talk like that about it all, Mathilde, why can't you yourself believe? I do and I *agree* with you!'

'If it were only that simple,' she said. For a moment, she was calm and thoughtful. 'The point is that *Durrand* believed it – believed what the Companionate stood for, and for nearly twenty years had cut off first a finger, then a toe, then an arm and then a leg to fit into this mould. After the spate of phone calls, made, I know, anonymously because he wasn't supposed to make them at all, there came a whole series of letters from Durrand. He was never a stylist at the best of times, but his letters had a jerky, robotic quality.

He seemed set on convincing me of the sacred truths embodied in Victor's pamphlets. Oh, he dripped with sanctimony!'

'He always did, Mathilde.'

'Ah, but this was different. These were not Durrand's own brand of pietistical mouthings. If they had been, I would have known how to deal with them. No, Durrand was far too gloomy and morbid to concoct these self-righteous outpourings. Every phrase jounced with clockwork optimism. He was like a Job's comforter in a tracksuit, urging me up from my fallen state, braying all the while about his own spiritual fitness, health, happiness. It was the greatest lie.'

*My sister, my own, my beloved, my dove. Your hand was on the latch and you opened unto me.* Durrand's voice surged through my brain, an acid bath of sarcasm.

Oh please God, please, please, please, I cried inwardly. Please stop him.

'Are there wolves in this forest?' someone asked Sonya.

Sonya said the wolf problem was getting under control. I made myself concentrate on the image of wolves padding through the undergrowth. I hummed the tune of 'Peter and the Wolf' inside my head. I tried to remember every detail of a school trip I had led to Portland to hear a performance of *Peter and the Wolf*. I made percussion noises to myself in order to drown out Durrand like a radio. Everyone in the bus looked out of the windows hoping for the sight of a wolf.

Mathilde seemed oblivious to this exchange and my discomfort. I was sure she could see me sweating with the effort not to hear the voice. She was oblivious too to the almost agonizing bursts of beauty, which thrust themselves through the forest in the shape of leaf or flower, in blurring bush and thicket.

'Durrand's religion narrowed him enough as it was,' she continued. 'He always imposed his own will on life, and never let it arrive with its own little theophanies; but, with Victor's even narrower convictions, with the power of

Victor's total belief weighing on him, Durrand had become almost a parody.'

I closed my eyes against the bursting wall of my consciousness, which groaned under the pressure of Durrand.

'The irony of it is,' she said, 'that the slavish emotion the Companionate induced in Durrand caused his downfall.'

*She . . .* Mathilde lit a cigarette *. . . did it all, not they.*

'Do you *mind*?' A haughty English voice sailed out from the seat behind us. The man's name was Hugh and he was travelling with a young man called Anthony. Without a backward glance, Mathilde crushed out her cigarette. Somehow, the piercing tenor of Hugh's voice dislodged the pressing inner resonance of Durrand. Like someone struggling in water, I gasped a mental breath. Mathilde went on.

'Durrand adored Victor. I'm convinced that he really did. It was as if Victor pulled Durrand's capacity to feel into life then had it slaughtered.' She paused, thoughtful for a moment, then resumed.

'Shortly before Christmas, Durrand turned up again in London. Although he gave me no warning that he was coming, he at least had the decency to knock this time. Something told me it was Durrand. I knew that it was Durrand at the door.

'I remember it was a very cold night, but Durrand wasn't wearing an overcoat. He didn't appear to feel the weather. I seem to recall that he was wearing dancing pumps – but he couldn't have been, could he? His shoes gleamed like beetles on the dark hall floor.'

The fir trees bristled by the Siberian road. A hare leapt in front of the wheels of the bus, then escaped into the thicket beyond. I had an impulse to say, and sharply, 'Why did you let him in?', and I would have had I not glimpsed Durrand at the door of my own heart. I have always had an animal instinct for flight – flight, or that paralysed stillness which is given to small creatures in peril from predators. Either Mathilde possessed no such instinct or she had needed Durrand too much then to heed it. I could feel how Durrand had torn her from the silken framework of her rooms, pulling her to the front door. I could feel the draught of her opening it, could sense how it sucked her hands over the threshold so that they flew like leaves to caress his expectant face. I could feel the terrible emotions he had called from her. As she spoke his name, they would have resounded harshly in her voice. *Durrand!*

'I let him in,' she continued. 'His face was pale and without expression. His eyes had that blank yet arrogant look which usually preceded a bout of sermonizing in him. As I let him in, I remembered his letters and braced myself for it: for Sunday Mass and Friday Fast, and where has Latin gone? For Benediction, birth control, and what have they done to Our Lady? For Fatima and Communism; for the beauty of womanhood fulfilled in much motherhood; for confession every Saturday, the discipline and Lourdes. I waited to be held personally responsible for the decline of Western Christianity.

'Instead, he told me he was starving. For a moment, I could not understand him. He stood in the hallway and blinked. "I'm starving," he said again. "I'm hungry. Don't you understand? I want a meal."

'The hour was late,' said Mathilde, glancing at me with some remembered indignation on her eyes. 'You know I am no cook, Reenie. I suggested we go to a restaurant, but Durrand would not have it. For some reason, he looked as if he were about to cry. Durrand never cared about food much, but he kept going on about chicken, how he wanted fried chicken, grits and cornbread. There was such intensity in this odd request that it frightened me.'

Mathilde opened her eyes wide as if to signify the fear she had felt. I doubted that she had been afraid. As children, Mathilde and Durrand had shared cravings for food as though they had one belly. Later on, when he became obsessed with practices of self-denial, she found it hard to eat and lost a lot of weight until she finally decided to taunt him by savouring their favourite foods in front of him. She would lick the spoon from a dish of pecan ice cream. 'Mmm . . .' she would say in his ear at the table as he pushed his plate away.

The bus jolted along the highway. Mathilde started to tell me a long story of how she had found a supermarket open, one which sold American food, how she had prepared a meal for Durrand . . . all this late at night.

'I stood,' she said, 'at the stove and he sat at the kitchen table, watching hungrily as I tossed the chicken in flour, as I immersed it in boiling oil. He watched me intently as I washed greens and shook them out and put them in the pot. It was so cold, that night, so cold. It was even too cold to snow. I remember. Icy gusts rattled the windows and you could feel the draught everywhere.

'Believe it or not, I had found corn-meal. I had no recipe books. I just remembered Lettie's hands, and followed and copied my memory. Durrand sat transfixed as I broke the egg into the meal. It was as if he were being baptized in the yolk. I could tell as I mixed it, his eyes were drowned in the yellow, in the glutinous white. I stirred and stirred rhythmically and he shut his eyes, listening to the grit of the meal against the bowl as the egg and water bound it and stuck it together. He watched as I put the pan in the oven – alert, not gluttonous.

'When dinner was finally ready, Durrand sat at the table. He started to eat. He stabilized his buttocks on the chair, put his legs apart and planted his feet firmly. He placed his forearm on the kitchen table and ate like a workman. When he was finished, he patted his mouth dry and asked me where the pecan pie was, but I had forgotten to buy this. It was freezing, freezing cold, and I refused to go out again. He shook his head in sorrow. "The meal," he said, "is incomplete."'

At this point, Mathilde became silent and seemed disconnected, even from her own narrative. It was apparent to me that Durrand's words about the dinner engrossed her: she had omitted something. In their different ways, both Mathilde and Durrand were perfectionists.

'But he had brought a bottle of Bourbon,' she said

suddenly. 'We drank that. I think that finished things off, don't you?' She did not wait for my reply, but looked comforted. 'It was only after the meal that I began to weigh and measure things in my mind and to question why he had suddenly arrived out of the blue like that. We took the whiskey into the living room, and that's when I started to laugh. I laughed and I laughed, and I said, "OK, Durrand, the game's up," because it occurred to me that all along he had been conning me. Chicken, grits and Bourbon. What sort of ass did he think I was?' Mathilde's eyes glittered with some inner triumph.

I really could not understand what she was talking about. I shook my head in real bewilderment.

'Don't you see?' she said scornfully. 'No, I suppose you don't. I omitted to mention that it was Friday. I didn't realize it was Friday until we were sitting down on the sofa. Did you ever know Durrand to eat meat on a Friday? He never, ever did – never at any point. No, Durrand would never have broken the fast without a purpose.'

'We don't have to fast on Friday anymore, Matty,' I said.

'*Durrand* did. So I asked myself what he was trying to achieve, and I reckoned he would have broken his rules only if the goal he had in mind justified these means. Durrand wanted something from me and what better way to get it than to demand from me something that would bring up our past? The past where we had the privilege of knowing each other utterly. Just thinking about this put me into a terrible fury and I started to yell and scream, "Come on, Durrand – own up, Come on!" And I kept on at him until he cracked.

'He said, "Mathilde, I'm in trouble."'

'And I replied, "I knew, I knew, I knew it."''

I saw the sign of water before us. The bus, having reached a graded curve in the road, came upon the shores of Lake Baikal. Sonya tapped the microphone. With barely concealed pride, she proclaimed the wonder of the lake. At the sound of her voice, Mathilde sank back into her seat. 'I knew it,' she said again softly, and she squeezed her eyes shut as if she had suddenly hit upon some immeasurable vision of the situation she had been describing, something even beyond her powers of speech.

'This is the deepest lake on earth,' said Sonya, 'the deepest.'

'Look at it, Mathilde. Look at it,' I said, but she was not to be distracted from her thoughts, and she shrugged away from the sound of my voice. The water, reflected in the sky, was the colour of liquid sapphires, half-molten, crammed together, flashing in the sun as they coagulated and melted. I could not take my eyes off it.

The bus drew up to the roadside next to a small village which bordered the water. A crowd of children stood and watched as we made our way out into the sunshine. Beyond them, lay a small area of common land where cows grazed or slept, and this was bordered by a little hamlet, consisting of irregularly placed wooden houses, decorated with fretwork gables. The settlement seemed set in the bosom of the earth and water like an amulet. Forests swathed the hills around it in apparently endless abundance.

Alice Trumpington trundled towards the children with a little yelp. She waved her loaded camera, talking as she went for all the world like a distressed grandmother at long last reunited with her family. Although she spoke only English, the children flocked around her as if she were some fabled personage from a book, and she started snapping their pictures and dispensing trifles amongst them.

The rest of us wandered about the grass, stretching our legs. Someone touched me on the shoulder. It was Dr Hartmann. 'She's just like one of those women who used to go down the Nile beating off crocodiles with an umbrella,' he said, indicating Alice. He bowed slightly, smiled briefly at Mathilde and me, then, as abruptly as he had joined us, he walked away, as if not wanting to presume or intrude. Mathilde looked as if he had woken her up, and she started wandering after him without much purpose or enthusiasm.

I drifted from the group towards the water's edge where I stood, contemplating its majesty and breathing in the pure air. Every time I thought about the sound of Durrand's voice in my head – the voice I had heard on the bus – I felt a quiver of fear. There was nothing blurred or indistinct about it. I perceived the voice as having had resonance, as having had tricks and ways about syllables. I decided that to think about it was to invite it again.

I looked round. John was standing next to me. Against the sky and water, he gave the impression of having arrived out of the blue. 'How are you today?' he asked. He looked out over the lake. I said I was all right, but as together we gazed at the natural wonder before us, I realized I was not. He turned, swiftly raised an eyebrow, then turned his glance once more towards the water. A sense of his presence kindled within me.

'It's a beautiful lake,' he said.

I was covered with confusion, for I felt an emotional warmth spring up between us, and I did not look at him in case it was not true, but then I did and I was not sure when he smiled at me quite what it meant, but I turned over inside and looked back at the water studiedly. For one idiotic moment, I opened my mouth, ready to tell him anything but what was conventional to tell a stranger. I wanted to tell him about Durrand, coiled and squeezed round my mind. But I shut my mouth. All the same, I trusted him. I could not get rid of the impression that he searched my thoughts. Simply standing there with him collected and connected the wires of my brain, and I felt an odd tranquillity. I *am* going mad, I thought, and I was humiliated that I had imagined the first stirrings of love between this man and myself.

Mathilde arrived and stood with us, then Alma joined us. For a moment, I felt unified with him against them, but shook off the absurdity of this. Alma gestured with light hands. 'Isn't this the most magical place?' she said. I noticed how Alma's face was almost characterless in repose. In response to something, it was like water. Expression lit it, rippled over her features so that they took on what one wanted to see in them. She smiled at John and me with something like delight.

At a small museum, further along the shore of the lake, a nervous young Russian woman with a sensitive face lectured us on the ecology of the lake. She catalogued the species of fauna and discussed plankton with much seriousness. She emphasized the purity of the water by telling us that she, in winter, had walked across the ice in terror she would drown; for although it was thick enough to hold a locomotive, the ice had been so pure that it had appeared to her that she was walking on water.

Dr Hartmann became animated. Indeed, he sprang to life, presented with so many exhibits in the little museum of stuffed birds and fish. With large gestures, he plied the poor young woman with questions she could not entirely answer. Seeing that she was embarrassed, he stopped and feigned a kind of ignorance himself about the habits of the *omul* and *golumyanka*. Silently, he inspected the cases, touching them with reverence, as if he regarded the taxidermy with peculiar awe. It was as if he made himself alone, hedged himself about with a sacred privacy which consisted of a wall of facts about the lake so that he thrilled to each new statistic.

'I feel nothing. I feel nothing. I am numb,' my sister said. We ate wild strawberries sold in cones of newspaper by old women in kerchiefs. The women had no teeth, the strawberries needed no sugar. The Russians and the tourists alike enjoyed them, and all stood about, eating them beside the water's edge.

'You are eating strawberries, though. You can taste them. You're alive,' I said.

After we had checked into the little hotel which was our destination, my sister and I walked down to the shore from the hill where the hotel stood overlooking the water.

Earlier, Sonya had taken us to this spot where the River Angara had its origin. She told us that it was the only one of the lake's rivers to flow away from it. At its source there was a large, protruding rock which Sonya called 'the Shaman Stone'. From ancient times, she said, the indigenous tribes had told how Father Baikal, the god of the lake, had heaved the stone at his daughter Angara as she rushed off, trying to escape him. The stone was supposed to have magical properties.

Mathilde and I stood and looked at the water. Her eyes were as blank as pebbles. She seemed wholly walled up in herself.

'And Durrand *was* in trouble,' she said, as if there had been no break at all in our previous conversation. 'I asked him what kind of trouble he was in, but he would not say. He just sat there on the sofa, staring into his drink, and even when I began to taunt him, he was silent.'

'Taunt him,' I said. She and he would wound each other. Standing before the lake, I had an impulse to put my hands over my ears as I had done in childhood when the mocking started. 'No,' I said. 'Mathilde. No.' I kept my hands by my side, however.

'Oh, but you must hear,' she said. 'I asked him if he had a woman. Durrand. A woman? Don't you think that's funny?'

'No,' I said.

'I bet you can't see Durrand with a woman,' she said, ignoring me. 'Boys – now that's something different. Could you imagine Durrand with a boy? I could. Now, that I could imagine. So I asked him if it was boys.'

'Mathilde, stop,' I said. But there was no stopping her. Her mouth had a kind of V-shape, as if she sensually enjoyed the memory of what she had said to Durrand. She shouted into the pure air and held up her arms exultantly. 'Boys, women, drink, drugs, horses – I catalogued them all. All.' She dropped her voice. 'So, he gave up, and he told me that he was in desperate need of money. Oh, yes. He needed money, and lots of it.' For a moment, I thought Mathilde was going to break into a little dance. There was an antic feeling about her, as if she were swept away into some private and savage thought. 'And I had all the money in the world,' she said.

In my mind's eye, I could see Durrand and Mathilde sitting together in her room in London, she beside herself with the power she had gained over him – or thought she had. But it would have been Durrand who had the upper hand. He liked nothing better than to entice Mathilde out of herself until she became sightless and berserk. He took an almost voluptuary pleasure then in having pure control over her.

I looked into the broad torrent which flowed from the lake. There was a little breeze and the water was flecked with white. It seemed wonderful that the river had escaped the confines of Baikal. I wished that I could have flown Mathilde, but her eyes were on me and I felt compelled to listen to her.

'So I asked him,' she continued, 'why he needed money, how he could possibly want money when he had taken holy orders, especially when his chosen hermitage looked like Claridges. "What could you need money for in a place like that?" I asked him, "where all your needs are supplied? Why, your habit is a silk shirt. I should think your cell is covered with Oriental rugs." He said nothing, but his eyes gleamed with contempt for me. He did not have to tell me that he thought anyone as unspiritual as I was could never understand the absolute righteousness of the Companionate.

'So I tried another tack. I said, "I know, Durrand. You want money from me so that you can give it to the poor. That's it, isn't it?" And, of course, Irene, you will remember what compassion he had for others. Now I think about it, in our nice, pious family you were the only one who ever gave anything away or felt sorry for anyone else.' She angled me a look, and I backed away, feeling uncomfortable. 'Oh, yes, *you* are a Christian, aren't you, pet? Take the whole thing seriously, go to Mass, things like that.'

'You told me only yesterday what a failure I was in that respect,' I said.

'Did I? How strange. I don't remember saying that.'

I let it pass, partly because it worried me to see that Mathilde had genuinely forgotten what she had said to me outside the church in Irkutsk.

'Can you imagine Durrand giving money to some needy person?' she continued sarcastically. 'Unmarried mothers, for instance. Can you imagine that? Oh, he loved a sinner like Christ from the Cross. He was always guided by love, wasn't he? And in its light he was drawn to the alleviation of pain and disorder everywhere. I said to him, "Oh, Durrand, you feel the tragedy of fallen man so keenly that I can't believe you want my money for any other purpose than to pick him up."

'Well, just as I thought he would never tell me, never give away his secret, he suddenly turned to me, looking as if he was about to be sick, and said, "Mathilde, I took fifty-thousand dollars from the bank."

'Can you believe it? I said, "You're kidding." He said nothing. I said, "Durrand, how on earth did you manage to do that? How could you possibly steal all that money?"

'He shook his head from side to side as if he himself did not really know, then he said, "I fiddled the books." A kind of smile spread over his face. He had, I think, a kind of involuntary pride in his ingenuity.

'I kept on asking him why he did it. I was awed. I said, "Why didn't you ask me for the money?" And I told him what I had suspected: that he had broken into my flat and tried to steal one of my icons and that I had seen his motive because he could not hide anything from me – not really. His eyes slid around. I said, "All you had to do was to ask me."

'He told me I wouldn't have understood, but of course I would have, because I thought then that his only motive for taking this large sum must have been so that he could escape from the Companionate. I told him I'd do anything to get him out of that place. I'd bankrupt myself.

'And this was the awful thing, Irene. This was the most dreadful thing of all. He looked at me with an anguish I will never forget. I did not know that Durrand could feel so . . . He clutched at himself as though he were burning, and said, "Mathilde, don't you see? The Companionate is my whole life. I didn't take the money to get away. I took it to give it to Victor . . . so that he would love me again. After Argentina no one would trust me. Victor wouldn't even speak to me. Victor. I would have done anything."

'That's what he said. It came out so tortured and hot that I could not speak at all for quite some time. Neither did Durrand. He sat there as if he were in a state of shock at having revealed to me his agonizing love. I realized that Durrand was in considerable danger.

'When I had sufficiently recovered I asked him if Victor was an accomplice in all this. But Durrand dashed even that faint hope. He said he had told Victor that the money came from a rich person who was interested in the Companionate and who might even join because of Durrand's influence. "That was the whole point," he said. "The whole point was to get him to believe that I could do that sort of thing, that I wasn't finished."

'And then, of course, I knew,' Mathilde said. 'The whole thing became very clear. I said, "You told him it was me, Durrand, didn't you? You told him it was me – that I was interested in your bloody cult, didn't you?" His shoulders collapsed and he put his head in his hands. He said, "Matty, the bank is beginning to suspect. They are going to hold an audit. I will be put in prison." But it wasn't prison that frightened him,' Mathilde said, looking at me. 'It was the idea of losing Victor forever.

'What could I do? After quite an inquisition, I got him to admit that he had used my name with Victor, but that could not be taken back – not then. I had no choice at all. Besides, if I was ever going to get him away from Victor, the money was all the leverage I had.'

I did not ask Mathilde why she felt she had to get Durrand away from Victor, because she would not have understood the question. Her eyes were quite passionate. 'Mathilde,' I said, trying to alter the course of her thoughts. 'How on earth could you trust Durrand with such a large sum?'

'Ah, clever girl,' she said. She bent and picked up a stone from the shore, looked at it briefly, then threw it in. 'I couldn't and I didn't. I told him that not one penny of my money was to go to Victor, and to ensure this, we would open a joint account at his bank so that I could oversee absolutely the process of his fiddling the money back. It took all night to work it out.' Mathilde's face suddenly chilled. 'But this – this very prudent measure was to prove our undoing, Durrand's and mine, Durrand's and mine.' She looked at me. 'You don't understand any of this, do you?' she said, and for some unknown reason, she abruptly left me and walked along the lakeshore. I watched her retreating figure until it vanished.

*Matty, Matty, Mathilde!* The voice of Durrand wailed. *Matty, Oh, Mathilde!*

# Chapter Fifteen

I stood for another moment looking at the water. The sound of Durrand's voice faded, and in its place came a profound wrenching, as if my spirit were being pulled, sucked by an oceanic, invisible undertow, which I could barely resist. *Mathilde! Mathilde!* I turned from the water's edge and fled up the hill towards the hotel, and, gaining our room, threw myself on the bed and lay there shaking with nervous exhaustion. At length, I fell asleep, and I must have stayed in this dark and dreamless state for quite a while, for, when I awoke, it was early evening, and I did not know where I was until I went to the window, which looked out over the lake. The majesty of water seemed spread beneath me and above me: I sensed myself as existing in the vanishing point where the horizon of sky and lake met. I felt hung there between the two – and alone.

From the garden below the window came the sound of

casual conversation. I looked down and saw Mathilde. She had changed for dinner, and was standing in the grounds of the hotel talking with Dr Hartmann. She wore a lavender shawl against the chill of the evening. Suddenly, a large bird broke the skin of the water and retrieved a fish from below the surface of the lake.

*There is no burial for me. Irene, I must wander.*

On the verge of screaming, I clapped my hands over my mouth in case Mathilde could hear me.

*My ashes are scattered to the wind, and you must tell her, tell her. No place for me.*

But I was huddled underneath the window while the dark walls of the dusky Russian room bulged and swayed and the floor sagged as I clutched at the thought of Christ walking on the water, through the storm on Galilee, and then there was the void. And then I heard a knock, and then again, and again – a knock and then a bang, and I sensed myself opening in the night of myself, either the lattice of myself or the door, but I do not know exactly what happened as a shadow was beside me and a hand grasped me, and then I saw John, and it was as if I were not drowning any longer. I fixed my eyes on him so that through the ruinous moment he led me out and up from the cavern as if he had found the mouth of it, and I was terrified that he would speak before I stood conscious and safe before him, delivered.

But he did not speak, not for the longest moment. We sat together in the dark room for a long time.

Why shouldn't this be a vision too? I thought, my stupid fantasy. The floor of my mind, however, gently reassembled itself and became firm.

'I brought you some food,' he said, at last.

'What is happening?' I asked him.

'Everyone has eaten and there is a lecture going on now.'

'Where is Mathilde?'

His face looked angry. 'Oh, she felt she had to attend the lecture. Alice Trumpington is giving a talk on Siberia. I'll admit I was quite surprised when Mathilde didn't seem to know where you were. But now I have found you, so it is all right.' He turned on the light and set a plate of fish in front of me. 'This is a very rare fish,' he said. 'It comes from the waters of the lake and is only found here. Eat it.'

But I could not eat.

'Are you thirsty?'

I shook my head.

'Does fresh air help?'

I nodded because I suddenly longed for fresh air.

'Come down to the lake with me. We'll walk. Then you'll feel better.'

There was a full moon and it had risen over the water. I did not know where to put myself. One foot followed another in irregular steps. John and I walked into the pure, silver light, which cut blue shadows – sharp – of aspen and of birch. We went down the hill towards the water, caught together in the throes of wilderness and moon. A young couple with a small child rose from a bend in the road and passed us on the other side; their slanted faces, tranquil, revealed no emotion. We walked down to the spot I had fled earlier. My eye fixed on the stone which marked the juncture of the lake and the River Angara. Silver runnels of water flowed past it, flashing as the lake disgorged into the stream.

John said, 'I have been wanting to speak with you alone since we were in Moscow.'

I heard him but could not believe he had really spoken. I thought I would rather drown myself in the lake than believe he had said such a thing when he had not. I felt ashamed and put out my hand as if to touch him for balance.

'There is the look of you and the thought of you,' he said. I thought, If I speak, I will only make a fool of myself. I turned and looked at his face, enamelled by the moon. There was the sound of a heavy, running animal in the wood above the road.

There was a short path to the shore of the lake. John indicated a declivity where we could descend to the water's edge. I felt disoriented, disjointed from time. I began to wonder if I had fallen through the slats in my mind and died. I sensed him as belonging to another reality, as if he were a guide to the dock of old Charon, or an angel bearing some happiness incommensurate with my just deserts.

There were some bushes by the lake that looked like large thorns. They stood out in sharp definition against the moonlight until I realized that the moonlight was not upon them at all so that I had seen them like a flashed negative. I became frightened of this circle of bramble. John, however, gave me his hand, and we passed the bushes. With confidence, I descended further with him to the dark and shallow bank of the lake. We reached some low rocks and sat down on them. The lake lay black before us except for the limpid streak of moon. A great loveliness and freshness in the air caught my lungs and filled me with wonder. I felt as if I partook of this place and the inhuman, cold moon, and the fishes, which trawled out in the deep beyond our fathoming. A nightbird screamed and pierced my recollection with fear: something jumped from the water, but then all again was still. John sat somewhat apart from me, contemplating the water.

'Why were you crying?' he asked me.

'When was I crying?'

'Don't you know? You were crying when I found you. I found you crying.'

As I looked at him, he took my hand and folded it into his own. It seemed to me that I must have died and gone beyond the reach of suffering forever. It seemed pointless ever to have wept, or, rather, it seemed that all weeping had been nothing if it had found this end. I perceived him as having all particulars of beauty, so that nail and eyelash, neck and smile, were illumined.

When I opened my mouth to speak to him, at last convinced that I could trust him with what was on my mind, the grating roar of Durrand filled my head to bursting:

*Tell him and you'll be sorry! It's for Mathilde. It's for Mathilde. You've got to tell Mathilde.*

'Oh my God,' I cried aloud, because I was truly terrified.

The voice came again, this time with a more insidious tone of threat, and so like Durrand that it was nearly impossible to believe he was not actually there. *Tell him, and he'll get you locked up. Tell her. It's for Mathilde.*

Across the water, I heard the approach of Durrand: the sound of oarlocks grating and the splash of water from the dark lake. Beyond John's shoulder, I saw the brief shadow of a figure standing in a boat, arms crossed over its chest, and then it disappeared: as if he had found entry to my skull, the pitch of Durrand crammed it. With all the strength I had I shouted, 'Help!' and I felt John's arms around me as I struggled and thrashed against the voice, which surrounded me with piercing filaments of sound so that I felt caught, as in the net of a gladiator. No longer did Durrand use cords of words to bind me. Like a monstrous fisherman, he seemed to have emerged from the dark water only to find another sort of depth in my mind where he trawled in deadly earnest for my sanity. I felt pulled mightily to the odious edge of wilderness within me, and as I stood on the cusp of madness, I saw in the barren moon an evil tranquillity of light.

From a distance at first, I heard John's voice calling my name and then I felt his hands on my face, then his arms around my struggle, holding me human against the inhuman sound of Durrand. Then all at once, the voice was gone, and I stayed huddled against John's chest for a long time until his healing, bodily warmth worked its way from my numbed limbs into my heart and mind.

'What is it?' he asked. 'What is it?'

I was shaking with the determination to tell him what had happened even if I risked losing him. If I were insane, I decided, I should be locked up anyway. If I were not and the voice had been real, it seemed the better course of action to disobey it in every particular.

'I think I hear Durrand,' I said. 'I think I am mad.'

'Durrand? Is this your brother you were talking about?'

'Durrand,' I said. 'It's . . .' and the effort to tell John about Durrand cost me much. It was like dragging myself from death. I had to do it quickly before the voice came back. 'You will never speak to me again when I tell you. I hear voices. I hear the voice of my dead brother Durrand. I *hear* him.'

He was silent for a moment and I was stunned with the feat of telling; yet, bit by bit, I saw the lake and the moon returning to their proper proportions. I breathed deeply, then quietly. 'It's not just epilepsy. I told you about that. I should have told you about Durrand too, from the very outset. I'm sorry. I'm very sorry. It has been unfair of me, not to tell you.' What I could not understand, even as I was saying this, was how I remembered with such clarity everything that had happened since John had come into my room. I stared hard at the water, not feeling I could face his pity or contempt.

'What does he say?' he asked. There was such simplicity in his tone that I turned and searched his face. His head was on one side, as if he were listening to some difficult piece of music and trying to catch the tune.

'What does he say? You mean the voice? Oh, it's very convincing. It sounds just like him. He, or it, seems to be trying to persuade me to tell Mathilde what I hear. He or it told me I must not tell you or you would have me locked up.'

John reached out and tucked a loose strand of hair behind my ear. 'You're so frightened . . .'

'I am. I am . . . wouldn't you be?'

'. . . of yourself. Do you really think you are mad, or not?'

'I even thought I saw Durrand for a moment. There on the lake.'

'I don't know whether you are mad,' he said. 'You don't strike me as being mad. You seem pretty lucid to me, in fact.'

I started to shiver. 'Durrand used to say I was possessed by the devil,' I said.

'Possessed by the devil. I see.'

'Yes. Because I had epilepsy. But this is all different. I used to see and hear things in a different way when I had . . . but maybe these are . . . maybe these are only fits.'

'I don't know about devils,' he said, 'or epilepsy, or madness. I know I am very drawn to you. I don't usually find myself attracted to mad women, but I suppose there is always a first time.'

I looked out over the placid water. His voice was so calm and even. 'I'm attracted to you, too,' I said and was surprised at myself.

'Good,' he said.

'Look,' I said, gaining boldness by the moment. 'Why is it – how – do you believe – don't act as if?' My words flopped and floundered over each other. 'Do you believe in ghosts?'

'I don't know,' he said. 'Do you?'

'I'm not sure,' I said, 'but I don't think it is rational. I have always tried to be very rational because of the confusion caused by the disease.'

'Maybe you should become less rational,' he said. 'Maybe that's the whole problem and you are not taking everything into account. Lots of irrational things happen. I told you that is why I go on journeys. To escape the logic of maps.'

We were silent for a while. Then he said, 'Look. Would you mind telling me when you started to hear these things? Did you hear him before the trip, or on the airplane from London while you were sitting with me? When did you first hear him?'

With what detachment I could muster, I recited as briefly as I could the history I have related so far.

When I had finished, he sat and thought for a long time. 'So you didn't hear him until you saw Mathilde at the airport in Moscow?'

'Yes. It was when I saw her. I thought the journey had brought it on.'

'You did not hear him, however, after this convulsion you talked about – the one you had the night he died.'

'No. I did not.' A small breeze had got up and the water chunked and lapped against the lake shore.

He drew a breath, looked at me sharply, then spoke. 'Tell me. Do you know if your sister is engaged in any political activity?' I could not understand what that could have to do with Durrand's voice, but he looked so earnestly troubled that I felt bound to answer him.

'Mathilde has contempt for politics,' I said. 'Why do you ask?'

'She isn't involved with anything shady to do with the icon trade, is she?'

'She may be, but I wouldn't think it would be worth her while. What has this got to do with what I have been telling you?'

John turned to me, his face impassive, and we looked at each other for a long time. Finally, he said, 'Ever since we arrived in Moscow, I have been convinced, for no very good reason, that we were being followed.'

'But that's what Mathilde said. She talked about a man in a black coat. Did you see him?' I still could not quite understand what he was driving at.

'That's just it. I didn't see him – not exactly.'

'What do you mean?' I asked.

'In the Kremlin, at the ballet, on the airplane to Irkutsk – someone. When I look for him, he is gone. At first, I thought it was my imagination, and maybe it is. It is really a question of your believing me when I tell you that I am not given to fantasies of this kind. As I say, for a long time I thought I was being silly. I associated the whole business with Mathilde, however, and this is why I am telling you because I got it into my head that you were being menaced in some way because of something she had done. I hate to tell you this, but I sense her as being a rather cruel and arrogant person. I could somehow see her pinning evidence on you or getting you to do her dirty work. In fact, this fantasy became so vivid to me that I followed you out onto the landing at Novosibirsk airport, thinking you were going to meet somebody — do a deal with this shadowy man — compromise yourself in some way in order to protect Mathilde. I wondered if you were being tempted to do something against your nature. I wondered if you had agreed to meet him and give him something.'

'You don't think it's Durrand, do you?' I put my hand to my mouth as this cold thought seeped through me.

'I really don't know,' said John. 'I hesitated to tell you because I thought you might be frightened. But that is better than thinking yourself mad, isn't it? Unless, of course, we both are. And that is a possibility. Whatever it is — secret agent, ghost — I would stay out of its way.'

'But I can't. It won't let me alone.'

'Oh, yes it will if you refuse to do business with it,' he said emphatically.

'What do you mean?'

'Make no concessions to it. Make no bargains with it and don't believe a word it says. No conversations with it or with Mathilde about it. None. Don't let it panic you into thinking you are mad or wicked or whatever. It is evil and wants to do you harm whether it is part of yourself, as you suspect, or whether it has an existence of its own. Don't give it an inch.'

'You did see it, didn't you? How else would you know what to say? How else would you know what I must do?' I started to shiver in the breeze.

'Out of the corner of my eye — something malevolent, yes.'

'In Novosibirsk, I was going to run away from it. That was what I was thinking of doing.'

'Can you? Run away from it? Look,' he said, 'I don't want you to think I am crazy either. Maybe it is nothing. I don't know. All I do know is that my instinct for danger has often preserved me. When I was in Cyprus and in the Gulf of Aden, there were moments when my peripheral vision saved me. On my journeys too there have been odd times when I have kept my wallet, missed the cobra, caught the train. I've been tailed here in Russia before, you know, and they usually do it so crudely one can tell. This time I sensed something different about it, and that is why your story worries me. It alerts me in a certain way. It's the door ajar, the dark passage, the runaway truck. You sense it as I sensed the unseen, so-called agent.'

All at once, I rounded on him. 'Suppose it turns out to be a coincidence. You will think I am crazy after all. You won't . . . You can't . . .' but I could not finish what I wanted to say.

His face softened. 'Oh, yes I can,' he said. 'This time, I really think I can. If you can, that is. I'm very lonely, you know, and I'm coming to the end of these trips.' He paused. 'Are you sorry you came?' he asked. 'Do you want to go home?'

# Chapter Sixteen

But I am at home. I am. It is as if this inaccessible place has provided . . . Mathilde lay abandoned to sleep on the bed . . . not only him, I thought. I could not sleep. I threw the window open wide and sat by it in the dark. I fed upon the consolation of pure air, the recent memory of subtle touch, glance and parting whisper. Everything seemed subdued to that immense order beyond our imagining. Stars had come out thickly and it was almost possible to see by them. I could not get it out of my mind that I had witnessed something familiar to me. I had no previous memory of the lake, of John, no sense of having had an earlier life in which the events of the evening had occurred and were now recurring. Still, I was unable to shake off the idea that part of the experience described a territory half known to me, as in a dream. I thought about the bulging floor of the room, the vision by the water. As if I were being rocked gently, my mind became still, my heart silent, and my being attentive – and then I came upon it. I had been having seizures – that was clear; yet I realized that I knew where I had been and had not blacked out as before. It was like the flare of a match, which lights in a dark cellar and then becomes extinguished. I began to recognize – see the map of – where I had been, and rememberd it. It was as if I had been there before a hundred times and had not known it: a voyager, until this journey, ravished past consciousness by sirens into a pool of their devouring. At length, I lay down and slept and woke rested from a pure space of peace.

We set off from Baikal early in order to catch the train from Irkutsk, which was to take us across the Russian border to Mongolia. The station seethed with the turmoil of arrival and departure. Russians getting off the train from Moscow embraced their relatives; Russians leaving for Ulan Bator lugged their baggage. Boxes and bags and trunks were heaved on and off the train, and our little enclave, the party of foreign tourists of which we were a part, were shunted first into one carriage then into another, until finally we discovered where we were supposed to be. Vinnie stood with a clipboard trying to organize people into compartments, but, as the train jolted off towards Mongolia, the complexity of his task seemed to grow in geometric proportions, so that finally he was forced to allow a free-for-all. No one was happy with any arrangement, except a group of Italians in our party whom I had not yet met, and had only seen from a distance. They spoke no English, but Mathilde had conversed with them in French the previous night at Baikal and had discovered that they were members of a society dedicated to Marco Polo. They, at least, were no problem to anyone, and seemed to get along with each other very well. Vinnie looked gratefully after them. Everyone else seemed out of sorts as the heavy baggage was being heaved up and down the corridors. Mathilde sat thin-lipped and silent throughout our bus ride to Irkutsk, and, once on the train, had insisted that she and I be left alone together in a compartment. As John trundled his luggage past our open door, she quivered, her whole being dense with anger. He and I looked at each other in silence for a moment until he was joined by Abel Hartmann, with whom, it appeared, he had agreed to travel. It was all I could do to resist jumping up and following him with my eyes down the corridor, but I sat still. I wondered if he had seen his 'agent'. I began to wonder seriously if there was anything to that.

The train went haltingly along, and at last, it arrived back at the lake. Slowly down the track, we skirted the water's edge. Finally, I did go into the corridor as Mathilde seemed to wish to punish me with lasting silence. John was nowhere to be seen, but a lone American woman from our party was standing by the door to the latrine and she was crying. I later discovered her name was Muriel and that she was travelling with her German lover with whom she continually quarrelled. She was in floods of tears. 'It's so dirty! It's so dirty!' she said to me brokenly. 'See for yourself!' I was very perplexed by this, but she wailed on and on until Vinnie arrived. Muriel pressed her head on her arms and sobbed by the window. Outside, birch and brush flashed by. It was the toilet. She was upset by the toilet. She had gone in there and stepped in a puddle of urine, but she cried as if she had seen a battlefield or witnessed a hanging. She was so helpless. She stood and wrung her hands.

A Russian soldier, who with his family had been travelling from Moscow for something near a week, opened the door and looked quizzically out at the row.

Vinnie turned to us both. 'I can't seem to explain to everyone that this is the way it *is*! I put it in the brochure – it was there in black and white. What can we do here? The guard is dead drunk, the samovar isn't lit, the blankets are filthy, but we just go on. We have to go on. What do they expect?'

The Russian soldier spoke English. I wondered if he had been following us, but it seemed absurd to think so. He offered to light the samovar himself, and did. It stood at the end of the carriage. He went into the guard's compartment and brought out some glasses in silvered holders. 'There,' he said. 'Make her some tea!' Together he and Vinnie laughed a little; but Muriel cried and cried until her boyfriend came. His name was Wilhelm. Throughout the journey, you could hear her calling, 'Villie, Villie!' in this plaintive, clutching tone.

I returned to our compartment and told Mathilde what had happened. She smoked and mused, then unbent a little. 'What did they come out into the wilderness to see? A reed shaken by the wind?' she asked, her eyes drifting out over the lake.

I wondered if she had herself expected manna – or purity from all that vastness, as if trackless space alone could constitute immaculate Jordan. Indeed, she looked at the landscape as if she could consume something of its pristine state and turn its passive energy towards her. I became frightened for Mathilde. She got up, stood at the window as the train started and stopped, crawled round the lake down the long, single track to Mongolia. She looked from tree to tree, from water to sky with a fearsome impatience.

'I can't wait to get there!' she said. 'I can't wait to get to Ulan Bator!'

I remember how huge her longing seemed then. I remember in the light of what befell her there that the immensity of her yearning seemed to flow out into the taiga.

'Why, Mathilde?'

'I don't know,' she said. 'I really don't know.' She paused. 'It seemed as far as I could go – farther. "Outer Mongolia" – it has a certain ring to it. Genghis Khan, Prester John, Marco Polo . . . Do you think it's a civilized place? I hope not. I don't want to have anything to do anymore with all of that.'

I listened to Mathilde as objectively as I could, but I did not think she had made the journey without purpose.

*Mathilde and I really must have a chat.* The voice of

Durrand was conversational. I slowly did the eight times table to block him out. Eight-eights are sixty-four. *As you said, she expects purity without purification* – seventy-two – *She thinks she can shed her sins like a filthy garment under which her flesh is white as snow* – eighty, eighty-eight – *Agent, am I? The question is, Agent of what?* – ninety-six – *six, six? Do you know? You don't know, do you?*

Mathilde said, 'What is it? What is it?'

All at once, John knocked and entered our compartment. There he stood, and I had been on the razor's edge of telling Mathilde about the voice. I focused and fixed my attention on his face. 'One hundred and four,' I said. 'It must be a hundred and four degrees in this carriage.' In fact, it had become quite hot, even though the train was now gathering speed along a straight stretch of shore. 'It's the heat,' I said, 'it's making me feel faint.' John left the carriage and returned with a water bottle. Mathilde watched carefully. When I had recovered, I lay down on the seat so that I concealed my jumping heart and pulse.

'I came in to ask if you would have dinner with Abel and me tonight,' John said.

'Yes!' I said, before Mathilde could open her mouth. She shrugged, and looked out of the window until John had gone away.

'You made quite an evening of it last night,' she said. 'Didn't you? All romantic and moonlit, eh? Makes a change – a nice holiday romance.'

I said nothing. The sun beat against the grubby window of the train. Mathilde kept fiddling with the hair on her neck. *Miserere nobis.* I fixed my eyes on her hair.

Her features blurred, and all became indistinct save the lock of hair twisting and twisting around her fingers.

Her voice seemed to come from a distance. 'I was talking about Durrand,' she said.

'Mathilde, I don't want to talk about Durrand. Please, I don't feel well.'

'But you must hear it all. You must listen.'

I lay still on the seat. 'Not now,' I said, and wondered

why I had never before been able to say such a thing to Mathilde. I pretended to sleep. All the while, however, I sensed her watching me, considering. I passed the greater part of the morning rigid in silent fear that she would speak and thus propel me into the grip of Durrand. At last, I did sleep. Mathilde woke me on her return from lunch.

'Are you better?' she asked.

I lay with my eyes closed, but she began to talk.

'The pitiful thing about Durrand,' she said, 'was that he never realized that all along the Companionate knew exactly what he was doing. There he was, toiling away in Paris on the assumption that he had got away with a crime and covered his tracks, while all along they were having him watched. It was Durrand's fatal flaw to think that if he hid from his own motives and actions, other people could not see them either.

'Do you remember how Mother used to jump down my throat for lying? It always made me laugh. Durrand could tell two lies for every one of mine, but he could always get away with it because he had the knack of convincing himself they were true. You never lied, did you?'

'I have other faults,' I said. At the back of my mind, an awful fear woke and moved that some past sin gave the voice of Durrand access to me.

'And the Companionate's philosophy dovetailed beautifully with Durrand's natural propensity for falsehood. Their monomania is the Church and the restoration of its authority. They want to form it into an indestructible power on earth, no matter what it takes. They have a siege mentality, just as Durrand himself had. What's a lie or two here and there if the goal is just? Tell me, Irene, do you think that is right? Do you think it is right to seek power in the name of God? To take surreptitious control of land, capital, property in order to dominate the world for its own good?'

I sat by the window, my heels drawn up as the taiga slipped past us. I hugged my knees, almost as if against the

184

threat of Durrand's return, and spoke through the threads of my unease. 'No, I do not think it is right. Of course it isn't right. You know that yourself.'

'Are you quite sure?' she asked me.

'It misses the meaning of the Church. It makes the Church an adulteress to Christ if it lies or arrogates power to itself beyond the power that Christ has given it. What publican or leper would want to dominate the world? Christ himself was tempted to do it and rejected the temptation. Any lie at all is abhorrent to God.'

'Quite a sermon,' said my sister.

*You deceive her when you don't tell her about me,* said the voice of Durrand. *I exist. I exist all right.*

Mathilde went crashing on. 'Well, whatever the rights and wrongs of it, my life went on as usual – after, that is, I had arranged my gift to Durrand – until one cold February day when once again I saw him. I saw him, and this time, he was not alone.

'It seemed to be a chance meeting, but I do not think they left anything up to chance. Whether or not they were tracing my movements, I do not know. Of course, once Durrand had told them how rich I was and had compromised me by giving the embezzled money to Victor in my name, I had had a fair old flood of tracts and literature sent to me. What he had done had put me in a very awkward position, for how could I show further interest in them without getting enmeshed more deeply? That's on the one hand. On the other hand, suppose I wrote to them and told them I had no interest in the Companionate? Wouldn't that have put Durrand in the soup? It seemed the best course of action was silence, and this is the one I took; but, quite honestly, it unnerved me to get all this bumf through the mail. My soul, my soul. I think they were trying to save it.' She laughed uncomfortably.

'Did you want it saved, Mathilde?' I asked.

She cut in abruptly. 'I don't know about that. I don't think so. I suppose there is an atavistic part of me that feels it needs saving. To live with that continual pursuit had a kind of mesmerizing quality. Suppose, I thought, they were interested in me . . . but, no, I can't say I wanted them to save me. More than anything, I worried about Durrand. I don't know. I worried about Durrand a lot those days, particularly as I hadn't heard from him directly.

'That's what made it odd, coming across him as I did one Sunday afternoon in Kensington Gardens. I was wholly caught up in thoughts of him as I crossed the park on my way home from a lunch I'd had with some prospective buyers of a beautiful icon I'd acquired – of the "Descent to Limbo". In the light of what happened afterwards, I think the Companionate must have been watching my movements. At any rate, I'm sure Durrand was in London to provide a lure. As I came towards the Round Pond on my way back to Bayswater, there he was, crouched by the stagnant water, looking into it. At first, I thought it was an illusion, that it was someone who merely looked like Durrand, so greatly had he been pressing on my thoughts, but he stood up, and our eyes met. There we were, quite still, saying nothing for a long while. "Durrand!" I cried. He had been drawing on the water with a stick, maybe looking for something in it. He dropped it. "Matty!" he replied.

'I went quickly to him. "Durrand! Were you coming to see me?" But he only shook his head and indicated an approaching figure, a man of about thirty or so with slick hair. "I'm not alone," he said. His companion drew level with us almost at once, so it was impossible for me to ask him anything of how the money ruse had worked. I thought, however, that he looked a little better – more relaxed.

'The young man appeared to be friendly with Durrand. He had some impossible European name which I didn't quite catch. Georges something-or-other. He spoke excellent English with an accent that gave his words a rich purr, like the motor of an expensive car. He seemed very interested to meet me and looked at me intently. Of course, I was used to that – used to being stared at when I was with Durrand.' Mathilde looked dreamily out of the window. 'I sometimes wonder what difference it would have made if we had been identical twins – if he had been a girl or I had been a boy. I sometimes think things would have been better – no, more clear, easier. Other people with fraternal twins seem to be able to forget them, whereas identical twins always *know*, always seem to know everything about each other. It seems the most peculiar accident that we had half knowledge, half truth. Things were half concealed. It's not as if we were half of the same cake, half of the same apple. There was something so infuriating, teasing about our resembling each other so much that people gawped at us when it never really was a true equation. And you'd have thought, really, that in middle age when life had treated us so differently for so long that we would have, at least, eroded in different ways. But no. No.' She pointed to a grey streak in her hair. 'Even that, that little bit of white just above my right temple – even down to that – we were the same height and build, we had the same lines on our foreheads. We stood without words while the young man watched us, as if we were some wonder of the world.

'After a while, Durrand started to talk, slowly; he always did talk slowly didn't he? That's a difference. I talk quickly. He started to explain that he and Georges were in London on business with Victor himself, who had plans to set up an English chapter of the Companionate. I searched his face but could make no sense of his expression. It was a chilly day and a fine rain started to fall. Beads of water clung to Durrand's hair and eyebrows, illuminating his features so that they became enigmatic like the image of some fierce saint or angel. I could not make up my mind what had happened, whether my gift had resolved his problems or not. "It's getting cold and wet," I said to him and Georges. "Won't you come up and have some tea? I live across the park . . ." But they declined. Georges started to move, indicating that it was time to go, and Durrand's body, almost unconsciously, followed. His eyes, however, hung on me. "Will we meet?" I asked. "We'll see," said Durrand,

and they made their way towards Kensington Palace, vanishing at last from my sight as I stood and looked after them.

'During the week that followed, I found myself listening intently for the telephone, but nothing happened. If I heard a strange noise in the hall, I jumped out of my skin. I must have smoked up to sixty cigarettes a day. Where was he? What was he doing? I began to wonder if I'd really seen him in the park or if I'd only dreamed it. At long last, he rang. His voice had a muffled, embarrassed tone, apologetic. He said he'd been unable to reach me and so on, yet he was fidgeting, fidgeting. I could tell. Finally, he got to the reason for his call. Victor, he said, had taken an interest in meeting me. Would I come to dinner the following evening? Some of Georges's relatives were coming too. Victor had taken a house in Holland Park, and would I please remember that everyone dressed for dinner. He gave me the address and directions, and then hung up abruptly. All night long, I tossed and turned, unable to erase from my mind the curious tone in his voice – a tone that held a signal in it: but what signal? What significance had it? Was I to impress them? Defend him? Not give his game away? Or was the note I detected a kind of jealousy? Was he trying to push as far away from himself as he could the deed he had done which had necessitated my intervention?

'The following night at eight sharp I arrived at the front door of a house which I vaguely remembered. That's the odd thing about it. I had the distinct feeling when I rang the bell that I had visited someone there before – perhaps to do with a painting. It bothers me still that when I entered, the place seemed so familiar to me, yet I could not recall who had lived there or why I had been. A servant let me into a dark hall replete with sleek oak banisters which reached up heavy stairs to a great landing above. The hall light looked garish against the gloom because the bulbs in the chandelier weren't bright enough. The place gave the air of a strange kind of poverty – not the genteel kind we remember, nor real poverty that has to do with going without things and terrible struggle ... I can't explain. The house was cold, for instance. Dreary oils hung in the panelling. They were grimy – mercifully so, because the dismal contents of the frames looked like a job lot someone had bought at an auction. There were badly executed hedge-rows and haywains, ships and dead aristocrats.

'The servant led me to the drawing room, opened the door, and I entered a large room obviously designed in the last century to be ostentatious to the last degree.

'And there, with his back to a raging baronial fire in the neo-baronial fireplace, stood Victor.

'It will seem odd to you, perhaps, that I hardly noticed Durrand, hardly noticed anything at all but Victor. I think I have described him to you before, but no description of him does justice to the man. He has a blinding look – that's the only way I can describe it. It is impossible not to look at him head on, impossible to avoid his gaze, and once you have met that, you have no recourse but to look away – then back again, then down.

'At length, Victor turned to Durrand and asked to be introduced to me. He was very formal. What can I say I felt? My heart beat faster than it had ever beat in my life. It was a very strange sensation, not unlike sexual attraction, but so unlike it – so unlike it. I can't explain it. The thought that I would physically touch the man, shake hands with him, filled me full of revulsion and desire at the same time. I went dry at the mouth. I can think of nothing like it except that I felt it would be the same thing to touch the dead body of a king or pope or someone famous. The feeling was that I couldn't help myself taking his hand but that I would wipe it off surreptitiously afterwards. He was that cold. I mean to say – now, I've got it, talking to you. He gave me the impression of being the coldest man I had ever seen who had yet survived, who had all the same survived, and how anyone so cold could survive puzzled me so that I wanted to touch him and say I had survived too, except that if I touched him I would be turned into

189

someone as cold as he was, even though I am not known among my familiars for emotional warmth. I know that, Irene, I know what you think of me, you see.

'He moved slightly towards me. He was dressed in dinner jacket and his shirt was so starched that it creaked and rustled. "Durrand!" I found myself saying. Only that. "Durrand!" And I looked at him. "Why?" I almost asked him, but I did not. All expression, all expression was moved into his eyes, and he met mine with one, electric charge of pure fear. He introduced us and Victor took my hand. His grasp, surprisingly warm and dry, very dry, made my hand sweat, and I found myself smearing it on my dress afterwards – stupidly, like an ill-bred child. He talked in a terribly grave and pompous way, saying something like, "I am delighted to meet such a great benefactress of the Holy Companionate. Now you must come and meet our other guests."'

Mathilde stopped for a moment and inclined her head to one side as if she were trying to struggle with perturbing memory. 'I know why I used the word "blinding" now. Blinding. Blinding. My eye travelled down the long room to where the other guests, Georges's relatives, stood near a high, mullioned window with opaque glass, some of it stained with phoney escutcheons and heraldic devices. Sitting on a large, beswagged sofa was a very elderly woman, who seemed to be looking straight at me until I realized she could not see me, for she was indeed blind. She was exceedingly old – withered – but she sat very straight. She held a black cane in her right hand and was dressed in a sort of olive, chiffon garment which looked quite new. Her white hair was freshly done in tight little curls, and she wore a striking Victorian jet necklace. "We must present Mathilde to Maman," said Durrand with reverential awe in his voice. I must have given him a look, because Victor said, "Ah, yes – Maman must meet your sister. She is my mother, but all of the Companions call her Maman. You see, she has gained everyone's affections." I was taken to the old woman who grasped my hand in hers, feeling it slightly. She let it go. Her lips worked together, pursing and unpursing themselves as if independent of her own volition. Then Victor said, "She's truly remarkable. She does so much of our work for us." But I could not think what he meant.

'No one seemed to be able to say much in the presence of such great age. Georges, the young man I had met in Kensington Gardens, nervously poured me some sherry while I met his aunt and uncle. They were a certain English type, and I could imagine they had a country house which made the absurd mansion where we were seem abominably pretentious. They looked as if they had strayed in from a hunt ball or had the bewildered, dazzled expression of unwilling tourists who had strayed too far into foreign territory without a guide book. It was soon established that Georges's mother had married into a European Catholic family, and though they did not say so, it was clear that her choice still filled them with some misgivings. Georges's uncle did something in the City, or had done.

'Once we were all assembled, and everyone had sherry, Victor said what a pleasure it was to have been able to draw together such a family gathering. He made a gesture describing a circle, and I felt it fell just a little short of presumption in its subtle implication that we were all related to one another somehow through him and might therefore relax. Georges's aunt looked a little uncomfortable, but the otherwordliness in Victor's expression made it hard to be precise in thinking he had gone too far. Looking at him out of the corner of my eye as he chatted away, I could see in his strange, detached expression the author of the pamphlets the Companionate had sent me. There was something both remote and smirking about his look — something of the heavy paterfamilias about him. Here was a man whose will was perfectly honed to the exercise of authority; yet beneath this stern, smiling face I sensed an underground nastiness, something lurid and intense buried in the character. How can I say I sensed this? How did he frighten me? I don't know. It was as if he burnt. His words were chosen for impact and distinctness, his brow furrowed in order to further empower his piercing gaze. His movements had a heft. He was tactile. His hand fell upon Georges's shoulder, his mother's arm as if through all things there burnt something, as if he were fuelled. All the while I watched in this indirect way, I could see the face of Durrand. Durrand, who seemed to quiver with some exalted feeling, who would not look at me directly.

'Through the patter of small talk, I felt that I was being slowly sucked into Victor's consciousness, so that while he talked intelligibly to Georges's uncle about business, he was thinking all the time of me, as swift looks to my neck and shoulders, face and eyes revealed. It was as if he was thinking, judging, assessing, *feeling* for probabilities, and from Durrand's face I knew that much hung on the evening, much . . .' Mathilde grew silent. The train had halted for a while on the single track. We had stopped amid trees and leaves and bushes. It was quiet and the carriage had become even hotter. Still, Mathilde shivered. I had the sudden, horrible apprehension of Durrand as a draught on my neck.

'Mathilde, I'm thirsty. I'm going to get some more water,' I said, but she did not appear to hear me. I went out into the corridor.

*Everything would have been so simple if she had only joined us*, said Durrand. *As it is* . . . And I saw a profound darkness of which I was very much afraid. I shook my head and shook it, then banged it against the train window. Was Durrand within or without me?

I made myself breathe deeply. I did not think I was having a seizure. There was no sense of seizure in it, no antic jumping lights or arcs, no burning almonds in my nose. 'What shall I do?' I thought. Suddenly, a short, dark, swiftly moving woman – one of our party I had not yet met – came briskly from the lavatory. She was wearing rubber gloves and had an air of cheerful efficiency. She peeled off a glove and shook my hand, introducing herself as Imogene Holt from Texas and she wanted me to know how glad she was to meet me. 'Listen,' she said. 'Do you hear something?'

I thought I was going to faint. 'Are you all right?' she asked. I nodded. 'It's that moaning! It's driving Frank and me crazy!' She pointed to one of the compartments. 'You know what that's all about, don't you? It's that poor girl Muriel in a state about the toilet. So I've cleaned it up now.' She thumped at the compartment door while I gathered my wits. I started to laugh with relief. It must have been the girl Muriel, or perhaps something else like that which had triggered my over-sensitive imagination into hearing Durrand. Muriel, heavy-eyed with sorrow, came to the door. 'It's all right now, Muriel,' said Imogene. 'You can go to the bathroom. I've washed it.' Together, Muriel and Imogene and I inspected her handiwork. Everything sparkled and shone. 'Frank and I get around a bit,' she said. 'At this point in time, he is dusting the interior of our compartment. We'll be fine in two shakes. You see? You have to put up with things or do something about them.' Muriel rested her head on the doorway. 'Oh, Imogene, thank you,' she said.

'Eventually, we were seated in a huge dining room at a large, polished table,' said Mathilde on my return. She continued as if there had been no break in her story and as if we were not sitting in a train in the middle of Siberia. 'We were attended by a maid of indeterminate national origin. She might have been Spanish, Portuguese or Italian. She wore a wig on top of which was perched a frilly hat. She might have been picked up in Athens airport or Milan station. She had the same shut look as women who wander around huge termini with brooms, women impervious to announcements over the tannoy.' Mathilde stood at the window smoking. The train lurched and started up again. She sat.

'We were joined by a priest – a Father Etienne – who said the blessing in Latin. I was seated next to Victor while his blind mother presided at the other end of the table. Although I had not been able to place the English couple's role in this gathering, it became apparent as the meal progressed that the Companionate had an interest in buying their house, and although they were clearly reluctant to part with it, their eyes gave away those uncertainties that people have when they are accustomed to much and are yet in need of money. The conversation revolved delicately around this topic for some time while a truly voluptuous meal was served and eaten.

'Victor's table manners fascinated me. Even though he appeared to concentrate on the subject of house and grounds, his approach to the food before him seemed of paramount importance. With icy reluctance, he dissected poultry, nibbled. Here was a man, his edgy fork proclaimed, for whom eating was more of a mortification than fasting; yet one could tell that such a man had appetites. It was as if he were playing his own game with the food. There were grapes in the sauce. He rolled them about. He patted his mouth often and sipped carefully at the wine.

'The menu was fit for a state dinner. Course after course arrived. The meal was ridiculous. Durrand chopped and swallowed, careful not to wolf his food. His eyes kept shifting around the dining room. I remembered our meal of chicken and grits. I wondered if he had confessed the meal to the priest – confessed the theft. I wondered if he had told anyone what was going on. It was almost unbearable to watch him eat with such choking restraint. The old lady blindly controlled forks and knives as if for her too eating were a dreadful effort and ritual. From fonds d'artichauts to the final tower of profiteroles, the assembled members of the Companionate seemed guided by inner rules of a hidden nature. They crossed, for instance, their silver in an odd way until finally I realized that this had a significance and resembled a crucifix. They all ate as if each mouthful of food violated them.

'At last, Victor cut the conversation short and turned to me as if he had weighted the agenda of the dinner party and decided to bring in the business he had with me at a specified time. "Something puzzles me about you," he said.

"Here you have given us so much money, and this is the first time we meet. I confess I have expected you daily, no, hourly in Paris. Your twin made you sound such a keen student of our activities."

'Durrand's face went slack with terror. Looking back on it, I think he was naive enough to suppose that the conversation would take a very different turn.

'Victor's heavy aspect frightened me as well, but I kept my nerve. I told him my work had prevented me, at which point he gave me an impudent, patronizing, amused look and asked me what job I could possibly be doing which could be as important as the burning sense of vocation which Durrand had given him to understand I had.

'I told him what I did, for some reason thinking it would impress him. I remember him leaning back in his chair and saying with a self-important smile that these art treasures were nothing to the treasure I would gain if I humbled myself and considered womanly duties. "Buying and selling?" he said. "It's a little aggressive." He went on to describe the scope of happiness I would have if I served the Companionate. Again, he wondered aloud how I could give such a large donation to them and not follow it up with immediate action.

'I suddenly conceived a deep hatred for the man. His hard eyes bored through me. It was almost as if he had a thorough sexual knowledge of me which had led him to regard me with loathing. Durrand's eyes wildly searched mine, but I was unable to look at him even though I could see he was in a state of total desperation. I fumbled about for something to say. At last, I said, "I have my taxes to think about, and it seems you are deductible. Durrand has very much exaggerated my interest in the Companionate. Basically, Durrand persuaded me that you were a worthy cause. He gets over-excited, that is all. He only thought I had more interest than I had because he wanted me to."

'I know this is what I said, Irene,' Mathilde looked somewhat wildly about. 'I know it is what I said, but I could not stop my voice from trembling.

'Victor just looked from me to Durrand. I realized that everyone at the table had stopped speaking as he toyed with us. "We will say no more at present," he said at last, and signalled the other guests to resume their conversation.'

# Chapter Seventeen

The workmen finished fixing the front stoop this morning and the whole house looks better for it. I have gone past the danger of it. ('Irene, you'll fall down those steps and break your neck.') John called me last night and we spoke long and late on the telephone. What shadows in this place can reprove love? In the craven manner of demons, my old tormentors flee before his words and mine, our silences and our connection. It is in this respect they are cast out and cannot enter me for they have no power over love. What I am saying is that I could fall and break my neck on the new, smooth, marble steps, could have seizures still, am mortal, fallible; but I am changed from my old self by this new beauty – I, who was never allowed to play the bride.

The crumbling step where I sat and watched Mathilde and Durrand mime their wedding was supposed to be my pew that June evening long ago. I remember sitting there and thinking 'no, this is not right – this is something I don't want to watch.' It was not love but death they wanted from each other. Now, I ask myself if Victor could have known how his hand moved the final number of their combination into place. Did he know what fusions were possible between them? If he had been any kind of leader, any guide of souls, he must have seen the loose, live, dangling wires in Durrand. Maybe he sought to earth them in Mathilde, but I think it is more likely that he underestimated the true nature of their bond – one they had once tried to struggle from. I do not think Victor knew what he was doing. Any attempt to consecrate Mathilde's life to Durrand's was bound to end as it did. It was as if their foolish children's wedding long ago had finally found a priest in Victor: their base and morbid rituals, their secret, gnostic, shared and inner life was given the necessary impetus to reify itself. What they did here in Baltimore on unhallowed ground found full flower, rose to the pitch of consummation, achieved almost artistic status in my brother's death, and though Victor cannot altogether be held responsible for it, he should have marked my sister better before he arrogated to himself the dangerous burden of their situation.

The train had left the chequered leaves and light of the taiga and was at last travelling over the broad steppe, which, covered with pale and undulating grasses, gave the impression of a hidden, inland sea.

Mathilde and I sat across from each other, traversing the wilderness as if it were not there. She seemed to withdraw into herself beyond my reach, even beyond her own thoughts. Even though she was not smoking, she appeared to be drawing on some noxious substance, as if her memory of the events surrounding Durrand's latter days had decomposed and turned into a gas.

'The meal,' she said at last, 'seemed to go on forever. I became aware that Victor had prepared for us unspecified torment. He had simply let the notion of my "gift" float out into the conversation, and with it the underlying threat that he was on to its real purpose. I did not dare to look at Durrand. In fact, I didn't need to. I sensed his panic as it grew and grew to gross and animal proportions. At any moment, I feared he might unleash it on the company — leap up, plunge around the room like a horse in a burning barn. Oh, Irene, this was *Walpurgis Nacht*. By the time we had finished dinner, the two of us were so reduced that it is impossible to say what either of us felt when at last Victor placed his napkin on the table, pushed back his chair and announced that he needed words with us in his office. The other guests seemed unmoved by this unconventional behaviour.

'Durrand cringed into the back of his chair, quite unwilling to leave the table, but Victor, with one motion of his thick hand, commanded him to rise, and so he did and we followed him down a short corridor to a little room where there was an old, oiled Spanish oak desk surrounded by tattered and uncomfortable chairs. I think I would have sold my soul to the devil to get away from him: Durrand, obviously used to the heavy man with his smug and weighted smile, stood transfixed, unable to take his eyes off Victor, who finally motioned us to sit. Durrand sort of slumped, and for a small moment I thought he was going to collapse.

'I remember the way Victor seemed to decide to call me by my first name. It was as if he selected it carefully from other possibilities he had in mind, and put it on his lips, so that, pursed up, they resembled the motion of kissing. "Mathilde," he said, "We all know what goes to make up a saint, do we not?"

'I thought to myself that I was going insane and that this was not happening. I asked him what he meant. I had expected him to talk about money and he spoke of sanctity.

'He said, "A saint is brave at renouncing all of those things which offend God. A saint gives everything to God. A saint lets God in on everything." His tone had a fondling insolence in it. I felt like a child again – a child being touched up by a smooth-talking uncle. He said, "Why do you look so troubled? If you told me your real reasons for giving us all that money, you would relieve your conscience."

'Durrand sat with his eyes closed; his whole body was shaking. Victor watched him.

'I found I could not think. Words just blurted out. I said, "Are you God?", but the moment I had spoken, I realized I had defied him to our peril.

'He answered me with utter conviction; he said, "For Durrand here I stand in the place of God, as Durrand knows full well." He let Durrand's terror come to the surface in his eyes before he went on. He waited for me, too, to show the unease I could not conceal. Then, he continued in a silky tone, saying, "But Durrand does not tell me all those little secrets he used to tell me. No. Durrand seems to have found another way of going about things. It is his way, but not the Companionate's way. I had rather counted on you to tell me the little sins your two hearts share."

'I told him he was not a priest, and for a moment I thought he looked uncomfortable, but he countered me by inviting me to consult Father Etienne if I were so scrupulous. "Make a full confession. Set your mind at rest," he said.

'Durrand suddenly cried out, "No!" Everyone was silent for a while.

'I said to Victor, "There is no secret I have that you are entitled to know."

'Victor turned to Durrand and said, "So this is the woman who was so eager to become a Companion. Oh, how sordid this all is. You have covered yourselves with lies and you have fallen far, very far – too far this time, I think."

'I asked him what on earth he was on about, but I could see it was too late. He knew. He had just been playing with us. He told me the bank had come across the discrepancy in their books, and the manager, "a very old and trusted friend of ours", he said, had noticed that the account opened by Durrand and me contained the exact sum which was missing. It had puzzled him because, as he said, "under the terms of Durrand's vows he is not allowed to have a bank account". His hands went hard and flat against the desk. "Our friend at the bank, of course, knew this, but I suppose that Durrand did not know he knew. We watched with interest as small sums of money trickled back – all recorded in the books by Durrand." Victor spoke to me the entire time as if Durrand hardly existed. His voice had a teasing, mocking tone when he asked me if I really thought that I could fool such a respectable organization as the bank, if I really thought I could fool him too. When he had finished, he sat back in his chair and it creaked under his weight.

'I turned to Durrand and he turned to me. We looked at each other for a long time. I do not know whether I spoke aloud or not, but I must have, because he answered me. Yes, I must have said, "Why?" I know I said, "Why didn't you tell me? Why didn't I know you were not entitled to an account? Why, Durrand?" The words just formed and formed, almost against my volition. His face, even though it was aghast, had a curious serenity on it. He said, "I dunno, Matty." And he didn't. He did not know.

'Victor cut in sharply and said, "I haven't many alternatives in this matter. It's beginning to become a question of not knowing what to do with you, Durrand." His voice was even, but it seemed to come from a deeper and more powerful source than Victor himself. It was as if Victor had access to some pure form of force. As he spoke, Durrand's head moved slowly, very slowly until his eyes were riveted to Victor. All the colour was drained from his face. "No," he said.

'I said, "What do you do here, you people? Are you torturers?" But neither Victor nor Durrand appeared to hear me.

'"It may be that you are unable to continue with us, Durrand," Victor said. "It may be that you are really questioning your vocation by doing this . . ."

'"No, please, no!" Durrand cried. "Please don't. Oh, please." And he started to weep in his hands while Victor looked on. A curious look of satisfaction came across Victor's face, and his hand twitched slightly on the desk. "Victor, I love you," Durrand said finally. "Please forgive me." He looked up at Victor, his inquisitor, and said, "I only did it for you."

'Then there was an awful silence. I thought I could no longer endure Durrand's pitch of self-abasement. But there was no stopping it. There he writhed like a caught fish. "And you thought I would accept stolen money," Victor said.

'"Oh please, please," Durrand said. "Please. She paid it back for me. It really was from her . . ." But he was too exhausted to argue any more.

'Victor turned his head to me. "Mathilde," he said, "I think I have a plan whereby we can avoid the unpleasant consequences of this deed. In fact, my idea would serve all three of us rather well. It is in no one's interests for Durrand to be exposed. We at the Companionate carefully guard our reputation, and of course, no one wishes Durrand to go to prison. Nor do I think you would find it convenient to be exposed for abetting a fraud. It might do your reputation as a dealer quite a lot of harm. What I suggest, therefore, is that you write a letter to our good Monsieur Salan, who has uncovered all of this, and make a declaration. Why not, for instance, say that you yourself had incurred great debts in a manner of which you were ashamed? You called on Durrand. Durrand heard. Anxious, desperately anxious to save the family honour, he stole the money, and you, grateful and repentant, restored it to him immediately, as soon as you could. This might give rise to some questions, I suppose, about why Durrand did not approach Monsieur Salan directly and ask him for a loan; but I think I could smooth that one over. Further evidence of your contrition would help, but I'm not sure it is entirely necessary. Monsieur Salan will know that we can effectively deal with Durrand here . . ."

'"So you won't expel me? You won't?" Durrand begged him, then me: "Matty, please! Matty, you will, won't you?"'

Abruptly, my sister stopped talking and gazed out of the window at the far horizon of the steppe. I sensed the presence of Durrand as having to do with that moment, having been caught in it. It frightened me more, somehow, that I did not hear the voice which any moment I thought might descend upon my inner ear.

'Did you, Mathilde?' I finally asked. She did not answer. 'Did you, Mathilde, or didn't you? Write the letter Victor suggested?'

Slowly, she turned to me. For a moment, I thought she was going to smile, but this, perhaps, was an illusion created by the afternoon light as it died away over the grasses, leaving each stalk defined in its gold illumination. The light was becoming to Mathilde and cast shadows upon her features so that for a moment they were caught in an almost ethereal look. She was not smiling, however. An expression rose from within her that seemed to be exhumed from her depths, and for a terrible moment I wondered if it would ever leave her. Her eye glittered and her lip drew back. 'No,' she said, 'No, I did not. No, I refused to put my name to such a lie.'

Before I knew what I was doing, I was on my feet and in the corridor outside the compartment. I closed the door behind me and left her sitting there alone. I did not know what to do with my hands or with the idea that Mathilde had done such a brutal thing to Durrand.

There's your ghost, I thought. The damage of that moment — sensed. My hands found the train window and I held them there, watching, with heavy misery in my heart, the landscape as we passed. In the middle distance, two large cranes with long legs stepped delicately about the grasses, and, as if with an instinct for maintaining their moment of privacy on the steppe, they suddenly took flight, and I saw them slowly climb into the violet reaches of the sky.

Could she not see that what she had done was wrong? I could not understand why she did not see it. What perversity in her could have committed that cruelty? To have seen her own twin brother weep and cringe and beg for mercy and refuse him the means of it seemed monstrous to me, no matter how corrupt he had become, no matter how he had been corrupted. I simply shook my head. It seemed beyond anything.

Suddenly, the sound of laughter erupted from the next compartment. The door slid back, and an elderly Italian rushed out in a state of embarrassment and confusion; he dashed past me down the corridor, and as he reached the end, a tiny woman in her fifties poked her head out from the carriage, and, seeing him, clapped her hands with delight. She slipped past me after him, uttering giggles and whoops. He gasped and bolted.

All at once, I gave way to the emotion that I had wanted to resist. Oh, Durrand! Poor Durrand! I felt seized by compassion towards him. Suddenly, I became aware of both his presence and volition – a spectral volume of air occupying space and capable of entering time. Like a column of the densest ice, he seemed to throb beside me with the deepest emanation of cold. Oh no! I cried, for I could see nothing and hear nothing, but could only sense for this second or two the terrible disturbance of air and it was gone. No, I said. I began to pray and I prayed, my eyes seared shut, until the sweat stood out upon my forehead.

# Chapter Eighteen

This morning, I paid a visit to the site of my first re-membered epileptic vision. I thought I would do so in order to ground myself against whatever possibility there can be of a return of Durrand or a wrong belief about what he might have been. I do not understand it. I do not. I have no wish or will to be a medium and had none. What happened to me there in the middle of nowhere? What did I really see and hear, passing through that emptiness?

When I was six, my sister took me to a birthday party and we had to go past the Francis Scott Key Monument up Sewell Avenue. I remember I was wearing my green velvet dress and my black patent leather shoes. I was carrying a present wrapped in blue tissue paper. As I passed the monument, I saw myself going the other way. The vision of myself was dressed as I was, but did not carry the present, nor was it accompanied by Mathilde. It seemed unaware that it had forgotten the gift, and as it passed me, descending as I ascended the hill, I became very agitated. If I was going the wrong way, then I would not get to the party, and if I did not have a gift, I would be embarrassed. I then began to wonder if there were two of me, and this distressed me more. Suppose my twin (of whom I had been unaware until that time) arrived at the party after all. Would there be enough ice-cream and cake? What would everyone say? Would everyone like her better than me? I would not tell Mathilde why I cried, and when I arrived at the party, I spent the better part of the afternoon hoping and praying that my double would not turn up. I decided that if she did, I would hide in the bathroom until she had gone. It took me several hours to realize that the vision I had had was not of my true self. I do not know why I knew it, but slowly it came clear to me that the little girl I had seen was not real and was no more to be worried over than a dream.

Years later, they told me that sightings of myself coming towards myself were psychomotor seizures: yet, I had always known, with instinct intact, not to believe me when I was approaching me. I even became fond of these visions and treated them as jokes. It seemed a lighter side of epilepsy to be able to see myself in such a way, and I sometimes used my disembodied self as a mirror, and would readjust my hair according to the information it gave me.

I do not feel qualified to decide what actually happened to me on that journey. But now I have returned and revisited this house, the tree-lined avenue where my brain played neurological pranks on me, I see it was not that. Not epilepsy. If it was madness, where did it go when I got home? Why do I no longer fear the cold and feral thing that spoke to me in syllables of Durrand? The house is free of it and so am I. It was as if for that space of time a thief had found a pathway to my mind, a thief who knew the latch, and fumbled for it darkly. My sensation of Durrand was profound.

I stood there helpless against my fear in the corridor of the train. Like a fly in a web, I was caught in the threading, binding horror of the thing I sensed as Durrand, as though I had been pitched beyond God's providence, beyond the place where God allowed himself to go. I reminded myself that I had neither called on Durrand nor willed Durrand to come, nor had I ever dabbled in any dark practice which might have left me open to a haunting. Was I possessed, then, by an evil I abhorred? Could such a thing happen without my consent to it? Or did God try me? Was I, like Job, blessed with a kind of curse so that I could learn pure patience? Learn to know light from its absolute absence?

Perhaps it was safer to think that I was mad, better to think this than to throw myself open to the unknowable and reachless power of God, who seemed to have abandoned me forever.

'Irene.' It was John. He touched my shoulder and I turned and saw him afresh. It was as if he were completely familiar to me; as if he had always been expected; as if, for no other reason but that it was so, he was there for me and I for him. I did not expect him to kiss me, but when he did, it touched me more deeply than I could have supposed. For a moment, there was a curious solemnity between us. As we separated from the embrace, though, the trap fell, and I rebounded from him, clamped in doubt.

'What is the matter?' he asked. 'I'm sorry . . . perhaps . . .' He looked confused and embarrassed.

'No,' I said, and took his hands. The part of me that wanted him pulled and gnawed at what was trapped in Durrand. 'Please.'

'Durrand?' he asked. He shook his head.

'You do think I'm crazy,' I said, and moved mistrustfully away.

'Maybe you want to be,' he said. 'Maybe it is easier for you than to hold on to yourself. Than to oppose Mathilde.' He looked away. 'I thought . . .'

'You were right,' I said.

His eyes became alert and they sought me as if he physically tried to peer through my confusion to the place where I crouched beneath it. I realized how frightened I was, and began to calm down. 'Suppose I told you that whatever happens to you is going to matter to me; I can't alter that feeling. It isn't a usual feeling. It is not a feeling I usually have. Don't ask me why I have it. Last night confirmed it and it has been on my mind all day.'

'You don't even know me,' I said.

'Well, I know myself,' he replied, and looking at him, I began to think that this might be true. He had the curious confidence of people who keep an exact account of themselves. 'But I suppose I can't expect you to trust me.' He turned to the window and watched the pristine landscape slip by, and I thought I could not bear it if he did not know how much I wanted to be free from all that held me back from him.

'Oh, I think . . .' I could not finish.

'I do not trust your sister,' he said, 'and from what you have told me, Durrand was her carbon copy. You are not an old-maid schoolteacher, nor anything else that they said you were. But maybe I have too great a conceit of myself. Maybe you have someone else at home. Maybe you think I do, but I don't.'

'I have no one . . .'

'And you were doubtless told that you never would have. How did it go? Epileptic, possessed . . . now it's crazy. Suppose I told you that I don't care whether or not you are sane. What then?'

We looked at each other almost angrily. 'All right, then,' I said. 'You win.'

'You don't seem to hear me,' he said. 'I'm saying that I love you as you are. Whether you suit anyone else or not is of no consequence to me.' His chin gave a little lift. He looked determinedly out of the window and cleared his throat.

'Do you?' I asked. 'Love me?' I peered at him. 'Really?'

Just then, the couple who had chased into the other carriage returned, and, with a wink, the Italian woman pulled her reluctant swain after her into the compartment.

John growled. 'It isn't like that and you are not a part of my itinerary.'

I could not help laughing. He looked at me swiftly out of the corner of his eye, and he too started to laugh.

'All right, then,' I said. 'You, too,' I said, and then was moved beyond anything into the first real happiness I had ever known. We stood there staring at each other, stupid with joy.

There is no Durrand, there is no Durrand, I kept telling myself; and even if there is, it doesn't matter now. But it did.

After a while, the compartments started to open; the tourists were getting ready for dinner and I thought I had better get Mathilde even though it meant stepping out of that encircling warmth of John and myself into her chilly ambit. I found her in a deep sleep and woke her with some difficulty. 'Durrand?' she said.

'No, Mathilde, it's me, Irene.'

She blinked, made one or two adjustments to her hair, and together we straggled into the dining car where John and Abel Hartmann had reserved a table for us. A fear oozed through me because she had used Durrand's name when she woke, but I managed to convince myself that this had been only natural, considering what she had told me earlier. She sat by the window, staring absently at the vast steppe which surrounded the train. The waitress brought soup and a bottle of Georgian wine which was sweet and sticky. Mathilde hardly touched her glass or the soup. Altogether, she emanated an awful desolation. Abel, who sat next to John, peered at her across the table as if she were a long way off. He had large, myopic eyes and a kindly expression. It was clear that he and John had hit it off very well, sharing as they did the same compartment. Abel seemed to have a naturally lively personality, perhaps a little quixotic. Although by no means egocentric, he was the sort of man who is used to having people listen to him. As the dusk deepened over the grassland, he spoke with verve about the trip, Vinnie, his own interest in Central Asia. It appeared that he was, after all, an anthropologist, and had developed an interest in zoology only after the death of his wife five years ago. From time to time, he glanced at Mathilde to see if he aroused any reaction in her at all, but it was not until he started to speak about his wife that she took any interest in him.

'She had cancer,' he said. 'It was terrible. We were devoted.'

Mathilde curtly interrupted him. 'You expect to find Przewalski's Horse.' Her flat voice cut across the subtle tone of grief in his voice so that his words alone stood. She made him sound self-pitying. Abel withdrew for a moment as if he had been bitten, but, to my surprise, he looked again at her, more closely as if to find an explanation for her behaviour – almost as if she were one of the wild creatures that so interested him.

'I couldn't hope to find the horse on a guided tour,' he said, 'not even one of Vinnie's. No, what I hope for is an invitation. No one can get a visa for an extended stay in Mongolia without a sponsor. Try as I might, I haven't been able to find one. If I can only make contact with someone in Ulan Bator who will help me, I may be able to get permission to return. The last herd was seen in the Altai Mountains. There have been some interesting rumours from nomads. Being an anthropologist, I think I know how to sift out the truth from such reports; I have access to information I am inclined to trust.'

'Being an anthropologist, you probably have a Rousseau-ist view of fundamental innocence,' said Mathilde. She gave him a not altogether unpleasant smile. 'Irene and I were brought up on original sin. Tell me, do Altaic nomads sin originally or in a commonplace way, or not at all, in your view?'

John's eyes mirrored my own surprise at this non-sequitur. My sister was sewn up in a bag of religion like a drowning kitten.

Whether or not in self-defence, Abel considered her question like a teacher with a particularly acute student. 'The concept of sin in Altaic nomads,' he said, 'is somewhat blurred. They still practise animism in parts of this area. An animist sees the numinous in things external to the self as we in the West understand it. The idea of sin presupposes a personal consciousness – a consciousness of personal destiny. Concepts like sin and redemption are lost on them. They don't differentiate themselves from nature and they see nature as imbued with a conscious will. This will in nature they reach through the medium of shamans and sacrifice. But I don't want to bore you.'

'You are not boring me!' Mathilde cried. She put her elbows on the table, having abandoned an attempt to disjoint a tough chicken leg. She stared at him intently. 'Tell me about shamans and sacrifice.'

'Well,' said Abel, looking rather pleased at Matty's interest. 'The *meaning* of pagan sacrifice is quite hard to convey to so-called civilized people, *especially* those brought up with an idea of original sin. You see, magic seeks to control events; it enters into an external relationship with the world. The end of magic is to dominate matter: to capture the spirit of matter and enter into a bond with it so that it will bend to the petitioner's will. In my view, it is a primitive form of science, and is completely distinct in its aim from the aim of sophisticated religion.'

'I'm not so sure about that,' said Mathilde. 'And I'm not so sure that magic is like science in its aims. I have always thought very highly of magic. I'm not so sure I have always thought so highly of science, or what you call the sophisticated religions. Doesn't Christianity, for instance, call for human sacrifice on a grander scale than primitive religion?'

'But it's on quite a different scale!' Abel cried jubilantly. 'It is redemptive and not repeatable. Let me tell you a story from these parts. I have it on good authority that as late as 1922, Mongolian soldiers tore out the living hearts of their Japanese prisoners in order to baptize their battle standards in blood . . .'

Mathilde was bug-eyed and I wanted to stop the conversation, but Abel, enjoying her attention, became more and more ecstatic with his idea.

'The sacrifice of Christ on the Cross at once acknowledges the need in mankind for ritual bloodshed – and takes it further. It is perhaps the most fundamental need, and Christ would not have been Christ if He had not accepted it. God never crucified him – the human race did it!'

'You're a Christian then?' Mathilde looked disappointed.

'No, no, no!' Abel cried. 'Not at all. I'm a Jew. Don't you see? I'm just trying to make sense of it. The Japanese soldier's death is for material gains in battle. The flags of the Mongolians used to be totems; the death of Jesus was undertaken by him for spiritual ends: so that man could form a proper relationship with God. To get it over with, once and for all."

'My brother,' said Mathilde, 'was sacrificed for material ends – for worldly success – by men who claimed to be, almost exclusively, the only true Christians in the world. It has formed a deep impression on me, his death. You don't suppose we could train my sister here – who is an epileptic – to be a shaman and bring him back to me? It would seem that she, who always had a visionary outlook, might well be capable. What do you think?'

There was a long silence. Mathilde's cold fury was not addressed to Abel. She looked at John.

'Why did you think I did not know Irene was an epileptic?' he asked.

'Oh, why don't you spend the night with her if you're so keen on convulsions!' she said. She banged her fist sharply on the table and tourists nearby fell silent and looked round. 'Oh, you animals! You animals!' she cried, and she struggled up and fled. I started after her.

'No.' John said. 'Don't go. Leave her alone.'

Abel said, 'Look, shall I try? I think I can . . . I'll try to talk with her. I'll stay with her tonight . . .' But I did not hear all that he said because I was so ashamed at her exposure of both disease and love.

'Irene, you must leave Mathilde alone.' John said, gripping my hand hard in his. Abel followed Mathilde back to our compartment.

'You don't think she knows? You don't think I told her without knowing it about the voice, about Durrand?'

'I don't think you did anything like that. Please, let Abel talk to her. Maybe he can make some sense of it — where you can't.'

'But Mathilde set Durrand's death in motion,' I said. 'She cannot see it, but she feels the guilt and puts it onto everybody else . . .'

'Are you in any fit state tonight to deal with that?' he asked. 'Let Abel try.'


# Chapter Nineteen


The shipment of Mathilde's icons has arrived at last. They seem overjoyed at the museum with the size and distinction of the collection. I did not tell them that I gave the icon of the Saviour to the Orthodox Church in London. I gave the Transfiguration to the parish of the priest who helped me so much after Mathilde's death. It seemed only fitting that those two, which had accompanied Matty at times of great perplexity, should belong to people who could understand them for what they are — not totems, but signs. I have kept nothing.

An art historian from Johns Hopkins spent the better part of the morning praising Mathilde's tact and skill as a restorer. She would have been so pleased to hear him. As I stood listening to him amongst the crates open and revealing treasures, I found myself almost unable to believe she was destroyed by Durrand. Mathilde – so clever – who had been on first-name terms with the whole world of the Byzantine. How could she have become obsessed with him to such an extent?

I am trying to get something done to the dining room in Ashby Street. The walls sag in there. The paper is peeling and torn. Under a flap, I discovered the old design we used to have before some tenant painted over it. It was a diamond pattern. The last time Durrand was here before Mother died, he had come home on leave from Vietnam. Mother had become, by that time, shadowy to the point of vanishing, alive only on the tortured point of fear that Durrand would be killed. I remember how he walked through the front door, flipped his hat on a hook in the vestibule, sat, smoked, smiled his grim, ironic smile. I remember being surprised that the war had not touched him, that it had not changed him. We sat at the dinner table. I remember the diamond pattern well because my eyes kept shifting to it during the meal. Mother's hands were shaking in an effort at sobriety, and Durrand spoke about Vietnam without any conscience at all – on one side or the other. I suddenly felt that the chaos of the war pleased him, and I realized in a liberating moment that he was a person without real size. What turned such a man into the awful Charybdis he became?

'Are you listening to Durrand?' John asked. We sat in his compartment in the dark. I had been silent for a long time. The tourists were settling down for the night as the train ploughed towards the Mongolian border.

'No, I am thinking about him,' I said. 'I am wondering if I should tell her after all about the voices, the sense of his presence.'

'No,' he said. 'You mustn't tell her.'

'Don't you think she already knows? I can't tell you what Mathilde used to put me through. To Durrand I was a devil: to her I was a medium.' His arm was around me and we sat close together, enfolded in the dark of the train. 'Shh,' he said.

Then he said, 'You *would* be that if you told her. Don't you think? Why must you live for other people's expectations of you? You're not a telephone.'

'Suppose he *is* real?'

'Suppose he is. They are only safe if they are apart from each other. From what you have told me, they are the worst possible thing that could have happened to each other. What use would it be whether he is real or unreal – for her to know about what you have perceived? She wants you to see him because she cannot bear to think he is dead. If she thought he wasn't, God knows what she'd do. It's your job to live past this time. Whatever she does is up to her.'

I sat up suddenly rigid. 'Suppose she killed him! If what she said back there in the compartment was true, and I think it is true, didn't she send him . . .?'

'Then the pitiless thing that talks to you wants a revenge you mustn't let it have. Even if it is only part of you, you cannot let that part of you punish Mathilde with the revelation that the one person she has loved in her life condemns her. That person is *you*, not Durrand. I think she hates Durrand as much as she hates herself.'

'Then I have failed her.'

'Irene, you are not God. And when I say I think she loves you, it is not what you mean by love – or what I mean by it. You heard her back there in the dining car: for her, the whole world is magic, an extension of herself which she expects to be infused with meaning. She cannot say "I" and she cannot say "you" because there is no connecting verb. It is a great compliment that Mathilde thinks you are a medium because a medium effects a contact, as it were, between two unconnected things. What she means when she says you are a medium is that you are capable of connection when she is not. It is a compliment, but it is one you must not accept if you are to do her any real good.'

'Do you really love me?' I asked. I was glad the carriage was dark. 'Because I think that I really love you.'

'Shh,' he said. 'Of course I do. I wouldn't have said it otherwise.'

'It's because I'm exotic,' I said.

'Do you know?' he said, 'I think you are absolutely right. You are without boundary and can never be completely explored.'

'We wouldn't be very happy then if I get well.'

'On the contrary,' he said. 'You would find a good deal of energy if you got beyond Durrand and Mathilde. For me.' He closed his eyes and I touched his hand. 'I could just as easily say that you believed you loved me because I accept you as you are. We could both find deeper motives, I suppose.'

'There's sex,' I said, so solemnly that he started to laugh and so did I. 'Yes, there's that,' he finally said, and in a silence opulent with feeling, I felt a heavy stirring of desire, strange for its sweetness.

I said, 'I don't think it would be right because . . .'

'You're religious.'

I felt a monstrous, starchy prude. He gripped my wrist.

'What glimmer of hope have you against Durrand if you lose one iota of your integrity?' he said. 'Integrity as you and Durrand would both perceive it.'

'John, are you real?'

'Irene, for God's sake!' he said.

When at last I slept, I dreamed of a jewel, his gift. It was a stone I had never seen before. I was deeply surprised that I should have it, but it was mine.

When I awoke, everyone in the whole train did too, because Russian soldiers were busily dismantling the carriage in search of contraband.

They were everywhere. There was a terrible babble of voices and everyone was frightened. We had reached the border, and before we were allowed to cross it, our luggage had to undergo a thorough search. They marshalled us into the corridor. Various members of the party looked at me and John with averted eyes and little smiles. My sister and Abel stood next to our compartment while a soldier ransacked it. He even pulled up the hard cushions on the seats. Finding nothing, he returned to our bags which he opened and went through.

Mathilde was wearing a white nightgown of fine muslin trimmed with lace. She hugged her lavender silk shawl around her shoulders. The Russians were staring at her in her shift. She had let down her long hair which curled around her shoulders, grey and gold.

Suddenly, one of the soldiers gripped Hugh by the shoulders and started to question him roughly. Hugh could not understand Russian. Vinnie started to argue with the soldiers. Mathilde sidled up to Hugh and said in a whisper, 'I think £50 should do it. They're just saving face because they can't find whatever it is they are looking for. A bit of hard currency will work wonders.'

Vinnie accompanied Hugh off the train. From the window, we could see them retreating into a customs shed.

No one spoke. We stood for a long time waiting for Hugh and Vinnie to return. In that inhuman hour of night, we stood united in the fear of what might be going on in the customs shed. Only Mathilde looked cool.

The merry Italian woman asked Mathilde in broken English if Hugh would be sent to a camp.

'Oh, they've picked him at random, I think, because he looks rich. He may have been selling pounds for roubles, but even so, nothing will happen to him. Vinnie is too good at his job to let anything happen.' And, indeed, the train shuddered and the engine started to grind. Vinnie and Hugh boarded the train, and when they had entered the carriage and we were on the move, Mathilde vanished back into our strewn compartment without a word and shut the door.

Abel touched my shoulder. We looked at each other in silence, and then looked out of the window as the train gathered speed down the track that crossed the no-man's-land between the Russian and Mongolian border.

'My God!' Hugh exclaimed. 'A hundred pounds. What effrontery!' He flung open his compartment door. His companion had quite vanished during the kerfuffle, but he now sat in a corner, his eyes shut and his hands shaking. There was an expression of deep relief upon his face. 'And it was all your fault!' Hugh cried.

The younger man opened his eyes. 'They didn't find the letter, though, did they?'

'Anthony here, if you please,' said Hugh, 'agreed to take a letter for a Jewish woman in Moscow. He said he would smuggle it out and post it in London when we got back . . .' A long, complicated wrangle ensued about the letter, the money, the years taken off life. Hugh slammed the compartment door and, loud voiced, continued for a while.

'It was Mathilde,' said Abel quietly.

'What do you mean?'

'She smuggled an icon – in her shawl. A very little one of "Christ the Saviour". She told me all about it. I watched her sew it in. I didn't know what to do.'

'Abel, that's terrible. You must have been very frightened.'

'Oh, there's something more frightening in Mathilde than that,' he said.

'What? What is it that frightens you?' I could barely get the words out.

'I can't explain.'

'I'll try to pay Hugh back his money. The soldiers must have had some reason to suspect about the icon.'

'She had a terrible dream, when finally she slept,' said Abel. 'Before the Russians boarded the train. She woke up screaming in a sweat. The dream had something to do with a proliferation of ant-like beings crawling all over the world. Then her dead brother Durrand appeared to her out of a shadow and told her something unintelligible. She cried and cried afterwards. I tried to tell her how awful I knew it was to lose someone – you know – but she wouldn't listen. The minute the soldiers were on the train, bang – she was icy calm.'

We were coming to another stopping place. We had crossed the no-man's-land and had entered the borders of Mongolia. There were arc lights and chain fences with barbed wire on the top.

'I wouldn't worry about shamans and so on. You looked very upset earlier this evening. I think a lot of it is to do with her grief. I'll tell you something. When my wife died, I saw an advertisement for a clairvoyant in the paper, and I nearly rang the number. In fact, my hand was on the receiver; but it seemed awful to betray my wife with that – to buy cheap assurances that she had survived death. I think Mathilde is going through the most intense and dreadful period of mourning, and she'll simply have to get through it.'

'Thank you Abel,' I said. 'I'd better get back to her, I suppose.'

'Don't. Not yet. Wait out the night and let things settle.'

'She's angry at me then.'

'It's all very confused. But let's see if I can get her to talk quietly.'

'She probably resents John,' I said. I had difficulty in pronouncing his name because it moved my heart.

'Do you know, Irene, I'm not sure she has even noticed him,' said Abel, peering at me through his spectacles.

Mongolian soldiers now boarded the train. They had planed, angled faces of a deep red-gold, jet-black hair and black eyes. They moved with the easy, physical confidence of people who spend life largely out of doors.

Everyone assembled for the checking of visas – everyone but Mathilde. I opened our compartment, but she was deeply asleep. I shook her, but she did not move. The soldiers checked her papers which I fished out from her bag.

'She hasn't taken any pills?' I asked Abel.

'I'm afraid I took the liberty of checking to see if she had any before. She hasn't.'

The soldiers finished their business quickly and dispersed into the night. The train left the borderland and plunged down the long, single track towards Ulan Bator.

'John!' I said. 'She *did* smuggle an icon. Maybe that's your agent! The one you thought you almost saw.' But somehow I was afraid it wasn't so, and he said nothing.

# Chapter Twenty

The light of the morning caught me and I rose to it. 'John, oh John, look!' I cried, not caring if I woke him. The early rays of dawn slid across his forehead and hands. His eyes were closed, but he was awake, for his body was held in deliberate stillness and was not abandoned to sleep. The light played over his face, the tendrils of hair on the backs of his hands and touched him with more accurate tenderness than I could have done myself. He opened his eyes as if he sensed my wish to be that light. We looked at one another and smiled. 'Look,' I said softly, and he sat and together we watched what passed before the train window.

The whole moorland was filled with dawn, and in the middle distance, beneath a mountain that rose sharply up without foothills, stood an encampment of spheroid tents, marvellous to behold for their smoothness and beauty of shape. In front of this nomadic settlement, a lone rider posted out after his flocks and his horse's heels threw up little puffs of dust. The herdsman rode with one unified movement, not constraining his animal. They seemed to share the same will, the same thought, and the horse's gait reflected the ease of its friendship with the rider.

I almost made an exclamation, for I was sublimely happy with the man and the horse and the tents and the limpid sunlight and John and the releasing vastness of the empty steppe, but I sensed his absorption in the beauty of the landscape and was silent. Like the rider, he did not strain after anything, but allowed conclusions about what he saw to evince themselves. I sensed in him no desire to possess the uncommonness of vision which offered itself from the Mongolian countryside. It was more as if he gave to what he saw. I imagined what his former travels had been like, and thought to myself that from Anapurna to the Amazon basin he had gone giving rocks and cataracts their proper names, engrossing himself only in their true identity. Together, we watched the flashing elements of the place from the train.

A little house with Siberian shutters displayed a large mural of a man on horseback leaping over what looked like a black river. We passed more felt tents bound with straps; smoke came out of the chimneys of some. The train slowed as it passed a group of people lined up next to the track. A number of old men stood in the group, their faces eroded by the weather and age into a strange, gaunt toughness. They wore fedora hats, incongruous with the Oriental dress everyone seemed to adopt – men, women and children – high collared robes belted at the waist with bright sashes. They all watched the train's slow passage with solemn and utter concentration.

John went to get us tea from the samovar and returned with the scalding, orange stuff. I drank the tea with gratitude.

'The guard is still drunk,' he said, 'but Vinnie and the Russian soldier have between them managed to light the samovar.'

'Have you seen Mathilde yet?'

'She hasn't emerged.'

'John,' I said.

'Irene.' We stood together with each other for a long moment in silence.

'I'm very frightened.'

'Durrand?'

'Abel gave me a perfectly good reason why she'd try to get in touch with his spirit but . . .'

'What?'

'Well, Durrand is gone.' As if he had been there in the first place. And I sensed him, out on the steppe, where, shiftless there in the waterless hinterland of that passageless place, he gathered force and density.

John said, 'Maybe it really was someone following her because of the icon. It's really the most reasonable explanation, you know.' But he looked distracted, uneasy.

We went into the corridor where the other tourists were gathered at the window watching as the train passed through the suburbs of Ulan Bator. Mathilde stood at the window too, looking intently at the crudely built apartment blocks and factories which lined the track. A number of Mongolians were going about ther daily business on horseback. From time to time, motorcycles whizzed by, but otherwise the scene was lifeless.

Mathilde was dressed too formally. She wore a suit and smelt of perfume. She looked as if she were about to get out at Grand Central Station in New York rather than whatever the station was at Ulan Bator. Abel was standing next to her, gazing at the horses. I thought it a little strange that a man with such a scholarly cast had developed such a fascination with a nearly extinct horse. His head looked as if it had bent to books from an early age, and his tall form had the appearance of a question mark. He turned and laughed, as if reading my thoughts. Apologetically, he said, 'The search for unicorns!'

'Mathilde?' I said.

She turned round. 'I have something to show you,' she said abruptly and beckoned me into the compartment with the look of a stranger on her face. My belongings still lay strewn about where the Russian soldiers had left them and so I started to stuff things into my suitcase.

With nimble fingers, she started to unpick a little patch sewn into her shawl. Out of it, she took a tiny icon, not much larger than a matchbox. It was in a silver case and she opened it. Inside the case was a minutely executed portrait of Christ, his right hand uplifted in blessing.'I got away with it,' she said. 'God! That took a lot of nerve.' Somehow, I was very frightened that Mathilde had purloined this picture, which was of great, great beauty.

'I've never done it before, you know,' she said, 'but I couldn't resist this time.' She stared at me. 'Oh, don't worry, they won't catch me now.'

'Mathilde! Don't *become* Durrand!' I found myself saying.

She looked at me with faint contempt. 'I'm not.' She sighed. 'Oh can't you see the adventure in it? You can be so boring. Little Miss Mealy-Mouth.'

'Mathilde,' I said. 'Stop it.'

The sky above Ulan Bator was unbearably blue. The sun seemed to pulse in the pure atmosphere. All solid objects cast a sharp shadow so that you could almost tell the time by yourself standing.

A group of Russians on the platform were greeting friends and relatives who energetically heaved boxes and packages off the train: presents, no doubt from Moscow. A lot of Russian soldiers, too, milled about. They looked young and vulnerable. But soon this European crowd dispersed, leaving our party alone with the empty train, which was going on to Peking. An elderly Chinese woman, clearly a worker, was checking the carriages. I could not think why she tottered down the platform so, until I saw her feet were bound. The feet were stumps and looked like stilts. The woman was heavy and her full body agonized as she walked, heaving her weight about on these deformities. Mathilde had seen it too. We looked at each other, saying nothing, but aghast. We were left with the impression of the woman's feet.

We waited. The station is a large, crudely built edifice designed to suggest the modern outlook of the nation; yet it looked unstable, as if it had been erected according to a series of wild guesses. Eventually, from it came a beautiful woman dressed in an olive *usteey deel* buttoned high at the neck. Her lustrous black hair was tied in a severe knot at the back of her neck. She exuded an air of self-discipline and containment.

Vinnie scratched his beard nervously when he saw her coming. 'That,' he announced to our group, 'is Madame Densima, commonly known as Dragon Lady, but don't say I said so. If she's looking after us, we'd better behave. No rude remarks. No bad manners. Last summer, she locked a party of Germans in the hotel until the train came to take them to China. She did not like their uncultured behaviour. So, watch out for her and do what she tells you.'

When she arrived, however, Vinnie greeted her familiarly, and she greeted him in the same way. She summed the rest of us up with a compelling stare.

'*Sain Bainu,*' my sister said, suddenly and quietly.

Madame Densima raised her eyebrows in acknowledgement. '*Sain Bainu,*' she replied, and her back relaxed. Vinnie smiled and winked at my sister, and she seemed childishly pleased. 'It's only a simple greeting,' she explained. 'The more complicated form involves inquiries about your animals and family.' She looked around herself, somewhat awed, it seemed, by Ulan Bator station, by having arrived there at last.

Abel knew the more complicated greeting and joyfully spouted it. Madame Densima's face broke into a smile of utter charm, then quickly resumed its habitual, humourless expression.

'We will go to your hotel,' she said, 'and there we will breakfast.' She marshalled us into a touring coach. The driver of it wore jeans and mirror sunglasses. He was a handsome man, aware of his good looks, and he hung his arms casually over the steering wheel like an actor in a Western. He smiled with amusement at the lumbering, occidental crowd. I noticed how clumsy and pink we looked – like hams.

'They're Indians.' Imogene whispered.

'Not quite!' Abel exclaimed. He began to launch into anthropological detail about Khalkas and Tungus for Imogene's benefit. The driver belonged in no casebook, however. He drove capably and with wide enjoyment of the task. He glanced at us from time to time in his mirror which mirrored his mirror glasses. Some nexus of ironies seemed to possess him, for he continued to be on the point of laughing.

As we bumped about, Madame Densima stood and lectured into a microphone. She dwelt upon the twentieth-century achievements of the city once called Urga. We passed a university, a row of Eastern European embassies, and a supermarket, which had the dismal aspect of a shopping centre launched into outer space and planted on the moon. All the buildings and thoroughfares seemed too big for the small population of the city. Like a doll's house with furniture out of scale, so Ulan Bator looks out of kilter. At length, as we drove into Sukhe Bator Square, this disproportion showed its fullest expression. Indeed, it is hard to think of it as a square at all, as five city blocks could fit comfortably into it. The vast, paved area was almost completely empty. A pillared, rectilinear government building took up a whole side of the square. Madame Densima told us that the blockade-like edifice in front of it was the tomb of the Red Hero, Sukhe Bator, the Liberator. In the centre of this acreage stands a statue of him. He sits astride a rampant horse. The stone limbs of the man and the animal have been put together in such a way that, were they to spring to life, it would be impossible for them to move.

The other sides of the square are flanked by curiously neo-classical buildings, which seem to bear little relationship to the history and culture of the Mongols. Madame Densima said they were put up by Japanese prisoners. She had a cold-blooded way of describing everything, as if she felt angry at having to show us around.

She announced that we were staying at the newly built tourist hotel, and we were driven there forthwith. The Italians murmured against this, because for some reason they had expected to stay at the old Altai Hotel which abuts the square. Madame Densima gave them a murderous look and they were silent.

Like schoolchildren, we debouched from the bus and straggled into the new hotel, a building of no character. We trooped after the ferocious woman, half-relieved to be obedient to her inexorable will.

Everyone was tired and creased by the journey. We had breakfast in a large dining room, sculpted on two tiers like a nightclub in a Hollywood film of the thirties. I sat next to Mathilde, who consumed bread rolls and yoghurt in greedy haste. There was a large blow-fly in my yoghurt. Madame Densima stood on the upper tier of the restaurant like a teacher invigilating an exam.

'You ought to complain about that fly,' Hugh said.

'Sh, the others will be wanting one too!'

'You're cheerful,' said Mathilde. 'In love?'

I turned to her on an impulse to give her news of the happiness that possessed me. Her eyelids half veiled a look of triumphant contempt. I felt I had been up to something smutty. I said nothing.

'I'd just like to be informed if you intend to move in with him for the rest of the trip, that's all,' she said.

'I wouldn't do that sort of thing,' I said, looking at my hands. She left me feeling ashamed and exposed.

'I forgot how principled you are,' she said. 'High-minded.'

'I'm not high-minded.'

'Tell me, what is love to you?' she asked. 'Love between men and women. What do you *think* of it?' She put her elbow on the table and rested her head on her hand, looking at me curiously, as if I were some sort of Martian to whom human sexual experience might be a subject for study in an objective way.

'Mathilde, I have no general thoughts and my own feelings are my business.' I said, I was really angry and I felt spots of colour appearing on my cheekbones.

'Abel is principled too,' she said. 'He refused to "take advantage of me". Isn't that Edwardian? I'm sure you heard all about it. I saw you whispering in the corridor last night.' Her chin trembled and I thought she was about to cry. 'He's a gentleman.' Suddenly, she looked pitiable: an ageing beauty holding the remnants of her femininity about herself like a much-mended gown. In her eyes, there was a subdued terror – as if, being bereft of her power to seduce, she was more naked than the seduction itself would have left her.

'He said nothing about that at all, Matty,' I said gently,

disarmed as I was by her vulnerability. 'He said how sorry he felt for you in your grief over Durrand.'

She winced. 'Durrand,' she said, 'comes to me in dreams.'

I met her gaze with difficulty, because the way she said his name had the powerful aspect of a charm. A prickling, which I dismissed as atavistic, crawled at the back of my neck. 'Tell me,' I said.

She shook it off. Tears squeezed from her eyes. 'You will spend the night with me. You promise? I don't like being alone anymore.'

'I promise,' I said.

There was a great scraping back of chairs. Madame Densima announced that the tour of Ulan Bator was about to begin.

'Everyone is leaving me,' Mathilde said under her breath, 'and everything has changed.'


# Chapter Twenty-one


Madame Densima gave us a whirlwind tour of Ulan Bator, because, she announced, we were to leave the following morning. The weather was about to break, she said, and if we did not take the train to China as soon as possible, it would be likely that we would not be able to take it for at least another week.

Abel sank into his seat and groaned, the Italians erupted into a chattering furore, and Alma began to cry silently. The rest of the party in the coach seemed indifferent to the news. I turned to Mathilde. She simply shook her head. 'We are not going,' she said. 'You'll see. It will not happen.' Her smile had a gnomic look, and her eyes were far away. There was something about her expression that made me feel she had achieved some obscure, personal goal by arriving in Mongolia – a goal without reference to an ostensible purpose.

I squeezed my eyes shut, suddenly more frightened of her than I had ever been before. I spoke to my wave of panic like Canute. Over and over, I assured myself we were going to China and that Mathilde could do nothing to stop it. All of the sudden, China seemed a safe place. It was quite irrational. When we get to China, it won't be able to touch us, I thought. It won't be able to find us in the crowd. I will get her back to London, and I will get professional help for both of us – bell, book and candle, psychiatric help. I don't care. I envisioned great exorcisms in clean, safe English buildings: white-coated, reassuring doctors, black-coated, reassuring priests.

'I don't mind, Mathilde,' I said. 'I don't mind going to China tomorrow the least bit.'

'But you won't go,' she said, smiling. Her tongue poked out, almost serpentine to lick her lips. 'It is meant. I *know*.'

Vinnie took the microphone from Madame Densima and tried to explain in a less cut and dried way that Mongolian weather was not an ordinary conversational topic, but extreme and resistant to modern technology. 'A flood is expected in the Gobi Desert,' he said, 'and the tracks may be washed away if we wait.'

John sat with Abel. I let the warmth from the previous night flood me. It had never struck me before how cold our family had been and how loveless.

We whizzed and bumped round the city. Madame Densima provided an over-voice of correct socialist commentary to all we saw. She excoriated the Chinese and praised the Russians. We lurched past the few remaining landmarks of the old Manchu Dynasty and the former palace of the eighth Jetsumbamba Khutuktu on whose memory our guide heaped loathing; yet somehow the buildings, with their complex pagoda roofs and intricate buttresses, came as a strange relief to the eye in this treeless place with its open spaces and hesitant modern architecture. We heard of the serfdom and thralldom of the past: how the feet of the Lama religion and the Chinese presence had stood on the necks of Mongolians before their liberation.

I thought, We will get out of here and we will go to China and I will be safe and with John, and Mathilde will be safe too.

Encampments of the mushroom tents called yurts were dotted round the city. From time immemorial the nomads would have congregated round this centre; perhaps from the time of Genghis Khan. Madame Densima showed us modern apartment buildings. 'Soon, everyone will have a flat,' she said.

'Does everybody want one?' Alice asked, but the guide let it pass.

We crossed a bridge over a dried river and parked near the War Memorial which was perched on a high hill in the shadow of some low mountains. Some saying or slogan had been carved into the rock in an ancient script. 'We have recently transliterated our language into the Cyrillic alphabet,' said Madame Densima upon being questioned on the meaning of the sign. 'It is more convenient.'

We ascended the steps of the memorial and looked out over the city. Factories belched smoke over the plain. The piercing blue sky had dulled over and threatened rain. The monument was decorated with a mosaic, showing a Mongolian woman presenting a Russian general with a gift on a ceremonial scarf. Madame Densima gave us a bracing description of the gratitude the Mongolian people had to the Soviet people for their help in the march towards socialism; for their support during the war.

I tried to listen to the buzz of argument and commentary. All I could do was to watch the darkening weather nervously. 'We're going to China,' I said to John. 'We are.'

Abel was courting Madame Densima with phrase-book Mongolian and smiles. A wind was getting up and it whipped my skirt around my knees. 'Do you think we'll get away tomorrow?' I asked John. 'The weather can't change that fast, can it?' We both looked at Mathilde, who was standing alone at the edge of the high memorial, lost in contemplation of the plain below.

'The Gobi Desert is five hundred miles away,' he said. 'So we can't know.'

'She knows. She says she *knows* we are not going,' I said. 'She can't know.'

'What frightens you about staying?'

'I have no idea.'

We went to visit a ceremonial yurt in the old Altai hotel, which smelt of rancid mutton fat. Russians were drinking vodka or tea in the lobby. The yurt had been erected on the top floor. Going to see it reminded me of visits to Santa Claus in Hutzler's department store when I was a child. Muriel and her German boyfriend were quarrelling about the war. Something was going on between them about the war. There was an exchange of glittering looks and hostile reactions as we sat in the tent on its lacquered furniture. The guide told us how swiftly the tent could be erected and dismantled. How convenient it was in the Mongolian weather. My sister stayed behind for a few moments, stroking the red-gold furniture with her hands, dreaming. I thought to myself, This is a genuinely interesting place, and why shouldn't she want to stay?

Over lunch, we sat with Madame Densima and ate tough mutton and the interminable cucumber salad. The guide had somewhat softened. She sat between Alma and Abel who had plied her the entire morning with educated questions. As we sat, Alma whispered in a dither of excitement that she had wrested a promise from Madame Densima that we would see the Gandan Monastery after lunch. 'I think it's really noble of her, considering her feelings about Lamaism,' said Alma, and cast an admiring glance at the guide

Mathilde seemed lost, isolated in her own thoughts. Suddenly, she interrupted the conversation without any apparent reason. 'What are the Mongolian customs for the burial of the dead?' she asked.

There was a silence at our table. 'Burial customs?' asked Madame Densima.

'Yes. I want to know about them.'

The guide's olive face flushed.

'It is not rudeness,' said Alma. 'We are all so interested to know about everything in your country. It is not rudeness in the West to ask.'

'We follow the Russian customs now,' said Madame Densima. Alma shot Mathilde a look. 'The old customs were as in Tibet. They were a little gruesome. "Gruesome"? Is that right?' she asked Alma, suddenly pleased with the word. When Alma nodded, it seemed to change her mood entirely. 'The old Buddhist way,' she continued, launching in, 'was to dismember a body and leave it for the vultures. That way nothing is wasted.'

'It is a mark of humility to do that,' Alma added.

'Hah!' said the guide. Nonetheless, she looked obscurely proud of something she was supposed to consider barbarous.

'Thank you,' said Mathilde curtly and devoured her meat without looking up from the plate again.

And I remembered that 'Durrand' had said, *There is no burial place for me*.

I began to count on the morning train to Peking like an article of faith.

Religion, Madame Densima advised us through the bus microphone, was the opiate of the people and a nasty one too. Correct in her zeal to keep us informed, she gave us a run-down of the Mongolian people's grievance against the lamas: their former wealth; the way they packed the lamaseries by taking a son from every family; their unscrupulous habits; the fear they promoted of demons, and their unchastity. Nevertheless, she gave Alma the opportunity to make some of her own comments and we heard how Tibetan Buddhism had come to Mongolia during the reign of Kublai Khan. A learned lecture followed as we approached the only remaining monastery in the country. It was set at the top of a gentle slope, lined with some long slogan or other written in red Cyrillic letters. No one bothered to construe it. I became fearful of seeing Durrand as shadow behind the billboards, but I shook the notion off. We entered through an imposing gate where there stood a complex of temples. To the far left of the compound, there was the painted statue of a lama in a yellow peaked cap. It had stopped raining. There appeared to be some religious ceremony in progress, for from the door of one of the temples came a low hum of voices. There was a stone censer outside alight with incense. Madame Densima neatly shuddered away from such goings-on, but indicated we might enter. Quite a number of Mongolians made their way into the temple, men, women and children. Everyone passed his or her hat through the incense smoke as they entered. I wanted very much to go in. Alma made a gesture of reverence, and it was clear she was deeply moved.

The sanctuary was full of people who crowded round the door. We all jostled a little. In front of us were rows of monks facing each other across a central aisle. They were wearing greasy saffron robes and they chanted from well-worn texts of scripture, which they tied and untied from grubby satchels of silk cloth. The bass recitation of prayer, deep to the point of growling, made an unceasing drone. One of the monks, whom I took to be the abbot, was seated on a raised dais; none of them took any notice of us or the other spectators. From time to time, the faithful in spontaneous bursts made circumambulations around the reposeful backs of the monks. All along the back and sides of the room were little statues which the Mongolians seemed to venerate. We ourselves started the circum-ambulation respectfully and on tiptoe. A monk entered with a huge teapot and started pouring a strange smelling liquid into bowls. Abel whispered that it was boiled brick tea made with yak butter and salt, and one of the tourists suppressed a titter. The monks did not interrupt their chanting except to take small sips of the steaming tea: they continued the same deep, harsh muttering until by the force of its hypnotic effect and the animal smell of the tea, and the crowd, it became impossible not to be drawn into relationship with the chanters themselves.

It was as if they formed words and unformed words with their lips in a sequence which was unending. The closing of their lips around the words and the releasing of the lips from the words was of equal importance. Their mouths seemed to empty and fill with the scripture from a source beneath themselves, so that the source seemed to come both from the self and not from the self. Not beautiful, the chant was abounding. It gave the feeling of the sea, guttural on stones, bounding and rebounding. It made a point about pointlessness and then unmade it. The heads of the monks were shaven, their faces made coarse by harsh weather. Whether they expressed reality or unreality, they went on.

I looked around me and saw the crowd had thinned. The other tourists had disappeared, and John was nowhere to be seen. My sister was leaning on the door post, watching me. When I caught her eye, she shrugged and went out into the courtyard. I felt at peace in the temple and was not even afraid of her intense gaze.

For some reason, I started thinking about how I had seen myself pass myself, how I had met myself going out of the house when I was entering the house, and of John and his goings and comings across the globe. Something in this foreign ritual gave expression and shape to the experience of being myself and not myself; I wondered if I could finally know John and give him what I was and was not.

A couple with a baby came in to seek a blessing, then a soldier. They walked around the motionless beings in dirty saffron robes. The monks were not chanting about anything. They were in and of themselves the chant. In a perilous moment, I passed beyond the growling prayers into an emptiness – the unvoiced void the singers served, where truth left truth and floated bodiless, and being and illusion clashed, confused.

The monks unwrapped and wrapped the texts. I looked at the curious crooks and scrolls of the lettering. All at once, the abbot smiled at me. I felt a kind of interview was over, but I had no knowledge then of what it presaged.

# Chapter Twenty-two

The courtyard of the Gandan Monastery has an association I would prefer to forget. The irony is that in the course of writing this account of what led up to my sister's death, I find that there is no forgetting. I am not forgetful. I have not forgotten anything, and what is more, I will not be able in the future to forget.

The memory of the courtyard must be remembered: is remembered no matter what it signifies.

I could not have thought that first day in Ulan Bator that the monastery compound, washed by the recent rain, could ever be anything but peaceful. When I stepped out into the pale sunlight, I could see no sign of the others. A drum-like prayer wheel stood to one side of the temple, and prayers, written on strips of cloth, fluttered in the breeze. An old man was sitting on a bench against a sheltering wall. He was soaking up what little sun there was. He motioned me to join him and I did. He smiled and gave me a little gift: a grainy, brown substance, wrapped up in a screw of paper. I did not know what it was, but I thanked him all the same.

Oh, my mind goes round like the drum of the prayer wheel. There is truth and there is illusion. There is the illusion of truth and the truth of illusion. But when are we *able* to choose those things we cannot properly discern?

Suddenly, a number of children gathered around me and the old man. They came in from a yurt encampment sited next to the monastery; they arrived like birds in response to a hidden signal. The little girls were spotlessly clean and wore their black hair in pony tails trimmed with huge, stiff bows. The little boys looked like tom cats. One of the girls put her hand out and gently touched me. She took her hand away and nodded to herself as if in solemn agreement with herself that I was, after all, real.

John arrived. He stood laughing in front of me and the children.

'Where is everybody?' I asked.

'There's another building, full of gold Buddhas,' he said. 'There's a wonderful Alpine horn, about twenty feet long.'

'Come on,' he said, 'I hear some music.' And indeed, there was a clash of cymbals and the groaning, whining noise of horns coming from within the temple. He took my hand, and we entered again. The abbot stood in the aisle dividing the monks. He held a shallow bowl, and from it he flung handfuls of grain onto the floor. There was the noise of shawms and a flock of birds flew from the rafters and ate the grain.

Rooted there together by this sight, we hardly heard the honking of the bus.

'I think you should avoid her,' he said as we went down the steps. 'I think you must.'

'I promised her. I promised her this morning I would stay with her. She is so frightened.'

'You gave your word?'

'Yes.'

'You mustn't forget last night.'

'Could I?'

'She would *make* you forget,' he said.

'Not any longer.' A sudden huge love leapt up after him.

'That's all right then,' he said, but he looked doubtful.

'I must finish telling you about Durrand,' Mathilde said on the bus.

The sky again had become a pea-soup colour. There was lightning and an ear-splitting crash of thunder. The heavens opened, and we were drenched as we ran into the hotel.

'Mathilde,' I said, 'I don't think we should talk about Durrand. I think we should talk about you.'

Our room overlooked a parking lot without cars. We were unpacking a few light things with a view to packing them up again the following morning. She took the smuggled icon out of her handbag and stood it for a moment on the bedside table. The gold and tawny Saviour flashed out, illuminating the plainly furnished room. Mathilde stared at the painting. She peeled off her wet clothes and stood in her slip. Suddenly, she began to wail. 'But I am talking about myself! Those people compromised me as well as Durrand!'

She sat on her bed and started to weep, then she stopped. Her hands were toiling around each other.

'I'm trying to understand,' I said. I kept thinking there must be some sort of clinic I could take her to in London. Maybe John would know a good doctor. I put my arm around her shoulder, but she twitched it off.

She said, 'You can never understand what there was between us. No one ever can.' She was silent for a while. 'They murdered Durrand. They compromised me and then they murdered him.'

She sat very still. Her voice ran up to a pitch, 'They took him back to Paris and they pushed him under a train. They pushed him under a train and got everyone to lie about what had happened!'

I did not know what to do. I said, 'Mathilde, I think you should perhaps confront them with this when you get home. We are not without means and together we could investigate this terrible thing.'

She said, 'They pushed him, and they have covered their tracks. There is no one to talk to. No one.'

'Well,' I said quietly, 'there is the bishop, I guess. I mean, if something as dreadful as that is even suggested of a religious order, the bishop would certainly want to know about it. Don't you think?'

She had the crafty look of the mad. 'I won't talk to any bishop. I'll never enter a church or an ecclesiastical building ever again. They killed Durrand. All of them. All are responsible. All.'

'Matty,' I said. 'Dear Matty. Maybe you are right. Maybe you should avoid such upsetting places. When we get back, I will see the bishop. Why don't I see him? I'm sure he would see me.'

'You,' she said, and laughed.

'Matty, I'm not so stupid as you think, and I have never been.' I regretted the emotion in my voice.

'No one ever thought you were stupid, Irene. You're a *fox*!' she said. 'Foxy, foxy. You're very foxy and you always were. You always *knew*. But you can't get the better of me.'

'Mathilde, I never could get the better of you. You know that. You know how clever you are. Always were the smartest in the family – you.' My words were edging round now as we spoke, edging round to get by her. She looked gratified when I said she had been the brightest in the family. Then, she looked into the middle distance again with no expression at all on her face.

'They killed him, and there is no justice,' she said.

'Mathilde, why – did they kill him?' I began to think in desperation that if only I could get her back to her narrative, she would return to some semblance of logical thought.

'Oh, isn't it obvious? Well, I suppose I'd better spell it out. They killed him because he was inconvenient to them, that's all. It's completely clear to me, anyway. He knew too much for them to let him go.

'It was only after that terrible dinner party that I realized what I must do. I realized more than I ever realized anything that I had to get Durrand out of that place forever. But how was I to do it? What was I to do? They had no telephone number I could call, and even if I could have called them, they would certainly not have let me get through to Durrand. I thought of a friend. Maybe I could get a friend to . . . but, I *had* no friends. I realized for the first time in my life that I had no friends to turn to.

'At last, I set up a watch – all by myself – outside the door of that house. I watched it day and night. I went without food or sleep. No one came out of the house. I kept thinking if the servant came out, I could smuggle in a message; but day turned into night and night to day and no one emerged. Finally, it occurred to me that there must be a back door. I circled the house until I found the bolted gate of a garage. There was a wall, and over the wall was a garden. I could not watch both doors at the same time. Taking a huge risk, I divided up my time between the two look-outs; and this, and this' – her voice rose and rose – 'was my undoing. Just as I was changing places, just as I was approaching the rear entrance, I noticed that the gate was open. A large limousine nosed out. I ran. And there he was. Wedged between Victor and Georges, his face was waxen with exhaustion and fright. I screamed, "Durrand! Durrand!" and in a moment, his face turned to me and our eyes met. "Durrand!" I shrieked. "They're going to kill you! Run! Make a run for it!" I gained the car, but, with a look of complete contempt, Victor motioned the chauffeur on and I was left completely on my own, standing there in the rain. It was the last time I saw him. I will never, never, forgive them.'

She and I were silent for a long time. 'Oh, Mathilde,' I said at last, 'that is a dreadful story.'

She looked at me as if a fly buzzed. 'Yes,' she said. 'Yes, it is.' She gave an ironic laugh. 'Of course, they took him back to Paris from there. You can't tell me that those whited sepulchres were going to let their reputation suffer. Not one whit. Oh no, not they. They weren't going to let themselves in for any exposure in the press – not they with their duchesses and mandarin airs. What they did, they did neatly, I am sure. I am sure they arranged the whole thing to look like a martyrdom. How they did it, I am not at all sure. What did they do? Did they lead him out into the snow and push him? Or did they drug him first and then do it. Maybe they got him drunk. Who knows? All I know is that they made away with him.'

I said, 'Oh, Matty.' I could not help but feel sorry for her.

'And you! You heard him die! In your head.'

I said, 'No.' I heard my voice saying, 'no, no, no!' But

my attention was elsewhere. I felt the breeze of Durrand's entry into the room.

'I'm going to get a drink!' she said suddenly. 'Would you like a drink?'

I shook my head. She got up, went to the bathroom, fetched a glass and swivelled the top off of a bottle of Mongolian vodka she had bought at the Friendship store. She poured a good measure and drank it.

'I want him back,' she said. There was an odd, fleshy look about her face. It was pallid and moon-shaped: heavy. 'Because nothing is more important to me than Durrand. Nothing. And I did not *know* it!'

'But you can't get him back,' I said. 'He's dead. Mathilde, you must accept that he is dead – really is, otherwise you'll never get better.'

*There you are, you did it! Liar, Liar!* I heard the voice, this time, outside of my head, a footfall by the window and the creak of a chair.

I watched Mathilde's face, but I realized she had not heard the voice.

'Oh God! Irene! Leave me in peace!' she cried.

I could not overmaster my intense fright. I had my face in my hands, hoping that she would not see how terrified I was.

'Get out of here!' she said.

And I felt the presence in the room as a negative density compelling me towards the door. Without thinking, I found my hand on the knob.

# Chapter Twenty-three

He will follow me, I thought, because it's true. I am the only one who can hear him, and he cannot reach Mathilde without me. I slipped from the room, leaving her there, and ran down the stairs out of the hotel into the gathering evening.

When I reached Sukhe Bator Square, I stopped. Alone, in the empty space, I gave vent to the cry uppermost in my throat. 'It's all my fault! It's all my fault! I am the one. Let it be me!'

The air, freshened by the rain, hit my senses. There was a sombre, clear light in the square. I looked around me. There were only a few people around, but even they were at a great distance and milled about the government building at the far end. Otherwise, I seemed to be by myself.

'She doesn't understand what she did to you,' I said. 'She doesn't know who you are. She doesn't know you are here. She cannot be blamed because she does not understand what she did. I will sacrifice myself if it will make you go away!'

Once I had loosed these words into the air, I began to think I had squandered them. I clenched my mind in my will and made myself reason. What could the ominous sound in the hotel, the sense of breeze, the voice of Durrand be, if I were not insane and if I were not having an epileptic fit? Surely Mathilde's story and her powerful feelings could have produced, on their own, this delusion which I had accepted with such credulity. I walked towards the improbable statue of the Red Hero in the middle of the square, and then took shelter against an evening breeze that made me shiver. Large pools of rain stood about in the bumpy asphalt underneath the stone warrior. A truck went by, and an elderly couple out for a stroll stared at me, then went on.

'But we're going to China tomorrow,' I said aloud.

Caught and bathed in the early evening light, I began to see something. No. I began to see that we were not going to China the following day. It was simple enough. It came to me, dawned on me.

'I am not and I won't be clairvoyant,' I said. The realization that we were not going to China serenely reasserted itself.

'Suppose we don't go to China,' I said to God. 'Where are you and what shall I do?' And I broke down in tears underneath the statue. 'Who is Durrand?' I asked, 'and why am I afflicted with him? Is it the devil? Am I really possessed by the devil?' I was silent for a moment. 'Is *Durrand* the devil?' I asked.

It is hard to explain what I knew about Durrand then. It was as if I had a brief, inner vision of what 'he' was trying to achieve. There 'he' was: the imponderable foot, wedged in the door of my consciousness, 'What sort of faith must I have to endure this?' I asked. 'What sort of faith do you require from me? Blind naked trust?' I was overwhelmed by a wish to die rather than hear Durrand another moment.

I heard no voice, but a suggestion came seductive on the air, that in the split second of my seizure the night he died, Durrand had slipped in a crack and had fed and grown like a ghastly pregnancy so that at last he had come to maturation and found entity in air. I said the Lord's Prayer. 'I won't and I'm not and I won't and I'm not,' I said afterwards, but I didn't really know what I meant that I would not do.

I decided it was time to go back to the hotel. I felt a little better and it was beginning to get dark. On the way, standing in front of a public building, was a large statue of Stalin. I hadn't noticed it before. His face was stern; yet on it was a smile of smug self-satisfaction. His chest protruded, and everything about the statue seemed to proclaim the rightness of all his works.

I knew that some cruelty was prepared for me, foreshadowed in that smile, and I huddled into myself against the chill and the dusky premonition that one of us, either Mathilde or I, would not get to China alive.

As soon as I entered the lobby, I saw that something had happened. The other tourists were assembled around Vinnie and Madame Densima. There was an air of consternation and a babble of voices. Some were clutching their tickets and others were holding onto their manners uncertainly.

Mathilde stood on the periphery of the group with Abel. 'Where were you?' she asked.

'I went out for some air.'

'The train to China has been delayed indefinitely,' she said. 'The Gobi Desert has flooded and Madame Densima says it is impossible to say when we can leave here. It might be a week or more. See, I told you so.'

And so, the cruelty had come. 'What about an airplane?'

'Mongolia has no diplomatic relations with China and they adamantly refuse to fly us out. They can't get permission to land at Peking airport.'

'Surely they can. Surely.'

'Apparently not,' Abel said.

I looked for John's face in the crowd, but I could not see him. I was possessed by a longing for him so extreme that it caused me physical pain. I could not account for the strength of the feeling or the intensity with which I sensed him seeking me as I sought him. It was as if his name, John, were a misnomer, as if it were a mere title of address beneath which there was another name inexpressible but known to me, and a ferocious, but inexplicable certainty about him made me tremble. I loved him with a kind of rage.

In the time since, I have asked myself whether I would have remained in darkness about my brother if John had not come in the door at that moment; for as soon as I felt the power of his presence, I saw Durrand.

How can I explain it or contain it? It must have happened in the space it took John to cover the distance across the lobby to me, but it seemed to be in another configuration of time altogether so that every detail is fresh to me.

Durrand was sitting in an obscure corner near the reception desk. He was waiting. I was swept by horror, and on reflection I believe this mainly came from the very ordinariness of his apparition. He wore no cloak; had no transparency. There was only the look of something shaded – something almost right but not quite right about him – that distinguished him from the living. Durrand was wearing a dark suit, and his cuffs gleamed especially white; in them, nestled our father's cufflinks, gemstones of a dull character set in gold. He seemed to sit in the gloom out of some predilection for it – this was my first reaction – because his eyes looked sore. On closer inspection, however, I saw that Durrand created the odd darkness around him and the chair in which he sat, and the potted plant under which he sat, so that the whole corner of the room seemed funnelled into the depth of shade by him: as if he extracted light from the atmosphere in order to be made visible.

As I say, his eyes looked sore. He did not glance at me, nor, precisely, at Mathilde. He sat in the attitude of one waiting, not unlike anybody else who waits for the arrival of an acquaintance in an hotel lobby. His hands were curiously folded and dangling between his knees, yet his body was erect. He looked exhumed, new-born from death, but not of the resurrection. Although he resembled nothing in nature, he was something like a new-hatched moth emergent from its chrysalis, its wings creased and damp. And yet for all of this, he looked as if he might very well open a newspaper, rustle it straight, and read it there in the lobby.

When the apparition gathered that I had seen it, it opened its mouth to speak. '*Tick . . . Tock,*' it said. It recomposed its face, then, in an immense blackness, it seemed to fold into itself and it was gone.

The vision of Durrand left me in abeyance. It was as if I had stepped into another catchment area of time where I was shocked for a moment on the barriers before I could return. It was as if linear time had rushed into the cavity of my apparent absence from it, gathered me up and thrown me on a shore where everything was jumbled and meaningless, in one sense. In another sense, I felt completely lucid. Coming down gently from the experience, I felt an overwhelming disgust at the image I had seen. More than anything, his voice filled me with loathing. It had had the rustling sound of beetles' wings, whirring near my face.

241

Why I knew that the spectre could not endure under the influence of John, is as yet unclear to me, but my awareness was acute that the moment his arm encircled me, it was bound to disappear, and indeed had disappeared as he had touched me. It was as if the configuration Durrand represented could not withstand him; and so I stood extremely puzzled both at the vision and its antidote.

'I've been looking for you everywhere,' he said.

I felt a complete sense of calm descend upon me, as if the irrational moment had made some ulterior sense like a bizarre painting made without rules which nonetheless one sees as having unity. I felt almost privileged that I had witnessed an obscure truth, but when I opened my mouth to speak, I found I could not say a word and I was pitched into an uncontrollable fit of shivering. The tourists were starting to go into dinner. The noise of their wrangling had subdued.

'I told you we weren't going to China,' Mathilde said.

I looked at her and at the corner of the room which the phantom had occupied. There was a deep look on her face, a deep look in her eyes. It was a mad, covert look, not hostile nor inimical to me, but knowing and oddly corrupt. It was her expression which-pierced me with a shaft: the spectre seemed to occupy her temples and her cheeks as if it had wrapped itself around her. 'What's the matter?' she asked.

'I think I caught a chill.'

John looked narrowly at Mathilde – a fleeting look that only grazed her. She shrugged it off like a horse shuddering a flank.

'We will get your cardigan,' he said.

In the elevator, he held me and breathed on me with animal warmth. He touched me with a sure gift of love. My teeth were chattering. 'I saw it,' I said. My face was muffled in his chest. I could hear each stroke of his heart. 'I saw the ghost of my brother Durrand.' As we ascended, I felt him absorb this news, taking it into himself and making it his own, as if he needed to know it and wanted to have it. 'Shh,' he said.

242

The elevator stopped. In front of the room, I fumbled with the key, but when it turned the wards of the lock, I found I could not open the door. In the moment I had lost my reason, I had been able to understand the vision as a kind of gift. Now that my reason returned, I was overwhelmed by a heavy turbulence of mind and I was filled with dread both that Durrand walked and that John was humouring me as a lunatic.

John turned the handle of the door and went in. Although the room was neat, the light seemed wrenched about by Durrand's traces. I was filled with revulsion not at the memory of the spirit this time, but at myself for having seen it.

'It is my fault,' I said. 'I have brought this whole thing about.'

'Because you can see what other people cannot see?'

He hung his head over my suitcase, picked up little things of mine tenderly and then replaced them.

'I am the unhappy medium,' I said, and started to laugh uncontrollably. 'And an unwilling one. I don't even believe in such things. It's against my own will that I see such things . . .'

'It's not against hers, though. Don't you see?' John said.

'She wants me to call him up – to call up his spirit.'

'And so you did.' He turned on me with ferocity, his hair fiery, his eyes dancing.

'I said, "Take me instead of her." And shortly after that, I saw him.'

'You idiot –' he said. 'You did forget. You forgot last night.'

'I thought you understood,' I said in tears.

'I understand you are being used,' he said. Then softly, his hand fell on my shoulder. 'But you won't be used by me. And you *mustn't* allow her to use you again.'

I spent myself against that sweated night in the vice of conflict. It was as if my own internal contents had been pulled from my mind and strewn about the bed in complete disorder. What elements were there? Into what had I

243

fragmented? On the one hand, there had been John, implacable during dinner, sitting across from me, eyeing me with something more critical than ardour; on the other hand, there had been Mathilde who swayed me with pity like a tree in the wind. She sort of gnawed on her meat, chewing it with her mouth partly open. She resembled a child or a very old person whose manners have become dishevelled out of some disdain for life. She looked both vacant and poisoned. Was she a person whose emptiness and toxicity had caused me to be avatar for Durrand? Was that correct? Was I the carrier? Or was she?

I went to bed early, pleading illness; she came to bed a long time after and I pretended to be asleep. She sat at the window, looking out of it and smoking while I prickled at not knowing what to do. I knew that I was willing to sacrifice anything to resolve the dilemma, but I had no inkling of what was required. Should I connect them? Should I connect her with what she so earnestly desired? Connect 'him' with what 'he' so urgently wanted? Or had I already in my person made this connection? That idea came upon me with a brutal force that hammered and bruised my conscience until freshly I came upon the opposing view that chained me to the mast of myself for a while and kept me from leaping out of bed and destroying myself: that what I could see was not of necessity what I was.

As the night progressed, I became numb in the toils of it. If sleep came for a moment, it would leave me staring wide awake, on the rebound from fitful dreams. What was I to do but get her to China? And how could I do that when the train would not come. At length, driven to slump against the slippery walls of thought I could not scale, I hunched into my consciousness in a final heap of resignation. For, around two or three in the morning, it seemed to me that my own death was imminent and that Durrand was its angel.

# Chapter Twenty-four

When day broke this morning over my eyelids, I opened them from sleep to a fresh and glittering knowledge that I saw him whom I sought, though darkly, and that I seek him and see him still. They no longer play brides in Ashby Street; where the whim of nature has produced wild flowers in the lush long grass of the untrimmed backyards, there is no one left to gather, twine and enrobe the bride with daisies or blossom – or even the odd rose purloined from the tended gardens. Children these days are severe in preparation for another sort of life.

I am the bride. After all these Lenten years, my Easter is prepared for me. I neither prepared for it nor expected it to come. I had no way of knowing I would dawn and become myself, no idea that I was given when conceived for this purpose. All the while I hid myself away, I was being found, and as I disguised myself I was divulged. When I doubted most I was believed, when running was confronted.

I sense him in the night in the released power of honeysuckle. I know him as inaudible music and as imageless beauty. When he comes, I will know the day and the hour and I will be dressed to greet him. It was I who had locked and bolted the door and called it integrity; I who chose a withering virginity from a terror of love; I who regularly told myself that the ordered ritual life I led was obedience, and I who built my own sepulchre – a narrow place where I conceived all goodness to consist in the avoidance of seizures and of sin. How I needed my perilous sister to keep me in that childlike state where none of these things could be challenged! And how I needed Durrand too to mock and control my heart so that I never needed to risk it! I neither deserved epilepsy nor did not deserve it. I cloaked myself in it and despised it, because I never saw a way in which the malady itself might transform me.

I wait now in stillness for John. There is no more seeping dread of Durrand. Although I tried to reason with myself, the queasy apprehension of my immolation in him did not vanish with that morning in Ulan Bator. I can only recollect now what was blurred and not completely evident then, but out of the corner of my eye, I felt somehow I was to be sacrificed like Andromeda on a rock.

'I must. I must do it,' I said to myself. 'I have to go instead of her, because I will never tell her about Durrand and she will never know.' Yet, each time I said it, I felt an active, purposeful loneliness invade my being.

'John can't understand it, he wouldn't understand it, he doesn't know,' I woodenly and with futile heart repeated. 'The ghost has come for me.'

Day followed day and night followed night. Still, the train did not come. Time seemed stretched taut as the skin over a drum and little incidents rebounded off of it, causing in my mind a series of unconnected resonances. My conviction that I had been predestined to die rose and built itself like a wall around me. As if I were in a sealed truck, bumping off to some place of execution, I resigned myself. I was dragged along an unknown route and pulled from my moorings.

I began to drift through time and no longer lived by the clock. The light in the room Mathilde and I shared took on a grainy, grey quality, whatever the hour. I washed and lay down; I got up and washed. I joined my lips around a glass or a cup without knowing what I was drinking. Arguments with myself about the phantom ceased. I no longer cared whether or not it had a true existence; the important thing seemed to be that I had seen it, and minute by minute, the cruelty sank in that whatever it was I had seen had waited to appear until I had fallen in love with

246

someone who loved me in return. As for John, he became silent and watchful. With pang after pang, I felt I betrayed him with my withdrawal. Wherever we went, he kept close by me, but my hand was listless. It was borne on me again and again that the vision of unholiness I had seen made me unfit for his clasp or touch.

Mathilde, on the other hand, seemed to become more sprightly every day. She was delighted that we were stranded in Mongolia. As if expectant of pleasure, she chatted away now to the various members of the group who were enjoying what the hospitality of the government had to offer them. She wasn't merry — she was excited.

We visited the king's palace where four colossal statues of guardian demons loomed about the entrance. Inside, there was a gold Buddha sensitively carved, as though entranced. We went to a carpet factory and watched a woollen rug advance over a loom. We picnicked in the countryside. Madame Densima caused a goat to be slaughtered and roasted whole for us. We sat on the grass and awaited the feast like a convention at a barbecue. I could not eat. After the lunch, our driver brought out a sturdy little pony and led the various tourists about on its back. Myra Bedrosian and Mathilde, Abel and Imogene rode the animal, but I sat still amid the ruins of the meal.

'Irene, I love you. Please speak to me,' John said. My sister, astride the horse, was being led around in circles by the driver while Abel pronounced on its resemblance to the primeval beast.

I looked through the cage of my responsibility to die and ignored John's remark. Sitting on the lush grass of the hills where we had been driven, I leaned against his shoulder. I did not care if I exposed myself before the others. They drank Mongolian beer and soda pop. I felt acutely the weave of his shirt on my cheek.

'What is going on?' John asked me, a little sharply.

'It's hard to say, really,' I answered. Before us lay pristine countryside. Strange, rounded rocks dotted the landscape.

A crowd of horsemen appeared on the hillside, stood for a tremulous moment and then were gone. Tears kept oozing from my eyes, but I made no attempt to dry them.

'He's not going to get you,' said John. 'I am.'

'What do you mean?' I didn't want to tell him what I thought.

'I mean I *will* win against Durrand, whether *she* wants me to or not!'

I said nothing, revealed nothing. It was as if somewhere beyond the sunrise, the sunset, the leaving of the hotel on the bus, the re-arriving at the hotel on the bus, the walks round Ulan Bator, the peering at sights, the consulting of watches, the chatter at dinner, the revenant had fixed me in its jaws, and I could move neither backwards nor forwards from the moment of his clenching.

My sister dismounted from the pony and made her way up the little hill were we sat. 'I enjoyed that,' she said. 'I haven't ridden in years.'

I said nothing.

We returned to Ulan Bator in silence.

Still, I waited. Nothing happened. I sensed that Durrand was not far, but he was silent.

Mathilde got drunk every night, evenly and steadily, without making a spectacle of herself. She left the story of his latter days, and began to talk confusedly of when Durrand was a child. She talked about games they had played together. She talked about a fabulous land she had invented where they had limitless adventure; how once he had wanted to be Superman and had tried to jump out of the window; how she had dared him to eat mud pie.

I remembered the time he had pushed a heavy thorn in my flesh to punish me for wetting myself. I remembered him saying 'let's play Bible stories' once and his taking my best doll and his whanging it against the bedstead. 'There,' he said, 'I'm Herod.' And he laughed. I said nothing. I said nothing to Mathilde at all, but only listened.

The night we returned from the picnic, Madame Densima had us served with koumis, a drink made of fermented mare's milk. Vinnie whispered to everyone that it would cause great offence not to drink it. By this time, people were taking no notice of Vinnie and someone said out loud that the koumis was disgusting.

The group had become fractious with the delay and had split into factions. Those who wanted to go to China started to dislike those who were happy to stay in Mongolia. Some had even tried to charter a plane, but the weather, according to Madame Densima, was impossible. A few disbelieved her and muttered darkly about the political situation. Madame Densima regally ignored all insults. Alma and Abel earnestly begged for more koumis and looked reprovingly at the surrounding tables.

I drank without knowing what I was drinking and ate without knowing what I was eating. I noted in an abstracted way that the guide and Alma had struck up a curious kind of friendship; they were talking in a spirited fashion about the Tibetan *Book of the Dead*. Alma recited passages from it in a subdued but moving tone of voice, describing small arcs in the air with her silvery hand. She detailed the soul's progress after death; the various stages of joy at being released from the bonds of flesh; horror at being confronted with the image of demons; the struggle required to maintain integrity before them, and the final arrival at reincarnation or Nirvana.

I wanted to burst out crying and tell everyone at the table what was happening to me. Instead, I sipped at the koumis, then pushed it away in case it befuddled me into revealing what I knew I should not.

A little smile quivered at the corners of Madame Densima's mouth. Her complexion was the colour of flushed gold. Her expression made a graceful but critical comment on Alma's throbbing enthusiasm. Like a calligraphic quirk, her black brow etched the picture of a woman whose thoughts on most matters were entirely her own.

Suddenly, Mathilde got up abruptly and left the table. It was a queer, jerky action. She looked like someone who has heard the summons of a distant telephone. As if there had been a chain joining our legs, I found myself moving after her. John's hand clamped my shoulder.

'Madame Densima,' he said, 'I am taking Irene out to look at the stars. I have read they are very beautiful here.'

She looked a little roguish from the koumis. 'You can only really see them in the Gobi,' she said, 'but never mind.'

I felt disoriented. He propelled me through the lobby past a group of Mongolians who were watching a Russian circus on the television, and we were out in the night under the oceanic sky, heavy with stars.

We walked aimlessly and in silence for a while and at length we arrived at the little bridge which crossed the river bed, now sluggishly full of the recent rains. Despite the stars, it was very dark. The moon had not yet arisen.

'Irene,' he said, 'are you offering yourself to Durrand?' His voice cut across my confusion, and revived me in a part of my ear which had been deafened.

'You're afraid to tell me, aren't you?'

I was so torn in my mind that I went from one side of the bridge to the other, back again and forward, clutching the rails and looking into the dark water beneath. Was he tempting me or was Durrand? What would happen to Mathilde if I told him? What would happen to me if I did not? A dissonant babble of distant Sunday sermons, of ill-digested pieties from books imparted nothing to me but further complication. What was the right and Christ-like thing to do? How could I choose when the choice was invisible? What path could I take when both were occluded?

He looked at me vividly. I could see his eye glittering.

'Pity me,' I said.

'I won't,' he replied. 'You don't love him more than me. You do not.'

I put my hands to my ears, and shook my head from side to side, and I started to cry.

All at once, there was the sound of a loudly cleared throat, and I jumped with the shock of it. Imogene Holt emerged from the darkness; she was walking briskly over the bridge from the direction of a yurt encampment which nestled in the hills above the city. I could barely make out their dome shapes above us in the dark.

'I have just been calling on the nicest family,' she said, as if no time had elapsed between this and previous conversations and as if she had not seen John and me exercising our madness in the dark. 'I made friends with the chambermaid at the hotel and she invited me to see her yurt. Her family gave me a gift. Wasn't that sweet of them?' And she extracted a little figurine from her handbag: a bronze god with many arms. 'Well, I won't keep you all,' she said. 'Good night.'

We stood on the bridge in silence and watched her go. The stars cast no shadows around us.

'Tell me,' he said. 'Do you think my love is a trivial thing? Why do you think you have it?'

I looked at him and though I could barely see him, I knew every aspect of his features as if by heart – as if, word by word, a psalm. I knew him as if he had been spoken to me, articulated not to my ear but to my being. As Durrand was perceived, so he was not.

'We do not know each other,' I said, contradicting what I had sensed. I caught from him a glint of deep reproach that I shall never forget, but what I had offended and whom, by my denial, I did not understand.

I thought deeply for a few moments. 'I am sorry,' I said. 'That isn't true.'

'We will marry,' he said.

'If I survive,' I cried out. The sound of my voice carried wild and muffled across the water.

I thought he would be angry. Instead, we became enfolded in each other, so that for a moment, there seemed no real difference between us. 'If you survive,' he said, curiously, 'I will. And you will.'

When I returned to the hotel, Mathilde was sitting alone. Her eyes seemed fixed on a point somewhere near the window. She was smiling crookedly and had been drinking vodka. She seemed deeply preoccupied by a pleasant thought.

'Tell me,' she said with sottish amiability. 'What do you think ought to be done to murderers? Do you think they should be executed or not?'

'I don't believe in executions,' I said.

'You believe in mercy. Hmmm!' she said.

'I do.'

'That is a truly Christian attitude,' she said. She took the little icon of Christ out of her pocket. 'This is supposed to embody the merciful Saviour,' she said. 'Do you think it is a fake?'

The picture, tiny as it was, exuded freshness and vigour. 'I don't think so,' I said, 'but you're the expert.'

'You don't think it's a fake? That's all I wanted to know,' she said. She did not speak for a long time, then suddenly, as if it explained everything, she said, 'I have no means. I have no means.'

# Chapter Twenty-five

My rigid watching of the night at length succumbed. I could no longer hold and finally fell asleep only to wake late. The atmosphere in the room was stale and trashy as if there had been a party and no one had cleared up after it. Mathilde was not in her bed. Her covers, sweaty and rumpled, had been thrown aside, and there was a peculiar silence — the kind that almost has a sound. I associated this profound absence of sound with something in my memory, but I could not identify it. A haze of smoke in the air signified that my sister had been up for some time. She never smoked the moment she arose, but always waited for a while.

'Mathilde,' I called. I was frightened by her absence and

jumped up, nerves atwist. 'Matty?' There was no answer. I saw to my relief that the bathroom door was shut; after a moment or two, I heard the sound of running water. 'Matty?' There was no reply. I could hear the water scattering round the bathtub and running down the drain, but the bath was not filling and the water kept on running.

'Mathilde, I want to get in there,' I said. All at once, there was an explosion of laughter. It stopped abruptly and she said nothing. Eventually, she emerged. She was dressed in white, a skirt and a shirt, but the clothes were wrinkled and not altogether clean. She seemed very preoccupied. 'It's all yours,' she said. She was fragrant from some cologne or other she had put on, but she smelt sweaty and I realized she had not washed.

The bathroom was in chaos, and her things lay around. Water was splashed all over the place. She sat demurely on a chair while I washed. She chattered on at me about the Buddhist tapestries we were about to see that day. Her cheerfulness unsettled me, because it seemed to come from nowhere inside herself, nor did she seem as if she were straining to achieve it. She was controlled but a little manic.

'We're supposed to see the tortures of hell,' she said. 'Good old Buddha.'

'Maybe the train is on its way,' I said.

'Oh, I don't want it to come,' she said. 'I like it here. Anyway, I want to see the tapestries.' She spoke as if it were a visit to the zoo.

When I was ready, she said she did not want any breakfast.

'I need to be alone for a while,' she said. 'Come for me when you are ready to go.' She got up and stood by the window. The way she arched and articulated her body made her seem almost beautiful. For a momer her face softened and there was a loveliness about it in the placid, morning light.

I thought: We are going to get out of this place.

As if propelled, I made my way down to the lobby

where Madame Densima was standing behind the counter. She was gloomily perusing a paperback book one of the tourists had given her. It was a novel by P. G. Wodehouse. 'I can't understand why this is supposed to be funny,' she said. 'Bertie? Algernon? I suppose it's very idiomatic.'

'Madame Densima, is there any news of the train?'

She leaned her elbows on the counter. 'The train has decided not to come,' she said, 'but tonight, you will meet the British Ambassador. He is giving you a reception to cheer everyone up. That is why I am reading this English book.'

'Madame Densima, I mean nothing offensive when I say I think we must leave Ulan Bator as soon as possible, my sister and I. I do not think she is very well.' I had the curious feeling that things were rocking about me as in the early stages of an earthquake.

'What? Is it stomach? If it is stomach she can see the doctor and he will wash it out.'

'No, it is not stomach. I think her mind is affected.'

'If you like you can go back to the Soviet Union,' she said, 'and fly from Moscow to wherever you want to be.'

I was overcome with relief. 'Oh please, I would be so grateful.'

'You are a nice tourist. I will see what I can do,' she said. 'There is a flight tomorrow morning if the weather holds.'

It had not occurred to me that this could happen so easily. I could hardly believe that I had done such an obvious, healthy and simple thing all by myself. I walked with balance into the dining room, sat down next to John and said, 'I have just discovered what to do. I am going to take Mathilde home tomorrow via Moscow.' We looked at each other. He said nothing for a moment.

'I have no idea what she'll do if we stay here,' I continued. 'I left her up there in the room. All at once, I knew she was – crazy. I knew she was, whether I was or not. All that Durrand thing has got to stop. I will take her home and I will get her put into a hospital – or something. Anything.'

He shook his head only once. 'She won't go,' he said.

'You don't want me to go . . .' It was an expression and a question.

'She won't,' he said.

'Will you help me? Help me to make her?' I saw my hands shaking and heard my voice shaking. The feeling of Durrand but not the presence of Durrand made my mind go like a knocked light, bounding and swerving off the ceiling.

'I'll even come with you,' he said. 'If she can be persuaded.'

There was the knowledge that something was radically, terribly wrong that morning. It was hard to shut it out. It was not a question of knowing what it was: it was as if my feet and voice had instinct where my mind had not. It is hard to report what the confusion was like. It was not a sense of dread so much as of an insurrection of the order of things.

When I returned to the room, there was again that peculiar silence in it. Mathilde came willingly enough, but she would not use the elevator, only the stairs. I wondered how to put it to her that we might return to London the following day. Mathilde looked inscrutable.

Our programme began with a visit to the State Museum. It was a particularly bright morning after a slew of rain from the night before. The rest of the tourists were in a high mood for some reason, and there was a lot of joking on the bus. It seemed to me that everything was wrong. Everything had the wrong perspective to it. The sunlight glinted off the driver's glasses and jagged into my eyes.

'I don't like it here, Matty,' I said. But she made no reply.

We entered a great, grey edifice which housed exhibits of Mongolian natural history and displays of anthropological interest. We walked past cases of stuffed wolves and birds of prey. We passed a bear rearing on its hind legs, a perfect specimen of taxidermy, its frozen eye alert. Everyone assembled around Abel, who began to lecture passionately on the displays.

'Mathilde, I want to go home,' I said. 'I was talking to Madame Densima this morning. It seems we can go back through Moscow. We can fly there tomorrow.'

'Go then,' she said absently.

We trooped into a vast hall. In the centre of it stood the colossal skelton of the Gobi Dinosaur.

'I want you to come with me.'

'Why?' she asked. 'I was never happier.'

The rampant dinosaur, having fine, bleached, sand-blown bones, seemed an X-ray picture of something lizard-like and slow that had danced out its existence a million years ago. Through its bones I saw John, who regarded it with interest. The others poked around the room looking into fossil cases and listened to Abel.

The rib cage of the dinosaur was held aloft by steel supports.

'For the love of God, let's leave this desperate place!' I said. The tail of the dinosaur was heavy, its white vertebrae finely articulated. I could feel its heavy tread. I could feel as if its heavy tread shook the earth in the gravel desert, as if the howling, grating wind harrowed it with sand and tumbleweed. I could see it swaying. I could see it as larger than Mathilde and me. Tears were running down my face. 'Please come with me,' I said.

'No,' she said. She seemed to be involved in her clothing. She looked down on herself and brushed away a crumb of something that had caught in her button.

At length, after drifting through halls of botanical displays, halls of ancient costumes worn by the old nobility of Urga, Madame Densima took us to the palace of pagoda roofs where the promised tapestries hung. John took Mathilde aside, and started talking to her with quiet urgency. 'No!' she said.

We entered the palace where there were yards and yards of silk hangings, for the most part painted with the ancient doom of hell. Smoothly ministering demons flayed wr100thing sinners and hung out their skins like washing on a line. Everywhere, pain and terror were evident. A glutton's guts strung out from his belly; a lecher was tortured in his genitals. Blue devils stuffed naked creatures into cauldrons or tore out eyes.

My sister did not appear to react to this dire iconography. Instead, she wandered about looking at the statues that stood along the walls. But Madame Densima regarded the images with contempt. 'You see!' she said to Alma. 'You see this vicious superstition! Why does it attract you? Our whole nation was subject to this fear.'

'It is only part of a whole system of thought,' said Alma. 'You cannot dismiss the light because it creates a shadow.' She stood with her back to a gold, cross-legged deity with a fiery sword. She was staring at a picture of a woman being disembowelled by fiends – rendered in appliqué.

'They are only after-images. They can't do any harm in themselves,' John said.

'Why did you say that!' Mathilde snapped at him.

'I don't know. I just see them that way,' he said.

At once, her eye seemed to catch something. She made her way through the door into a gorgeously caparisoned room and stood very still looking fixedly at a small gold image on a plinth. The room was dominated by a cush-ioned throne on a dais, but Mathilde looked only at the statue. I went to join her. The image was of great sublimity, delicately wrought: a jewelled god with many arms was conjoined to his goddess, their faces and limbs expressing an exalted sexual ecstasy. Mathilde turned a cold face to-wards me and looked at me with contempt. She said nothing, but turned on her heel and made for the outside of the palace. I followed her swiftly. She was trembling all over. I felt an awful compassion for her. 'Matty,' I said, 'let's go back to Paris together. We really will find out what happened to Durrand. I'll make myself responsible for it. I promise you.' I put my hand out to touch her arm, but she withdrew from me with disgust.

'Why were you ever born?' she said. 'Why?'

I opened my mouth partly out of pain, but partly to speak.

'I want to be alone. Is that understood? I want you to leave me completely alone.'

John stepped out from the shadow of the porch and held my arm while she walked quickly and purposefully away.

I felt giddy and unstructured and was silent. We walked to the Park of Culture and Rest, a barren stretch of land, not very successfully cultivated with occasional military rows of flowers. Pools of water from the previous night's rain lay in declivities in the asphalt. All at once, loud-speakers set on poles throughout the park began to crackle, and Tchaikovsky's First Piano Concerto started to blare out of them. Everywhere we walked, there was this music, but apart from a few desultory Mongolians, we were alone.

'Where did I go wrong in this? Something has gone wrong,' I said. The recorded piano banged away obstinately, accompanying my sense that everything was askew.

'What do you mean?'

'Did I try to escape – the sacrifice I felt – I felt I was to be?' I could not seem to string words together properly and they came out breathily. My voice sounded obscure to me.

'Irene, no.'

'It was just this morning I felt something so odd about *her*. I knew all at once I had to take *her* right away . . . I can't explain. There was something, something, and I can't find it. Something about her face, her behaviour – some-thing, and I knew we had to go, but now I'm afraid. There's something – something . . .'

'Irene, dear, your purpose was not to sacrifice . . . Your purpose was not that here. You are with me. Look at me.' The lush harmonies of the broadcast music gave the cra-ziness of my growing panic a kind of shape. What there was authentic in him, I cannot say, but as I looked at him, I knew and remembered.

'It was the silence in the room this morning,' I said. 'The peculiar silence – when they were young. Oh no, oh no!'

'Don't go! Don't go!' he shouted after me, but it was too late.

The sequence of events which followed is both vivid and unclear in my memory. I remember the whirr in my ears of the crashing, blaring, earnest music as I ran from the park and bolted for the hotel. Taking the stairs two at a time, I banged on our door and called her name, but there was no answer. The room was open; I almost fell into it, half expecting to see her stretched out dead. It was completely empty, and the chambermaid had done the beds. I ran downstairs to the lobby. 'Where is Madame Densima? Where is the party?' I cried to the man at the desk, but he spoke no English at all. The dining room was silent and empty. There was no one about. She must be with the others. She must have gone out, I thought, but still my feet impelled me and I found myself back in the odd park where an Oriental marching tune had replaced the Tchaikovsky. I had lost John and I could not think what to do – or so it seems to me because the sense of everything being out of kilter was uppermost. John tells me now that as he ran after me, he had come across Abel, who said he had seen Mathilde in Sukhe Bator Square, so thinking it was wisest to find her and bring her back, he had gone there, only to lose both of us.

I ran until, out of breath, I came upon a small stadium situated at the end of the park. A group of young Mongolians were practising archery against targets. They regarded my breathless, shaking form impassively, and when I sat down to gather my wits and decide what to do next, they did not object.

Both boys and girls were armed with massive quivers. The arrows, finely fleched, rattled against each other. Everything to do with the archery seemed direct, seemed something I could focus on, seemed balanced and intact. The bows creaked when drawn. The wood of the bows strained at the powerful stretch. Once shot, the arrows filled the air with whispers; embedded in the target, the arrows thocked and trembled. In an endless stream, the mute archers drew and released their bows, seeking with an almost casual eye the targets. The arrows always seemed to find their way, and the archers were silent, expressionless, impersonal. No one seemed to tot up scores or care about who excelled. The archers retrieved their own arrows from the targets while others among them fired more and more arrows. No one dodged or laughed or made mock fright; each simply wove in or out of the whizzing missiles lightly and with confidence.

Caught in this spectacle of the delicate, ancient art of war, I began to get hold of myself and the stupid panic I felt receded until I came to a still point where watching the weave of arrows took me up and consumed me with interest for a while. I watched; and then there was a moment when I watched and knew; and then there was a moment when I turned my head and saw, having known; and then there was the moment when there was really Durrand, and there he sat, so close to me that I could have touched him, locking me in the death-look of his eyes. I rose in one unified movement like someone in deep water unable to stay down, and as I did so, his image vanished and traversed me and was on the ground near the targets, then vanishing again, reassembled itself beyond the archers; and I found myself running without thinking, for a moment almost into the volley of arrows, but then out of the stadium and onto the road where I made, as through water, a slow and dreadful flight. And he was on the road in a black coat, and he was on a wall sitting, and he was behind me. His image had this bizarre trajectory so that it fell by the wayside or came in front of me as I ran.

Vivid and peculiar, I saw the curl of a pagoda roof, a black dog, a building where people milled in and out while the image of Durrand like lightning struck here, there, everywhere at random. As I ran I thought of God and of all the saints and angels, and I thought of them and I thought of them as I made my way up the long road lined with huge Cyrillic letters towards the monastery. And I thought only of God and of the Mother of God and of all the angels and of all the saints, and I turned myself inwardly towards them, and at last swung into the gate of the monastery.

An old woman was making prostrations on a platform outside the temple. I stood and I stood in the empty courtyard, and then there was the stillness, and then there was what I saw: emanating from nowhere but from the very ground before me was the pulsing, growing image of Mathilde, the whole and awful spectre of my sister, dressed as she had been dressed that morning, but with the curious difference of eyes and hands, reaching out, beseeching – not me but beyond me towards the gate behind me. And then it came. I do not know when but the sulphurous confusion lifted through my nose and head.

## Chapter Twenty-six

I saw her: she came, and was gone, came and was gone. Her image flashed across the courtyard like winking lightning. She looked like a chalk drawing against black sky – an inconsequential scrawling on the dark. And then I heard the scream I did not know I screamed.

I do not remember anything. There was something vague, then nothing again, then a far-off engine sound. There was nothing at all for a long time; neither life nor death. There was a grey, grainy John, and then collapse.

I regained full consciousness two days later. The convulsions had left my limbs and nerves in pain, but the aftermath of curious well-being that often follows seizures gave me a mental lightness I should have mistrusted.

Madame Densima came to visit me and sat with an unselfconscious air beside my bed. She brought me koumis and insisted that I drink it for my health. It was famous, she said, for curing all ills. She had another novel in her hand – this time, an Agatha Christie. She wanted to know if I liked detective stories, and amiably expounded to me the plot of *The Murder of Roger Ackroyd*. I drank the koumis. I was grateful for her concern, more so in a way because she veiled it behind her habitual stern expression.

I asked her where Mathilde was, for all I had was the recollection of having seen her in the monastery compound. She said, 'Shhh . . .' and put her finger to her lips. The fermented milk did have a good effect, and I sank calmly into sleep.

That night, I woke to find John in Mathilde's bed. 'What are you doing here?' I asked him. 'Where's Mathilde?' He sat next to me. 'Mathilde should be here. Mathilde is dead. Where is she? You know she is dead and you are not telling me!'

'Mathilde is not here anymore,' he said, and he put his arm under my head.

The next morning, he said, 'Mathilde has vanished. She cannot be found.'

This time I did hear myself scream.

A Russian doctor looked after me – a motherly woman, but she spoke no English.

Madame Densima conferred with her and it was decided I would be better off at the British Embassy.

'Can John stay with me?' I asked the guide.

'He has stayed with you all the time,' she said. 'Vinnie left with the others. It was decided. I do not think he will go away from you.' I wondered if she liked romances too, for she looked slightly misty.

'What has happened about Mathilde?' I kept asking day after day. Everyone said I must rest. The British Ambassador and his wife were very restful people. We drank tea in the afternoons by a portrait of the Queen in a silver frame. She wore a tiara and a blue sash with medals on it. They kept up a quiet, polite patter of conversation and were only a little disappointed when John and I said we did not play bridge.

All along, I sensed that lakes were being dragged and nomads questioned; that horsemen combed the country-side.

There was a gazebo in the garden, a summer house. John and I walked there. Eventually, he said, 'Mathilde was not at the monastery when you saw her there.'

'What do you mean?' I had kept on telling everyone that I had seen my sister.

'That you "saw" her there has caused some confusion,' John said. 'You know there is an awful political row brewing over this. I think you ought to keep out of that as much as you can.'

'Well, where was she – last seen?'

'They have taken very careful evidence, both from Vinnie's lot before they were released, and from Mongolian witnesses. Irene, Imogene Holt saw Mathilde about an hour after Abel had seen her in Sukhe Bator Square. Imogene was coming from the yurt encampment down the hill towards the bridge – the one we stood on that night – and there, according to her evidence, was your sister in the company of a man of the same height and build. He was wearing a dark coat. They were deep in conversation. Imogene did not get a good look at his face, but she saw enough to realize he was a European and not a member of our party. She tried to hail Mathilde, but Mathilde did not answer . . .'

'No!' I said. 'No!'

'I didn't want to tell you until you were very much better. The doctor has told everyone that you should not be upset.'

I clung onto him. 'Who else saw? What did they see?'

'Irene,' he said. 'Don't jump to conclusions. The real suspicion is on the Russians. Mathilde, of course, spoke Russian, didn't she? Very fluently.'

'Who else saw?'

'I'm coming to that. It seems that a Mongolian lad on a motorbike about a hundred miles south of here saw a strange-looking European couple walking down a dusty road towards the railway station. Again, the man's face was very unclear, but the woman answered Mathilde's description.'

'Didn't he stop them? Ask them what they were doing?'

'He went off to get someone who could speak Russian. In fact, they were expecting an agricultural adviser there and he supposed two had come. They had no luggage. Anyway, he returned to find them gone.'

'But she must be alive! She must be!'

'That was a week ago,' he said. 'I hope she's alive.'

John and the ambassadress discussed England, looking for points in common. Did he know so and so? Had she seen such and such? A movie arrived on a plane from London via Moscow. We watched Peter Sellers fall into a lake, bump into doors. Everyone treated my anxiety as a dignifying mark.

The ambassador had a great interest in the Mongolian people and their culture. He spoke very well about it. He was translating some poetry into English and read it to us. It had a lot to do with movement and animals.

No one spoke to me about what went on behind closed doors, but it became pretty evident that people were beginning to think Mathilde was an agent. For whom, no one could discover. Both the Russians and the Americans denied that she had been working for them, but neither would believe the other's story.

I kept thinking she must be found. The thought that Durrand had become actual and had spirited her away was so terrible that I refused to think about it. Numbness blocked my passages of thought and every day she was not found became longer. Each moment had the awfulness of a sealed envelope containing certain and irrevocable news.

She was found dead in the Gobi Desert. They are still asking questions about how she got there. The desert lies five hundred miles from Ulan Bator, and no one would have thought of looking for her there. It is a gravel desert, subject to roaring winds and freak weather. Camels and tumbleweed survive. The nomads have found a way to negotiate it, and Russians, because of the desert's proximity to the Chinese border, regularly patrol the place. It was one of these soldiers who found her when he went to inspect a flock of vultures. Something of Mathilde was left, but mostly she was stripped of herself. She was identified finally by the small icon of the Saviour she still held clutched in the bones of her hand – by the icon, her bright hair, and by a piece of her clothing.

The questioning and questioning began, pierced by my mourning. I only wish my grief had been complete. I loved but did not miss her.

What could I tell them about Mathilde in such an inquiry? About Durrand? I could only say that she had been in a very distressed state of mind during the journey owing to his death. I was borne out here by Madame Densima, who acknowledged that I had wanted to repatriate her.

Had she mentioned selling the icon to anyone? The one she had smuggled? Was she a regular smuggler? (In fact, it took me the better part of six months to establish that her collection, and the other paintings she had restored and sold, had been acquired legitimately.) I wrung my hands. Oh, it went on and on. Investigators were flown in, facts were sought, exhaustive searches were made, alibis were checked. No one could think how she had managed to get to the desert without being seen. Hungarian diplomats and workers were searched and questioned; Czechs, Poles. Who was the man? No one could say.

At last, I thought I really must tell them about my visions of Durrand. They listened politely as I struggled to be as lucid and plain as I could. 'Thank you, Miss Ward, that's all very interesting,' they said, and turned to Matty's politics again. Why had she spent so much time in the Soviet Union? Who were her contacts? Finally, they gave up on me.

Madame Densima accompanied John and me and Mathilde's pitiful bones to the train. We decided to go to Peking and from there fly to London. She turned her head slightly to me as the engine slowly arrived at the platform.

'It is a very strange story,' she said. 'This is what I heard from my relative near Sain Shanda in the Gobi. A venerable old man was standing near the fence of his collective a few weeks after your sister's body was found. The light was not good, and his eyes were bad, but he says he saw two Europeans standing in the desert, not very far away from him. The man was dressed in black, the woman was in white. She called softly to him in a language he did not understand. He was a little frightened. He turned to go for help, then turned back to look at them again – but they were gone.'

She inclined her head and I, mine. We parted with mutual gestures of respect, saying nothing.

For a day and a night, we crossed the steppe on the Chinese train that bore us away past the lonely and seemingly endless vista of land until we reached the desert where we had to proceed slowly because of the retreating flood. Rootless grass had sprung up because of the inundation. Was it here or there she died? I looked out over the green expanse to the point where there seemed no vanishing at all, only the equivocal nexus of horizon and sky in that place of unclear border. 'Where are you Mathilde?' I asked. Over the terrible makeshift coffin, I wanted to gather her bones to me, hold them to myself, release her from all wretched desperate acts and thoughts in one last and inexpressible embrace.

We broached the Great Wall. Its handsome, ancient gates flanked us, and soon we arrived at the jagged mountains near Kalgan and followed the winding track towards Da Tong. It was early evening and there was a new voice which opened my heart with its consuming beauty. 'In your pain I have tried you and in fire have I purified so that death shall have no dominion and whom I forgive is healed twice over – once for the wound and again for the joy in my own mercy. There is no death – only my deep abiding where what is lost is found.'

And so I left behind me the talk of law and inharmonious conjecture when I heard these unmistakable clarities. John, who was standing near me, suddenly said, 'Irene!' – for no reason at all.

266

# Epilogue

This is the story of Mathilde's life and death as I know it. I hope some clarity may emerge from it. I myself do not draw any particular conclusion from it; indeed, there are several conclusions which may be drawn without contradicting one another. I realize that any history as personal as this has, as its limitation, the vision of only one observer. I feel better from having completed my task, although I am not really sure why. Perhaps I no longer feel responsible for having survived. Durrand and Mathilde, Mathilde and Durrand.

In a sense, I realize there was no victim, no sacrifice. When I said, 'Let it be me!' I thought I was required, but slowly I have come to see I was not needed – had never been needed, either for or between those two.

Durrand committed suicide.

It still gives me the little jump of shock whenever I think of it. I found out only a few days before I left London when the ex-member of Fraternitas I had consulted earlier came to see me at Mathilde's flat just as I was packing up. The walls were bare, the place was clean, the funeral over. He stepped into the hall and cast his eyes around; he creased and uncreased a newspaper he was carrying. It was clear that he had something difficult to say.

One of his few remaining friends in the organization had come to see him, and during the course of the conversation, my informant mentioned that he had met me and that we had discussed Durrand. 'You know, I think I'm leaving too,' said his friend, 'after all. Not that I had much time for Durrand. It's just that they refused to see his death for what it was.'

Apparently, when Durrand returned to Paris from

London, his behaviour became grossly disturbed. He would not eat, he could not sleep, he was found wandering around the house in the middle of the night muttering to himself. He lashed out, lost his temper, then became morose and would not speak at all. He was treated like a wilful child, admonished for his pessimistic outlook. Everyone could see that he was in terrible trouble with the authorities.

At length, one night he disappeared. He left a note which was destroyed after his body was discovered on the railroad track from the Gare St Lazare to the west. He had executed himself under the wheels of the oncoming train.

If there was a victim, it was perhaps Durrand.

My informant and I sat and looked at each other while the news sank in.

I cleared my throat. 'At least, they did give him a decent burial,' I said. I could think of nothing else to say.

'I wouldn't be too sure of that,' said my informant. He splayed his hands on his knees. 'He had a regulation Fraternitas Requiem, all right; but Victor's attitude to suicide is pretty rigid. He's not buried in the Fraternitas vault. My friend checked. They have a big ritual surrounding the deaths of their people. Victor has extended his family burial place so that everybody gets walled up with him when he goes. He says he treats the members like a family in life and death. I don't know where Durrand is buried. I suppose you could investigate it.'

'Do you think Mathilde knew? Do you think my sister could have known he killed himself?' I had explained to him briefly what had happened about the money.

'I really don't know. It depends on what Victor felt at the time. He is, oddly enough, a whimsical man. She may have known. She may not have known.'

I suddenly realized that I had been crying. 'Should I try to find him?' I asked.

He looked at me pityingly. 'Leave that to us,' he said. 'Leave that to my friend.'

'And the cover up? They covered it up.'

'Oh, they're quite capable of it, but I'm sure they would

have seen it in another light. It was hardly edifying for people to know that a member had killed himself – a worse evil, don't you see? They might even have said the cover-up was an act of mercy.'

My teeth chattered on my tea cup. Oh, Durrand, oh, caught in a twist of malice, longing and despair. I have had a Requiem said for both of them. They were very kind about it at the Cathedral. I only wished I had been able to tell Father Mowbray, but he is dead.

I am sitting as close to the bay window as I can. I have been straining my eyes and ears for him all morning. Every car is his taxi, every footstep his. In the distance, walking up Ashby Street, I think I see him. It is John! It is! He *is* coming and I am done with this. I will run to meet him. I will meet him – and not meet myself. I will meet him walking up the street.

# Acknowledgments:

I wish to thank Valerie Hylton for generously sharing with me her expertise on epilepsy.

# Arena

| | | |
|---|---|---|
| ☐ The History Man | Malcolm Bradbury | £2.95 |
| ☐ Rates of Exchange | Malcolm Bradbury | £3.50 |
| ☐ The Painted Cage | Meira Chand | £3.95 |
| ☐ Ten Years in an Open Necked Shirt | John Cooper Clarke | £3.95 |
| ☐ Boswell | Stanley Elkin | £4.50 |
| ☐ The Family of Max Desir | Robert Ferro | £2.95 |
| ☐ Kiss of the Spiderwoman | Manuel Puig | £2.95 |
| ☐ The Clock Winder | Anne Tyler | £2.95 |
| ☐ Roots | Alex Haley | £5.95 |
| ☐ Jeeves and the Feudal Spirit | P. G. Wodehouse | £2.50 |
| ☐ Cold Dog Soup | Stephen Dobyns | £3.50 |
| ☐ Season of Anomy | Wole Soyinka | £3.99 |
| ☐ The Milagro Beanfield War | John Nichols | £3.99 |
| ☐ Walter | David Cook | £2.50 |
| ☐ The Wayward Bus | John Steinbeck | £3.50 |

Prices and other details are liable to change

---

ARROW BOOKS, BOOKSERVICE BY POST, PO BOX 29, DOUGLAS, ISLE OF MAN, BRITISH ISLES

NAME. . . . . . . . . . . . . . . . . . . . . . . . . . . . . . . . . . . . . . . . . . . . . . . . . . . . . . . . . . . . . . . . . . . . .

ADDRESS . . . . . . . . . . . . . . . . . . . . . . . . . . . . . . . . . . . . . . . . . . . . . . . . . . . . . . . . . . . . . . . . . .

. . . . . . . . . . . . . . . . . . . . . . . . . . . . . . . . . . . . . . . . . . . . . . . . . . . . . . . . . . . . . . . . . . . . . . . . . . .

. . . . . . . . . . . . . . . . . . . . . . . . . . . . . . . . . . . . . . . . . . . . . . . . . . . . . . . . . . . . . . . . . . . . . . . . . . .

Please enclose a cheque or postal order made out to Arrow Books Ltd. for the amount due and allow the following for postage and packing.

U.K. CUSTOMERS: Please allow 22p per book to a maximum of £3.00.

B.F.P.O. & EIRE: Please allow 22p per book to a maximum of £3.00

OVERSEAS CUSTOMERS: Please allow 22p per book.

Whilst every effort is made to keep prices low it is sometimes necessary to increase cover prices at short notice. Arrow Books reserve the right to show new retail prices on covers which may differ from those previously advertised in the text or elsewhere.